Other Titles by Hanes Segler:

Patriot

The Paradise Key

Always Unfaithful

A Lie Told Often

Becomes the Truth

The Truth Hurts

Spoils of the Desert

Hanes Segler

SPOILS OF THE DESERT

iUniverse books may be ordered through booksellers or by contacting:

iUniverse
1663 Liberty Drive
Bloomington, IN 47403
www.iuniverse.com
1-800-Authors (1-800-288-4677)

Because of the dynamic nature of the Internet, any web addresses or links contained in this book may have changed since publication and may no longer be valid. The views expressed in this work are solely those of the author and do not necessarily reflect the views of the publisher, and the publisher hereby disclaims any responsibility for them.

Any people depicted in stock imagery provided by Getty Images are models, and such images are being used for illustrative purposes only.
Certain stock imagery © Getty Images.

ISBN: 978-1-5320-5129-6 (sc)
ISBN: 978-1-5320-5130-2 (e)

Print information available on the last page.

iUniverse rev. date: 06/05/2018

CHAPTER 1

▼

Mike Conner lowered his book and looked out at the swimming pool. Despite sunglasses, the late afternoon sun caused him to squint and divert his gaze for a few seconds. He shifted his deck chair to the right and shielded his eyes, trying to see the entire courtyard.

Heat waves danced and shimmered above the tiles, blurring and unsettling the scene, creating an atmosphere that might have been designed by hotel management to make it look dreamy—it had worked on the staff. A waiter, stripped of his jacket, string tie loosened, snoozed against the ice storage bin in the outdoor bar. It had been a while since he had made rounds at the pool to take drink orders, and it didn't look like he'd be doing so anytime soon.

Directly across the pool a gorgeous brunette lay on her stomach with her top unhooked, while her Muscle Beach companion flexed and strutted around the deck. Common to the genetically gifted, both wore bored, arrogant expressions of disdain for the rest of the world. At intervals of about five minutes, Muscles strode over to apply more sunscreen to her lovely bronze back and legs, momentarily obscuring Mike's view. Seconds later the fragrance of the coconut lotion drifted over on the hot breeze.

Watching Muscles concentrate on the pleasant task at hand, Mike figured Bronze Lovely's chances of sunburn to be just about nil. But even while he envied Muscles' current position of Sunscreen Applicator, he found himself darkly wishing a case of sunstroke—or worse—for both of the showboats.

That's not very nice of you, Mike.

He contemplated going over to the bar for a drink, but the trip seemed a long journey across hot tiles. No need to rush things. Besides, why wake the bartender?

Butterflies fluttered in the oleander bushes bordering the pool deck. For a while Mike watched their wobbling antics and tried to time their stay at each blossom to detect any pattern. This entomological research was difficult, since his eyes kept drifting back to Bronze Lovely—just in case a horsefly bit her, causing her, hopefully, to jump up without re-hooking her top.

You're a dreamer, Mike, you know it?

Newly-arrived guests, a middle-aged couple accompanied by the bell captain himself, crossed the pool area on the way to their room. *El Capitán* was helpfully pointing out the restaurant and bar when he spied the sleeping barkeep and scowled, a gesture lost on the unconscious employee. Deftly steering the luggage cart around some inflatable pool toys, he turned the corner, heading for the new guests' room. As they skirted the pool, the husband held his gaze on Bronze Lovely long enough to stub his toe on a chair about the time his wife caught him gawking. The chair skittered and screeched, metal on tile, and the man pitched forward, catching himself before he fell face-first onto the pool deck. Seeing the look on his wife's face, Mike figured the guy would be better off in the hospital with a broken nose than he would be when they reached their room.

The bartender was awakened by the commotion and proceeded to busy himself wiping the bar and looking for his pen and order pad. Muscles pulled a towel over Bronze Lovely's loveliest parts, and the spell was broken.

In another patio of the same hotel—separated from the pool courtyard by the restaurant and a wing of rooms—two men sat at a table sipping beers. They were the only occupants of the area, which was intended for breakfast, when it was shaded. At this time of day the sun beat down mercilessly in the alcove, but the men had insisted, over polite protestations of restaurant staff, that they sit there alone.

The two men were oddly dressed for the setting. While the pool-goers and other guests wandering through the courtyards were outfitted for the tropics, one of the men wore jeans and boots with a starched shirt and leather vest. Sweat circles had formed under his arms and he looked uncomfortable. His cowboy boots were propped on a chair, the sloppy posture of one not accustomed to using proper public decorum. His medium height and build, along with non-descript brown hair, would have made him invisible in a crowd of two—except for the know-it-all, lop-sided sneer plastered on his face. His expression said he'd sipped one beer too many and was about to inform the world of an important fact known only to him.

The other man was heavier and older, maybe mid-fifties, clean shaven, with iron-gray hair cropped short. At two hundred pounds and shorter than his cowboy companion, he looked powerful, with meaty arms pulled in close to his side, as though self-conscious of his bulk. Dressed in khaki pants and shirt, he looked like a retired military man, unable or unwilling to shake old habits. He sat hunched over the table, cradling his beer and talking intently to his companion. "I think we should stay somewhere else," he said. "We know what his car looks like, and we can find it later, maybe when he goes to the warehouse. I don't like being this close to him right now."

"Naw, this place is as good as any. Hell, there's a couple hundred rooms at this joint. *Everybody* stays here. I ain't stayin' at some dump out on the freeway. And besides, he ain't gonna spot us 'cause he don't know what we look like." He paused for a long pull on his beer. "Shit, we don't even know what *he* looks like, not exactly, except that he's tall and skinny and got blond hair. That don't exactly narrow it down, so we gotta get a positive ID on his car. All she knew was the name of this place; said he usually stays here. And all she knew about his car was the make and color, but I want to lay eyes on it, see what it looks like and get the damn license number. We need to be able to spot it fast, even if there's a shitload of traffic around."

At the mention of the female pronoun, Soldier launched again, as though suddenly reminded that "she" was the root of their problems. "And I don't like getting that woman in on this job! She's unreliable and goofy as a tree frog. She won't go along to the end without ratting us in and causing a problem."

"Bullshit. She knows what's good for her. She was supposed to stop this from even happening, but she didn't, so if she screws up just once more, she's finished, and I'll make damn sure she knows that from the git-go."

"Well, I still don't like depending on her to get this done."

"Let's get your mind off that by pulling a little recon mission down in the parking garage. Besides, it's hotter'n a little pistol in a big battle out here."

Down in the garage, it took a few minutes to locate what they were looking for. Parked facing the inside wall, a white sport utility vehicle of foreign make, several years old, was the only vehicle that fit the minimal description. It had an El Paso automobile dealer's name on the back.

"This must be it," Cowboy said, noting the license number and peering at the bike rack on top.

"Must be."

"See how simple that was?" said Cowboy. "With the tag number and that deal sticking up there on top, we can pick it out anywhere, anytime. I wonder what he puts on that thing."

"I hope so. Oh, that? It's a bicycle rack, you dumbass."

Satisfied, they climbed the stairs and emerged from the hallway between rooms near the pool. It was almost deserted. A tall, thin man with sunglasses propped on his forehead rose from his deck chair and fished through his wallet, pulling a ten-dollar bill for the bartender carrying a Coors Light in his direction. The only evidence that anyone else had been there was a scattering of water puddles splashed onto the tiles, and in the air, the faint scent of coconut.

Mike paid and tipped the bartender who, worried about being caught asleep, had fairly trotted the beer across the courtyard. Leaning back in his chair and sipping his beer, Mike contemplated tomorrow's business. He was scheduled to meet with the warehouse manager, a guy named Robles, sometime after lunch. If things went well, Mike Conner would be El Paso's new distributor for Morales Products, a move that he hoped would increase sales for his import shop. The little shop of antiques, art, trendy building materials, and archeological items made him a reasonable living, but adding the exclusive Morales line would really give it a boost—or so he hoped.

The trip to Laredo had been necessary because the Morales stuff couldn't be bought in Juarez for any less than full retail price. After a few inquiries among decorators and builders, Mike learned that only the manufacturer, Morales, warehoused the preferred line of goods, and the nearest one was in Nuevo Laredo. So, there it was. An exclusive product with high demand and sales potential, one manufacturer, limited warehouses, and they didn't ship to his part of the world—not to him, anyway.

Mike gave up trying to figure out Mexican business, finished his drink and headed for his room. He showered and plopped down on the bed, remote in hand. Surfing the channels, he checked the inn's events calendar and decided on supper at the hotel restaurant. Dining across the border could wait until tomorrow, after his business meeting. He would pick up Sandra at the airport and take her across for drinks and dinner at his favorite place. With any luck, she wouldn't insist on hitting that big dance club next door.

Forget it, Mikey, ol' boy. She'll hear the music, so just get ready to dance.

Donning a T-shirt and shorts, he stepped out on the balcony to watch the activity below. Guests were coming and going, and one large group was starting early on the evening's festivities. Seated around the tables in the courtyard, they were laughing and slurping margaritas, getting louder by the minute.

From outside the courtyard, the traffic noise blended into a non-stop symphony. The drone was occasionally interrupted by a horn blast, probably the least effective driving tactic in Texas, unless one wanted a one-finger salute, or maybe a fisticuff. Across the border in Mexico, horns were more useful. Over there, it was used to communicate with other drivers on the poorly marked streets, some no wider than alleys in the States.

Across the border was different.

CHAPTER 2

▼

Across the border. To the uninitiated, the two-hundred-yard walk across the bridge spanning the Rio Grande seemed like a movie set. Despite U.S. border towns' overwhelming Hispanic population, only by crossing over the muddy river could one really experience The Border.

And that was exactly what was happening to Mike right now, with the international bridge traffic alternating between slow creep and dead standstill. He was jammed between a dilapidated dump truck leaking hydraulic fluid all over the road and a van filled with loud college boys, already drunk and ready for action.

He had anticipated the mess and left the hotel well before noon to give him time to locate the Morales warehouse. Eventually, an official waved him through, but stopped the van and motioned the young rowdies to a nearby parking lot. Mike smiled, remembering his own adventures on this side of the river during a misspent youth.

He turned right onto a street which bypassed the busy downtown area and intersected with the Monterrey Highway on the south side of the city. Mike knew only that the Morales operation was located on *Carretera Monterrey*, somewhere in an area populated by commercial ventures. Apparently, none of the businesses was too concerned about being found, since few of the buildings had names and even fewer displayed address numbers. After passing it twice, he spotted a faded sign proclaiming *Productos Morales, S.A., numero*

1804 on the opposite side of the road from other even-numbered buildings, a fact that didn't surprise him in the least.

Sure. Why not? Makes perfect sense across the border.

Mike drove by again, turned around and pulled into a gravel parking lot inhabited by an old Ford sedan, a vintage Datsun pickup with a flat tire, and a late-model Mercedes, which undoubtedly belonged to Señor Robles. *Morales, S.A.'s* building was the only thing in sight which looked even remotely like a warehouse. Neighboring businesses appeared to house everything from auto repair to farm produce, along with a *pollo frito* stand which, in addition to greasy fried chicken, also sold plumbing supplies and duct tape. The Morales building was bordered by a baseball field on one side and a horse pen on the other.

Zoning laws are a bit different in Mexico.

The Benz sat adjacent to the short flight of concrete steps leading to a steel door that looked as though it had taken more than a hit or two by would-be bandits. Just before Mike reached the door, a swirl of wind blew dust and debris in his face, along with the odor of the horse stable. It reminded him of why he didn't like horses, but it was preferable to the scent of greasy fried chicken.

Esteban Robles was a very short, rotund individual with gold, wire-rimmed glasses and a two-pound Rolex on his wrist. Mike introduced himself, shaking Robles' pudgy hand and expressing his thanks for the personal meeting. At Robles' invitation, he took a seat on a metal folding chair in front of a cluttered desk, while his host perched himself on its edge. Mike wondered if the move was designed to give him a superior bargaining position over his seated customer; if so, it wouldn't work too well, since Mike, at a couple of inches over six feet, was still almost eye-to-eye with the diminutive Robles. Grinning inwardly at the tactic, he was relieved that Robles spoke reasonable (though heavily accented) English; his own Spanish was adequate for getting around the country as a traveler or tourist, but not for the nuances of business dealings.

Robles squirmed around on the desk in an attempt to get comfortable and issued an embarrassed wave at his surroundings. "So much to do, I have given up already having clean my desk," he declared, pointing at the mound of papers and clutter covering the top.

"That shows you have a lot of business, and that's good," Mike said, wondering if Robles was using "clean" as an adjective or a verb. "When my desk is clear, I haven't been working enough." That Mike didn't even have a desk of his own wasn't important. In reality, he sat infrequently at a metal monster his store manager used for doing daily paperwork chores, but he wanted Robles to see him as a "hands-on" manager, here to bargain in order to further his business.

They chatted briefly before Mike explained his business, relating to Robles the increasing demand in the El Paso area for high-quality building and decorative materials. "I hear that the Morales line is superior, *Señor* Robles," he said. "And I'd like to carry several of your products, but I must buy at a good price."

"We have many customers who insist on the very best, and I tell them that they must buy Morales—it is the same for tiles, *chimeneas*, adobe bricks, it is the same for all—*todo es mejor*," Robles bubbled, waving his hands expansively and slipping into his native tongue.

Mike noticed that his endorsement didn't address the matter of pricing. He tried again. "I want to buy from you and have the goods shipped across to Laredo, then forwarded to my shop in El Paso. I have to get a better price than I can by buying from Morales' man in Juarez—low enough to offset those shipping costs."

At first, Robles seemed puzzled, but when Mike told him about the Juarez warehouse operator's refusal to sell at wholesale prices, he brightened and said, "*Sí*, yes, I see now that you are having difficulty with this. Perhaps you can buy at a better price from me."

Mike produced a sheet listing the items he wanted to buy, along with the prices he wished to pay. Robles studied the paper for a few minutes, shaking his head at some figures and merely blinking at others. It was impossible to tell if his homework was making any impression, good or bad, but he leaned back and kept quiet while Robles continued with his facial concert. He finally sighed, took off his glasses and began polishing them vigorously on his tie.

Mike took that as a sign he was finished reviewing the written proposal, so he straightened in his chair and pulled out a blank draft form and a letter of recommendation from his bank. Then he proceeded to cap the spiel with what he hoped would be a winning incentive: "Of course, you will receive your money immediately upon my bank's receipt of this bank draft with a detailed invoice enclosed and priced as we have agreed. The funds will be wired directly to your bank, into your account that same day. I am paying with a wire transfer, the same as cash for you at your bank, in U.S. dollars. I would ask the best exchange rate from you, better than I can get in the *casa de cambio.* I don't want the exchange house to make a profit on this. Please feel free to call my bank and speak to the official who signed this letter."

Robles scrutinized the letter closely, then nodded and looked back at the information on his desk. Mike watched as Robles pondered the figures again and penciled in his own indecipherable scratching. Robles was obviously trying to figure out how to make the proposed sale while keeping prices high enough to skim *and* please his boss. The scene reminded Mike of his old friend, the automobile dealer who opined that everyone should "leave a little meat on the bone for the next guy, let him dip his beak."

Robles was evidently calculating how much meat to leave on the bone and how deep he could dip his *own* beak. After several minutes, he looked up, alternately frowning and grimacing, gesturing at the figures before him. "I can do some of these, maybe, but some items I am unable to sell at the prices you want," he declared.

Mike took his turn frowning, then pressed ahead gently, offering to sweeten the deal slightly on those items Robles couldn't live with. After more than an hour, in which Robles had re-traded his "final" deal about six times, he rose to shake hands enthusiastically, his face shining with sweat.

Mike was sweating too; nervous from the impact this meeting had on his finances, plus his natural aversion to bargaining. To him, the process all too closely resembled the negotiations with prostitutes in Nuevo Laredo's red light district only a mile from this very location, but many years removed from his current life. He hadn't liked it then, and he didn't like it now, but this time the bargaining was necessary for his business.

And this time, he wouldn't end up with a hangover, or worrying about picking up more than he had bargained for...

CHAPTER 3

▼

While Mike bargained with Robles, Sandra Payne squeezed forward in the boarding line for the afternoon flight from El Paso to Laredo. There was a stop in San Antonio, but no plane change for Sandra to continue on to Laredo. She carried only a single overnight bag, which would surprise Mike. Besides, she had secreted another fully-stocked emergency bag into his car before he left, containing everything from toe rings to tampons.

She finally found a seat on the aircraft's non-assigned-seating cattle car and crammed her bag into the overhead bin, plopped into the seat, leaned back and closed her eyes as the plane was pushed away from the gate. Within a few minutes, the engines throttled up and hurtled the aircraft down the tarmac and into the Texas sky. A gentle right-hand bank lined the plane up with San Antonio's north-side airport over five hundred traffic-free miles away, an easy jaunt for the experienced crew, who cheerfully promised a smooth, quick trip due to a favorable tailwind.

Settled in for the flight, Sandra's thoughts turned to Mike and this short vacation. She knew they would have a good time; he always saw to that. Now if she could just get a commitment out of him for the future—their future...*together*. Sure, the recent months had been great, especially compared to her married years, which had nearly driven her crazy. Her life had been transformed from a veritable nightmare into one she never knew existed, not for anyone, and certainly not for Cassandra Payne. She had fun, went places, saw new things, new people, and never had to worry about saying the wrong thing at the wrong time, a constant dread during her tumultuous marriage.

The contrast was unbelievable, a fact vividly illustrated when she had recently seen some people from her past life during a visit to her hometown. She'd become depressed and returned to El Paso two days early. She was so happy to see Mike that she'd cooked his favorite meal, treated him to a movie, and held him captive overnight at his own place. The next morning, he informed her she should go home for a visit and return early more often.

She turned to the window and reluctantly let her mind drift to her trip back home. What could she have done differently? She'd gone to a party with old friends, which was fine until certain people from her past showed up. Even that part was okay for a while, until the conversation turned to their interest in shady activities—activities that had long troubled Sandra and weighed heavily in her decision to divorce in order to avoid contact with something she felt was wrong, at least for her. Not that she felt superior to them—or did she?

Maybe it was the other thing, the request—or was it an assignment?—she stopped cold and refused to think about *that*. Or how about the agreement to report?—she pushed that thought aside too. How had her life become so entangled with people and activities she wanted to forget? If her entire past would just disappear, she thought, the present and future would be a lot easier to navigate…

The questions her friends had asked were bad enough, without her jackass ex-husband and his cronies pressing her for more. She wondered if she seemed different to them, and if so, what they said about her later. Whatever it was, she couldn't change it now. Instead, she consoled herself with the thought that life had been passing her by while she lived there, something she didn't feel now. The move to El Paso had been right—for a lot of reasons.

While the reunion with old acquaintances reminded her there was no benefit in associating with them, she still wondered about Mike Conner. His idea of their future consisted of the long weekend in New England and a hiking vacation in Yellowstone, both planned for the end of this summer. And while that was great, she needed a little more—okay, a *lot* more.

So what exactly was the long-term benefit of dating Mike Conner? Where is this going, and how long will it take to get there? Are we going to keep on "just having fun?"

It had occurred to Sandra that Mike's emotional attachment skills were suspect, to say the least, and she sighed to herself at the thought as she watched the expanse of West Texas slide by below her.

Mike turned left into the airport entrance and started looking for short-term parking. He thought about parking at the curb, but signs everywhere warned that unattended vehicles would be towed after thirty minutes—and when was the last time a flight was on time?

He had returned from his meeting with Robles at mid-afternoon, and after another brief dip in the hotel pool and a quick shower, he headed for the airport to meet Sandra's flight from San Antonio. Tomorrow, he would take her around the town with him to see the sights and make the final arrangements for shipment of the goods to El Paso.

But tonight would be different, he vowed to himself. No business, not even a mention of such matters. He would take her across the border for an evening of dining and drinking, and, perhaps, God help me, even *dancing*. He groaned inwardly at the thought.

He circled the lot again and lucked out this time, finding a space big enough for the Land Cruiser near the back of the short-term parking lot. Being a little early, he stopped for a cup of coffee in the terminal restaurant before wandering toward the arrival area in time to check the arrivals-departures screen. As a rare treat, he saw that the flight from San Antonio was, in fact, on time; a good omen, he thought.

Seated near the back of the aircraft, Sandra was one of the last to emerge. Mike spotted her blonde hair bouncing as she weaved in and out of the crowd. As soon as she saw Mike, she dashed toward him. "I'm glad you're here," she said, giving him a big hug and kiss. "I was afraid you'd still be tied up with the Morales guy, and I'd have to cab it to the hotel. Or maybe you'd just forget about me, leave me stuck out here at the airport."

"Not a chance. How could I forget my favorite girl—uh, *Sarah*, isn't it?" The smart remark cost him a gouge to the ribs, Sandra's standard tactic for his foolishness. He decided to straighten up. "I'm glad to see you, too," he said, meaning it and kissing her again. "I've missed you. Where's your claim check? The baggage pickup area is down this corridor to the left. You might need it to claim your bag and carry it out of there."

"This *is* my baggage. All of it," she added with a proud grin.

"Sounds like a clever excuse to go shopping, leaving all your clothes behind."

"You *know* you like to go shopping." Her outrageous lie was accompanied by a sly grin.

"Oh, sure I do! I had something else in mind, but it seems my date has left all her clothes at home, so we'll just have to sit in the hotel tonight."

"Okay, Smooth Talker, I'm convinced. No shopping. Let's go wine and dine. Maybe I can find *something* to wear. Oh, and can we go dancing?"

Mike smiled weakly, but avoided the question by launching into a recap of his business meeting, despite his earlier promise to himself. "It took four hours of haggling with a guy named Esteban Robles, but you are now looking at the new El Paso distributor for the Morales line. And it's going to be profitable for Conner's Imports as soon as I get the first shipment, so the bargaining was worth my time." When she didn't reply, Mike looked over at her. She seemed to be concentrating on something far away. Her blue eyes were even bigger than usual, but a worried frown ruined the effect.

She turned to look at him, appearing flustered by his stare, and she struggled to recover. "Um, when do you get the merchandise?"

"I gave him a bank draft already, but I'll meet with him at his bank tomorrow in case he wants his banker to call and confirm my credit line. That should close the deal, and it'll be shipped out tomorrow, I guess. The first shipment, anyway. He'll just ship it straight to the shop."

"*Tomorrow?* That soon? I mean, just like that, you don't go look at it or anything?"

"Yep. That soon. I don't need to see it, I just need to stock it. Every builder and decorator in El Paso has been hounding me to get the line. I had the list you helped me with, so I ordered from that."

She didn't respond, which further puzzled Mike since she'd known he was going to complete the transaction in person, if possible. That was the reason for the two-day drive down here, that and an opportunity to entertain her. She'd jumped at the invitation to fly down and ride back with him, and Mike was looking forward to the time together.

Maybe she's just irritated because I brought up business. I'd better concentrate on entertaining her, like I intended.

Since meeting her after a marathon race last summer, entertaining her had become his favorite pastime. It didn't take long to find out that Sandra Payne, recently divorced, had neither traveled much, nor experienced much fun in her previous life. She seemed delighted to go on trips and have Mike show her things and places she didn't know about. Mike couldn't tell if she was enthralled with *him*, but she appeared to enjoy the new-found lifestyle. He certainly did, and he hoped this business/pleasure trip hadn't been a mistake.

As they neared the car, Mike opened the passenger door, then put her bag in the back. As he unlocked the driver's door, two men walked by him. One looked at him and nodded, grunting something unintelligible and walking on. Just as Mike reached for the door handle, both men pivoted, turned toward him and stepped apart. Facing him, they produced handguns and pointed them at him. One of the weapons, wielded by a young guy dressed in jeans and boots, was an automatic. The other man, older and heavier with gray hair, pointed a revolver with a short barrel at his chest.

For a few seconds, nothing happened. It was as though no one knew what to do next. Mike surely didn't. It was such a surprise he didn't even become frightened immediately, but then he remembered Sandra was in the car. He began to get scared, *really* scared.

These guys just looked like two guys in a crowd to whom he wouldn't have given a second thought. Now they were pointing guns at him, and he had no idea why, or what they could possibly want.

Maybe you could ask them, Mike.

"What do you want?" he asked with more force and conviction than he felt.

"Get in the car and we'll take us a little ride," the cowboy said. We got *beaucoup* to talk about. Now get your ass in, most *riki-tiki*."

Mike wished he could signal to Sandra to get out and run, but the older man had already opened the back door and was getting in. Sandra, her eyes wide with fright, withdrew against the dashboard and stared in disbelief as he leaned past her to lock her door. He was brandishing the pistol, not in a particularly threatening fashion, but it was evident that he was comfortable with it and could bring it into play any second.

Mike had his door open, and the cowboy reached to close that door also, jamming it against Mike's leg before he could get completely in. Then he sauntered to the rear passenger door, climbed into the back seat, and slammed his door before issuing another terse order. "Okay, drive. We're going to get our stuff back, so flog this heap all the way to El Paso."

At the mention of his home town, a new wave of panic swept over Mike; they obviously knew of his connection to El Paso. Plus, they must know something he didn't to be pulling this stunt. This was no plain carjacking or robbery.

What the hell is happening?

He drove to the entrance and, on impulse, turned left on the highway, the wrong direction to get to El Paso. He tensed, waiting for a shout from the back informing him he had turned the wrong way. Incredibly, no sound came. Did they not know the way? Or worse, did the gunmen not care, since they were just going out in the country to kill them? At that thought, Mike panicked again, thinking he had unnecessarily endangered himself and Sandra.

Way to go, Dumbass. They'll probably kill you for that smart move.

The miles eased by, and Mike took a chance to steal a glance over at Sandra. She was sitting on the front edge of the seat, staring straight ahead, her white knuckles clenched in her lap. Neither of them had buckled their seat belts. For a while, Mike had hoped that a highway cop would notice and pull them over, but the hope faded along with the evening light.

He was reluctant even to peek in his mirror, but he wished desperately he could look closely at the men to see if he knew them. The cowboy had mentioned El Paso—could it have just been a chance remark, like "all the way to Timbuktu?" Maybe he had just meant they would go as far as needed "to get their stuff back," whatever that meant.

As the miles stacked up, Mike relaxed slightly and decided to try to find out. "What stuff is it you're trying to get back?" he asked, looking in the mirror at the cowboy seated directly behind him.

"The goddamned stuff you got from Morales' warehouse!"

Mike hesitated a second, then said, "I haven't gotten anything from Morales. I went to set up business with them, but they haven't shipped anything yet. I was only there today."

"But they've already arranged to ship you some stuff, and it just happens to have our stuff in it."

Mike tried to analyze this mysterious statement, but the tension of the situation made it impossible to concentrate. He tried again. "Look, I don't have your stuff. I ordered some merchandise and it's going to be shipped to me, but I have no idea what you're talking about, 'your stuff in my stuff.'"

This is sounding like an Abbot and Costello routine. It would be funny, except these guys have weapons.

"You just get us to your place in El Paso, and we'll worry about that."

Darkness was falling fast now, and Mike turned on his headlights. At that instant, a road sign reflected the damning information: CORPUS CHRISTI—94.

"Where the fuck are you going?" came the shout in Mike's ear. "We're going the wrong damn way! Turn around, goddammit!"

Mike eased over to the shoulder, swung out and U-turned, heading back toward Laredo.

"I oughta' blow your fucking head off!" Cowboy screamed.

"You didn't say which way to go. And you didn't exactly give me a chance to look at a road map," he said, trying to keep his voice strong.

"Just shut up and drive! You know where El Paso is. Kick this thing in the ass, Wiseguy."

Mike sped back toward Laredo. All this time, not a word came from the other man. Out of the corner of his eye, Mike could see him, motionless, directly behind Sandra. Mike sensed that he was being still for the same reason hunters remain motionless—so they can kill something. It was unnerving, having one raving lunatic yelling in his ear and another one who seemed even more dangerous just sitting there, waiting.

CHAPTER 4

▼

Mike somehow had to interrupt the trip, stop what was likely a one-way journey to their demise. Maybe with time, the kidnappers would drop their guard and he and Sandra could get away, though nothing came to mind. He knew only that he was scared, for both him and Sandra.

For the past half hour, Cowboy had become increasingly restless, fidgeting in his seat and waving the gun around. Mike knew his intentional wrong turn had been dangerous. Cowboy was hot to get to El Paso, and the lost time was making him antsy. "Drive this Jap piece of shit faster, Asshole."

"You want to get pulled over for speeding?" Mike asked, looking in the mirror.

"You want a bullet in the head?"

"Not any more than you want to get stopped."

"I have to go to the bathroom," Sandra interrupted.

"Shut the fuck up and hold it!" screamed Cowboy. For a few seconds, the tension in the car was palpable, and no sound was heard other than the engine and tires. Then, in an instant, Cowboy's demeanor changed. He leaned forward, a sly grin on his face. "On second thought, maybe I can hold it for you," he said sarcastically, reaching across her lap. Sandra cringed and withdrew onto the front corner of the seat, glaring at him. At her reaction, Cowboy's irritation seemed to subside completely, and he sat back to watch the road.

Mike hoped Sandra had noticed how Cowboy's actions were instantly changed by feeding his macho attitude, even if he had to do the feeding himself by making vulgar remarks. He obviously enjoyed the discomfort he caused, especially with a woman. The effect might come in handy, Mike thought.

Re-entering the Laredo city limits, Mike cautiously glanced at the fuel gauge. Touching empty, he noted hopefully. If he could get into city traffic before running out completely, maybe they could bail out at a stop light. He'd have to signal the plan to Sandra, and they'd have to run opposite directions, and—his jumbled thoughts were interrupted by Cowboy's grating voice in his ear.

"Find a place to gas up. Don't want to run out of gas, now do we? And find one that's on the right. Don't want you to get confused and turn the wrong way again."

A half mile farther, Mike spotted a Diamond Shamrock Corner Store. He pulled in, eased up to the pump and reached for the door handle.

"Just stay put," Cowboy ordered. "Get out and fill this thing up, Sarge," he added, handing him a fifty-dollar bill and indicating the middle pump to his silent companion.

Sarge? What's with this military talk?

Mike remembered his earlier comment about "most riki-tiki" and "beaucoup shit," terms he hadn't heard since his own brief stint in the military, and then only from the older guys in his unit, ones who had been around since the end of the Vietnam era. Why was this goon still using jargon from decades ago? He was too young to remember those expressions.

Sarge walked into the store to pay. Delayed by the busy time at the cash register, it was several minutes before he returned and gassed up the vehicle and gestured for Mike to run down his window. "Gimme seven dollars," he ordered gruffly, the first words he had spoken. "Fifty didn't cover it, but they let the pump run."

Growing tired of being ordered around, Mike countered, "Check under the hood, will ya' Buddy? And catch that windshield, too, while you're at it."

"Save it, Wiseass," came from the back. "Here, go pay for the rest," he said, shoving some bills past Mike's head to the one he called Sarge. The uncommunicative kidnapper snatched the money and stalked toward the store.

When Sarge returned, Sandra spoke up meekly as he closed his door. "I have to go to the restroom. I want something to drink, too."

Cowboy mulled it over for a moment. "Y'all can go to the restroom one at a time. If you're not back in five minutes, we leave here with your friend and drive straight into the country for a little execution duty and burial detail."

That military-speak again. What's with this throw-back idiot?

Goofy sounding or not, Mike knew that he would likely carry out the threat. Whatever "stuff" he was bent on recovering was important enough to wave pistols around and commit kidnapping, a felony good for many years in the slammer. Too much was at stake for these guys to flinch at killing a couple of people after having gone this far, he thought.

At that realization, a feeling of dread came over him; he could feel it in his stomach—that little flip one experiences just before a fistfight or a car wreck. He had first placed high hopes on running out of gas. Then he switched to hoping for some kind of break at the gas stop, and now it appeared that escape would have to come later, if at all.

"You first," Cowboy gestured to Sandra, followed by another lewd remark about "holding it."

Watching the patrons of the convenience store steadily coming and going, Mike noticed with no surprise that everyone was Hispanic, including the two night clerks. The customers tended to mind their own business as they pulled in to fill up and buy junk food, beer, and lottery tickets. They weren't interested in some gringo's problem. They wouldn't have cared even if he could fully explain their situation. He could have yelled his head off, and gotten no more than a militant stare from the bystanders; then, from Cowboy, a bullet for him or Sandra.

And as luck would have it, no passing police cruiser pulled in for coffee. Mike didn't think he would have been able to alert them anyway, given the close proximity of Cowboy and Sarge. The talkative lunatic's threats seemed real enough, and his mood was too volatile to take any foolish chances.

When Sandra returned, Cowboy gestured for Mike to take his turn. As she got in and closed the door, Mike saw she had bought two bottles of water in addition to the one she was already drinking. "Don't drink so much," Cowboy warned. "I don't want you having to piss every five miles."

Sandra didn't say anything, but Mike noticed she placed one of the bottles on his side of the console and took a swig from hers while he got out. As he walked to the restroom in back of the store, he wondered about the water. Did she have something in mind?

He thought of creating a disturbance so the clerks would call the police, or even leaving a message in hopes of someone, *anyone*, finding it and delivering it to the police, but that would be a long shot. Writing HELP,

I'M KIDNAPPED on the restroom wall sounded so ridiculous he almost laughed out loud. Besides, Cowboy and Sarge would be taking their turns in the restroom and might find any message, no matter how cryptic.

When he came out of the restroom, he bought two more bottles of water, hoping he could pass it off as being dehydrated from a night of drinking if Cowboy became suspicious. It didn't seem likely that their trip would be interrupted at this stop. Something had to happen soon, before they got too far away from the city. Mike had driven through this country many times, and any problem or breakdown would simply leave them stranded in the boondocks together. While that would be better than this current trip to doom, it wouldn't separate them from the kidnappers.

As he walked back to the car, he thought about the open country to the north. What was it, what was the ultimate foolproof breakdown that wouldn't be his fault and, hopefully, wouldn't elicit a bullet from Cowboy? As he opened the door to the vehicle, his eyes strayed to the hood, and he grasped the beginning of a plan.

"What is it with all the water?" Cowboy demanded. "Why the hell are y'all so thirsty?"

"Had a few too many margaritas last night," Mike said, trying to stay calm while Cowboy glowered first at him, then Sandra.

"Guess you had too many, too, huh, Baby?" he leered over the seat at Sandra. "Were you out boozin' with your other boyfriend?"

"None of your business."

Mike cringed in his seat.

She's been watching too many movies about tough gals being able to fade the heat against bad guys. This is no movie, this is real, dammit! I wish she'd shut up and quit antagonizing this idiot!

"Shut the fuck up!" Cowboy yelled, causing both Mike and Sandra to jump.

Well, at least we're in agreement on something.

They drove north out of Laredo, skirting the city itself, picking up Interstate 35 along with a steady caravan of eighteen-wheelers. About fifteen miles out of Laredo, Highway 83 veers to the northwest toward the vastness of West Texas, first passing through miles of fields growing a variety of crops, including corn. It was the corn fields Mike awaited. And a chance to undo some driving skills he had learned long ago.

Seeing numerous deer beside the road, Mike realized that his feeble plan to disable the car wouldn't be as simple as he at first thought. Smacking a deer at seventy miles an hour would cause quite a jolt, and as each animal appeared in the headlights, he felt himself steeling for a move to the brake or a quick steering correction to avoid hitting one. To do what he wanted—put one right into the grill and, hopefully, well into the radiator—he would have to overcome his long-ingrained habit of dodging them. Several deer had looked up expectantly as the car approached, one taking tentative steps toward the road, prompting him to brake reflexively and angle away from its projected path; others leaped the barbed-wire fence to safety. Most, however, simply kept nibbling the grass at the side of the road.

Mike could see this was going to be tough. He had driven thousands of miles dodging the deer, armadillos, jackrabbits, and the occasional javelina which wandered into his path. Mostly, he had been successful in avoiding collisions with wildlife, except for two deer and countless armadillos. Remembering those encounters, he held his speed steady and searched for the opportunity to do what he had always tried to avoid. For several more miles, nothing of importance appeared even close to the road. A rattlesnake slithered off to the right shoulder, and a few rabbits popped in and out of the ditches. Then a group of four or five deer on the left side of the road raised their heads, eyes shining eerily greenish-white. They stood stock-still as Mike sped by, forcing himself not to look their direction while hoping Cowboy noted his inattentive driving style. If he could pull this off—hitting a deer and disabling the car—he couldn't let Cowboy suspect it was done purposely. Even at best, the kidnapper would be enraged at the delay and probably vent his anger on his captives, but his appearance and accent indicated he also had driven in Texas and wouldn't be overly surprised at hitting a deer.

When miles passed uneventfully and it seemed the plan would not succeed, Mike began to relax at the wheel and shifted his mind to some other solution. Maybe at the next gas stop, he could feign checking under the hood and damage some component enough to fail later. He quickly dismissed the idea—the redneck cowboy surely had worked on cars, and would know enough to see through that ploy immediately. And the other guy was just plain spooky. As jumpy as they had seemed at the stop in Laredo, they certainly wouldn't leave him alone to fumble around under the hood of their only means of transportation. Besides, the next gas stop would be three hundred miles away, almost five hours of tension and uncertainty.

Already, the two had begun to talk quietly in the back. Mike could only catch a word or two over the engine and the country music station that

Cowboy had insisted on tuning in. The tone of the conversation suggested disagreement between the two, perhaps a discussion of changing the plan, whatever it was. While Mike didn't think the final outcome could be any worse for him and Sandra than what he already envisioned, he didn't relish the thought of having even less time to come up with a plan. What if they were discussing simply killing them and taking the vehicle? They really didn't need hostages now—they had his car, a road map, and enough information about him and Sandra to do whatever they were planning without their help.

Approaching a small community, Mike wondered if he could slow down enough for him and Sandra to jump from the car. But how to signal to Sandra what he was planning? And even if they could get away, the residents would be suspicious of anyone pounding on the doors at this time of night. They might be recaptured or killed by the gunmen before the door was answered. Besides, the door might be answered with a shotgun, he thought. In Texas, self-defense and defense of one's home are still sacred. Texas' state motto might be "The Friendship State," but late at night, common sense always takes priority when dealing with strangers in the middle of nowhere.

The little community receded in the mirror, and Mike searched for some means to get out of the car, away from these two lunatics and back to civilization. If we could just break away on foot, he thought, Cowboy and Sarge could easily be outdistanced in the darkness, provided the car was sufficiently disabled to strand them. And it wouldn't be that hard to survive the night in the thorny, hostile land, rattlesnakes and all. That was no problem compared to armed kidnappers. But how to get that first few feet of darkness between them?

CHAPTER 5

▼

Two hours later, the drive had entered the tedium stage of most late-night automobile trips. Even the nerve-wracking tension had dissipated, replaced by the hum of tires on pavement. They passed through Uvalde, turning left onto U. S. Highway 90, which heads west to Del Rio and crosses Lake Amistad before entering the northern reaches of the Chihuahuan Desert.

Northwest of the upper end of the lake, about ten miles beyond where the Pecos River joins the Rio Grande, sits the tiny tourist stop of Langtry. Supposedly named for Lilly Langtry, a nineteenth-century English actress, by its founder, Judge Roy Bean, it now is the location of the fabled jurist's courthouse/saloon and a state-operated museum. Passing the sign to the museum, Mike wished he could invoke some of the old judge's harsh justice upon the two kidnappers who had commandeered him, his girlfriend, and his car without any explanation.

He deliberated, then decided to take advantage of the relative calm, try again to make sense of the capture and what was going on. Reaching up, he adjusted the mirror to see Cowboy's face. "Perhaps you could explain to me exactly what it is you think I have and how I can help you recover it," he said. "Maybe then we can cooperate and resolve your problem."

"Well now, I don't think you have much choice in cooperating, do you?" came the reply, enhanced by a wave of the automatic.

"You wouldn't need that gun to get whatever it is you want. If it's your stuff, I'd love to see you have it, then you could get the fuck out of my car *and* my life," Mike said, his voice gaining strength and venom.

"It's like this, Asshole," Cowboy leaned forward in the seat, placing the gun against Mike's right temple. "The order you placed with Morales, it comes from Monterrey, right? Well, I get my Morales goods from Monterrey through Robles' warehouse, too. Only I buy special goods, *real* special goods."

"Yeah, I'm sure you buy only the best," Mike said sarcastically. "But what's that got to do with me? And why do you think you need to take mine? Just go to Robles and tell him you want to buy some more of those real special goods they've been peddling."

"You don't *comprende*, Pardner," said Cowboy, relaxing a bit and leaning back in his seat. "They're *so* special that Robles don't even know how special. He thinks all the shops he ships to are Morales outlets, but he's wrong. He just ships them out by certain Mexican truckers who haul them to towns up and down the border. We know which ones, and we shop in those little towns and buy the goods from the stores just like good tourists should."

Mike didn't try to keep the disdain from his response. "You mean you buy the stuff from retail outlets? No wonder you want to steal mine. You got a lot to learn about the pottery business—*Pardner.*"

Cowboy continued, ignoring Mike's comment. "Only we give a little more money, so the shopkeepers keep the Morales stuff for us, in the back of the shop, so some dickhead school teacher from Indianapolis don't buy it. When we buy it and get it across, we have a good market for it with certain friends, because the stuff has more to it than just clay and paint—it's got special ingredients."

"Yeah, so I'm told. I have customers who specifically request the Morales line, in fact."

"Well, my people want the Morales line, too. In fact, they insist on it. Just ain't interested in any other brand."

"So you think that justifies sticking a gun in my face and kidnapping two people just because I might sell some in El Paso? For cryin' out loud, El Paso's several hundred miles from here! How much market area do you want?"

"My market area is pretty big," Cowboy said, smirking at Mike in the rear-view mirror. "From here to L.A., in fact."

"Well, maybe I can just sell you my Morales stuff at a price where you can still make a good profit. For that matter, I will sell you the first and final shipment at my cost, if it's that important to you," Mike said, hoping to make a deal with this nut just to get him and Sandra away from these maniacs.

"The pottery items have hollow spaces. They're filled with cocaine."

The two sentences, delivered in a quiet monotone from Mike's right, so surprised him that several silent seconds went by before he could grasp what he was hearing. The shock of the information was exceeded only by its source. For a few seconds, he was so confused he didn't even know where to begin. He turned to stare at Sandra. "What are you talking about? How do you know that?"

Sandra continued to look straight ahead, her hands still clenched in her lap.

"What are you talking about?" Mike repeated, louder this time.

Silence continued for almost a full minute. Finally, she began to speak quietly. "I thought...I didn't think...they would do this. They just wanted to know what you did." Sandra's voice quivered and trailed off at the end, leaving him straining to hear.

Mike was overwhelmed by what he was hearing—not only did he have two adversaries in his car, Sandra was in on this, or at least knew *something* about it. He felt his face flush as his emotions ran the full gamut, from anger to jealousy to disappointment, and finally, to embarrassment. The steering wheel felt slippery, his hands breaking into a sweat, and he had difficulty controlling his breathing. All these months with her, and not a hint that she was involved with a couple of common...*drug dealers*? How in hell did she even *know* these two creeps? How could he have so badly misjudged her character? He was gritting his teeth and could barely see the road ahead; his anger was as tangible as the pavement stretching before the hood of the car. The terror, the tension, the concern for *her* safety; what in the hell for? At least now he knew whose safety was important. "Maybe you'd better enlighten me as to what's going on," he said quietly, doing a better job than he thought possible.

"They're from Graham, my hometown, up by Wichita Falls. A while back when I went there for the weekend, I saw them at a party. They're just some people from the past I know through my friends."

"Is this what all your old friends do for entertainment? I'm glad I haven't met any more of them!"

"No, they just asked me what you did and where you bought your merchandise. When I mentioned you were going to set up the deal with the Morales Company in Nuevo Laredo, they told me to discourage you. I told them you were set on buying the Morales merchandise, that it was popular and you wanted to carry it in your shop. I didn't know why it was important to them, but I just said I'd try to change your mind, anything to change the subject."

"What business is it of theirs where I buy my merchandise? Like I just told this guy, he should go to Robles and cut his own deal. And I don't know anything about drugs being hidden in the stuff. I'm a pottery salesman, remember?"

"Mike, I thought the talk about drugs was just bragging or drunk talk, so I didn't take it seriously. I didn't fully understand the connection until now. I should have told you, but I didn't—the time just never seemed right. And when they found out you were going through with negotiations to buy from Robles, they said they wanted to talk to you, just talk, that's all." Her voice was rising now, the words rushing out. "I thought they just wanted to buy something or sell you something, something to do with business, I—"

"You knew they were in the drug business," Mike interrupted. "You seem real informed about how that part works." He continued the conversation as though the two men weren't even in the car. What could they do? Shoot him? Big deal, he thought; I'm driving, so we can all just run off the road together. At least now Sandra could worry about herself.

Surprisingly, a sense of security started to grow as Mike grasped the implications of Sandra's involvement in this. Whatever else he had lost in these last few minutes, at least he had regained his old standby—depending entirely on himself, not worrying about anybody else. The ultimate freedom.

Freedom. Nothing left to lose, as the song goes.

"I knew you wouldn't have anything to do with the drug business," she began again. "They just wanted to know what your car looked like, they said they would find you at Robles' warehouse and discuss it—just discuss it. Mike, that's all they said." Her words were rushing out again.

"Well, I hope you're happy, because this is how they discuss things." Mike waved his hand at the men in the back. "You pick some great people to discuss business with, the cream of the crop. How'd you ever pick me? I seldom stick a gun in your face." Mike was doing his best now to hurt her, to point out the error of dealing with people like the two thugs behind them. Even as he said it, though, it occurred to him that they really hadn't physically hurt her, or him either—yet. She sat still in her seat, tears running down her face.

"She just told us where you'd be and about your car," Cowboy said from the back seat. "Hell, if Jack hadn'a been drunk, he wouldn't have mentioned the drugs. He was just showing off for her."

At the mention of someone named Jack, Mike wondered why Cowboy had used the name of one of his cohorts. There was no way it could mean anything to Mike, but he asked anyway. "Who's Jack?"

"She said she'd try to get you not to buy the Morales line," Sarge said. "If she had done that, and if you'd listened, you wouldn't be in our territory."

Mike's question went unanswered.

Sarge's views might be interesting, Mike thought, since he sounds a lot smarter than this cowboy shithead. But he couldn't think how to further the conversation, so he was left to wonder about the mysterious Jack—and why they hadn't answered him after *they'd* brought up the name. Was he supposed to know him, just because Sandra did? That fact alone, Sandra knowing these jerks, was more than he could stand. He was blind with jealousy, he knew that—and could hardly breathe, much less apply reasoning to this mess.

"I'd be glad to stay out of your territory," Mike said. "In fact, the *three* of you can just part ways with me at the next town, and I promise you'll never have to worry about me or your territory again. *Never.*" He looked over at Sandra, who continued to cry, still staring straight ahead at the road.

"Now Mikey, ol' boy, don't be so hard-assed!" Cowboy taunted. "She was just up there visitin' for old times' sake and ran into her old crowd. We got to talkin' and she tells us that her boyfriend was fixin' to buy from Morales, so we asked her where. When she said Nuevo Laredo, Jack knew you'd get some of our goods, sooner or later. We just wanted to talk you out of doing the business with Robles. After we talked with Robles this afternoon, we could tell by the size of your first order that you was goin' to get some of our merchandise. He said he'd already cut his deal with you and was fixin' to ship it, the greedy beaner."

"I told you I haven't arranged shipping," Mike said hotly.

"Well, that peso-gougin' meskin must'a done it for you. He said the shipment was headed for your place in El Paso tonight."

Mike couldn't imagine how this could occur; Robles couldn't have received payment yet, although he had the bank draft, signed by Mike, and a letter from his bank assuring any acceptor that Mike Conner had a line of credit in place. Robles might enclose his invoice, overnight it to the El Paso bank and get money in a day or so via wire transfer, but that wasn't likely. He must have included a sufficient margin in his price negotiations to justify putting off these idiots with a story about the goods already being sold. He'd already arranged the shipping, or so he'd told Cowboy. Robles thought of everything to protect his deal with Mike. Something was drastically wrong with this story. Nothing ever worked smoothly in Mexico, and now it had worked so well it was about to get him killed—over merchandise he hadn't even paid for yet.

"We didn't let on to Robles what our interest in the stuff is, not exactly," Cowboy continued. "See, he don't know about the extra stuff that goes into the Morales goods—and we don't want him to. So, we can either hijack every truck goin' your way to look for our stuff or we can go to your place in El Paso and get it off the truck in a couple of days."

Some of this was beginning to make sense now. These two goons and their partners had an arrangement with someone on the manufacturer's end, at the Morales factory. But Robles evidently knew nothing about the drugs or the routing of the contraband to shops where they sold exclusively to these guys. He just ran his warehouse and had seen a chance to sell merchandise to Mike and line his pockets, like any good businessman.

But what about Sandra's involvement? As if to seek an explanation from her, he glanced over at her, looking for any sign this was not really happening, that it was all some crazy dream or joke or hallucination.

Hallucination—that was it. For at that instant, Sandra's eyes opened wide and she screamed, just like some psycho in a bad movie. Mike, driving seventy miles an hour, was still staring at Sandra, wondering why she was screaming, when the crash occurred.

In addition to natural wildlife roaming the roads of Texas, drivers also have to contend with wild hogs, feral descendants of domestic hogs. Their numbers have increased dramatically in recent years, boosted by the availability of food in farming areas, where they destroy crops and root up the land. In desert areas, they subsist on the occasional ranchers' feed crops and gardens, as well as native desert flora, grubs, and small animals. Roving in bands numbering several animals, they are a real menace to drivers, as well as farmers and ranchers. Though infrequent, collisions with hogs cause a lot of damage due to the animals' solid structure and weight.

Mike's current mental state deprived him of the ability to evaluate and act quickly. Before his foot had even left the accelerator, the vehicle hit the two-hundred-pound hog, rolling it under the chassis and briefly launching the car off the pavement. But even as the vehicle was out of control, Mike's mind suddenly cleared and reverted to its earlier strategy of hitting a deer. All the occupants flew forward, but Mike, with a grip on the wheel and feet braced, weathered the jolt better than the others. Whipping the wheel to the right, his finger sought the manual door lock for his door. Before the vehicle screeched to a halt, he opened his door and re-locked all the doors with the power lock button. He jumped out, slamming the door behind him and locking the others in the vehicle. Then he realized he should have grabbed the key, but it was too late to worry about it now.

He ran to the left side of the road and scrambled down the ditch, up the embankment and groped blindly for the fence. He didn't locate it immediately, but he did find a catclaw bush. He squelched a yell when the thorns pierced his hand, and the entire branch clung to him, attached at several places in his palm and index finger. He finally managed to tear free, painful as it was. He struck out again for the fence, more carefully this time. Then he heard someone scrambling up the embankment behind him.

"Mike!" Sandra half-whispered, half-gasped.

At first he didn't answer. He only wanted to get away from the two kidnappers and everything connected to them—and that included Sandra.

"Mike! Please! Wait for me!"

He stood motionless, wondering what to do, still shocked over the last few minutes' revelations. Scanning the darkness, he spotted her silhouette outlined by the headlights of his car sitting sideways in the road. Down on the highway, he could see movement inside the vehicle, the kidnappers dimly illuminated by the instrument panel lights. She was alone, having made it out of the car quickly by knowing exactly where the door lock button and door handle were positioned. Also, she would have been braced for the impact, whereas the back seat passengers hadn't seen the hog. Maybe they were dazed. Mike hoped they were dead, but the movement he saw in the vehicle belied that hope. "Over here," he answered cautiously.

"Mike, please, you've got to listen to me," she continued in a breathless whisper, growing closer as she neared the top of the embankment.

"Let's just get out of here," he said between clenched teeth. "I've had more than enough of your friends and quite enough of you. But come on, if you're going with me."

He realized as he said it that his conflicting statements closely matched the conflict in his mind. He wanted to get her out of here, out of danger, away from this. But he could not forget the treachery she had imposed on him, even if unwittingly. That she would have anything to do with a bunch of losers telling her about their drug business made him so angry he couldn't think straight. He knew he must put it out of his mind for the present and get as far away as possible. At least he didn't think Sandra's presence was a physical danger, not like the guys with guns.

He tried another spot and was rewarded with the feel of barbed wire and a fence post. He climbed the fence and dropped to the other side, then parted the middle strands of wire for Sandra. Standing on the other side of the fence, they faced each other for a few seconds of silence.

This is the first time since we met that I have absolutely nothing to say to her.

The thought made Mike angry and sad at the same time, but he couldn't dwell on it now. They first needed to put some distance between them and the kidnappers, a task he and Sandra could easily perform. Facing the enormity of the desert badlands before them would be nothing compared to the last few hours during which they'd had no control over their fates. Out here, their physical conditioning would kick in, the long hours of training runs would pay off. Hopefully, it would save their lives.

By now their eyes were adjusting to the moonlight, and they could see the vast desert before them, a forbidding expanse of land stretching south to the border and way beyond. Compared to the danger in the highway behind them, the hostile, eerily-lighted land looked downright inviting.

CHAPTER 6

▼

Breaking into a slow trot, Mike knew they'd be safe within minutes. The kidnappers' eyes wouldn't be any better adjusted to the darkness, and they had to contend with the catclaw, cactus thorns, and barbed wire, just as he and Sandra had. And while Cowboy may have been physically fit, Sarge looked too heavy to run very far, no matter what condition he was in.

"Stay directly behind me," he called softly to Sandra. "I'll try to pick us a good line."

The gravel crunched beneath their feet loud as gunshots, but each step was taking them farther from their captors, and the sound would soon be lost in the emptiness of West Texas. Mike calculated that, as the crow flies, they were only about ten miles from the Rio Grande. Unfortunately, they weren't crows. Already, they had run across rocky areas, some of the stones protruding just above the surface and hard to see in the dim light. After tripping and nearly falling face-first, he slowed the pace slightly; a twisted ankle wouldn't help matters right now.

He knew the guys behind them faced the same obstacles and at least one of them was wearing cowboy boots, so they weren't going to be very fast in their pursuit. Mike and Sandra were both wearing running shoes, especially lucky tonight. Mike had changed from his pool sandals, and Sandra hadn't arrived at the airport in high heels. Either of them having the wrong shoes would have greatly reduced their chances of escaping on foot in this rugged country.

About time something went right.

Back at the vehicle, Cowboy was dazed and bleeding slightly from a cut on his forehead, the result of smacking the door post after impact. Sarge was okay, but still fumbling around with the door lock. When he finally located it, he jumped from the vehicle and ran to the left side of the road, where he had glimpsed Mike sprinting only seconds after the wreck. He stopped at the roadside ditch and heard steps beyond the fence on the embankment, but couldn't be sure if the sound came from two sets of feet. Whether the pair had managed to join up wasn't that important; neither of them was in sight, and he saw the futility of pursuing them on foot, especially the guy.

Trotting back to the car, he helped Cowboy out of the vehicle. A few seconds later, Cowboy shook off Sarge's steadying hand and wandered around to the front of the vehicle where dizziness again overcame him, forcing him to lean against the fender.

Sarge searched around for a flashlight, then looked under the car to assess the damage. He knew the Land Cruiser was specifically built for off-road use, so he had hopes that it had survived the collision with the hog well enough to be driven. Shining the light on the underside, he couldn't see anything except the under-chassis steel skid plate that had served to launch the car like a ski ramp when it struck the animal. The tough steel shield had effectively prevented any mechanical damage to the steering mechanism or drive train.

Satisfied, he got into the driver's seat and restarted the engine. He pulled over to the shoulder and parked, leaving the engine running. Cowboy walked slowly to the passenger side and crawled in, easing his battered body carefully into the seat. As he closed the door, Sarge began ranting, "Goddamit, I told you that woman would cause trouble, and now she's gone, too! I heard them running away. They both hauled ass like a pair of fucking deer. And she's already told him more than he needed to know. He'll damn well get the rest of the story out of her now. Jack shouldn't have told her all that shit in the first place."

"It won't make any difference, because neither one of them is going to live to tell anybody else. The only place they can go is back to that little town a few miles back. And we're going to be waitin' for them when they get there."

Sarge pulled the vehicle into gear and made a U-turn. Dodging the hog's mangled body, he headed east, back toward Langtry.

Even at a slowed pace, Mike and Sandra were several hundred yards from the road when Sarge made the U-turn. In his peripheral vision, Mike saw that his vehicle was heading back in the direction they'd come from. The kidnappers would wait for them in Langtry, thinking it was the only place he and Sandra could possibly go. Unfortunately, they were right. As logical as it had seemed only a few minutes before, running to the border wouldn't accomplish much, not in this part of the state. They might find a fisherman on the upper reaches of Amistad Reservoir. If not, the rocky, barren shoreline didn't offer much except a place to swim to Mexico, where they would find another rocky, barren shoreline.

Some choice.

Mike slowed to a stop and turned to face Sandra. "Did you see the headlights?" he asked.

"No, which way did they go?"

"They headed back to Langtry. They've figured out it's the only place where we can go to get back to civilization. We could cut through here, go south to the lake, but that won't do us much good."

"Couldn't we contact the sheriff or somebody if we got to the lake?" Sandra asked.

"Maybe. We're more likely to find a game warden, *if* we can get to the lake, *if* anyone's in shouting distance, *if* we can get a ride…lots of ifs. And it's a long way, ten, twelve miles straight line, a good bit farther on foot. We have to cross some deep ravines as we get closer to the river. It's plenty rugged down there."

The discussion went on for several minutes, neither choice seeming very good. For the moment, though, it felt good to be out of immediate danger, away from the guys waving guns around. Mike almost wished they had pursued them on foot. He and Sandra had hiked across similar terrain many times, and he knew they could easily outlast most people, certainly those two who now had his car. Come daylight, the sun would soon heat the surface to well over one hundred degrees. Only a few hours of trekking in that environment separates the weak from the survivors. He would love to see the look on those two goons' faces when the heat and exhaustion overcame them, while he and Sandra, due to long training runs—and having recently consumed two bottles of water—would have many miles left in them. Seeing those two assholes gasping and convulsing on the verge of a heat stroke might be sufficient repayment for the past few hours, he thought.

But he didn't know what to do about Sandra. Where was she in all this mess? Had it really been just loose talk at a party, or was she working with them, sent up the embankment to stay with him, to lead him back to the captors? Mike decided to get it into the open; his doubts and reservations about her needed to be resolved here and now. He couldn't even decide which direction to walk without knowing the whole story.

He turned to face her in the darkness. "Look, I know this seems like a strange time to discuss the finer points of our relationship, but I'm not going anywhere without knowing how you fit into this drug business. I can't believe all the time we've spent together in the past several months, and in one hour I feel like I don't know you at all. I feel like a complete idiot, the dumbest sonofabitch in the world. Two assholes stick guns in my face, kidnap us, steal my car, and it turns out you *know* them!" His anger was growing again as he talked and recalled the past few frightening hours; the guns, the feeling of helplessness. He continued the attack. "Yeah, ol' buddies of yours! All the time, I was so concerned about what they might do to *you*. Well, I needn't have worried. It appears to me that you're all big buds, you and the *pistoleros*.

"Sandra, if you're not prepared to tell me the entire truth about these guys and how you came to know them and their business, I'm walking out of here without you. You just need to go back to the road, get to Langtry and find those guys. I'll make it on my own, without you or my car."

Sandra said nothing for a long moment, blinking and fighting to hold back tears. In the darkness, Mike could barely see her face and hear her swallowing hard to stifle a sob. "I don't know why I ever talked to them about your business," she began. "When I went back to Graham for a visit about six weeks ago—remember when I came back early? Anyway, I went to a party with my friends. Jack and his buddies were there, and I didn't want to bail on my friends, just because those jerks showed up. I thought I'd look stupid, like Jack was controlling me, just like he always did."

"Who's Jack?" Mike asked for the second time that night.

"He's my ex-husband. I told you about him, but I don't recall that I ever told you his name. Anyway, you never seemed very interested in my past life."

"No, I guess I wasn't too interested in the name of some guy who hit you, cheated on you, and made every effort to ruin your life. I had gotten the impression in the past several months you wanted to leave that part of your life behind, forget it and everyone associated with it. That's why I never asked you about your past or your marriage. I thought you wanted it that way."

"I did. I *do*. I realize now I made a mistake going back there to visit."

"Well, hooray for ol' Controlling Jack! It looks like he's controlling both of us now. We're stuck out here in the desert, and they've got my car and our belongings. And if they can find us, they're going to kill us. That sounds fairly controlling to me."

The tears which had subsided a bit began again in earnest with Mike's verbal jabs. "Mike, I'm sorry! I made a mistake and compounded it by not telling you about it, so you could be prepared."

"How did my name even come into the conversation? And how did that entail describing my business to them?"

"I don't know. The conversation started off...*casually*—you know, 'how are you?', 'how's El Paso?', 'you dating anybody?', 'what's he do for a living?'— that kind of talk. When I said you imported products from Mexico, Jack asked who you bought from. I told him you were trying to set up business with Morales. How could I have known that Morales was the same company they buy from, the company that smuggles drugs in by hiding it in pottery sold to drug-dealing importers?"

"I suppose you couldn't," Mike admitted. "But that's the problem with associating with people like that. They always have an ulterior motive, something they're trying to find out, somebody to scam."

"I know that now. Anyway, Jack and Dirk—that's the cowboy who kidnapped us—started telling me about their business in great detail, about the drugs and how they bought some items with cocaine inside, and I tried to just change the subject. I didn't really want to know what they were doing and the less I heard, the better. Except I had agreed to report—"

"Report on your boyfriend, so they could stick us up and steal my car and my merchandise?" Mike interrupted sarcastically.

"No! I told you, I was trying to change the subject. I thought talking about you would let them know that I had no interest in them, that I was more interested in Mike Conner and what he did, not their damn drug business, or how Morales hides cocaine in pottery so it can be smuggled into the States."

"We don't really know for sure. That's what those jerks were telling you, and what they were telling us just before the wreck, but their story may be entirely fabricated."

"That's what I thought. Or they were just drunk that night and showing off. Anyway, they said they would like to talk to you about buying from Morales—what could I say? I'd already mentioned it in the course of the conversation, so I couldn't suddenly deny you were going to buy from that company. They weren't *that* drunk."

"You could have explained that your boyfriend deals in pottery, not drugs."

"I told them if you thought Morales had anything to do with drug smuggling, you wouldn't buy from them. I see now they took that to mean I would cooperate and talk you out of buying anything from Morales, now or in the future."

"Why didn't you tell me about all this?"

"Mike, that night I thought they were just drunk, bragging about smuggling drugs and would forget it when they sobered up. Then, a couple of days ago, Dirk called me at work and asked me when you were going to arrange buying from Nuevo Laredo. I then realized they hadn't forgotten and it wasn't just drunk talk, all the crap about drugs and how they do it."

"How did he know where you worked?"

"I don't know. I guess he asked one of my friends in Graham, one of the girls I was visiting. Under normal circumstances, it isn't something I would keep secret, you know."

"I know, Sandra. It's just that they've used everything you told them to their advantage. They even knew my *car*, for crying out loud!"

Sandra thought for a minute before responding. "God, I remember now, that night at the party, he even asked me what kind of car you drove, just another innocent question; you know, acting curious about the guy I was seeing. I am such a bigmouth!"

"No wonder they were able to spot us at the airport and kidnap us. Why didn't you make them a key to it? Then they could have waited inside, run the air conditioner, waited for us in comfort." Mike paused for a moment in his tirade and said in a softer voice, "You shouldn't have told them anything, but now I understand how the conversation evolved. But you should have told *me*, Sandra."

"I know, Mike. I didn't know how *not* to tell him, so I told him you were coming down last weekend and I would fly in to meet you. I was afraid if I didn't tell him, he would do something. I knew I should tell you, but I didn't know how. I was hoping it would come to me on the trip down. I knew you'd be mad, and I just hoped it would all…go away. Anyway, the minute I got off the plane, you told me it was a done deal, so it was too late to change your mind. And I was terrified if you found out I'd even talked to Jack, you would end our relationship."

"Well, I'm not all that delighted. I didn't realize you were so enamored with him that you would run back home and look him up, get drunk with him, talk about his drug business, and make me a target for two jackass helpers of his. Why didn't you just paint a bull's-eye on the back of my shirt?" Mike was getting angry again, his voice rising, hurling the ridiculous questions at her faster than she could respond.

"That's not the way it was, I didn't *look him up!*" she sobbed. "I told you, Jack and Dirk just showed up at a party. He just happened to be there. Mike, please, you've got to believe me, I am so sorry any of this happened. I..." At that point, the sobbing turned into a flood of tears and she couldn't talk. She sat down on the rocky ground and began to cry uncontrollably.

Mike suddenly felt overcome by a different emotion and regretted his earlier remarks. Seeing her this upset, he realized how much he cared for her. But how could she endanger him; no, *both* of them, how could she be so silly and careless around people she already *knew* couldn't be trusted? And why had she put herself in the same place with any of the people she knew during her marriage, a marriage that had been so rotten? Even as those questions raced through his mind, Mike conceded that her explanation sounded plausible enough. She was basically shy, and if someone hounded her or intimidated her, she would be unable to tell them to get lost, especially the overbearing jerks from her past.

He sat down beside her and put his arms around her, pulling her close. The crying subsided somewhat and, after a few minutes, ceased altogether. "Sandra," he began carefully, "just tell me why you were spending time with anyone from your past. You've told me how miserable you were the whole time—why would you want to expose yourself to that environment, those people, that kind of life?"

"They seemed so interested in me," she sniffed. "A few months ago, the first time I went home to visit, I ran into two girlfriends from school, and they couldn't seem to get enough information about how I was, what I was doing, all about you, lots of things. And they told me all about their lives, everything they had been doing, what they planned, on and on. I could tell they really cared. That's why I agreed to visit again a few weeks ago, when all this mess started."

"I can understand that your relationship with those people is different, but I never thought you'd prefer it to ours. I guess I've misjudged my ability to please you," he added bitterly.

"You *do* please me, Mike. But some of my old friends seem to take a personal interest in me. I'm not talking about Jack and Dirk, I mean my girlfriends, ones I grew up with. They seem to want to be *close*. Not like us, you and me. You do a lot of things for me and you spend time with me and sometimes I think you really do care for me, but you keep your distance. You insulate yourself and your life from me. You don't discuss anything intimate. I want to be closer to you, but you don't allow it. I guess I need that part of human contact, and you don't."

"I've always been the same with you. I've not hidden anything, I act the same way all the time. No deceptions. No lies. Everything I tell you is the absolute truth. And I haven't seen any other woman in months, because I don't *want* to. I love spending time with you, because I thought we had a great relationship. It would appear I was mistaken." He said the last sentence with more force than he intended, but he couldn't help growing angry again as he recounted what he thought were his good qualities. Care, concern, devotion, fidelity—was there no reward, or even *recognition* for those qualities, the ones all women claimed to be looking for? Maybe if he had knocked a few teeth loose, like her husband did, or rifled through her purse for beer money, maybe she would have taken that as being interested in her, he thought bitterly.

"I know all that," she said, starting to cry again. "And that's why I feel so bad about getting us—you—into this mess." The flow of tears increased.

Drop it, Mike. Don't even try to make sense of it.

CHAPTER 7

▼

The Ford Super Cab pulled a long, open-bed trailer into the lumber yard parking lot and dieseled to a stop near the loading dock. The driver got out and sauntered in to pick out materials to be loaded.

At just over six feet and two hundred pounds, with a store mannequin's proportions, Jack Pearson had always used his ready smile and cocky demeanor to charm everyone he met. With his Stetson cocked jauntily back over a main of dark hair, Jack still cut a handsome figure, although the weight was starting to shift from the shoulders to the stomach, a 'pound pilgrimage' that exacerbated the comedic appearance of his stride.

Indeed, to an observer, it would seem that Jack suffered from painful, sun-burned underarms; hands held well away from the body, arms swinging like stiff pendulums, a bit too jerky and exaggerated for the speed and cadence of the walk. Actually, the stride had been purposely affected during Jack's youth, swaggering through beer joints and dance halls in an imitation of the rodeo cowboys he admired.

Now, swinging arms in full action in the bulk lumber section, he approached a roving clerk pushing a big four-wheel cart, proffered a long list of items, and began discussing his order. After a lengthy exchange, the clerk abandoned the dolly in mid-aisle and scurried off to fill the order.

A half hour later, after verification and loading of the supplies, the clerk handed Jack an invoice and pointed to a contractors' check-out area. As Jack approached the register, he pulled a wad of bills from his front pocket and peeled off several hundreds. In smaller towns, merchants seldom saw big purchases made with cash, but here on the west side of Fort Worth, no one would question a large amount of currency, In the commercial lumber business, sales counted, not audit trails.

Jack Pearson had entered the construction business like many other semi-skilled, blue-collar young men of his generation. Jack had excelled at all the peripheries of the trade: drinking beer, using colorful language, driving a pickup, and working with a hangover. But he had also developed a real sense of getting the job done, a trait which drew the attention of the boss, a retired military man everyone called Sarge.

Sarge put Jack in charge of a crew of three men, including a reliable, if not too bright young guy named Dirk Benson. At Sarge's direction, they moved from job site to job site, doing house remodeling projects. Throughout the building boom of the eighties, Jack made Sarge a lot of money and gained experience in all aspects of the trade, including the intricacies of finances in the construction industry. It was Jack's knowledge of finance as it related to the construction trade that prompted Sarge to send him on sales excursions, soliciting work to keep them all busy in the future. Jack could sell jobs at a higher price, even as a credit crunch and banking crisis wiped out many small companies, including Sarge's. In an odd twist of events, Sarge then went to work for the ever-successful Jack.

During that period of soliciting jobs, Jack met Reynaldo Gomez, a mysterious resident of Wichita Falls, whom local rumor-mongers had labeled a "rich Mexican National" who sought refuge from the violence in Mexico in this conservative part of North Texas. Gomez was sometimes seen in the company of a younger woman, a dark-haired beauty named Eva, who immediately mesmerized Jack.

Gomez was evidently well-heeled, driving expensive cars and living in a veritable mansion with which Eva was never satisfied. Her demands to redecorate her living abode led to the hiring of one Jack Pearson and the development of an unusual relationship between him and the glamorous Gomez couple. It also strained Jack's relationship with his wife, Sandra.

Jack spent more and more time with the Gomez couple, lunching with Reynaldo one day and driving to Dallas with Eva to pick out wallpaper the next. At some juncture, talk among the newly-formed friendship turned to money and how to make more of it. Eventually, Jack was introduced to a certain illicit trade with Reynaldo's contacts in Mexico.

Jack was attracted to the handsome, urbane Reynaldo and the gorgeous, bitchy Eva. In turn, Reynaldo saw Jack as an asset to his trade: smart, industrious, knowledgeable about mechanical things, able to travel with pickup and trailer anywhere, anytime. He also saw in Jack's business the one critical link for any illegal gains operation—the ability to wash money. The very same factor which had enabled Jack to price his work shrewdly would serve to wash large amounts of money for Reynaldo's trade. The price of material could vary greatly, invoices could be changed, altered, or destroyed. The amount of money received for work could easily change with the customers' expressed desires; it could be padded with additional currency, decreased, increased, expensed out, banked—a smorgasbord of options existed to turn dirty money into clean, taxable profit of a small, successful construction company.

The relationship continued for a couple of years, with Jack providing the jobs as a vehicle for Reynaldo to wash money, and Reynaldo compensating Jack well for his role in presenting a viable, tax-paying entity as a business front. Jack met others in the hierarchy of Reynaldo's chain and occasionally spent time in lush Mexican resorts being wined and dined. He also was entertained by Eva during this period, putting more strain on his already rocky marriage to Sandra.

Sandra, though pretty and bright, was no match for the sexy, sultry Eva, who apparently plied her wiles on Jack with great success. Jack became more and more distant; he felt constrained by his marriage. Jack thought Sandra had unreasonable expectations regarding another woman's lipstick on his shirts, the scent of perfume in the car, and credit card receipts from hotels they'd never stayed in together. Those incidents and more placed the relationship in jeopardy, eventually leading to divorce and Sandra's departure.

Sandra had stayed in the area, working as a mortgage lender for a local financial services firm. She found new friends, took up running, began exercising on a regular basis, and generally changed her life to a calmer and healthier, though less exciting, one. Eventually, she had moved to El Paso, returning to her hometown a couple of times to visit old friends. During one of these visits, Jack had seen her and learned of her connection to a guy in El Paso, a guy who also had an unfortunate, though completely innocent, connection to Jack and Reynaldo's business. That connection had presented a minor problem, albeit a solvable one—according to Jack.

Returning from Fort Worth, Jack unloaded the materials at a construction site, then drove to his office. Propping his feet on his desk, he shuffled through some paperwork and began checking his phone messages. Pressing the button for successive calls, he erased most of them and listened completely to only one. Jack re-played it twice more before slamming his hand down on his desk, causing the phone to jump. "Goddammit! I should have known those dumbasses would screw it up!" he ranted to the empty office.

He jumped from his chair and stalked around the office, deliberating on what to do next. The "minor problem" was now spiraling out of control. Reaching for the phone again, he dialed the number left in the recording.

After only one ring, Cowboy picked up. *"Where are they?"* Jack snapped. *"And how the hell did they get away?"*

"Jack, we had a wreck, we hit a fucking hog in the road and they got out and ran, both of them."

"Well, goddammit, why didn't you chase them, run their asses down? Did you two just sit there and watch them run off?"

"Shit, they ran like goddam deer, Jack! They just hauled ass across the pasture, headed south. Hell, you remember those people Sandra came to the party with, they was all runners, they run miles and miles, every day, just for fun…on foot!"

"That's how most running is done, Dirk."

"Huh? Oh, yeah. Anyway, you even said something about how fucked up they all was, standing around at the party, drinking nothing but water. Which reminds me, goddammit, they both bought a shitload of water when we stopped for gas. I guess they wanted to tank up in case they got away. It's hot as hell and plenty dry out here, but they got a good supply before they ran. Anyhow, we figured they'd have to come back to this little burg sooner or later, no matter how much water they drank. They also got to piss and sweat, so they'll get thirsty again. It's the only place anywhere near here where they could even get a drink." After a moment's silence in which Jack didn't respond, he added, *"We been waitin' here all night and half the day already."*

"You're gonna wait longer," Jack snapped. *"Y'all shouldn't have let them get away, dammit. You knew damn good and well they could outrun your lazy asses if they got half a chance. You should have tied them up. Now, where is that shit he bought from Morales?"*

"He said he didn't even close the deal yet. But we went and asked Robles and he told us he'd already shipped it on to El Paso, the same damn day. That greedy Meskin saw a chance to sell a shitload of stuff for sure payment and decided to ship it out before Conner could change his mind. Conner must have seemed like the type who had the money arranged and would come back and pay him in full.

Anyway, we couldn't find out exactly which truck it left on, but it was the Zamora Trucking Company out of Nuevo Laredo."

"Well, then we can't grab it in transit. I'll have to get someone on to El Paso to buy the stuff from his shop. It'll take two or three days to get there, and I'll have to pay full price from that fucking shop of his to avoid raising any suspicion with whoever he's got running the place."

The thought of Sandra's boyfriend making full profit from merchandise which he shouldn't even have bought made Jack livid, but his contact at Morales headquarters had told him that a large portion of the items warehoused in Robles' place had hollow compartments filled with product. Gomez would go ballistic if a bunch of clay pots crammed with cocaine were sold to a vacationing accountant from Des Moines, and Jack didn't want to face that.

"You wait until I get there," Jack continued. *"I'll go see Gomez right now. Maybe some of his guys out of El Paso can handle getting the stuff back so we don't have to pay for it."*

"Okay, Jack. We're sittin' at the pay phone here by the tourist center, but we can see the whole damn town from here. There ain't nothing here but this place and a memorial museum for Judge Roy Bean. We parked his car down the street. We can't hang around too close to it, in case he reported it stolen."

"I don't know how he'd do that, stuck out there in the badlands. There ain't shit out there west of Langtry, no cell phone service for sure. They have to come back there or die of thirst."

"All right, we'll wait here for them. What do we do with them if they show up?" Cowboy asked."

"Just get them in the car and wait for me. And don't let them get away again, you hear me? I'm gonna have enough trouble explaining this one to Gomez. Where's Sarge?"

"He's leaning up against a mesquite tree over there taking a snooze. You want to talk to him?"

"Nah, just be sure one of you stays awake and get those two rounded up when they show. Come to think of it, Gomez may even want to come down there with me and personally oversee their disposal. Anyway, I'll call and let you know about what time we'll be getting there."

"Okay, no problem." After a slight pause, Dirk added, *"Shit, Jack, I feel like I been rode hard and put away wet."*

"Well, Dirk, that's better than the other way around, ain't it?"

CHAPTER 8

▼

Mike peered over the *cenizo* bush toward the ramshackle buildings on the south edge of Langtry, straining his eyes to see if he could spot Cowboy and Sarge among the scattered tourists. No luck. No Land Cruiser, either. From this angle, he couldn't see the museum or the visitors' center parking lot. In fact, from here, he couldn't see anything except a mangy dog licking itself on the sidewalk.

That dog is the only one that knows what he's doing.

"I don't see either of them, or the car," he said quietly to Sandra.

"Maybe they went on to Del Rio. Or maybe they turned around and decided to go to El Paso. It's the merchandise they really want, not us. Right?"

"They know we might go to the law. They've got to find us first, before we get to a place where we can contact the Sheriff's Department. Let's circle around to the east, so we can see down that main street in front of the museum."

It was late morning, and the sun was climbing steadily, along with the temperature. This was the fourth vantage point they had tried, and the only part of town left unchecked was the main street in front of the tourist attractions. If the car wasn't there, Mike was quickly running out of ideas.

They had walked through the night, their progress slowed by the increasingly rougher landscape west of the little settlement. Oddly, driving through the region allowed one to see for miles to the horizon in any direction, giving the illusion that the land was fairly flat. On foot, the gently rolling hills weren't so gentle; instead, they obscure rocky outcroppings, gullies, and deep ravines cut by centuries of flood waters rushing to the Rio Grande. Patches of knee-high, thorny vegetation cropped up in any area that wasn't solid rock, making travel on foot a tough undertaking.

During the long walk, the pair had discussed how to get their car back, avoid recapture and get the two thugs arrested. Mike reminded her that even if they found a law enforcement officer, the two kidnappers would have concocted a story by now. "What exactly do we say? Those guys forced us into our own car at gunpoint? And when we finally escaped, we walked miles through the desert to come here, to face them unarmed?"

"Well, that's what happened."

"Sure, but they know our full names and enough about us to tell a good story, like we were all together and then argued after I hit the hog. They'll say I was drunk and they took the keys from me for all our sakes. They'll walk, I promise you."

"Mike, they held guns on us! They *kidnapped* us!"

"They'd just deny it. I'm sure they have permits to carry those guns, just like I do. Since the car's registered to me, we'll get it back sooner or later, but I promise you, those two won't go to jail over this."

"Mike, this is unbelievable! How can they do that and not go to prison?"

"It's our word against theirs, and our story is no better than the one I just concocted. Every day, law enforcement officers hear wild stories, most of them pure fabrication. All you have to do is ask any cop, and he'll tell you that *everybody* has a story and they're *all* victims. We wouldn't be any different, just two more nuts with a crazy story."

"But Mike, we know the truth. I—"

"Sandra, that shipment of pottery is invoiced to me and is heading to my shop. Those two could easily point out that fact to the police, and I'd have a hell of a time convincing them it's not *my* nose candy hidden inside the pieces. And even with our knowledge of what has been going on, you might start telling the story and get tied in with them."

"But I can explain my connection to those people—"

"Like you did to me? Under the circumstances, I was pretty hard to convince, and I know you. I *care* for you. You want to explain your relationship with those mutts to a couple of hard-nosed cops who've never seen you?"

Sandra started to say something else, but thought better of it. Mike was right. No matter what the story, some cynical, overworked cop wasn't going to buy it—not even the *real* story, not right now.

Beyond that grim assessment, they hadn't devised anything concrete; there were too many unknowns about the situation to implement a plan until they could see if, and where, Dirk and Sarge were waiting. It did seem best to get the car, get completely away from the kidnappers and straighten it out under a scenario of their own choosing. Mike had a spare key under the vehicle, so if they could get to it, retrieve the key from its magnetic box and get in, escape should be easy. But first, they had to have some good fortune in locating the vehicle. Given the general trend of events in the past twenty or so hours, it seemed a lot to ask.

Now, as they circled to the east side of town, Mike told Sandra his plan for getting the car back. "Remember how that Dirk guy kept making remarks and leering at you? If it comes down to it, we may have to capitalize on that. You're going to have to deal with him, not the one called Sarge. He's smarter than the cowboy."

"That's not saying much, but you're right. I can handle Dirk easier than Sarge."

"You can convince Dirk you've returned to them, but that I've gone south to the border and left you. Make an excuse to get into the car by yourself—tell him you want to get your stuff, change clothes or something—and use the opportunity to get the magnetic key box. I can't imagine he would just hand you the key they've got, so if he walks you to the car to unlock it for you, tell him you need some privacy. Wait until he walks away to go for the key box."

Sandra wrinkled her nose at this suggestion; doing anything with the sneering, pig-minded Dirk in her presence was distasteful. But she knew she had to do something. This whole thing was a result of her talking to Dirk and his buddies in the first place, so she'd have to figure out something.

Mike described exactly where the box was stuck to the frame. "Just look at the gap between the front fender and the door. It's under the car body at that point, about eight inches under, sticking to the outside of the frame," he explained, pantomiming reaching under the car to retrieve the key box.

"This is about eight inches, right?" Sandra interrupted, smirking and holding her thumb and forefinger barely two inches apart. "At least that's what men keep telling women."

Mike rolled his eyes at her bawdy comment and shook an admonishing finger at her. "No, no, that's more like *nine* inches, Sweetheart. Women just never learn measurements. But more about that later. Listen, the box has a slide lid, so look at it quickly to see which way to open it. The key is wrapped in a piece of oilcloth, so you'll have to unwrap it. Even a few seconds counts, so just do it carefully and don't get in a panic. If you drop it, it'll only take longer."

Luckily for Mike and Sandra, the little town had a steady stream of tourists, so two more people, though dusty and disheveled, were not especially alarming. Before noon, they had worked in a huge semi-circle around to the northeast end of town, where three junk cars sat rusting near a shack. Mike still couldn't see directly into the museum parking lot, so he moved farther north, staying behind the junked cars. Raising his head slowly, he saw his Land Cruiser parked in the end of the lot nearest him. Unfortunately, the squat figure sitting nearby on the curb was undoubtedly Sarge, and Dirk couldn't be too far away.

Sure enough, about two minutes later Dirk ambled up and said something to the larger man. He must have returned to relieve Sarge, because the heavy man strode off toward the visitor center entrance, while Dirk leaned against the car. Mike waited until he turned his head the other way, then sprinted back to Sandra. "I spotted the car at the museum, but they're not going to leave it unguarded. They may suspect we have another key on us or hidden under the car. We can't even get into the convenience store or the museum without being seen. You've got to trick Dirk into letting you use the car to change clothes. Then you'll have to drop something beside the car and get the key while you're stooping to pick it up."

"I'll just have to play it out," Sandra agreed. "Dirk's not the brightest light in the room, and I think I can get him to leave me alone in the car. I just hope that Sarge guy doesn't come back. He's smarter and a lot more dangerous. Jack used him to collect some money a couple of times. I think he roughed up some people, did a real job on them."

At that remark, Mike began to rethink his plan. "On second thought, I don't like this. What if they don't believe you? What if they've talked to Jack, and he wants to do something different, like shoot both of us on sight? Who's going to miss us? If they do that, they can go on to El Paso at their leisure and take the stuff away from the shop the same way. That couple who run the shop for me wouldn't suspect a thing until it's too late, and I'd hate to get Mr. and Mrs. Hanson hurt over this. Come to think of it, they'd kill them just to silence *all* of us for good, I'm certain of that. Plus, they'd get their shipment back, paid for by me."

"But Mike, without being caught in the act, the law will never connect them to the drug scam. Like you said—*you're* more connected to the drugs than they are. We've got to be the ones to explain this mess voluntarily and privately to a law enforcement officer, not in front of Dirk and Sarge."

Even as she made the observation, it occurred to Mike that Dirk and Sarge had grilled Robles, so they undoubtedly knew which trucking company was hauling the drug-filled pottery. Dirk and Sarge might even be in line for a reward for revealing that information, either to the law or some other drug dealer. After all, they didn't care that it was supposed to have been Jack's shipment; they'd collect no matter who got to the stuff first.

"I know is seems risky, but I've got to do something," Sandra continued. "I got us in this mess, and I can help get us out."

As dangerous as it might be to put Sandra with Dirk, they both knew they had to retrieve the vehicle and get away until they could contact the authorities under their own terms. They went over the plan again, Sandra firm in her belief that she could manipulate Dirk.

Mike finally agreed and pointed out a spot on the main street through town where Sandra could pick him up. "Be sure to unlock the passenger door," he grinned. "I don't want to hang onto the mirror all the way back to Del Rio."

"Well, don't just stroll over to the car," she countered. "Get your butt in gear when I get headed in this direction. If I wanted to wait around all day for a slow, out-of-shape guy, I'd wait for a fat one, not some skinny dude like you."

Mike faked a scowl at her, then let it shift to a grin. He pulled her close and said, "Sandra, be careful. If it looks like it's going bad, just get away from that jerk. I know he seems too goofy to be a cold-blooded killer, but who knows what someone will do for the kind of money the shipment's worth?"

"I know, I know. But I can handle him, Mike, I really can. I've got to do this," she added, standing on her tiptoes to kiss him, then quickly turning to go before he could say anything more.

A few minutes later, she had worked her way back to the south end of town so she could appear on the scene walking from the direction they had traveled, not from Mike's location. She forced herself to stroll slowly past the convenience store and turned right toward the parking lot. Thankfully, Sarge was nowhere in sight, but Dirk was propped up against the front fender, trying to stay in the thin shade of a mesquite tree.

"Dirk!" Sandra called out as she neared the vehicle.

He spun around and looked at her like she was an apparition arisen from a graveyard. Regaining his composure, he glanced up the street for Sarge.

Sandra came closer and said, "Get my stuff out of the car, will you?" Sensing that going on the offensive was the only tool she had, she put as much force in her voice as she could muster, adding, "I'll catch my own ride out of here. I'm through with this mess and everyone involved in it."

"Well now," Dirk drawled, "it seems to me you're in no position to be making demands, seein' as how you chose your side last night. Why don't you just get your boyfriend to buy you some new stuff? Or is the mall a little too far away?" He sneered, giggling at his own joke.

"He chose his own side last night, left me alone and headed for the border. Said he could be back in El Paso before you got there and that he'd be ready for your arrival," she ad-libbed, throwing in the last part with a smirk.

"That's bullshit, there's nothing out there but miles and miles of more miles. All he's gonna get out there is thirsty," he declared with a wave of his hand toward the south.

"He's a good long-distance runner, so the distance is nothing to him. He said he was going to walk to the upper end of the lake and get a ride with someone to a fishing camp near Del Rio. From there, I guess he'll rent a car and drive to El Paso. But I don't care, he made it quite clear I wasn't going with him. I've had enough of all of you, you're all nothing but trouble, so just let me get my stuff."

Dirk hesitated, leering as Sandra walked up to him. Her blouse was unbuttoned, and he seemed to be having a little trouble concentrating. After a few seconds of blatantly staring at her breasts, he said, "Nope. No dice. You should've thought of that when you were with us last night. All you had to do was go along for the ride and then convince ol' Mikey boy not to buy any more from Morales. We was goin' to get our stuff and leave both y'all alone after that. But now you waltz in here and want to re-trade the deal. Well, I don't appreciate being second place." He unfolded his arms and pushed away from the car. "On the other hand, if you *really* want your stuff, we can work something out, and any place with you is fine with me."

As he stepped closer, his eyes traveled down her blouse and back up again. Sandra had to clench her teeth at the disgust she felt, but she knew it would take a commitment from her, right now, to get him to go along. Something needed to happen, and fast, before Sarge came back. Her unbuttoned blouse was clouding Dirk's judgment for the moment, and she had to make the best of it. "It might be fine with me too, but not here, and not now," she said.

Feeling like an actress in a bad soap opera, she pushed her hair back from her face and gazed at him seductively. Despite the desperation of the moment, she nearly laughed out loud when she remembered she was covered with dirt and dust, hadn't slept in two days, and would have given fifty dollars to brush her teeth.

And she hoped to God she'd never have to do anything like this again.

CHAPTER 9

▼

The poolside phone rang several times before the woman cursed, reached back to re-hook her top and rose to answer it. Eva's skin was very dark, like her hair, and her eyes, if one could have seen them through the huge sunglasses, would have provided a perfect match for the rest of her—dark and sexy.

Eva's annoyance disappeared when it was Jack on the other end. *"Oh, hi! No, no. I was just getting some sun."*

A low chuckle on the other end, a remark about getting something else.

"Well, come on over then!" she said.

"I'd love to Baby, but some other time, maybe. Look, I really need to talk to Reynaldo. Is he around?"

"No, he's gone downtown to his office, but you can come over here and wait for him," she purred. *"He said he'd come home for lunch."*

"Darlin', as inviting as that sounds, I better try to catch him before he leaves his office. I got something going on that needs his attention."

"Okay, but don't say I didn't ask!"

After a few more suggestive comments back and forth between them, Jack hung up and called Reynaldo's office. He was told that Mr. Gomez was in conference, so he decided to drive up and catch him before he left for lunch. This matter called for a face-to-face meeting anyway. He asked the secretary to get him in just before lunch, then headed north to Wichita Falls.

During the drive to Reynaldo's office, Jack pondered the problems: Mike and Sandra's escape, the merchandise in shipment, and their ongoing business with Morales. Apparently, Sandra hadn't been able to dissuade Mike from buying from Morales. Jack had been certain she'd change her boyfriend's mind to buy from someone else. He also figured she'd been scared by his description of the drug import activity and would come up with a plausible explanation to the guy without disclosing any details about the hidden drugs. She didn't like anything not on the up-and-up; she never had. That had been her problem all along, Jack thought, she just wouldn't agree to go along with things he liked. But he could tell by her expression that night at the party that he could still intimidate her.

Dirk had related the previous night's events to him, including how Sandra had blurted out to Mike about Morales' special exports. Now, both of them had to be silenced, Jack thought grimly. Dammit, he mused, I should have gone myself. I'd never have let it get this far. As soon as Sandra mentioned the hidden drugs, both she and her boyfriend should have been eliminated and their bodies drug out into the rocky wasteland for the buzzards to take care of. That shithead Dirk was worthless as tits on a boar hog, and Sarge, though handy at physical tasks, needed constant supervision.

As usual, Jack was convinced he could handle everything better than anyone else; anyone, that is, except Reynaldo Gomez. Jack hated having to tell Reynaldo of the trouble, because he'd assured him soon after hearing about Mike's new supplier that it would be taken care of immediately. It hadn't been, and now it was in a mess. But Reynaldo would be even angrier if it carried on without a resolution. He'd want to be informed and involved until the problem was fixed.

At the moment Mike and Sandra were arriving at the outskirts of Langtry to find their vehicle, Reynaldo greeted Jack at the door of his plush office. "So Jack, my friend," he said, "what brings you all the way up here? Not just to see old Reynaldo, is it? You probably have been over to *mi casa* to visit Eva, no?"

"No, no, Reynaldo, nothing like that!" Jack laughed at their ongoing joke. "I'd sure like nothing better than to see her lovely face, but something important has come up, and I need your help with it."

"Of course, of course, my friend. Come on in. Have a seat." Reynaldo led Jack into the office and motioned to a sofa, rather than sitting behind his desk and seating his partner in front, like a borrower at the bank. He wanted Jack to feel comfortable, and be open with whatever he wished to discuss, and that meant he needed to feel equal in stature and importance. It was a tactic that had served Gomez well; when people were made to feel important, they often imparted information they'd never intended to, information that gave him a strategic advantage.

Although both men knew Gomez was the real power in the relationship, that fact rarely surfaced between them, at least not in an overt form. Whatever Jack's shortcomings, and despite some recent troubling information, Gomez knew Jack was generally a problem solver in his business. It would be interesting to hear what situation justified this face-to-face meeting. He had an inkling, though, and it didn't take long to find out.

"What can I do for you, Jack? How can I help?"

"Reynaldo, we have a real problem with that Conner guy I told you was setting up a buying relationship with Morales. Sandra didn't wave him off of the deal, so I sent Dirk and Sarge down there to meet him in Laredo and talk with him one-on-one to discourage his purchasing from Morales.

"Well, kiss my ass and call me Shorty if the son of a bitch hadn't already bought a shitload of stuff—and that goddam Robles shipped it out for him, same day! Dirk and Sarge met up with them to talk a little turkey and decided to haul them to El Paso to get the stuff."

When Reynaldo frowned, Jack couldn't tell whether the displeasure was with his handling of the matter or just the resulting complications, but he forged ahead with the truth, knowing better than to do otherwise. "Dirk and Sarge was sittin' in the back so they could watch them, and Conner was driving. On the way, he hits a fucking hog in the road, damn near turns the car over, and in the confusion, he and Sandra jump out and haul ass."

"Where are they now?" Gomez interrupted, leaning forward, a trace of hardness entering his normally cultured voice.

"Out in that God-awful wasteland just up the river from Del Rio, close to Amistad Reservoir. Dirk and Sarge are waiting for them to come back to some little shit town where they've got his car. They figure they got to show up back there—hell, there's nothing for a hundred miles anywhere near there."

"Show me," Gomez ordered, producing a road map from his desk drawer.

The missing topographic detail somewhat belied the enormity of trying to find someone in the desolate area surrounding Langtry. Nevertheless, Gomez knew a great deal about the border area, and his quick perusal of the map told him it would be a huge task to search for two people in a remote area of southwest Texas; it would certainly be better if they just showed up. But unlike Jack, he didn't think the two runaways would cooperate. Perhaps,

Gomez thought, they are tougher than Jack knows. Jack's major weakness was underestimating others. Maybe they would die in the heat and dust. Or maybe they would get lucky and hitch a ride out of the desert. But he could not take the chance that they would survive to tell anyone about the specialty items produced by Morales.

Pulling a telephone toward him, Gomez first placed an international call to Nuevo Laredo, left a message, then called Eva. After speaking with her for a few minutes, he placed a third call, to the operator of a flying service at the Wichita Falls airport. He arranged for a charter flight to Del Rio, leaving in forty-five minutes.

Jack sat quietly, trying to gauge Gomez' mood, but he couldn't tell if Gomez was angry at him or not. Jack had rarely seen this, and it was unsettling, not knowing what was going through Reynaldo's mind. He knew he and Reynaldo shared several things (besides Eva): a love of the good life, spending money, and generally being flamboyant. But there the resemblance ended. Jack blustered his way into everything, reasoning that more noise and action would settle whatever needed his attention. He saw himself as an important, big-picture man.

Gomez was different, especially when it came to business. Despite his flashy appearance, Gomez was no-nonsense about commercial matters; he analyzed and studied each problem, looking at details, looking for the obvious, as well as any hidden subtleties. It was the behavior he had exhibited a few minutes earlier—not simply flying into a rage over the escape of the pair, none of the colorful language used by Jack, but immediately seeking a solution by studying a common road map.

Like many successful men, Gomez had learned that the best way to handle anything difficult was to do it himself. And while he recognized Jack's abilities in certain areas, he knew his greedy, loud-mouthed partner's limitations. This was beginning to look like one of the times he should have taken charge. Maybe Jack is losing his edge, Gomez thought...or perhaps he has something else in mind.

The drug importer also knew all about Jack and Eva, but like every other set of circumstances in his life, he was using it to further his needs elsewhere. Let Jack think he was fooling old Reynaldo; Gomez let it continue only because he wished it so. It might solve a problem he had seen coming for months. He also wished this current problem to be eradicated once and for all, and quickly. He would take Jack and go see this Mike Conner for himself.

"Jack," Reynaldo said, again turning his attention to his partner, "we are going on a little trip, you and I. We will meet some people I know in Del Rio who can help us with this little *problema*. We will fly down to Del Rio, then go out to this Langtry place. If Dirk and *Sargento* have already got them back, our task will be easier. If not, we will hunt for them ourselves. And no matter which, we will have some dinner in *Ciudad Acuña* and maybe some entertainment afterward. You have your passport?"

"Sure do. You know me, Reynaldo, always ready for action," Jack answered.

Reynaldo excused himself, went into the adjoining executive restroom where he kept changes of clothes and emerged a few minutes later wearing jeans and boots, dressed not unlike Jack or Dirk. Jack wasn't surprised; he'd seen this type of transformation before. Gomez had the background and experience to become a variety of things at a moment's notice, whether it be a working cowboy in Wichita Falls, a sophisticated businessman in Mexico City, or a slick drug dealer in Los Angeles. During his relationship with Gomez, Jack had seen all those, and more.

Donning a pair of expensive mirrored sunglasses, he gestured for Jack to precede him out of the office. Reynaldo paused to adjust the leg of his jeans over his boot top, concealing the ankle holster with the .38 Colt snub-nosed revolver. After spending a few minutes with his secretary in the outer office issuing instructions, the pair went down the elevator and headed for the airport in Jack's pickup. On the way, Reynaldo made two more calls on his cell phone, speaking softly in Spanish.

Jack, who understood almost no Spanish, wondered about the emphasis his boss placed on the phrase *"matarlos."*

He had no idea that it meant "kill them."

CHAPTER 10

▼

Sandra casually unbuttoned one more button on her blouse and stepped closer, turning sideways to move between Dirk and the car. "If you'll let me in there to change clothes," she said, smiling, "you can go talk to Sarge about getting lost for a while." She let the remark sink in before adding. "Then I just want to take my stuff and leave. I can catch a ride with some tourist heading for Del Rio."

"Aw, Baby, you might not want to leave after all!" Dirk whined.

"We'll see. But I don't want Sarge around, and I don't want him to know what we're doing."

As if to make her point, Sandra glanced nervously around Dirk's shoulder and up the street toward the museum where Sarge had disappeared. She hoped Dirk interpreted her aversion to Sarge as modesty, but she knew that Sarge, sharper than Dirk, would know immediately what she was up to. Dirk was busy staring at her exposed breasts, but surely he realized nothing was going to happen until he delayed Sarge's return.

"Okay, I'll be back in a few minutes. I'll send Sarge down to that little restaurant and tell him to go ahead and eat, and that I'll go when he gets back. The way Sarge eats, we'll have plenty of time." Dirk laughed loudly at his joke, nervous at this chance to get his hands on Sandra. Like most loud-mouthed, self-proclaimed Lotharios, he wasn't nearly as cool and composed as he liked to pretend.

He reached into his pocket for the key and unlocked the driver's door.

Sandra squeezed past him and climbed into the driver's seat on her knees and bent over to search the passenger side floor for her purse. Even though Mike had placed her single piece of luggage in the back when they were leaving the airport, it was her purse she really wanted. And all Dirk wanted was to stand there and stare as she bent over the center console.

She emerged, clutching her purse and pushing Dirk away from her and the vehicle. "Now go, get rid of Sarge before he comes back."

Dirk turned to go, then partially recovered his senses and whirled to grab her wrist. "Better let me take a little look inside that purse, Darlin'. Don't want you to come out with any surprises, do we?" he sneered.

Peering into the purse, Dirk saw nothing unusual, but extracted her car keys from a side pouch. "I don't know what these fit, but I'm not taking the chance that you have an extra key for this Jap trap on your cute little key ring," he continued in his sarcastic tone. Then he handed back her purse and gave her a wink before turning to go look for Sarge.

Sandra set the purse on the driver's seat and resumed fumbling around in it, stalling for time. Dirk hadn't gone twenty feet when he turned around and said, "I'm going to keep an eye on you, just in case, so don't try anything funny."

Sandra took his statement as a cue to act. She pulled the purse toward her and—blocked from Dirk's view by her body—dumped its contents on the pavement. "Oh, damn!" she exclaimed, bending to recover the items. She kept her body between Dirk and the vehicle, presenting him with a view designed to divert his attention from her hands. She found the frame easily enough, but at first she couldn't feel the key box. Then she remembered its alignment with the door edge and moved her left hand forward along the frame, while her right hand was busy gathering the spilled contents. In her haste, she bumped the key box from its resting place and it hit the pavement with a metallic clunk. She could only scoop it into her purse and hope Dirk hadn't heard it. She stood and turned to check Dirk's position, but he had disappeared from her view.

Sandra got into the vehicle and closed the door. Reaching into her purse, she struggled with the key box and wrapping material, her hands shaking uncontrollably. Her earlier sway over Dirk had depended on the prospect of sex, but if he had a few minutes to cool off, he might suspect her intentions. As a weak safeguard against his unexpected return, she pressed the door lock button, finished unwrapping the key, and took a deep breath before inserting it into the ignition switch and starting the engine.

As she pulled the transmission into reverse, she glimpsed Dirk dashing up the sidewalk toward her, pulling his pistol as he ran. Although he had walked away to find Sarge, he hadn't had time, so it was obvious he had lingered around behind another car parked up the street and peeked around it to see what she was doing.

Sandra accelerated back from the curb, then pulled the gear selector to Drive. On impulse, instead of driving away from the running Dirk, she turned toward him and accelerated again, jumping the right tire onto the sidewalk and bearing down on him.

The look on Dirk's face almost made the past hours of being frightened worth it. His grim, determined, tough-guy look changed to surprise, then wide-eyed fear as the big vehicle bore down on him so close now as to preclude even the chance of a lucky shot taking out the menacing driver before he was run over. At the last possible instant, Sandra whipped the wheel to the left in an attempt to merely brush Dirk with the right fender. Even with everything that had happened in the past twenty-odd hours, somehow she just couldn't run him down.

As for Dirk, whatever his failings, clumsiness wasn't among them. He danced sideways just in time to avoid the fate of last night's wild hog, but fell hard and couldn't recover his feet before she had made a U-turn in the street and sped off.

About a hundred yards up the street, Sandra saw Mike running from behind the same junk car he had used to spot the Land Cruiser. He was aiming for a point in the roadway well ahead of her, like a defensive back getting an angle on a fast receiver. Sandra slowed as she approached his path, and Mike reached for the passenger door handle. She had eased almost to a stop, but for some reason, Mike wasn't getting in the car—he was shouting and pointing at something on her door. She looked left to see to see what he was pointing at and saw Dirk in the mirror, running full speed and, surprisingly, gaining on her. Despite the cowboy boots, Dirk had already sprinted several dozen yards in a very short time. He would be at her door in a few more seconds; luckily, it was locked. That would keep him out of the car, but it wouldn't stop a bullet.

In full panic mode, she looked pleadingly at Mike, who now was pointing at the passenger door handle and mouthing something indecipherable. Finally, she realized he was pointing at the door lock control. Of course! she thought. All the doors were locked and he couldn't get in! As she turned back to look at Mike, she nearly burst out laughing in spite of their plight. He was doing exactly what he'd said he didn't want to do—hanging on the mirror because he couldn't open the door.

She unlocked the doors, but Mike had already wrapped both arms around the heavy-duty mirror and was holding his body off the ground. He wildly gestured with shakes of his head for Sandra to go, so she did.

After about two hundred yards, with Dirk tiring quickly and fading from view, she pulled over to let Mike get in. He loosened his grip on the mirror and opened the door, bailing in and slamming it shut while shouting for Sandra to go. He couldn't see behind the vehicle to notice Dirk's fading pursuit, and wasn't taking any chances on a wild shot spoiling their getaway.

Sandra kept her eyes on the road and drove, waiting for Mike's outburst. Almost a minute had passed when his rapid breathing morphed into a fit of laughter. Sandra too, started laughing hysterically, both at the comedy of the scene and relief that Mike saw humor in her error.

"I can't believe you locked me out!" he gasped.

"Mike, I really am sorry, but I told you not to just stroll out to the car. You were supposed to get your butt in gear and get in the car, not hang on the mirror like a monkey!" Then she burst into another round of laughter as Mike tickled her ribs with one hand and mock-strangled her with the other.

When they reached the highway, she pulled to a stop and asked, "Which way, right?"

"Yeah, let's go back to Del Rio where we can sit down to discuss the whole thing with someone in authority. It's going to be hard enough to explain all this to anyone, let alone some poor patrolman who just wants to drive around, eat donuts, and get his shift over with."

"Maybe we should get the Drug Enforcement Agency or Border Patrol," Sandra suggested, "since this involves drugs and international smuggling."

"I'm sure the local police will call in the appropriate parties. You're right, this is going to get one or more federal agencies involved, plus international drug-combating forces. This will be a big deal for them. The DEA in Del Rio may work out of the local police station or the sheriff's office. Either way, they won't be hard to find."

"What about the stuff that's on its way to El Paso?"

Mike grimaced. "That'll take plenty of explaining on my part, but I want to make sure it's out in the open. I don't want the law ransacking my shop and terrorizing Ralph and Bernie. The Hansons are nice people, they don't need that. Besides, I don't pay them enough to deal with this type of activity.

"When Dirk and Sarge are picked up, their first response will be that I'm the *real* drug smuggler, so we've got to get there first and tell what's going on. I think your testimony about the conversation at the party and Jack's insistence that I change my mind about buying from Morales will be important to the case."

Sandra didn't respond, and he wondered if she was still intimidated by Jack, even in his absence. Maybe she's just concentrating on driving, he thought. Leaning over to look at the speedometer, he saw she was driving just over seventy, her eyes locked on the road. He urged her to speed up. "Dirk and Sarge may hijack another car back in Langtry. It'd be easy to grab one from a tourist, so we need to get a big head start."

Sandra glanced over at him and shuddered at the thought of ever facing Dirk again, then pressed the accelerator harder until the needle touched ninety. Neither wanted any more dealing with the kidnappers, but Mike knew Sandra's recent encounter with the sneering, disgusting Dirk must have been miserable. He opened his mouth to ask the details, but thought better of it.

Traffic was lighter than usual on Highway 90. Truckers coming out of Del Rio from across the border at *Ciudad Acuña* used the route to travel west and intersect with Interstate 10 at Van Horn almost three hundred miles to the west. From there, it was a straight shot to the West Coast, not even a stoplight until the interstate turns into the Santa Monica Freeway and ends at the surface streets leading to the famous pier.

After only a few miles, weariness set in and the drive, though fast, became almost routine, the excitement of the escape waning. Luckily, they found an unopened bottle of water and another partially filled one remaining from what they had bought in Laredo.

"Not too cold, but it sure is good. I guess you want some?" Mike asked, grinning at her.

Sandra reached for the bottle and took a swig. "Sure wish you'd cooled it off. Is this the best you can do?"

"Nope. The *best* I can do is drink it all myself. Now give it back."

Sandra shook her head and switched the bottle to her left hand, away from Mike and out of his reach. The ensuing wrestling match almost resulted in the last of the water being spilled on the seats. The fun of the tussle and the relief at being free of their captors made the tension of the past hours fade. Both of them began to relax a bit and realize how sleepy they were. Mike cranked up the volume on a Mexican radio station to keep Sandra alert.

"Turn that down! I'm not that sleepy."

"I was hoping you'd want to dance."

"Yeah, sure. I could tell by the reaction at the airport that you're really fired up on dancing—as usual."

"Sandra, I really wanted to go dancing, but I thought you'd rather be kidnapped instead, so here we are."

This ongoing tug-of-war in their relationship was interrupted by a violent lurch of the Land Cruiser, nearly causing Sandra to lose control as the right front wheel fell off the pavement. "Damn! What—"

"Don't jerk the wheel!" Mike warned. "Move back on the road slowly!"

The helicopter had swooped over them from behind, passing about thirty feet above the Land Cruiser. The powerful wind from the rotor rocked it hard to the right, almost wrenching the wheel from her hands as the front tire dropped off the pavement edge. By the time Sandra had eased the vehicle back onto the blacktop, the chopper had pulled ahead, turned around during an altitude-gain maneuver, and headed toward them head-on, dropping to an even lower level than the first pass.

It seemed so bizarre for a helicopter to zoom in on top of their car out here in the middle of nowhere that it didn't immediately occur to them what was happening. But when the first bullets came through the top of the car, it was apparent their adventure was beginning anew, with a different, better-armed enemy.

Dirk and Sarge couldn't have hijacked a helicopter in the last twenty minutes, Mike thought, so someone else had been given their vehicle description. It didn't appear that the occupants of the aircraft were going to discuss matters; as he had earlier surmised, this business was serious enough to justify immediately killing anyone who might be a threat to the clever smuggling operation. And while Dirk and Sarge had been unnerving, this new, faceless opponent in the air was terrifying. Even though the first round had entered behind the front seats, the sound of the impact and the resulting hole in the headliner demonstrated what the shooter could do.

The first two guys had waved their pistols around, and Dirk had a loud, threatening mouth, but they hadn't actually inflicted any physical damage. Mike had done all the damage by hitting the hog and slamming Dirk's head into the door post. This was different. The shooter in the helicopter intended to kill them, here and now. As if to validate that fear, a second round smacked Mike's outside mirror, shattering the glass and passing through the right front fender, causing him to flinch and fall to his left, over the console and nearly into Sandra's lap.

"Mike, what do I do?" she screamed, turning to look at him. Seeing the frightened look on his face didn't help. *"Mike! Tell me what to do!"*

"Just keep driving—no, turn off up here before the bridge!"

The bridge over the huge river bed canyon represented the only cover available to them. They couldn't stay out here on the open highway. Even at ninety miles an hour, it was only a matter of time before a round from the large-caliber weapon hit him or Sandra, or penetrated a vital part of the vehicle. Proving the point, another round, then another quickly followed, one clipping the hood and the other smacking the right rear door.

"Get to the left shoulder!" Mike shouted. "The old road comes out of the river bottom on this side of the bridge. I don't know if we can get to it from here, but we've got to get off the highway. Slow down! *Slow down!*"

"Where? Mike, that's a ditch!"

"Right here. Angle to the left. There's the old road, way the hell over there. Veer more to the left. No, Sandra, the *left*!"

"But it's the wrong—that's…"

"I know it's the wrong side of the road, Sandra, but this isn't your driver's test! *Just get over there!*"

Luckily, there was no oncoming traffic as Sandra drove down the wrong side of the highway. She braked the vehicle to a manageable speed just as Mike saw the abandoned roadbed about fifty yards away. The route to the old pavement was going to be rough; the steep hill was littered with rocks as big as bowling balls, and a decrepit old fence that stretched before them would become victim to the big Toyota.

"Mike, I don't think we can make it. There's a fence!"

"We don't have a choice. Go through it!"

She veered into the ditch, over a berm and accelerated through the fence, breaking the top strands of barbed-wire, but snagging the mesh wire on the bottom with the bumper. A twenty-foot section, complete with a couple of mesquite fence posts, trailed behind, hanging on rocks and cactus until it, too, finally snapped. The roadway was now only a few yards away, but the terrain looked too rough, even for the Land Cruiser. It looked like the end, but Mike pointed to a narrow break in the rocks.

"There's not enough room!"

"Take it. There's no other way to get there!"

Sandra goosed the accelerator, mowing down a creosote bush and two small mesquites before bouncing over the remaining rocks and beginning an uncontrolled slide down a thirty-foot embankment toward the old pavement.

"Turn right at the bottom! Turn right!" Mike shouted, before the sliding vehicle had even reached the old roadway. "Try to make it under the bridge!"

She had to turn sharply to avoid shooting across the old road and plunging into the river over a hundred feet below. The Cruiser slewed under the hard right turn, then steadied as she accelerated toward the bridge.

"Good girl! Now haul ass!"

Mike winced as another round came through the roof and made a muted pop exiting his side of the windshield. The shooter was trying to hit them through the roof, rather than seeking window shots. Two more rounds missed, passing through the cowling in front of the windshield, and Mike realized they had been taking rounds all along; they just hadn't heard them above the noise of the straining engine and the clatter of rocks beneath the chassis.

Even at this slower speed, they were harder to hit since the shooter had to outguess Sandra's intended path. Also, in the hot afternoon air, updrafts from the nearby gorge were wreaking havoc on control of the aircraft, and the shooter's aim deteriorated as they neared the edge of the canyon. The next shot missed the passenger compartment completely, popping the front of the hood. Unfortunately, the bullet passed through the radiator.

Mike instantly recognized the sweet odor of hot engine coolant, signaling quick death for an automobile in this heat. It might run for a while, but the climbing temperature would soon cause the engine to seize and the car would stop moving, period. Then they'd be easy targets, ones this guy wouldn't miss. Mike wanted to control where they came to rest, and that didn't include the middle of the road, certainly not this old road which was about as wide as a single lane of the modern highway some fifty feet above them.

"Sandra, we've got to stop soon, before the engine seizes up! We don't have enough speed to keep air flowing over the radiator, and we're dead if it quits out here in the open."

"Where to?"

"Try to make it to that big rock pile under the bridge and pull in close. The bridge is the only cover we've got. We've got to bail out *now*."

She blasted through a gate across the roadway and zeroed in on the rocky mound, pulling up close, resulting in the passenger door being only inches away from the heap. She looked over as Mike as she jammed the brakes and held the car there.

"Back up, back up! Just enough to get out on this side!" he yelled. "We can't get out over there without being targets and you're too close for this door to open."

"Well, dammit, then you get over here and drive!" she screamed back at him, but did as he said anyway, backing up just enough for them to squeeze out on the passenger side.

"Go ahead, climb over me and get to the top of that rock pile," Mike said.

She scuttled up the rocks while prop wash from the helicopter sent up a stinging storm of dust and debris. In an attempt to give his shooter a closer vantage point, the pilot had inadvertently stirred up the dust, hiding the targets. He moved the chopper back out over the canyon, but strong updrafts again whipped across the control surfaces, rendering stability nearly impossible. For the moment, it appeared the fleeing pair had leveled the playing field.

Seeing the break in the assault, Mike scrambled over the back of his seat and jerked open the storage compartment, retrieving Sandra's overnight bag. Just before he slid from the car, he remembered his pistol. Bailing back into the front seat and yanking off the fuse box cover, he retrieved the little .22 automatic and shoved it into his front pocket. He'd almost forgotten about it being in the car. In truth, it wasn't much, certainly not against the high-powered rifle being used on them, but it was better than nothing.

He squirmed from the car, sliding headfirst to the rocky ground, where the flinty rocks scraped hide from his palms. Clutching the bag, he climbed the rock pile toward Sandra. From here, at least the shooter couldn't hit them. The helicopter would have to descend into the canyon to see them, and the updrafts would make that a daunting task for the pilot, any pilot. And even if he could get into position, the shooter couldn't get off a shot before he and Sandra moved to the opposite side of the rocks. So, for the moment, they were relatively safe.

"What are we going to do?" Sandra yelled over the noise of the helicopter.

"How the hell should I know? What am I, James Bond or something? I don't have a handy helicopter destroyer button on my watch!" Seeing her shocked look at his outburst, he added with a grin, "As soon as they surrender to us, we can get them to give us a lift into Del Rio, where the law can lock them up and buy us a steak.

"By the way, that was one hell of a driving job you did. In case you don't know it, you just saved our lives."

CHAPTER 11

▼

Jack's stomach flip-flopped, matching the motions of the helicopter as it dived and swooped over the canyon. The pilot was fighting the controls, trying to get the shooter in a position to see the pair below, and the resulting ride was taking its toll on at least one passenger. Jack looked over at Reynaldo, but could discern nothing in the impassive face, his eyes hidden behind the mirrored sunglasses.

After the fourth pass, the vehicle had driven under the bridge and the occupants jumped out. Then the scene below had disappeared in a swirl of dust and dirt as the rotors pushed the debris against the bridge footing where it ricocheted off the rocks, obliterating everything from view. Their quarry could be escaping under cover of the dust storm, but Jack was beyond caring at this moment. He just wanted the motion to stop.

The trip from Wichita Falls to Del Rio had taken just over two hours. During the flight, Reynaldo had the pilot radio to make sure the helicopter pilot and shooter would be ready to go. As soon as they landed, he and Jack exited the Beechcraft King Air and hurried to the waiting helicopter, which sat on the tarmac with its engine idling and rotor turning lazily. Jack hadn't met the two men already seated in front, but Reynaldo motioned him into the back and they took off without introductions. Flying north, they intersected U. S. Highway 90 and turned west, following the road at an altitude which allowed them to compare oncoming vehicles against Dirk's description.

Dirk had been vague about how the pair had regained control of the car, but Jack didn't press it. He knew Reynaldo was going to be angry upon learning that two unarmed people, one of them a woman, had somehow wrested their vehicle back from two armed men who were supposed to be guarding it. Now they would be searching for a moving vehicle on a public highway, not two stragglers dying of thirst in the middle of the desert.

Jack was right; Reynaldo was livid that Mike and Sandra were now driving the very vehicle Dirk and Sarge had commandeered the night before. "What in the hell were those two doing?" he demanded. "They both have guns, they are watching the vehicle, and two people who have walked all night just get in it and drive away? Did the dumb bastards leave the keys in it? Maybe they left it running and sitting in the road with the doors open, maybe a sign in the window, *hey, take me!* Goddammit, why did you send those two idiots to handle it?"

Reynaldo's anger manifested itself in his speech. He now sounded more like a Laredo taxi driver in a traffic jam than the smooth, States-educated businessman Jack knew. Another side of the man was being displayed, a side that troubled Jack. While he accepted that his own lifestyle was based upon corruption and violence—and expressions of anger and profanity were common—it was disquieting to see it in action, especially since it seemed directed at him at this moment. Reynaldo Gomez was showing the true source of his power and influence. This wasn't a quiet phone call or murmured instructions to an underling that magically gets things done beneath the surface. This Reynaldo was profane and demanding; a powerful man used to getting his way.

Jack's discomfort was increased by the two men in the helicopter. Upon their arrival in Del Rio he and Reynaldo had joined the men at the chopper, which was parked only yards from the flight service building. They had spoken briefly with Reynaldo, but didn't even acknowledge Jack as they all boarded the craft. He felt he was trailing along like an insignificant bystander, a mere hired hand. Accustomed to being important in the overall scheme of things, this development bothered Jack almost as much as the demeanor of the men themselves.

During the flight from Del Rio, Jack observed the men from his rear seat, trying to determine what Reynaldo saw in the two quiet, middle-aged enforcers. They hardly spoke, not even to each other. Each seemed to know what the other was thinking, and they worked as a team. In other words, they were nothing like Dirk and Sarge.

And now, after several terrifying moments of being tossed around in the sky and hearing high-powered rifle rounds being fired, it was apparent to Jack that setting out to eliminate two people was simply these guys' job—and they performed it without expression or emotion, which made the somber pair seem more dangerous and sinister. Clearly, the two had done this before... and so had Reynaldo.

"Reynaldo, I don't know," Jack had begun his explanation. "I can't explain it. I understand how those two got away after having a wreck, but I told my men to watch the damn car, that they would have to come back to Langtry because there ain't shit anywhere near there."

"Well, they did a hell of a job! Who trained them—you? It may be time to get a new training manual, Jack. Or do they need a new trainer?"

"I thought I trained them just fine. But I train them to do those sham construction jobs that make things work so well for both of us."

"Maybe you are losing your touch, Jack."

"Now Reynaldo, you know this isn't what I usually have these guys do. Sarge has done a good muscle job in the past, and Dirk always shows up and does what I tell him. This job was a little different, but I'm damned if I know how some weenie-assed shopkeeper and a woman could take the car back from them."

Privately, however, Jack had a suspicion about what had happened. Sandra had probably wrapped Dirk around her finger and somehow talked her way into the car. Understandable enough. Dirk liked women and would go to great lengths in his pursuit of just one more. Jack himself was pretty much the same, but had the dumb bastard just handed over the key? And where did her boyfriend come in?

Whatever the case, Jack knew they had to find them and eliminate them for good before it got out of hand. This pair of amateurs who should have been so easy to brush aside had turned into a real problem.

A few miles west of the Pecos River, the pilot spotted an oncoming white SUV and dropped down to check it out. On the head-on pass, it appeared to hold at least two occupants and it was almost certainly a Land Cruiser. The pilot executed a U-turn and swooped in from behind even lower, enabling the shooter to check the license plate with his rifle scope. "That's it," he proclaimed, loosening his safety harness to give him more maneuverability.

The pilot turned around yet again, dropped down to what Jack though was perilously close to the pavement, then slowed the forward speed almost to a standstill. He turned the craft slightly sideways, while the gunman leaned out the open doorway, took aim, and squeezed off a shot. A slight lurch of the chopper ruined his aim and the shot went high, into the roof of the car. A second shot, placed too quickly, struck the right-hand mirror.

The vehicle sped below them, and the helicopter, facing its oncoming path, now had to turn to pursue it. Although the chopper could reach speeds of well over one hundred miles per hour, the main advantage of pursuing a car on the road by cutting curves was lost on this stretch of straight highway. The Land Cruiser must have been pushing ninety, because almost a minute passed before the chopper again overtook the car.

As they approached the Pecos River Bridge, the vehicle suddenly swerved to the right, then turned hard to the left, abandoning the open highway. Trying to match the SUV's erratic path, the pilot soon discovered the driver was trickier than he had anticipated. Taking refuge near the canyon would make it impossible to get the shooter into position. The hot updrafts destabilized the craft, and when he tried to get lower, the blast from the rotors churned up such a dust storm the targets disappeared from view.

Reynaldo assessed the situation and leaned forward to speak to the pilot, "We'll have to land and go in for them. They can wait under the bridge for hours, and we'll run out of fuel before they stick their heads out."

The pilot nodded in agreement and pulled back, gaining altitude to study the surrounding area. Drifting out over the gorge, he spotted a level area in the river bottom, a gravel bar with sufficient room to land. It lay several hundred yards south of the bridge, and he turned the craft toward it.

Mike peered out from their vantage point as the helicopter moved out above the canyon and departed south over the bridge. At first, he thought they had given up and his spirits rose. But the chopper began to descend almost immediately, and he saw its intended destination: a gravel bar downstream, and on the same side of the river as their impromptu refuge. He judged the distance to be almost a half mile away and far below him and Sandra. The pursuers would soon be on foot, coming toward their rock pile safe-haven.

"They're landing on this side of the river, and it won't take them long to get here," he told Sandra.

Mike's grim observation was needless. Sandra was watching intently over his shoulder, and their pursuers' actions were easy enough to predict. They had to think of something fast. If they just sat here, the hunters would be on them in ten or fifteen minutes. The old highway terminated in the river bottom only a few yards from the gravel bar, and the killers would soon see the road provided a paved path up to their quarry. Even as Mike and Sandra watched, the helicopter settled its skids onto the gravel bar. All four men jumped out and, sure enough, started in their direction at a trot.

"They can't keep that up for long, not in this heat," Mike announced, "not up that incline." *Or can they?* Aloud, he added, "I hope they run till they puke. It shouldn't take long at that pace."

"They've got to slow down soon," Sandra agreed hopefully.

Mike studied the distance of the path and figured it would take them less than ten minutes at their present pace to reach them. Of course, the shooter would be in range much sooner, if he wasn't already. They could only hope they continued to charge up the incline, so as to be too winded to aim carefully. Both knew from experience that running uphill in the heat is plenty tough, even for someone in good physical shape. And while he couldn't tell from this distance, he doubted that cocaine smugglers spent much time in endurance training—*or did they?* He'd been wrong about a lot so far, he reminded himself.

He did know, however, that he and Sandra, though tired from the chase, could still cover ground on foot faster than most people. It seemed their only advantage, and it would be gone if they didn't act on it soon, like in the next minute or so. He looked around frantically for an escape route while Sandra kept her eyes on the road below, seemingly hypnotized by the sight of the advancing men. Their pace had slowed considerably, but the final outcome seemed inevitable.

"Mike, we've got to do something!" she shrieked.

"No shit!"

"Well, think of *something*! Even if it's wrong, we can't sit here and let them get much closer."

"I'm thinking, dammit!"

Looking at the crippled Land Cruiser, he considered back-tracking out the way they drove in, but they would have to stay well ahead of the shooter who was undoubtedly using a long-range rifle with a scope to match. Being inside the car would eliminate the possibility of any evasive maneuver like zig-zagging or ducking behind a rock; indeed, it would give the gunman a definite target to which he could send a hail of bullets and hope for a hit. With a good rest on a rock, he might be able to hit them at several hundred yards.

Plus, the engine wouldn't make it far with no coolant, probably not even far enough to escape the pursuers' line of sight.

Another troubling thought occurred to Mike: they may have placed others up at the highway, contemplating just such a move. Otherwise, all four of them wouldn't have left the chopper to storm up the hill. If Dirk and Sarge had been able to get transportation by now, they would likely be the ones to box them off. They would be holding the high ground up at the highway, he thought, and plenty pissed at being tricked by Sandra.

Again studying the vehicle parked at the foot of the rock pile, he tried desperately to come up with a plan. The bullet that had pierced the radiator had released the pressure and no more coolant was spewing out, though the smell lingered in the hot air. But in its overheated condition, it might not even climb the embankment back to the highway, even without the radiator problem. Gravity had been a big help in getting them to this point. Even with the rough ride, downhill was easier than going up.

This is no time to think about physics class, Mike. You nearly failed it, remember?

Then it hit him; *downhill*—that was the answer. The idea unfolded before him, made evident by the sight of the four pursuers still coming up the hill, but having slowed even more in the past minute or so. They were down to a walk, and a labored one at that. More significantly, they were walking abreast, leaving little room on the narrow old road to either side of their group. To their right, the canyon dropped straight down over a hundred feet. To their left, the sheer canyon wall loomed above them, leaving no escape from something rolling down the old road toward them—something like a Toyota Land Cruiser.

He turned and grabbed Sandra's hand, pulling her close to him. "Sandra, listen to me. We're going to get in the car and blast right down the old road, straight for those guys. It's the last thing they'd expect."

She opened her mouth to protest the idiocy of the two of them attacking four armed men, but Mike cut her off. "It's got to be now! If we get in, drive straight toward them as fast as I can make it go, they'll have no place to go except over the side or be flattened against the canyon wall."

Though the plan terrified Sandra, she knew he was right, but pleaded against it with her eyes anyway, saying nothing.

The fear in her eyes prompted Mike to try again. "Sandra, we're trapped here, and we can't let them get any closer. They're going to kill us. We've got to go, now!"

She inhaled deeply and nodded. "I know, I know. I'm just scared."

"I'll get in the driver's seat, start the engine, and pull it into gear. You get in the back and lie down on the floor. Hang on to the most solid thing you can find—the seatbelt anchors, or the seat itself. Brace your legs against the seats. I'm going to accelerate straight toward them. This has to be all in one move, or we lose our advantage."

She nodded again and swallowed hard, terror evident in her face.

Mike pulled her close and hugged her, whispering fiercely in her ear. "Okay, let's go!"

They clambered off the opposite side of the rock pile, shielded from the view of the men. Mike sprinted to the rear passenger door, throwing Sandra's bag in the floor and reaching back for her hand in one motion. Pulling her in, he slammed the door and bailed over into the driver's seat. Recalling his advice to her, he buckled his seat belt.

Sandra was firmly anchored against the seats when Mike pulled the transmission selector into Drive. He resisted gunning the hot engine, but picked up speed as the road sloped down the canyon. Leaning to the right as far as he could, he peeked over the dash, through the bottom of the windshield and steered toward the road. Gunfire would start any second, and he hoped the big vehicle had lots of solid metal between the grill and passenger compartment. Lower-placed rounds were no problem; the engine would deflect them. But a carefully placed round might still skim the hood and enter the windshield at face level. He tightened his grip on the wheel and tried to stay in the middle of the old pot-holed pavement. If he veered even a few feet to his left, the killers' job would be done for them, without a single bullet hole in their bodies. The canyon floor was a long way down.

Mike kept his foot on the gas and did his best to steer the car directly in the center of the road. He wanted to create as much confusion as possible as to which way the men should jump to avoid being hit. Cracks in the old pavement grabbed at the tires and rocks strewn across the roadway jarred the vehicle off its path, but he held tight, correcting his course by steering with only his left hand and gripping the dash with his right for support. Within seconds, he heard the metallic pop of rounds striking the vehicle. He held his breath, waiting for the one which would find its way through the charging labyrinth of metal, glass, wires, and plastic to core into his body, but it didn't happen, and he exhaled after the fourth round. He had the ridiculous thought of contacting Toyota and praising their products' bulletproof qualities, but dismissed it quickly for more pressing matters, like checking their progress.

Although he couldn't see very well from dashboard level, the sight was well worth the effort it took to raise up for a peek. All four men tried to get out of the path at the same instant, and all four ran together in the middle of the road. The heavy-set one fell down and, in trying to right himself, tripped the shooter. The last thing Mike saw was the rifle disappearing over the canyon wall. As the Toyota blasted through the men, he heard one satisfying *thump* and felt a couple of jolts as the tires bounced over something, much like running over an armadillo.

"You okay?" he shouted at Sandra, exhilaration in his voice.

"Yes!" came the muffled reply.

As he straightened up in the seat and slowed down, a sick feeling came over him. The excitement of his plan working and the elation he had first felt at defeating their tormentors was replaced by a dread feeling any normal human being experiences upon taking another's life. He'd run over one or more of the men, and the others had either jumped over the edge or been plastered against the canyon wall. Although the results were what he had planned, replaying the sounds of the carnage in his head repulsed him.

Mike Conner had never envisioned himself as a killer. He wasn't a tough guy, a fighter, or a rounder. He struggled to justify the act—he didn't like it, but he'd done the only thing he could to save their lives, his and Sandra's. Those guys hadn't been coming up the road just to talk, he reasoned. They must have thought they could just march up the hill and put a bullet in their heads, and the matter would be resolved.

Well, it didn't work out that way, boys.

For such tough guys, evidently competent at their work, they had underestimated their amateur adversaries. Nevertheless, Mike regretted having to kill someone; it wasn't his idea of doing the right thing. Informing the authorities would have been better, but the thugs scattered behind them hadn't let that happen, and his conscience would bear the burden caused by their violent intentions.

When they reached the bottom of the gorge, the temperature gauge was pegged into the red area, and Mike shut off the engine. They couldn't go any farther in this direction anyway, and the vehicle wouldn't climb the hill back to the highway without overheating to destruction, if at all. Their tormentors had been dealt with; now he and Sandra had to figure out what to do.

Sandra scrambled over into the front seat, breathing hard, her eyes still wide with fear. She'd undoubtedly heard and felt the impact on the trip down; like Mike, she was a normal person from a caring, middle-class background, and to have felt and heard someone being killed or maimed was beyond her ability to grasp. The tension of the kidnapping, the fatigue from the previous night's trek, the car chase, and now this was taking a heavy emotional toll on both of them. She started to cry, and Mike was shaking so badly he had to grip the steering wheel to steady himself.

Mike drew several deep breaths and forced himself to calm down, to slow his heartbeat and to concentrate on their next move. First, he reached over for Sandra and pulled her to him, enfolding her in his arms until her sobbing subsided. "It's okay, Sandra," he began. "We had to do it, otherwise we'd be dead now. Right now, we've got to figure out how to get out of here so we can contact the law."

She straightened in her seat, took a deep breath and tried to compose herself. "I know. I know it saved our lives, but I'm not used to any of this." After a pause, she continued. "So how do we get out of here?"

"Amistad Recreation Area is just downstream on the Rio Grande, which we'll run into in a few hundred yards, where the Pecos runs into it. Our best bet would be to hike down to the camping area to see if anyone has a phone or two-way radio. I think there will be a few fishermen there. Or, if we're lucky, we can find a park ranger. But we can't take a chance on going back up to the highway, since Dirk and Sarge could be waiting there."

"Then let's go now, in case those two saw all this and are coming down here. I've had all of Dirk I can stand for one lifetime."

"You're right. They're bound to be plenty pissed after being suckered out of the Land Cruiser, so they won't just wave pistols around and threaten us. And they can't let us stay alive to tell anyone, especially since you know them, know their names, and the deal about the pottery. They've *got* to kill us."

"If they saw this, at least they'll see we're not afraid to do something, like run over them," Sandra offered hopefully.

"Yeah, but if they saw their buddies get run over, they'll be more cautious—and more dangerous. They'll do what the helicopter guys did, shoot us on sight."

Sandra sighed. "You have any more good news?"

"Afraid not."

"Okay, then let's go."

CHAPTER 12

▼

When the engine started, the four men were too far away to hear it. A hot wind was howling up the canyon from the south, carrying the sound away from them, and all four were trudging up the incline, heads down and breathing hard. Only when the Land Cruiser was less than one hundred, yards away did Reynaldo sense something and glance up. He shouted, and the others jerked up their heads and stared in disbelief at the approaching vehicle, which was gaining speed by the second.

The shooter raised his rifle and squeezed off a round at the driver's side of the windshield, but to no effect. He tried another round, aiming slightly lower. The sun glaring off the windshield made it impossible to see where the rounds were hitting, or even where they should be aimed. By his third shot, the others had pulled their pistols and begun firing randomly. None of the shots slowed the vehicle, which was now only thirty yards away and approaching at forty miles an hour. They had to move, or they'd be mowed down in seconds.

Jack, always one to save his own skin, jumped first, colliding with Reynaldo. Both went down, and the shooter tripped over Jack's outstretched leg and dropped the rifle. He managed to scramble over Jack to the canyon's edge, where he clung to a remnant of the long-gone guard rail as the vehicle roared toward them. The expensive rifle fell ten feet, where it landed on a protruding rock ledge, incredibly balanced there, threatening another hundred-feet fall.

Meanwhile, Jack and Reynaldo had somehow untangled from their comedic embrace and fled to opposite sides of the narrow roadway. The chopper pilot was knocked backward into the path of the speeding vehicle. The last thing he saw was the license plate he had so adroitly spotted on the highway minutes before, identifying it as his prey.

Jack managed to dive against the canyon wall, his right arm taking only a glancing blow from the side mirror. He was stunned, but he quickly realized he was not seriously hurt. Looking across the road, he saw Reynaldo had rolled very near the edge, but had stopped before suffering the fate of the rifle. In the middle of the road, a mangled heap lay bloody and motionless. From the odd angle of limbs with splintered bones sticking out, it was clear that one of their bunch was beyond help.

Scraped and bruised but otherwise uninjured, Reynaldo clambered on all fours toward the shooter, who was clinging to a steel pipe; a piece of the old guard rail still performing its intended duty after almost a century. Reynaldo gripped his wrist and pulled him away from the canyon's edge, where he sat up and stared dumbly at the body in the road.

Reynaldo still held his pistol, and as he struggled to his feet, he flailed the air with both arms like a drunk driver flunking a roadside sobriety test. Jack spotted his weapon some twenty yards down the road, scratched, but still in one piece. He retrieved it, checked the action, and headed for his companions.

The shooter stood with the assistance of Reynaldo and Jack, and all three watched the Land Cruiser reach the bottom of the gorge and pull to the right of the old roadway, not twenty yards from the helicopter. Then the two people they had been pursuing emerged and set out walking, first passing by the resting aircraft, then returning to poke around inside. None of the stunned men watching them spoke a word.

Mike and Sandra got out of the Land Cruiser and started walking, passing by the helicopter perched on the gravel bar like a huge dragonfly. It looked strangely out of place here in the canyon, its menacing appearance enhanced by the occasional ticking of contracting metal coming from the still-hot engine.

After walking only a few yards beyond the aircraft, Mike stopped and said, "Let's see if there's anything in it we might use to help us get out of here."

Sandra turned and headed back toward the chopper. "I sure could use some water. My mouth is so dry—I guess it's from being scared."

"Me too. Water is going to get critical if we don't get out of here soon. Surely they had some."

They rummaged around inside, but found no water. The stream trickling along a few yards away looked good, but drinking water from the Pecos after its trip through hundreds of miles of ranchland livestock would likely be disastrous. The search did produce a map under the pilot's seat, an aerial topography map of the region, including a large area of northern Mexico just across the Rio Grande. Mike tucked it inside Sandra's bag. Before leaving, he wondered about disabling the craft and finally settled for jerking out a handful of wires from under the instrument panel. Not knowing what would quickly and completely ground the craft, he opted not to waste any more time.

After covering only a few hundred yards, Mike noticed the deepening water and decided to cross the Pecos before nearing its junction with the Rio Grande, where they'd have to swim. He didn't relish the thought of being caught in mid-stream by Dirk and Sarge, or any other buddies the killers might have had in tow.

Quickly taking off shoes and socks and rolling up pants, he and Sandra waded into the stream, which was knee-deep at this point. "God, I sure could use a swim," Sandra said, slogging through the water. "This feels *so* good on my feet. I've got enough dirt on me to grow tomatoes."

"Me too, but we'd better keep moving. Who knows whether those jackasses up on the road survived or not, but I don't want to wait to find out. We've got to get to a law enforcement officer and tell our story first."

Once across, Mike set out at a brisk pace, following the river toward its confluence with the Rio Grande. As they walked, Mike scanned the canyon walls to their left for a way to get to the recreational area east of the river, but it was Sandra who spotted a switchback trail that led to a plateau topping the bluffs.

"You dumb son of a bitch! How the hell did you let her get in the car with the key?" Sarge screamed.

Dirk said nothing and stayed in the same position, hands on his knees, wheezing and gasping from his fruitless sprint. And even if he'd had the breath to answer, he wouldn't have. How could he tell Sarge he just wanted to get in her pants, so he let her get in the car to change clothes, based on some vague promise; no, a *hint*, that she would have sex with him if she could just change clothes in privacy? And where did she get a key? He'd congratulated himself at the time for taking that bunch from her purse—must have been one in the car, the sneaky bitch. He really didn't have to explain anything to Sarge, but he knew he'd better have a good story when it came time to face Jack.

He limped back to the museum parking area and fumbled through his pocket for change to call Jack. Finally reaching him on his cell phone, Dirk flatly told Jack that they got away.

"Got away?" Jack asked, glancing over at Reynaldo then quickly shifting his eyes elsewhere. *"What do you mean, they got away? Got away, where?"* Jack still didn't understand that Mike and Sandra had regained possession of their own vehicle. *"What are they driving?"*

"They're on the highway toward Del Rio, that's the direction they turned when they left here," Dirk answered, ignoring the specifics of Jack's last question. *"We're going to Del Rio ourselves. Sarge says we can get a ride on the river down to one of those fishing camps at the reservoir, then hitch a ride into town."*

Exactly what that would accomplish wasn't clear to Jack, but he felt it wise to just drop it. It would be bad enough explaining to Reynaldo how their prey had escaped after he'd assured him they could easily be recaptured in Langtry. Maybe those two dumb bastards will drown on the journey, he thought. *"Okay, dammit, we're on our way out there now. What color is the car and what the hell is it, anyway?"*

"It's a Toyota Suburban, it's white and got Texas Plates, DGY oh, six, six."

"You mean a Toyota 4-Runner or a Land Cruiser? Toyota don't' make a goddam Suburban, Dirk!"

"Shit, I don't know! It looks like a Suburban, it's one of them SOBs, dammit."

"You mean an SUV, Dirk. Okay, we're headed out the highway now to see if we can intercept them. You two get your asses back to the Super Eight Motel in Del Rio and wait until you hear from me, okay?"

"Sure thing, Jack."

Dirk and Sarge walked down to the river, where they found several fishermen who had ventured up from the reservoir. After approaching one boater who didn't want to go, two guys in a Ranger bass boat with a two-hundred-horsepower Merc engine agreed to run them to the upper end of the reservoir. For fifty bucks.

And run them they did. Recent heavy rains in Mexico, rare for this time of year, had fed the Rio Grande's upstream tributaries and provided adequate water for the bass fishermen to venture far upstream. These two with a fancy boat rocketed down the Rio Grande at breakneck speed, artfully dodging driftwood, rocks, and the occasional animal carcass. Dirk and Sarge hunkered down and hung on while the driver and his companion babbled incessantly about fishing, oblivious to the discomfort of their passengers.

Their chatter continued all the way to the lake, leaving Dirk and Sarge relieved when they finally slowed and approached a boat dock at the recreational area. The driver edged the boat up to the dock, reversing the prop at the last instant to avoid slamming into the old tires tied to the side for bumpers. The maneuver nearly threw Dirk out of the boat, but Sarge grabbed for him, almost pulling both of them in.

"Whooee!" yelled the driver. "Damn, you boys are sure enough in a hurry! Shit, there ain't nothin' here to get in a hurry about. Better just stay with us and help us clean these fish."

"Uh, we'd like to, but we got to get going," Sarge mumbled as he gripped Dirk's arm and propelled him onto the dock. They scurried away from the two babbling drunks, waving and mumbling thanks as they retreated.

"I don't see what good we're gonna do here, Sarge," Dirk began, jogging to catch up with his companion, who was already striding up the embankment towards the RV park.

"Goddammit, I told you. We've got to get back to Del Rio to get transportation. You didn't see a car rental place in Langtry, did you? And there damn sure isn't one here. This is an RV park, Dirk."

"Well, no, I didn't see one, but—"

"Oh, for Christ's sake, Dirk, you didn't see anything but that gal's tits."

"Just lay off, Sarge! So fucking what? I guess you never looked at any?"

Sarge gave up and changed subjects. "In case you've forgotten, my car is sitting at the Laredo airport parking lot costing me eight bucks a day. Since Jack and Reynaldo met those helicopter guys at the Del Rio airport, we can just go there and wait for them to get back."

"Jack said to check into the Super Eight, the one out on Highway 90, and wait for him to call," Dirk said. "Maybe we'd better just do that."

Ignoring the suggestion, Sarge continued. "Maybe they'll give us a lift back to Laredo, or maybe they need us to help with those two shitheads you let get away. Either way, we weren't doing any good stuck in Langtry, and we can't do anything here, not on foot." Then, as an afterthought to cap his argument he added, "We'd better be ready to do something useful, 'cause I got a feeling Jack is plenty pissed about this."

Dirk wasn't eager to explain the escape to Jack, but knew there was no way out of it. Now he'd lost his position as the informal leader of the duo, but he still questioned Sarge's insistence on going to the Del Rio airport. "If we ain't going to the Super 8 like Jack said, we oughta get some wheels and help recapture those fuckers, Sarge."

Sarge looked at him and shook his head. "How the hell are we going to help? You couldn't run her down, could you? And if you could, you'd need to think with the big head on your shoulders, not the little one in your pants. They can find them from the air without us, and I'm sure Reynaldo has a shooter to handle it."

Dirk still wished there was some way he could redeem himself for his mistake before facing Jack, but he couldn't disagree with Sarge's statement about thinking with the correct body parts.

As the two walked up the path toward the camp sites, it occurred to Dirk why transportation was so important. Though only several hundred yards away, it seemed like a long trek in the oppressive heat. Neither liked walking very much, but they had little choice at this stage, heat or not. Trudging along behind Sarge, Dirk looked like a whipped schoolboy, hands jammed into his jeans pockets, head down, boots scuffling in the gravel. As they neared the RV parking area, he noticed two other people walking about a hundred yards away—the only other people in sight. As the distance between them narrowed, Dirk saw it was a man and woman who appeared to be looking for something. When the woman turned toward Dirk, he realized it was Sandra. In the same instant, Sandra's sudden stop told him that she'd made them.

"Sarge! There they are! Ten o'clock, one-zero-zero meters!" Dirk rattled off in the military jargon Sarge had taught him. He grabbed Sarge's arm, swinging him around to his left and pointing to the distant pair.

Sarge pulled his pistol and started directly toward the couple. Startled by the immediate action, Dirk hesitated, then pulled his piece from his boot and sprinted after him.

"Mike!" Sandra screamed. "It's Dirk and the other one, Sarge! There, over there!"

She was pointing, but by then Mike had seen them running straight toward them. His brief stint of accomplishment evaporated instantly.

How in the hell did this happen? The biggest, emptiest area in the state, and we run into these two assholes again! Jeez, are we cursed or what?

Had he taken time to reflect on it, this was one of the only spots of civilization between Langtry and Del Rio, this and a few other fishing camps.

And since they were all trying to get to Del Rio, it wasn't impossible that they would run into them along the way, but he'd mentally dismissed an encounter with them, at least for a while. And he didn't think they'd almost literally run into them. *Damn, I'm tired of being wrong all the time!*

Grabbing Sandra's hand, he headed back toward the canyon, quickly pulling away from their tired pursuers. Unlike the shooter in the canyon, their pistols didn't have the range to hit them from any great distance, so he felt safe within seconds. Besides, they had gained some insight into the ability, or lack thereof, of Dirk and Sarge. Earlier, when held captive in the vehicle, Mike had been terrified of the two. Yelling and brandishing pistols, they had been plenty scary. Now, it was downright exhilarating to glance back at the stumbling goons, who were fading fast.

Mike and Sandra's lead increased to two hundred yards, then three hundred and more as they neared the canyon trail. Mike looked back and saw Sarge had given up, and Dirk, though still moving, had slowed dramatically. In a few more yards, their adversaries would stop completely, unable to follow.

Mike kept jogging for another minute, picking their way through a rocky area near the entry into the canyon. "Be careful," he called to Sandra. "This is no time to twist an ankle."

"I know, I'm watching. Mike, this is crazy. We've got to find a way to lose these people, once and for all."

"Well, I don't know what else to do. Every move is determined by geography out here."

"Can't we go another direction until they give up?"

"We've got to be careful about just striking out into the desert. We go too far in, and we'll die of thirst. Their job will be done for them by Mother Nature."

They had slowed to a brisk walk, heading back down into the canyon. Mike knew the two men following them would have stopped by now, not caring if they moved another inch. But if he and Sandra didn't soon get some water, they too, would be incapacitated. When the muscles ceased to work, it made no difference how well-trained or tough an endurance athlete was, or what the motivation. The body simply quit.

"We've got to find some water soon," Mike said.

"Oh!" Sandra answered.

"What? What's the matter?"

"Um, let's look through my bag," she answered, a sheepish grin on her face.

Marveling at her suggestion, he slipped the bag off his back and started unzipping it, but Sandra reached for it. "Here, let me look," she said, digging into her belongings, which Mike now saw was mostly clothes and makeup. He was beginning to wonder why he'd opted to carry the bag out of the canyon when, from the very bottom, she triumphantly hoisted a big bottle of water.

Mike grinned, but shook his head. "I can't believe we've been dying of thirst, and you've let me carry all this crap *in addition to* a bottle of water! Maybe I could just carry it a little farther. We certainly don't want to do anything silly, like drink it," he continued sarcastically.

"I couldn't remember if I'd put another bottle in there or not," she explained. "And I haven't exactly had time to look. Anyway, you're the one who just grabbed the bag and brought it. You didn't ask me what was in it."

Mike looked at her incredulously and slowly shook his head.

Well, I did pick up her bag. And I didn't ask what was in it, true enough. Of course it's my fault, I can clearly see that now!

They split the bottle, each downing half in a few gulps. Carrying water in the body was easier than lugging it along in a bottle and rationing it a few sips at a time. Although it didn't slake their thirst, it would keep them moving.

Mike suggested they hide the bag behind a boulder off the path, but Sandra insisted they keep it, jettisoning only the makeup and hair dryer. "That's the heavy stuff," she said. "I need my clothes and toothbrush."

Mike was astounded, but followed her instructions and wisely kept his thoughts to himself.

I can see the newspaper blurb now: "Two El Pasoans with clean teeth and numerous pairs of panties found dead in Chihuahuan Desert." Women always know what's most important.

"Let's go," he said aloud. "They're just a few hundred yards back, and we need to get away completely this time, instead of stumbling around the desert bumping into each other. I'm really getting tired of those guys."

He hefted the bag onto his shoulders and started down the trail. He didn't have any idea where they would go, but maybe after dark they could reverse directions and slip by Dirk and Sarge. Dumb-asses they might be, and exhausted ones at the moment, but they would surely be out to make up for being fooled by Sandra, and they would not hesitate to shoot them.

Suddenly remembering the .22 in his pocket, Mike had another thought for handling their tormentors. He'd had enough of this running through the desert, being shot at, having his car destroyed and his life and girlfriend threatened. The more he thought about it, the more he wanted to turn around and have it out with the two followers.

I can ambush those two fuckers and shoot them stone-cold dead before they know what's happening. I've already killed a couple of them, maybe more. What's two more?

Just as he turned to tell Sandra his plan, his anger and his reverie were interrupted by a hard voice not twenty feet away.

"Stop right there! Don't move another step."

CHAPTER 13

▼

Three men stood facing them from below, standing abreast in the trail to the canyon. Two were holding guns, while the third leaned against a boulder, a contemptuous smile on his hard face. Actually, *sneer* better described the unarmed man's facial expression. Nearly being swatted off the canyon road and considerably scuffed up a while ago hadn't left much to smile about.

The speaker's voice sounded slightly Hispanic, evidently having come from the dark, handsome man in the middle holding a snub-nosed revolver at waist level. To his left, a tall, paunchy, western-dressed Anglo glared at them, wielding an automatic and nervously pointing its barrel first at Mike, then Sandra, as if contemplating which to shoot first.

At the command, Mike stopped short and stared in disbelief at the men, thinking he had killed, or at least permanently maimed them all only an hour or so ago. His former regret at having run over the men was replaced by a feeling of failure. He hadn't done much damage after all, he thought, though one of the four was missing.

Mike knew this would not go well. There was no question these guys he had tried in earnest to kill were not going to extend much kindness now. Seeing no chance of escape at this point, he knew to keep quiet, see what was in store, and hope for a chance to do something. His thoughts went briefly to the pistol in his pocket, and also that he and Sandra again held the high ground, something that had helped them before. Although the men stood well below them on this steep section of the trail, the two armed ones were watching warily, and the eyes of all three bored into him and Sandra. He couldn't possibly pull the little weapon quickly enough, and if he could, he wasn't sure he could hit all of them at this distance, maybe not even the two armed ones. And Sneer Face might also have a weapon, although he didn't look like he needed one. Best to wait for a better opportunity to use the gun and hope they didn't search him or notice the slight bulge in his right pocket.

The Hispanic spoke. "You two have caused me a lot of trouble. Trouble that could have been avoided if you had only listened to what they were saying." He nodded his head as though "they" were standing nearby.

"They didn't just talk," Mike responded. "They stuck guns in our faces, kidnapped us, and forced us to drive them out here. Then they stole my car."

"Goddammit, Sandra, you were supposed to stop him from buying the Morales stuff!" the nervous Anglo shouted. "It's your fault for not doing what I told you."

So *this* is Jack, Mike thought. At long last, after hearing only snippets about him over the last several months, then far too much in the last twenty-four hours, he finally was looking at Jack Pearson. And, true to his reputation, he was yelling at Sandra and blaming someone else for what had happened.

Sandra glared at Jack, but said nothing. He started to speak again, but a glance from the handsome one silenced him. By his air of authority, this Hispanic guy must be the leader, Mike thought. He at least seemed calm, in contrast to Jack, who was still wobbling the gun back and forth. Had the Hispanic not been there, Mike would have been a lot more concerned that Jack might do something really trigger-happy in the company of his ex-wife with her boyfriend—the pair who had created a lot of trouble in his drug business. Not that their future looked very bright anyway; he knew these guys intended to silence him and Sandra.

Mike could only hope the boss' remark about causing trouble and not listening meant he was more interested in business than quibbling over the Toyota Attack. Maybe he could convince him he would be glad to quit dealing with the Morales Company. Slim as that seemed, it was their only hope—that, or some other unforeseen, crazy occurrence changing everything. The past twenty-four hours had certainly proven that could happen.

"Come on, let's go," the Hispanic ordered. He waved his weapon for Mike and Sandra to come down the trail, then pass in front of him to lead the way back into the canyon.

As they neared Sneer Face, he reached out and shoved Mike as if to hurry him. It took all of Mike's will power to resist pulling the .22 and shooting him in the face, but he knew he couldn't take all of them before being killed. Instead, he feigned a stumble, then straightened up from a crouch with all the power he could muster, slamming his right fist into the guy's nose. A satisfying crack was followed by a spurt of blood and the guy went down.

Jack ran over to Mike and shoved his gun into his face, screaming, "I'm gonna blow your fucking head off!"

Spurred on by the one-punch defeat of the guy who shoved him, Mike screamed back, "Well, just do it, tough guy! You're so goddam tough! Just do it! Or put the fucking gun down, and let's see how tough you are!"

Jack stopped, confused, unsure of how to proceed. He was a born bully and had always thought himself quite the tough guy, but intimidation hadn't worked this time. And in those few seconds, he remembered how he had felt threatened earlier by the demeanor of the helicopter pilot and the shooter— the *same* pilot who now lay dead on the other side of the canyon, and the *same* shooter who now lay bleeding and moaning at his feet, both taken out by this screaming maniac. He really didn't know whether to take up the challenge or shoot him, and the delay was making him look like a fool.

The decision was taken from him by the Hispanic's roar. "Stop it! *You!*" he shouted, pointing at Mike. "Get down here!"

Mike turned to see the gun leveled at him, the hammer cocked and the man's finger tightening on the trigger.

"And you, Shithead!" he yelled at Jack. "Help him up. And don't make threats you can't keep!"

With the harsh rebuke, Jack shrunk back, then leaned down to help Sneer Face to his feet, the second time in an hour the battered man had been assisted off the ground by his companions. When he was fully upright, he glared at Mike with hatred and swiped at his bloody face with his shirt sleeve.

Mike and Sandra led the way down the winding path back into the canyon, the leader of the gunmen closely behind, followed by Jack and the still-bleeding Sneer Face. As they descended lower, the breeze from the southeast was blocked. The sun was blazing in the west, and the temperature soared to well over one hundred degrees. It was like hiking in a heated vacuum chamber.

While it was bad for him and Sandra, Mike knew it had to be punishing their captors even more. Sharing the big water bottle earlier with Sandra had been a tremendous help. Recalling the futile search of the helicopter for water, he surmised the gunmen may not have drunk for hours, dangerous in this environment. And at least a couple of the guys wore cowboy boots, not the best footwear for this terrain. Periodically, he could hear a sliding scuffle and mumbled grunt or curse behind him as one of the captors slipped on the gravelly path.

Leading, he gradually increased the pace and hoped Sandra would see it and follow suit, like she had done every time they had trained together. Keeping the increase imperceptible, Sandra stuck behind him, right in his footsteps. The sounds of slipping increased behind him and, at one point, Jack fell down, pulling Sneer Face with him. Mike was delighted.

Serves them right. I hope they broke their fucking necks.

After a while, the trail neared the bottom of the canyon and began to flatten as they approached the river. Mike could hear the boss behind him, breathing hard and making an effort to place his feet on the less treacherous parts of the trail. Finally, he called out to Mike. "Slow down, this is no race. You in a big hurry to die?"

That remark took the pleasure out of Mike's tiny mental victory over their captors. Unless given the opportunity to walk them to death, the gunmen were going to win, and he and Sandra were going to die. Unlike Dirk and Sarge, these guys weren't about to fall for some trick. Mike's mind raced to come up with a plan, but nothing materialized.

Rounding the last bend, the helicopter came into view a quarter mile ahead. When they reached their earlier wading point, Mike again sat down and removed shoes and socks for the crossing. Sandra did the same, and the gunmen didn't complain at the delay. They were still breathing too hard to gripe about any respite from the pace. Mike noted they apparently hadn't bothered to remove their footwear on the first trip across, because he had heard squishing and sloshing almost every step down the trail. He could only hope the resulting blisters would somehow work to his and Sandra's advantage, though he couldn't imagine how.

Sad to think our lives depend on blisters on our adversaries' feet.

While they walked toward the chopper, the gunmen spoke among themselves for the first time. "Dan, can you fly this thing?" the boss asked Sneer Face.

"Sure thing, Reynaldo. Vince taught me to fly choppers, and I gave him some pointers on shooting when we were in Iraq in the first Gulf War. He said I had a knack for it, more than he did for shooting. I got pretty good at driving one of these things."

"I certainly hope so. I used Vince many times in the past, but he can't do it now, or even help, so I just want you to be sure you can get us where I want to go without a problem."

At the mention of Vince's absence, Sneer Face Dan's features hardened. "Yeah, I can get there, no problem. My only problem is that fucker in front of you. I'm going to shoot his ass and drop his body over Mexico, along with his girlfriend. Better yet, I'll just push them out from a couple thousand feet. That way, they'll have time to think about running over Vince and taking a swing at me. Hell, Vince and I did that to ragheads all the time in Iraq. The look on their faces made that whole fuckin' war worthwhile."

Hearing the confessed war crime, Mike cringed inwardly.

With that attitude, we should have won the war a lot sooner.

As the group approached the helicopter, the leader, now identified as Reynaldo, motioned for Mike and Sandra to step aside while Sneer Face— Reynaldo had called him Dan—checked the aircraft for readiness. "Take off the backpack," he ordered Mike. "Look in it, Jack, and see what they've got that's so important he carries it around the desert."

Jack snatched the bag before Mike could disentangle from the straps, nearly jerking him off balance. Mike caught himself and turned to glare at Jack, but said nothing. Jack unzipped the bag and rifled through it, smirking at the clothes and sheer underwear, then tossed it back to Mike with a lot more force than necessary.

Still trying to show how tough he is, Mike thought. He had evidently been looking for a weapon, or something more significant than underwear and toothbrushes, but he failed to find the map Mike had taken earlier and stuffed into a side compartment.

"Nothing in there but skivvies and a toothbrush kit," he announced. "Looks like Romeo and Juliet here had a real intimate party in mind. I didn't find any clothes for him. Hell, Reynaldo, on second thought, maybe some of those panties are his."

With that remark, Jack laughed loudly, and Sandra glared at him with renewed bitterness. Mike remained silent, watching for the right moment to make his move. Maybe he'd have an opportunity while boarding the helicopter, he thought, or perhaps as they disembarked. The leader, this Reynaldo guy, had mentioned "where I want to go" when inquiring of Dan's ability to fly the craft. Mike wondered where the destination was, although it didn't really make much difference; his and Sandra's fate was already determined, no matter what the location. At least that harsh knowledge took the pressure off of making a decision whether or not to try to escape. There was no choice—they *had* to try.

After digging around in the cabin for a minute or two, Dan flipped various switches and checked some instruments. His perplexed look got Reynaldo's attention. "What's the matter?" he asked.

"I dunno, but the radio doesn't work. Can't tell why it's inop, but I guess we don't need it. We damn sure don't need to communicate with anyone," he said with a snort. "Maybe Vince had it wired on the same circuit as the transponder. He never left it turned on during the ops, so he probably killed both of them after we left Del Rio. Could be another switch somewhere, but I don't see it."

"Well, check out the mechanical part," Reynaldo ordered, "and we'll worry about that later."

The new pilot fiddled around for another few minutes, manipulating controls and re-checking the instruments. Apparently satisfied, he declared he was ready for takeoff by giving a thumbs-up to Reynaldo, who approached the pilot's seat and spoke quietly to him while Jack trained his pistol first on Mike, then Sandra. Their voices were too low to hear, but Mike knew they weren't discussing what to get him for Christmas from the look he was getting from Dan and the grim answering nod from Reynaldo.

Reynaldo stood aside, motioning for Mike and Sandra to get in the back. He squeezed in next to Sandra, squatting on the floor in front of her seat, facing Mike. With his pistol in his right hand, away from Sandra, he sat cross-legged in the floor and leaned against a frame support just behind the door opening. Jack climbed in the front, buckled up, then turned in his seat to join his boss in watching them.

Dan switched on the ignition and started the engine. He let it idle for a few minutes with the rotor turning slowly while he re-checked the instruments, then gave the engine more throttle. With a slight shudder, the chopper tilted up and forward, until the front tips of the skids left the ground and they were airborne.

Reynaldo must have told Dan which direction to go, since he never turned to inquire. As the chopper gained altitude, he swung it around to the south, staying below the rim of the canyon. Once they reached the Rio Grande, he turned the craft to the right, in a westerly direction, staying low and meandering along the path of the muddy river below.

After flying for about twenty minutes, the cliffs on the Mexico side flattened out, and the pilot veered to the left, toward the interior of Mexico.

The scrub vegetation thinned out, the landscape below growing increasingly barren with each mile that slid below them.

Mike tried to read the airspeed indicator and compass without anyone noticing. It looked like they were traveling at around one hundred knots on a heading of two hundred degrees, so they would be over one hundred miles south of the border in an hour. Looking out the window, all he could see were scrub cactus, rocks, and desert.

At one point, the chopper carried them over a canyon of considerable size which appeared to have a trickle of water in the bottom. Several gullies leading to it from the south soon played out and the landscape again flattened. Mike was growing wearier by the minute, the drone and vibration of the helicopter lulling him to sleep. He hadn't slept in almost forty hours, and it was beginning to take its toll. A glance at Sandra told him she was in the same shape. Maybe we can both get a few winks in, he thought. Whatever was going to happen, they couldn't do anything about it right now, and it wouldn't hurt to be rested.

Just as he allowed his eyes to close, a jolt and a sickening dip brought him back to reality. The tone of the engine had changed, and the rotor was beating the air with an odd-sounding pitch. At first, he thought they were landing, but a look forward told him a different story. Dan was gripping the controls and looking frantically at the instruments. The engine sputtered, coughed, revved up for a few seconds, then settled into a rough idle. He eased the stick forward and began manipulating the foot controls, apparently trying to steady their flight. Jack was leaning over toward the pilot, saying something Mike couldn't hear, but the look on Dan's face indicated that the words weren't very calming. Reynaldo pulled himself to a squatting position and looked over Sandra's shoulder to the instrument panel between Jack and Dan.

"Look at the fuel gauge!" he yelled at Dan above the noise of the rough-running engine. "Goddammit, it's empty!"

"I know! I switched tanks a few minutes ago, but the engine's still not getting fuel. Something's wrong with that tank's fuel pump, so I switched back to the original tank. Now I can't get either pump to work, and both tanks read empty!" Panic was creeping into Dan's voice with the last statement.

Hearing the explanation, it took several seconds for Mike to realize the problem was likely due to the wires he'd jerked out trying to disable the craft, not both tanks actually being empty. In the tense situation boarding the chopper, he had forgotten the attempted sabotage. Now it was clear he had created a problem that would have surfaced only after they were airborne and running out of fuel in one tank.

The ground was coming up fast, and the chopper was lazily turning round and round, trying to rotate around the under-powered rotor, instead of the other way around. Mike vaguely recalled "auto-rotate," or some such term, but he didn't know if Dan was familiar with how to accomplish the maneuver. However, he knew the thing wouldn't stay in the air very long due to lack of lift from a fully-powered main rotor. And if the tail rotor quit turning completely, the craft would start spinning around, and they would be out of control. Dan probably didn't have much experience in emergency situations, and this was beginning to look like a real emergency.

Mike cinched his harness even tighter and did the same to Sandra's. Reynaldo had moved in behind him and Sandra and gripped the harness anchors, one in each hand, then braced his feet against the seat frames. As they neared the ground at an alarming rate, the craft tilted slightly to the left. Dan tried to right the thing, but the rotor struck the ground a glancing blow, knocking them back to the right with a similar result when the rotor struck the ground again, harder this time. He muscled the controls, and momentarily regained a level attitude, but the craft suddenly spun and rolled toward its right side again.

On this, the third impact, the chopper spun and smacked hard into the desert floor on its right skid. The rotor hit the ground on its next revolution, this time too hard to survive. The resulting jolt was like nothing Mike had ever felt, so jarring he felt his insides were being wrenched loose. His mind went to Sandra, but he couldn't see her or even focus his eyes to try.

The next few seconds were a blur, filled with screeching, screaming, and grinding sounds, along with gravel and dust flying about the cabin like bullets. Despite the harnesses, bodies were flung around like rags against the restraints. In full panic mode, Mike wondered whether the screaming noises were mechanical or coming from him and the other passengers, but he couldn't tell.

Finally, the motion stopped. Mike would later recall it must have made two full flips before skidding forward another fifty or sixty yards on its side, though he couldn't be sure. But at this moment, realizing he was alive and the horrible motion had stopped, he was certain of two things:

This airline gets no more of my business! And never, ever again will I jerk wires from an aircraft I may have to ride in.

Mike was hanging from the left side, which was now the top. He reached down toward Sandra, who was shaken and wide-eyed, and thrashing wildly against her harness. He took that as a good sign, indicating little or no injury. The extra tightening of her safety harness just before impact had completely immobilized her, protecting her from injury, but now the claustrophobic atmosphere inside the wrecked, dust-filled cabin was making her desperate to escape its grip.

"Hold still, hold still," he instructed her. "Let me loosen your seat belt and harness."

From his own still-secured position, it took a minute to reach the buckle so Sandra could squirm out from under him before unsnapping his own. He promptly fell in a heap on the seat where she had been pinned, cracking his head against the seat frame in the process.

"Ow! Shit! Dammit!" He struggled to untangle himself, rubbing his head and looking forward to where Sandra was now crammed by the front passenger seat. She was staring at Dan's body, the shooter-turned-pilot, who now had joined his buddy Vince in Helicopter Heaven, the Final LZ. Hanging from his seat belt, his head was crushed like an egg, turned at an impossible angle to his body.

Mike looked about the cabin and spotted the Hispanic guy, Reynaldo, leaned against the rear bulkhead of the craft, his face bloody from a gash in his hairline. His eyes were closed, but he was moaning and stirring slightly. Jack was nowhere to be seen, probably thrown from the wreckage during one of the flips. If so, he certainly couldn't have fared well, Mike thought.

Too damn bad, but I won't lose any sleep over it.

Sandra had pushed herself up from her stooped position, reaching for the opening above them. Mike pushed on her behind to boost her up until she could grasp the frame around the opening. He guided her feet onto his shoulders so she could pull herself up and scramble over the side.

"Be careful, watch out for sharp edges!" Mike called out as she clambered over the edge and slid to the ground. He watched her through the dusty Plexiglas as she took a few shaky steps. She seemed to be okay, but still hadn't uttered a word. "You okay?" he asked, watching her face.

She turned to look at him inside the craft, a confused look on her face. "I think so. I don't think anything's broken, because I can move alright. How about you?"

"Just banged up a bit. Re-tightening those belts was the trick, I think. Remind me of this next time I get in a car and gripe about wearing a seat belt." He turned to the back of the craft and reached a hand toward Reynaldo.

His eyes were open, but he looked dazed and disoriented. "Can you move?" he asked.

"Yes, perhaps." He struggled to his knees and wriggled toward Mike, who managed to guide him up through the opening much as he had done with Sandra, although it took a lot more effort to get the man over the edge. Reynaldo lacked the strength and lightness that had enabled Sandra to exit easily, and his injury didn't help matters. The task took several minutes, and Mike fell back, exhausted. Sandra helped Reynaldo down from the top of the chopper, where he leaned against the wreckage and closed his eyes. His head had taken a pretty good shot, and he was obviously still dazed.

After a few minutes' rest, Mike stood on the edge of the passenger seat, grasped the edge of the opening and pulled himself up enough to hook his right leg over the pilot's seat. From there, he was able to propel his body up through the opening. He half-slid, half-fell off the wreckage, landing beside Reynaldo.

Assessing the damage, he was amazed they had survived. That he and Sandra were unhurt was nothing short of a miracle. Although the cabin remained fairly intact, the tail boom was gone and the rotor was snapped off, the pieces nowhere in sight. The path of the sliding wreckage was clearly marked in the desert gravel, leading back almost a hundred yards to the point of the first impact.

Mike began back-tracking the swath of destruction, looking for any sign of Jack Pearson. After covering the entire wreckage area, he turned back toward the helicopter, but saw nothing on the return trip. He concluded that Jack's body must have been flung farther from the wreckage path, so he expanded his search area, checking several yards out from either side of the path. Still no Jack.

Mike wondered if he could have survived. Nor likely, but it was also unlikely he and Sandra would survive walking out of the desert, certainly not if he wasted any more time or energy looking for him. But where the hell was he?

Mike walked back to the wreckage where Sandra had propped Reynaldo up against the shaded side of the cabin and made him as comfortable as possible. Lacking any water to cleanse his wounds, she had used her sleeve to wipe blood from his face. He was sitting upright and looking better than before, but still did not appear to be in any condition to travel. Sandra's diagnosis confirmed it.

"I don't think he can walk at all," she told Mike. "It seems like some ribs are broken and his ankle is twisted pretty badly, maybe even broken. It's so swollen I couldn't get his boot off to look at it."

Mike squatted down to examine the injuries. The cut on Reynaldo's head had stopped bleeding and didn't appear too serious. But he had both arms wrapped tightly around himself, and his breath was coming in short, measured gasps. Clearly, he was in a lot of pain and wouldn't be walking anywhere. "How do you feel?" Mike asked, knowing the answer already.

"Not so well, I'm afraid."

"Do you know where we are? How far are we from water?"

"We should have been nearing our destination under normal flying conditions. Sitting on the floor, I did not see exactly where we were, but another twenty minutes or so should have brought us to the ranch. I have a manager at the ranch, and of course, there is water. I don't know if there is any closer source."

Mike quickly calculated the roughly one-hundred knot air speed with insignificant headwinds would mean about one hundred fifteen miles, more or less, in an hour. So another twenty minutes would have covered almost forty miles. Pretty long walk in mid-summer with no water.

Pretty long walk, period.

He looked around for a better spot to sit while determining their next move. The sun was still high enough to render the shade provided by the wrecked cabin pretty slim. Only then did it occur to him the aircraft might burst into flames any second, if one were to believe the movies. So far, their accident looked to be a dud in that department, for which he was grateful. No fire, no explosion; just a wreck. Maybe the chopper *had* been completely out of fuel, not enough left in the tanks to splash out on impact and cause a fire. But the way everything else was going, he wasn't going to take a chance.

He looked in the direction they'd been traveling and spotted a gully about forty yards away that would provide shelter from the sun. With no small effort, he and Sandra helped Reynaldo to the new resting place. Even the short journey was a strain, and Reynaldo's face was ashen by the time they had him leaning against the embankment.

Mike returned to the chopper to look for anything useful. Wrapping his shirt tail over the exposed edge of the windshield, he carefully pulled a broken portion of the Plexiglas out to get a better look. He located a first aid kit, which was strapped under the passenger seat. He used his pocketknife to unscrew the overhead compass from it bracket. He also found a penlight and booklet in a storage compartment he had overlooked earlier. A single can of Coke had rolled to a stop against the passenger seat anchor. Should be well-shaken by now, he thought, but even hot and shaken, the liquid might mean the difference between life and death out here. He stuffed it into his back pocket.

Glancing warily at the body hanging grotesquely from its seat harness, Mike realized the difference for Dan was of no importance now. Despite the hatred that had immediately surfaced between them, Mike had to admire the man's efforts during the last terrifying seconds to bring the craft in safely. It had enabled him and Sandra to walk away from the crash—and maybe out of this jam with the drug dealers. After all, Dan and Vince were dead, and the leader of this bunch was laid up with a badly broken body. Dirk and Sarge were left far behind, and pistol-waving Jack was missing from the scene.

The thought reminded Mike to look around the cabin for Reynaldo's gun, but he gave up after about five fruitless minutes. Even if Reynaldo still had it on him, he wasn't going to shoot the only people in the world who could possibly get him help.

By then, Mike was soaked with sweat, not only from the heat build-up inside the cabin, but the nervousness at being trapped inside with the possibility of a fire and the reality of a body hanging over him. Finding nothing else of use, he backed out of the craft, glad to be outside again. Standing up, he wondered again about Jack. He stooped and looked back inside the cabin at the unbuckled passenger seat harness. Had Jack unbuckled it before the crash? During the crash? Had it unbuckled itself on impact? He hadn't found Reynaldo's revolver, or the automatic that Jack had waved around so much; so wherever he was, the gun was probably with him. Mike hoped he was in no shape to wave it around—or even pick it up, for that matter.

He walked back to Sandra and Reynaldo with the first aid kit. Sandra used the small bottle of antiseptic to cleanse the gash on his head and taped a sterile pad over the wound by wrapping tape around his jaw. He looked like a poorly outfitted mummy, but at least it would keep the wound clean. There was little to be done about the broken ribs or the ankle. Mike considered trying again to remove his boot, ostensibly to examine the ankle, but also to see if he had hidden the gun there before the crash. Looking at him holding his ribs, barely able to move, he decided against it. They were going to leave him to go for help anyway, and a gun in the injured man's possession seemed of little consequence now.

Mike squatted to talk with Reynaldo, watching his face for any indication he was sandbagging on the injury. The pain in his eyes told him he wasn't.

"The heading we were traveling was about two hundred degrees, south, southwest. Were we on a direct line to the ranch?"

Mike's question must have told Reynaldo about Dan's fate. He turned his head toward the crash scene and hesitated before looking back at Mike and responding. "Yes, I believe so. We have made this trip in the past, and the route looked familiar, although the terrain lacks distinguishing features. I can only assume that Dan was heading straight to the ranch headquarters. Proceeding in the same direction should take you to a fence line on the north side of the ranch. Turn right and follow it. Since the ranch house is located in the northwest corner, you will spot it before you reach the corner forming the west boundary."

Mike was pleased to hear Reynaldo's explicit description of the ranch layout. They at least had a sure destination for finding help. Of course, getting help would benefit Reynaldo more than anyone. He was in pretty rough shape, the effort of just giving the directions showing now in his face, which was distorted in pain.

But what about getting help and coming back out here? The ranch manager was likely involved in the drug business with Reynaldo and might silence him and Sandra before they could explain, especially if he had been forewarned of their delivery for execution. The ranch probably held a number of unmarked graves of those who had crossed paths with Reynaldo in the past. The ranch manager was probably the Regional Manager of the Silencing Division for the whole operation, Mike thought grimly. Obviously, it would be wiser to get help elsewhere and send assistance to Reynaldo, rather than approaching one of his employees. He and Sandra hadn't had very good luck dealing with Reynaldo and Company. But where exactly was "elsewhere," and how did they get there?

Reynaldo must have read his mind. "I know you are apprehensive about getting help for someone who recently planned to kill you. I wouldn't blame you for simply walking out of here and leaving me here to die. You two probably can do it if anyone can. You have already shown resourcefulness and physical endurance beyond what I expected from Jack's information about you—"

"We're not going to leave you here to die," Sandra interrupted. "We'll go for help, but in exchange, you must give us assurance that your ranch manager will take us to safety. In return for that, we'll forget your operation, and Mike will quit buying from Morales."

Reynaldo gave a pained smile, showing perfect teeth. "I am in no position to bargain, and I accept your terms. However, I am surprised you are willing to deal with me. After all, my business—"

"I don't care what business you're in, so long as it doesn't involve me or Mike. I've always been opposed to drugs and those who deal in them, but I know it's going to happen, no matter what I think or do. And putting you out of business wouldn't make any difference in the long run. Somebody else will just take your place, fill the gap. There's too much money involved."

"You seem to have a thorough knowledge of my business. Your assessment is correct. It surprises me that your distaste for it is matched only by your cynicism."

"We just want to be rid of you for good, but you'll just have to trust us on that part. And I want to know we did the right thing for another human being."

Mike was surprised at her outburst. He fully expected she would insist on getting help for the injured man. But vocalizing her viewpoint on the drug business was a new twist, something he didn't expect from her. He knew she was smart and more informed about seamy matters than she exhibited, but this philosophical, even cynical, outlook on the inevitability of drug smuggling opened his eyes.

She wasn't through. "And maybe you should listen to someone besides Jack. I've known him longer than you have, even before he started screwing your wife. He's always been long on talk and short on information."

The news about Jack and his wife didn't seem to surprise Reynaldo, but coming from this source and at this time, it appeared to stir something in him. His eyes again took on a pained expression, and even Mike flinched as she imparted the information. He wasn't sure this was the best time to advance her hometown soap opera.

When are women most likely to twist the knife? When you've got broken ribs, of course!

CHAPTER 14

▼

At the sudden change in pitch from the engine and rotor, Jack looked over to see Dan frowning and looking from gauge to gauge. At first, the situation appeared minor; Dan flipped a couple of switches and reached under the seat to change something, then resumed his study of the gauges. For a few seconds, the engine regained its power, and the sound of the rotor resumed its former pitch. Jack leaned back in his seat and tried to relax.

Then the chopper started losing altitude. Dan struggled with the controls to stop a gradual turning motion which, along with fear, was already making Jack dizzy. He could tell the helicopter was out of Dan's full control and decided then and there to get out of the aircraft as fast as possible. Though he saw that Dan was trying to correct the flying problem, he wished the new pilot would just put the thing on the ground. Anything was better than this wallowing around in the sky.

"Put this thing down! Get me on the ground, now!" he screamed at Dan, gesturing wildly and pointing toward the earth below as if Dan didn't know in which direction it lay. Gone was the earlier intimidation he had felt with Reynaldo's grim-faced enforcer-turned-pilot. He had witnessed the hired killer being knocked over by a Toyota, flattened by its owner's fist, and now, less than an hour later, the look of terror on his face at this new impending disaster. For all his earlier outward appearance of being a cool, calm, hard-eyed hit man, he was obviously scared—and *that* scared Jack more than anything.

Jack wished they were closer to the ground so he could just jump out and take his chances. He was more terrified of being stuck inside the chopper than crashing. If they crashed, so be it; but he wasn't about to be trapped inside a burning aircraft with his seat belt buckled tightly under his paunch. He unbuckled it and braced his feet against the framework under his side of the instrument panel, then gripped the underside of his seat by clenching his hands around the frame and pulling upward with all his strength, much like preparing for a bull ride.

On the second contact with the ground, the aircraft smacked hard on its right skid. Jack lost his grip on the seat frame, and inertia launched him out the door, straight into a large *cenizo* bush. Being one of the few items in the Chihuahuan Desert that doesn't bite, sting, prick, gouge, inflame or otherwise destroy the skin of anything making contact with it, he couldn't have been luckier than to land in the *purple desert sage*, as it is also known. And a last-second sideways lurch dumped him almost gently into the bush, instead of slamming him into the ground.

Once again, fate had been kind to Jack Pearson. He sat dazed for a few seconds while the helicopter struck the ground a final time, separating the fuselage from the tail boom. His senses seemed to slow time while he observed the bizarre event unfolding. He vaguely noticed the rear section parting from the body and pole-vaulting itself over a rise a hundred feet away. The shattered rotor scattered over the desert, and he instinctively ducked farther into the bush as the cabin slid across the gravel, moving away from him. Amazingly, he even saw the remaining passengers through the Plexiglas. It reminded him of watching clothes being tossed about inside a dryer. He couldn't believe that only seconds before he had been a part of the horrible action he was now witnessing.

When the chopper finally stopped moving, Jack watched, mesmerized by the sight, while the dust slowly settled and silence returned to the desert. A few minutes later, someone's head poked up through the top of the crashed cabin. It was too far away and still too dusty to tell for sure, but judging by the size, it was almost certainly Sandra. He continued to watch while another person struggled for a long time to clamber over the edge of the cabin and slip to the ground. He couldn't determine who it was, but it looked like Reynaldo.

After another long wait, a third survivor appeared. Jack squinted into the bright sunlight and recognized Mike's thin frame. He kept looking at the top of the wrecked cabin, but no one else appeared, and the three people standing and sitting outside didn't seem concerned with anyone else in the craft. Somebody must be dead, Jack thought, since they're making no effort to get the last person out. Had to be the pilot.

When Mike started walking back along the path of the crash, Jack, for some reason unknown even to him at the moment, remained perfectly still. Though dazed and still unsure if he was injured, something told him to keep his position (and thus even his survival) a secret for the time being. The tables had turned once again in this ongoing, see-saw contest between him and Mike, and Jack wanted to evaluate what this meant before showing his face.

As Mike returned to the wreckage after two sweeps of the crash area, Jack tried to focus his thoughts. Mike and Sandra could probably go for help, but Reynaldo was injured, judging by Sandra's nursing efforts over the still form. Would they go for help, or capitalize on this event and use their physical capabilities to walk away? And how would he, Jack, handle the two of them if he walked out of the bush right now and used his gun to take control again? Take control of *what*? There was no water to fight over. Certainly, the only chance was to go for outside help and water, and he couldn't very well force them to do it for him. To maintain control over Mike and Sandra, he'd have to go with them, not a likely prospect.

He'd been to the ranch once before with Reynaldo, and while he didn't know exactly where the crash had stranded them, it certainly wasn't close to civilization. Cocksure as he was, deep inside, Jack knew his limitations, and walking twenty or more miles in the desert was beyond his scope. He was already thirsty as hell and his feet hurt. He wasn't sure anyone could do it, but suspected Mike and Sandra's distance training might enable them to succeed. Hell, they'd worn his ass out just walking back to the helicopter, he thought, and that was after they'd already been hiking for hours.

Jack was grudgingly forming a new opinion of Sandra's boyfriend. There was more to this weenie-assed shopkeeper than he'd first thought. And Sandra too, for that matter. Quiet and meek as she had always acted, she was turning out to be tough as a boot. Between them, those two had bailed out of a car in the middle of nowhere, walked back to Langtry, taken the car away from Dirk and Sarge, run over Vince in the canyon, knocked the living shit out of tough-guy Dan, and survived a helicopter crash. And now, they'd probably walk out of this God-forsaken land.

Watching through the bush, Jack could now see the three were talking, but he had no idea of what was being said. He could, however, readily tell that Mike and Sandra now had the upper hand. First one, then the other, stooped to talk with Reynaldo, as though lecturing him.

But why would they bother? All they had to do was walk away. Judging by his slumped pose against the wreckage and the effort it took to move him to the gully, Reynaldo was in no shape to do anything about it.

Jack reasoned Mike and Sandra surely knew there was no Mexican Air Patrol or FAA on its way to help—hell, this was Mexico. Government agencies could barely take care of their own citizens, much less some dumbass *gringos* crashing in the desert. Besides, Dan had kept the chopper at a low altitude, below the cliffs along the river, before turning south toward the ranch. That would have avoided detection by radar, which was used only sporadically in this area to combat drug and alien smuggling. And Jack was certain that Vince hadn't filed a flight plan before leaving Del Rio; his line of work precluded record-keeping of any kind, and the helicopter belonged to Reynaldo's operation anyway. As far as Mike and Sandra knew, the only thing that could discover Reynaldo were the vultures wheeling lazily overhead. So why the long discussion?

As Jack continued to observe, Mike and Sandra both squatted in front of Reynaldo and appeared to be studying something between them. He couldn't see it was the aerial map that Mike had taken from the chopper. What he did witness, though, was more discussion, interspersed by pointing in several directions. It was apparent that they weren't sure of exactly where they were or where to go. But by including Reynaldo in the talk, it appeared they were planning to send assistance, rather than abandon him to the vultures. And if they went to get help, Jack wanted to benefit from it. Showing himself now might change their minds. Even if he used his weapon and forced one to go while holding the other as hostage, things might not go as well as he wished—the messenger might return with more than he wanted.

So for now, Jack decided to stay put in the sage bush, wishing he could take off his boots and have a long visit at the water jug.

CHAPTER 15

▼

Spreading the map between them, Mike and Sandra discussed their probable location with Reynaldo. It was soon apparent that distance was a formidable barrier to their survival, compounded by heat and lack of water. The map showed the ranch's landing strip to be located southwest of the canyon Mike had noticed from the air before the crash. Not knowing where on the course they had crashed, they could be at any point between the canyon and the ranch, which would place them thirty to fifty miles from the ranch house. That would not be a comfortable distance under any circumstances, but without water, the walk would prove dangerous, possibly fatal. They could only hope the distance turned out to be on the lesser side of Mike's calculation, or that they found water along the way. But it didn't make any difference how daunting the trip seemed—to stay here was to die.

"The map does not look very encouraging, does it?" Reynaldo asked, looking from Mike to Sandra, then back again. "And I did not give my ranch foreman any notice that we were coming, so he has no reason to mount a search for us."

"That's why we've got to take our best shot now," Mike said. "We won't find any water just sitting here."

"Are you sure we can we just set out walking and run into the ranch house?" Sandra asked. "What if we miss it?"

"We miss it, and we'll die of thirst," Mike responded. "If it's anywhere near as far as we think, even a small deviation from a direct line to the ranch house will be compounded by the distance, so we could miss it by miles. We really can't afford just to take off in the general direction we were flying and hope for the best, but that's what we're faced with. We have the compass, but without knowing the exact bearing from here to the ranch house, it's pretty iffy."

Reynaldo exhaled deeply, pain showing in his face. "It's all we have though, right? That, and your physical ability. Cell phones don't work out here, and as you might guess, this particular route is not a popular one. I have not traveled this area on foot or by horseback, though I have flown over it many times. I know it is quite inhospitable. That much is evident just by looking around." He raised his hand in a feeble gesture to point out that fact, but the effort made him grimace.

"It's not an area anyone would travel through on foot if they had another choice," Sandra agreed. "Not on purpose, anyway."

Her grim observation halted the conversation for a moment. All three were thinking of the obstacles between them and salvation, the one-shot effort they had to make with little navigational skill to help them. It was going to take some extraordinary luck to live through this, and even more good fortune to get help and water back to Reynaldo in time. Even if they got lucky and struck the fence line Reynaldo had described, it could still be miles to the ranch house. And what if the ranch caretaker was gone, out tending livestock or gone to town for supplies? They had to be able to return quickly with water and transportation for Reynaldo, or he would suffer the same fate as if they failed altogether; it would just take a little longer.

Mike stood and pondered what other options they might have. He recalled seeing slivers of sunlight reflected off a stream of water in the bottom of the canyon, but it was miles back. He decided it would be too risky to go that direction for water, even though it might be closer. In the first place, they would still be a long way from civilization, perhaps farther than they were right now. Plus, they had nothing to carry water, even if they found it. And Reynaldo needed medical attention and transportation to a facility that could properly tend to him if he were to survive. He decided not to mention it.

Reynaldo broke the silence. "The ranch foreman's name is Alberto. He will be able to return to this spot by horseback with your guidance. He has lived in this area all his life. I am sure he will know where you are talking about when you mention the big canyon."

"Does Alberto speak English?" Mike asked. "My Spanish is pretty limited."

"Mine too," Sandra added. "This is a different assignment than we ever had in Spanish class."

"Unfortunately, no, he does not," Reynaldo replied. "I can give you a few basic phrases to describe the situation, and the mention of my name will lend credibility, although he may foresee a possible trap, a treachery on the part of a competitor of mine, or retaliation by a politician to whom I have not adequately contributed. It will be up to you to convince him."

"I can't imagine any of your enemies staggering up to your ranch house trying to pull off a kidnapping of *El Patrón*," Sandra quipped, managing a laugh.

"Probably not likely, but Alberto is most protective. He has run my ranch for years, and he is very loyal to me. And although he never asks questions about any of my other business, he is much wiser than his station in life would suggest, so he will know you are not there to look over my livestock."

Sandra had a better working knowledge of Spanish than Mike, but they both repeated the key phrases Reynaldo gave them to communicate the dilemma to Alberto. He grinned weakly at their recitations, but assured them it would be satisfactory to deliver the message. Mike and Sandra laughed, despite their dire circumstances.

They walked away, toward the chopper, repeating the words again while stretching their leg muscles in preparation for the walk. Mike fished around in his pocket and produced the Coca Cola he had found in the wreckage. "This is all we've got to drink," he said. "It would be better with ice, but I'm fresh out right now. Drink up."

He pulled the tab, knowing it would spew all over the place after bouncing around the cabin in the crash. It did, but at least it was wet. Even rodeo-cold, it tasted good. He downed some, then offered the can to Sandra. She declined to drink any, suggesting they leave it with Reynaldo. Mike agreed, and they turned back toward the shade of the gully and the injured man. Without saying it, both knew the single can of soda was all that separated the immobile Reynaldo from a meeting with the buzzards.

Reynaldo gratefully took the can and took a sip. "I must apologize for the lack of hospitality on my aircraft. One hot soft drink doesn't exactly qualify it for luxury status." He took another drink and offered the can back to Mike, who shook his head.

"You drink the rest. With luck, we may even run on to some water on the way. Right now, I've got to pinpoint the direction we want to travel and figure out how to stay on track. We've got to get moving."

Mike knew little about navigation and had to think for a few minutes about how to best utilize the compass he had salvaged from the crashed helicopter. "According to the map, we've got to stay on a course of two hundred degrees and hope it's right," he told Sandra. "I don't know what else to check to determine exactly what our original course was, so we've just got to go with this, imperfect as it is. You've got to help me with this and remember what we're viewing in case you have to go on alone."

He moved to the open area atop the gully's bank and had Sandra hold the instrument by its mounting bracket before him at just above eye level. He moved around it until he faced a bearing of two hundred degrees, then sighted directly under it toward their destination to find a prominent landmark on the horizon. Luckily, the first low hills of the *Sierra del Huacha* were visible, and he was able to pinpoint a fairly deep cleft between two matching, rounded peaks. If they got off course, simply taking another two hundred-degree reading would no longer be accurate; they had to remain focused on the cleft and hope it didn't change appearance with the change in distance or the angle from which they would be viewing it.

Then he stepped to the opposite side of the compass to find a landmark lining up on the reciprocal of their destination, twenty degrees, and was dumbfounded to see nothing but flat desert. He had no reference point in that direction; nothing he could look back to and re-check for purposes of staying on a straight line.

Now how in the hell was this supposed to work?

He explained the problem to Sandra. "All we can do is keep the mountain cleft in sight and concentrate on getting to it," he said. "This compass business is guesswork, and there are too many unknowns to be absolutely sure of anything, but that's our target."

The late afternoon light was becoming less harsh, and Mike wanted to make some real progress before darkness fell. If the moon gave enough light to see the ground before them and the landmark, they could walk easier, even if slower, in the cool of the night. If not, they would have to stop and begin again at first light. Wandering off their intended course would be a waste of time and energy they could not afford.

They returned to Reynaldo, who sat sipping on the Coke, breathing slower and more evenly due to finding a somewhat comfortable position against the embankment. Seeing his improved condition, Mike figured the injuries wouldn't cause him much trouble if he remained still. "We're going to make as much distance as we can before dark," he announced. "So we'd better get going. Survival is going to be touch and go, no matter what."

"I have every confidence that you will succeed," Reynaldo said. "My fate is up to you, obviously. Even if you reach safety, I am literally at your disposal. What can I say? I am embarrassed to be in this position, my life dependent upon the whim of those whom I have threatened. I—"

"Don't worry about that," Mike interrupted. "Just hope we succeed, for all our sakes. If we do, you have Sandra to thank. I can't say that I wouldn't just leave your ass out here to rot, but she's reminded me I'm really not that way, either. But if we get out of this, I don't ever want to see or hear from you again. And you will never hear from us again, I assure you. You and your business is of no importance to us. But my life and Sandra's life *are* important. I want you and your drug-dealing buddies to stay the fuck out of it."

Reynaldo looked Mike in the eye to respond. "You have my word. And in spite of what you think of me and my activities, my word is good. I do what I say I will do. Good luck."

Mike set out at a moderate pace, Sandra agreeing that he should lead for now, so long as he didn't take long strides and force her into a constant catch-up pace. "The minute you do, I'm going to lead. I can't stand having to run every ten feet or so, just so I can catch up," she reminded him.

"You've got more endurance than I. You'll end up in front before this is over, anyway, just like you always do, so what are you worried about?" Mike was grinning as he said it, but wisely chose not to glance back at the look she was giving him.

Vegetation was sparse, and the gravel crunching beneath their feet was packed and stable; pretty good footing for pushing off on each step and making good time. The land was generally flat, with a few gullies crisscrossing the landscape, but nothing that would drastically impede their progress or divert them from a fairly straight path toward the cleft between the hilltops to the southwest. Mike wanted to get as many miles as possible between them and the crash site before darkness fell. Even if they got lucky with good moonlight, their pace would slow after dark. Also, an eerie feeling had come over him just before they departed, and he hoped to shake it by covering some ground.

Mike still felt uncomfortable about the missing Jack Pearson. How the hell could he just disappear? While he hadn't exactly scoured the area in his search, he should have been able to spot a body lying somewhere within the path of the wreckage. Well, if he's dead, it makes no difference, just as it didn't with Dan, he thought. They'll both rot in the desert heat. And if the son of a bitch is still alive, maybe Alberto can find him when we return. *If* we return.

Only a half hour into the walk, and Mike was rethinking the plan to get help for Reynaldo. The farther they walked from the crash, the more Mike wanted to walk away for good. He started to say something to Sandra about it, but decided against it, for the moment, anyway. They were a long way from extracting themselves from trouble, much less worrying about some drug dealer who'd gotten them into it.

Mike found himself fuming again about their predicament and the unsavory group from Sandra's past. Although he'd already pointed out to her that dealing with these people was dangerous—exactly what got them into this mess to begin with—she didn't seem to comprehend that some people were just plain trouble, no matter what the situation. It wasn't in her nature to condemn anyone lightly, and Mike admired that trait, but she had to recognize this entire debacle had started with a mere run-in at a casual party she had attended. Who would have guessed it would nearly cost them their lives? Several times, in fact.

And the lead guy, Reynaldo. His smooth manners, educated speech, and chartered aircraft may have cost a lot of money and look cool to an observer, but he was still a drug dealer. Like Sandra, Mike realized the extent of drugs in American culture and the inevitability of crime given the vast profit potential. But in his opinion, anyone involved with drugs was a loser, and no amount of money would instill any class into their miserable lives. They weren't worth saving. Why couldn't Sandra see that?

He progressed from fuming to downright angry again just thinking about the boss of this bunch. Until her recent outburst, he hadn't been aware that she indirectly knew Reynaldo, or at least knew him to be the spouse of her husband's lover. Mike hadn't exactly had time to discuss her entire history with this group, but he was itching to demonstrate to her what happened when you fell in with their type. He remembered the words of an old banker he had done business with in the past: *"Mike, when you lie down with dogs, you get up with fleas."* He couldn't recall the conversation or the context of the remark, but he'd liked the saying, and right now, it seemed apropos in describing Sandra's connection with these people.

Once again, someone from her not-so-pleasant past was dictating her actions, and, by extension, *his* actions. Rather than walking out of here and just saving themselves, they were going to try to convince a ranch foreman to backtrack into the harsh landscape to save his injured boss, the very man who had ordered them both dead. And, in all likelihood, they'd have to accompany Alberto back to the crash site. No matter how well the rancher knew the country, he couldn't find Reynaldo in a gully twenty miles away by simply being pointed in the right direction. That is, not unless he got within a few miles and spotted the buzzards circling, which was certainly a possibility.

Despite the mental turmoil, Mike realized his dislike of Sandra's connection with this bunch was prompted by jealousy. And didn't that mean he really cared for her? Why else would he want to protect her? Then he recalled a passage from a book he'd read that said something like "caring for someone is just selfishness in disguise." It had surprised him at the time that a generally positive emotion was labeled as a negative trait. The recollection caused him to reconsider the merits of caring for someone, but only briefly.

Maybe I'm just selfish.

In the past two days, Mike had developed an overwhelming need within himself to protect her from pushy, forceful people, especially anyone connected to illegal activities, for the obvious reasons. He despised the fact that some people flaunted the laws, while he felt inclined to obey them. He didn't consider himself an elitist or a snob, but he hoped when it came down to it, Sandra would see that *any* contact with those people would turn her into a loser, just like they were.

And if that makes me selfish, then so be it.

CHAPTER 16

▼

The fading light from the sun left a glow in the western sky that gave Mike and Sandra more time to keep their destination landmark in sight. In fact, the rays shining on the hills highlighted the cleft for quite some time after sunset, creating a beacon in contrast to the darker, lower hills to the southwest. Their target seemed tantalizingly close, beckoning to them from the horizon, but in reality, many miles away.

The relentless hot wind had ceased, slowed to a slight breeze. The temperature had dropped considerably, and Mike wished it would stay this way for the entire trek, however far it was. It was the ideal time for walking in the desert, and he pushed the pace accordingly.

But as full darkness fell, the view of the hills faded, then disappeared altogether. Mike looked over his shoulder every few minutes, anxiously awaiting the moon's appearance. He recalled it having been high in the sky and fairly bright as they hiked from the Toyota-hog crash scene to Langtry, but that had been late at night.

"I wish the moon would rise," he said.

"I remember it was pretty bright last night, but I didn't pay particular attention to it. Doesn't it rise later every night?"

"Yeah, I think so. If it comes up any time soon, we can make pretty good time tonight. We have to really cover some ground while it's cool enough to walk fast. I don't look forward to continuing this little hike in the sun tomorrow."

They trudged on in silence for a few more minutes before Sandra asked, "Can you see the hills at all?"

"Not anymore. I've stayed in a pretty straight line for the last quarter mile, but I see some dark spots, maybe big cactus patches ahead. We've got to concentrate on keeping our overall direction correct. We can't just wander around out here, wasting energy."

They had covered only another half mile or so when the landscape changed. The ground was getting progressively harder and flatter, but the scattering of thorny bushes and cactus intensified on the land in front of them. It became impossible to walk more than a few steps without having to dodge the thorny obstacles, and Mike worried they would get off course. It was time to stop and hope for an early moonrise.

"Let's rest here," he said. "I'd like to make some distance, but I can't see well enough to keep moving."

"Me either. I can barely see the horizon, much less where our landmark is. Maybe starlight will get brighter later on."

They sat down cross-legged on a tiny patch of ground barren of cactus, facing each other in the clear night.

"Damn, I'm tired," Mike announced, yawning and leaning back on his elbows.

"Well, we haven't slept in over two days. I could go to sleep sitting right here, but I'm too thirsty."

"Yeah, this water shortage is getting to be serious. Good thing we stocked up when we stopped in Laredo. And without that bottle you had in your bag, we'd never have made it this far. Sure am glad we drank that before those guys went through your stuff, or they might have fought over it. Water would have been more interesting than your underwear."

"Boy, you *must* be thirsty!" she giggled.

"I meant *they* would have found it more interesting. They covered three or four miles in the heat, and none of those guys was in shape to do that, not in any environment."

A period of silence followed, and Mike knew Sandra was thinking what he was—some of those guys are not in shape to do *anything* now. He remembered her staring at Dan, hanging from his safety harness, his head cracked like an Easter egg. She'd also heard the crunch as he ran over the first helicopter pilot while coming down the old road. Mike, too, had only to think of the event to hear the sickening sound again. He pushed the thought aside, but another troubling item replaced it—*what was she thinking about her ex-husband's fate?*

Soon after the crash, when Mike told her he couldn't find him, she had become quiet, gazing over his shoulder toward the wreckage. Was it relief he had seen in her eyes, or hope? Was it resignation, as though she had known all along that Jack Pearson would come to no good end? Was this simply a continuation of their stormy relationship; the uncertainty, the turmoil she had hated? Or maybe he'd just imagined those emotional signals, his jealousy playing tricks on him, putting expression into her face that wasn't really there. For a moment, he considered asking her, but abandoned that idea.

Anything I say about Jack will come out wrong.

This past forty-eight hours had been a grueling experience for both of them. Mike didn't see himself as a tough guy, immune to the effects of seeing people killed—or killing them. He was a normal guy who preferred things to run smoothly and to get along with those around him. But that philosophy had not worked with Jack and his cronies, who tried to intimidate everyone they came in contact with. They'd given him no chance to change his mind about the Morales business; no discussion, no options other than going along with an armed kidnapping. They just barged into his life via Sandra and commenced to screw things up in a grand way. For Mike, despite his easygoing manner, it made for a quick trip from surprise to fear to hate.

The first two thugs, Dirk and Sarge, were pitiful excuses for human beings, and they weren't even very capable bad guys, yet they were able to kidnap him and Sandra because they had guns and used threats of violence. Mike was angry at himself for falling victim to two boneheads who wouldn't even have elicited a second glance from him under other circumstances. But when they produced guns, and their violent intentions were made known, he truly despised them for it.

The second crew, the helicopter band, were truly dangerous. They were scary men who had been bent on killing him and Sandra, no doubt about it. Even so, to be responsible or instrumental in their deaths was another matter altogether. Mike thought it put him in the same category as they were. Where did that leave him now? This dangerous hike through the desert should be enough price to pay. If not, what *was* the penalty, anyway?

Maybe the punishment was to be a sentence of "stripped and thrown to the wolves," he thought wryly, like in some European fairy tale. After all, the wolves were here already, weren't they?

He could hear them howling in the distance, plaintive at first, then barks and growls, followed by another long howl. They were closer now. He could hear them in the darkness, just beyond his field of view, but he couldn't see them. Suddenly, he felt the first bite—from behind. It was on the back of his arm, and he jerked it away, trying to twist his head to look behind him for the next attack. Nothing there but darkness. He looked forward again and strained to see or hear where they might next approach from. And again, the flash of pain in the back of his arm, and then another on his shoulder.

He awoke with a start. It wasn't wolves he was hearing—no wolves in the Chihuahuan Desert—it was a coyote pack. And the bites he felt weren't canine fangs, but jabs being inflicted by a thorny *cholla* cactus his exhausted body had chanced to slump into. Sandra was leaned against him, her arms around his middle and her head in his lap. She too awoke with a jerk when Mike stirred. The coyotes sounded near; the breeze had carried the pack's serenade to them, and Mike's subconscious had melded their sound with his sleepy thoughts into a bizarre dream of wolf-pack punishment for bad people, himself included.

"We've got to get moving," he mumbled to Sandra, who had re-settled into a snuggling position.

"You go on," came her sleepy response. "I'll be along later."

"Fat chance. Come on, the moon's up. Let's travel."

The moon had already risen to about twenty degrees above the eastern horizon, reflecting stark bluish light across the desert. It was almost full and so bright Mike could again see the hilltops and the distinct cleft between them, miles upon miles in the distance. Struggling to get up, he winced at the stiffness of his tired, dehydrated muscles. Sandra rose slowly too, stretching and yawning in the night before looking to the western horizon to check the visibility of their destination.

"There it is, plain as day. Sure doesn't look any closer, though," she said, defeat creeping into her voice.

"Well, I guess not! You fell asleep, and you are hereby charged with dereliction of duty for letting me fall asleep, too. It won't look any closer until you get a move on and start walking toward it."

She poked him in the ribs, an action always guaranteed to get his attention. He hated to be poked in the ribs, a secret he should never have divulged, since she used it every chance she got. He jumped backward into a dagger plant and yelped as its sharp tip imbedded in his leg.

"Ow! Quit! Use some of that energy to get us to the horizon."

"You're the one who fell asleep first, sitting there, staring into space while I was trying to carry on an intimate conversation with you," she chided him. "I gave up and used you for a pillow when I saw you weren't responding."

"Okay, I'll answer you now. As long as you keep a good pace and don't make the questions too difficult. I can't think clearly when I'm tired and thirsty."

"Did you look in my bag? You found some water last time you looked there."

"You'd better hope I'm not lugging around more water while you trot along up front, unfettered and unweighted."

"I think there's another bottle in there, but I'm saving it for a man who won't fall asleep on me."

The good-natured exchange served as a diversion from the stress and encouraged them to keep going in what both knew could soon become a test just to stay alive. They both needed something, someone, to live for—and who better than each other?

Beneath the banter was a respect for each other's qualities. Sandra admired Mike's tenacity at completing tasks, knowing it was a bigger factor in his life than he admitted. In spite of his seemingly nonchalant attitude about a lot of things (like their relationship!) she knew he quickly determined what was important, even if he didn't voice it. Since saving their lives was important, his ability to focus would be a valuable asset in the next several hours. Giving up wasn't an option in the desert. Combined with their physical stamina, she had faith they would somehow survive.

Likewise, Mike held Sandra as his standard of the ideal woman—smart, attractive, keenly feminine in some ways, yet tough as nails in the physical conditioning department. He had recognized it the day he met her, and was immediately smitten. Nor was she a whiner or complainer, as Mike had discovered on their training runs. She was a blend of feminine mystique and real physical capability that Mike Conner couldn't resist.

But while mutual admiration and respect were good for personal relationships, both knew it was going to take all the physical abilities they possessed, plus some luck, to make the trek ahead of them. Heat, thirst, and exhaustion don't show favor to good personality traits…the desert just doesn't care.

Mike thought they were covering maybe three miles an hour on the good ground, slowing in places where *arroyos* had washed into the rocky terrain. If they could maintain that pace all night they might have covered twenty miles or more by daybreak. If help lay very far beyond that distance, it might just as well be located on the moon now shining brightly in the sky—it would be just as unreachable.

After another hour of walking, the conversation lagged as both faced the grim fact—without voicing it—they had to get most of the journey behind them by sunrise. Soon after the sun began its climb, the temperature would rise just as steadily, and the hot wind would begin from the south, robbing them of the slight advantage the coolness of night presented. Thirsty and dehydrated as they were, at least the cooler temperature made it possible for their muscles to continue functioning. With tomorrow's daytime heat and wind, what little moisture remained in their muscle tissue would soon dissipate. When the resulting cramps set in, they would no longer be able to put one foot in front of the other. All the toughness and training would be for naught—dry muscles simply don't work, and the walk to salvation would be over. They had been on the move with minimal rest and water and no food for over forty-eight hours, hiking, dodging, and running in harsh conditions. Good physical condition or not, there wasn't much left in their tired bodies.

Sandra trudged up a slight rise, leaning forward so as not to have to bend her legs so much. Watching her stiff-legged gait from behind, Mike felt even more awkward, his stomach muscles tightening and his steps becoming shorter. Evidently, Sandra hadn't entered that phase yet, because her stride was now longer than Mike's, and he struggled to stay up with her. The result was an uneasy move toward the first vestiges of panic, the realization that he and Sandra might very well die before they next day passed.

The moon was sliding toward the west, falling gently onto the hills, hills that seemed only slightly nearer than they had hours before. The beauty of the stark, moonlit scene was lost on the pair; they couldn't see anything beyond the ground lying just one step ahead. Always one step ahead. Whereas the point between the two hilltops on the horizon had lured them earlier, their focus had now shortened to just a few feet, and even that seemed almost impossible.

Conversation had long since ceased. There'd been no talk between them for hours aside from an occasional grunt when one of them stubbed a toe or stumbled on the rocky ground. Every ounce of energy was being expended to take another step, just one more stride toward the hills and, hopefully, rescue. Except now it wasn't even rescue on their minds. That lofty goal had shrunk to the single step lying just ahead. If either could have uttered a coherent statement, it would not have been about rescue. It could have come out "one more step, just one more step." Their brains had stopped processing the information about finding the fence line, turning right, following it to the ranch house, beseeching Alberto to provide them with transportation back to Reynaldo. Their brains only sent messages to their legs to take one more step.

Hours or days or years later, Mike was leading again, or trying to, when he became disoriented and confused. He couldn't move forward any more. He had been slogging along, pitifully slow, but now something was physically holding him back, pushing against his thighs and stomach. Even by leaning forward with all his weight, he couldn't move. Sandra had pushed up against him from behind and used her weight to help him forge ahead, still to no avail. Neither could concentrate on the problem long enough to find the answer. Under different circumstances, they would have found it hilarious, the two of them, seemingly drunk, leaning and pushing to overcome some unseen obstacle in the dark.

Mike raised his hands, which were so swollen he couldn't feel anything. He moved his hands forward a few inches and felt a vague stab in his forearm. Looking down and squinting in the gloom, he saw that a barb had raked along his arm. For a moment, the significance of this escaped him, then relief took over as he realized what held them back.

"My God, it's the fence."

He reached back and pulled Sandra forward so she could see for herself, as though she might not believe him. Maybe she wouldn't have, or maybe she was simply beyond caring. For a few minutes they stood there, trying to remember what they needed to do now. Whether subconsciously remembering to turn right or by pure accident, Mike didn't know and would never recall. But groping along the wire strands to their right was the path he chose. Neither knew how long they stumbled along before seeing the light.

It appeared in the gray dawn, the square of yellow illumination ahead and just over the fence. Had it not been shining, the pair could easily have stumbled on beyond the house, following the fence line in the darkness to their deaths.

Mike tried to call out, but his voice was no more than a hoarse whisper. Sandra's voice was a little better, but even their combined efforts resulted in barely enough volume to carry the few dozen yards to the house. A few more minutes passed; maybe it was longer, since pink streaks were visible in the east when the door opened and a thin figure stepped onto the porch.

They called out again, their voices a bit stronger, perhaps reinvigorated by the appearance of possible salvation. *"Alberto, nececitamos ayuda, por favor!"*

Upon hearing his name, the man stepped off the porch and slowly moved towards the fence, raising his arms as he approached them. At about twenty feet away, Mike could see the outline of the ancient .30/.30 Winchester pointed in his general direction, but he was too exhausted to worry about it. On the plus side, his tired brain told him this thin man must be Alberto and they must be in the right place.

"Hola, Señor. Por favor, nececitamos ayuda, comida y agua. Y tambien para su patrón, Señor Gomez."

Mike used his poor Spanish to describe their situation, since both had forgotten the phrases suggested by Reynaldo. Alberto slowly lowered the rifle and said something in Spanish, but as Mike had mentioned earlier, it was a lot different than conjugating verbs in Spanish class. They couldn't understand a word.

Sandra tried her hand, telling him their names and that Reynaldo was injured about twenty miles away. Alberto walked up to the fence to get a better look at these two stragglers, apparently knowing there had to be some element of truth in their tale, since the nearest water beyond the ranch's wells was far beyond the distance any sane person would venture on foot. The pair had to be either honest or stupid to be out here at dawn after walking all night. He motioned for them to come to the house.

It took a few minutes to maneuver their stiff, tired bodies through the fence and shuffle toward the house, where they stood groggily in the bare yard. Alberto went inside and returned with a bucket of water and a dipper. He dipped water for Sandra first, offering it up to her cracked lips, saying something in Spanish that Mike took to be "drink slowly." She obeyed for the first few sips, then greedily sucked away at the dipper until it was empty.

Alberto repeated the process with Mike, getting the same results. After the first dipper, Mike couldn't tell any difference in his thirst. He reached out clumsily for the retreating dipper, almost knocking it from his hand. But Alberto was in control, and he administered the next dipper to Sandra. She was in the same shape, but didn't have the strength to grab at the dipper. After two more dippers each, Alberto refused them any more water, issuing a long string of insistent Spanish. Mike only understood "no more," "later," and "sick."

I can't be much sicker, Mike thought. Was he refusing to give them more because he was short on water himself? The vague thought nearly made him panic, but he was too tired to concentrate on the problem for long. He took Sandra's hand and pulled her with him over to the side of the house, where they both sprawled on the porch.

They were too tired and numb to sleep. Instead, they fell into a stupor for over an hour, regaining full consciousness only because of Mike's painful muscle cramps, and for Sandra, a headache. Alberto had disappeared for a while, but returned as they stirred, bringing more water and some food. They each devoured a tortilla wrapped around some beans and accepted another slim ration of water from Alberto's stingy dipper before resuming supine positions on the porch.

Within thirty minutes, both began to feel better, although the cramps in Mike's legs and lower back were causing him to twitch and jerk involuntarily. Sandra's headache remained, and she was nauseous, but managed to keep her food down by leaning against the wall and sitting very still. Gradually, the nourishment hit their bloodstreams and enabled them to think about the problem they had left out in the desert.

"We've got to get Alberto to round up horses and supplies to go for Reynaldo," Sandra said. "Even if he's sitting still, he'll be close to dehydration by now. As the day heats up, he may not make it."

Mike thought carefully before responding. "Sandra, do we really want to go back into the desert to save someone who was bent on killing us less than twenty-four hours ago?" He knew her humanitarian convictions and wanted her to think it through, not see his remark as outright opposition to the plan. She didn't answer immediately, and he tried again. "I thought about it during that ordeal last night, and I wonder if we can trust him. If we guide Alberto out there and save his ass, will it cost us our lives? Maybe next month, or six months from now, will we step out of our car and get blasted by his new batch of henchmen?"

Sandra sighed and answered slowly. "I see the danger you're talking about. But how can we just leave him out there to die, especially after promising him we would get Alberto to come for him?"

"I know, I know," Mike responded irritably. He was angry at himself because of this mess and his inability to come up with the right answers, the ones that would make Sandra see his point. He continued, "I agree with you from the humanitarian viewpoint, but remember how scared we were when those jerks were waving guns around, threatening to kill us? And the little shooting spree out on the highway while you were driving—you haven't forgotten that, have you? Do you want to take a chance on that happening again? Next time, it won't be threats or wild shots, they'll just kill us outright. I just don't think Reynaldo can risk our going to the authorities with this story."

"But we can't let him die, can we? Doesn't that make us the same as they, sort of?"

Mike thought about his nightmare of being eaten by wolves as punishment for indulging in criminal, albeit necessary, behavior. "I suppose," he answered reluctantly. "But I don't like trusting him with our lives."

Their dilemma was interrupted by Alberto as he rounded the corner with four horses, two laden with packs. It was apparent that he'd understood about Reynaldo and intended to make a trip to get *El Patrón*.

"Estamos listos," he announced.

It was a statement, not a question. *"We are ready"* clearly included Mike and Sandra and left little opportunity for discussion. One would have thought he did this every day, set out on an expedition to save someone's life. Maybe he does, Mike thought. This land was harsh and unforgiving, filled with heat, thirst, snakes, and vast distances. Rescue missions might happen all the time, all in a day's work for the faithful ranch foreman.

In any event, Alberto was surely a kindly soul; even when confronted at dawn by two alien-looking strangers, he'd barely hesitated before providing them food and water. Reynaldo's warning that he might be distrustful of two *gringos* had proven unnecessary; Alberto was a better judge of people than his employer had thought, and Mike felt his reluctance to return to Reynaldo slipping.

What the hell; if this tough old buzzard is kind enough to feed two strangers, no questions asked, I should be kind enough to help save his boss. Even if it kills me.

CHAPTER 17

▼

Alberto obviously intended for Mike and Sandra to accompany him, and that Reynaldo would ride back on the extra horse. Mike thought he'd better try to let him know that Reynaldo wasn't going to be up to twenty or more miles of bouncing along on horseback. *"Señor Alberto, Reynaldo está herido muy mal. Creo que no es posible montár un caballo,"* he said haltingly, struggling to explain the extent of Reynaldo's injuries, thus rendering him unable to ride a horse. He knew the sentence structure wasn't perfect, but Alberto nodded as if in understanding. To bolster his explanation, Mike pointed to his own ribs and grimaced as if in pain.

Undeterred, Alberto nodded again and rapidly mumbled something about *"troca"* and *"caballos,"* which Mike and Sandra picked up as "truck" and "horses." Beyond that, his statement was a mystery. They looked at each other, shrugged, and looked questioningly back at Alberto. *"Favor de hablar mas despacio,"* Mike said, asking him to slow his incoherent jumble.

Looking frustrated, Alberto repeated what he had said, but it came out neither clearer nor slower, as Mike had requested. Sandra tried to ask him about a wagon, but the ranch foreman had already headed toward the barn with all four horses in tow. He emerged a few minutes later with one horse hooked up to a single-horse surrey of sorts, and leading the other three by their reins. Pulling his entourage up to the porch, he removed the saddlebags from the horses and transferred them to the rear of the buggy. Looking at the

- 118 -

suspension on the rig, Mike wasn't so sure it was a great improvement, but it would have to do.

"Sure will be a rough ride for Reynaldo," Mike commented as he and Sandra eyed the contraption.

"Not as rough as staying out in the desert. I just hope he hangs on until we can get there with some water. And I didn't know what to do about the gash in his head, except clean it. He needed a doctor."

"Alberto will probably know that when he sees him. If there's medical help available anywhere in the area, he'll figure out a way to get his boss there."

"A donde?" Alberto asked, interrupting their discussion.

Where to, indeed. Mike unfolded the map and spread it on the porch. Alberto moved in close and peered at it while Mike pointed out the ranch house landing strip and declared the ranch house to be *"casa aquí."* He moved his finger along the map toward the canyon for a distance equaling a little less than twenty miles. *"Reynaldo está aquí,"* he informed Alberto, who nodded in acknowledgment and handed Mike the reins to one of the horses.

Alberto held Sandra's reins while she mounted up, then swung easily into his own saddle. Mike did the same thing, but with a lot more effort. Alberto led the way in a brisk walk, a jarring pace seemingly designed to punish the riders. After their earlier trials, being bounced around should have been minor, but Mike thought the experience was pure torture. Sandra bounced along, looking at the landscape and appearing oblivious to the pounding. Watching her, Mike noticed that she supported herself slightly in the stirrups to lessen the impact. Copying the technique, he was amazed at the improvement, but no more enamored with horses.

Alberto stopped after traveling only a couple of miles and produced a canteen. Mike didn't hesitate to reach for it. *"Muchas gracias,"* he said, taking a long pull and resisting the urge to finish it off in a few gulps, handing it over to Sandra instead.

"I never thought plain old water could taste so good," she said, handing the nearly empty canteen back to Alberto.

"I did, but I was beginning to think we'd never find out. I don't know about you, but I was nearly done when we hit the fence. If the house had been any farther, or if that light hadn't been on, it wouldn't be going so well for us right now."

"You said it would take luck to make it. Keeping our direction, having enough moonlight, running into the fence—so many things had to go right."

"It's about time. After the past two days, we were overdue for some *good* luck for a change. The best luck was probably the distance. After we got tired last night, our pace slowed considerably, so we may have covered only fifteen or sixteen miles. Looking at the map, it looked like it could have been over twenty. We'd never have made it."

"*Vamos,*" Alberto ordered. He set off in the same brisk walk, looking straight ahead. Mike wondered if he were going to try to pick up some sign of their passage the night before in order to track their way directly back to Reynaldo, but it didn't look like it. Instead, it appeared that they were veering too far to the north. Mike thought a more easterly direction was correct and he pulled up beside Albert and pointed to their right. Alberto nodded in agreement, but said something else about "*troca.*" Frustrated, Mike asked him to repeat himself and strained to understand.

"*Sí, Patrón está allí, pero la troca está por alla,*" he said, a touch of frustration in his own voice as he pointed first toward Mike's chosen path, then back to their current direction. He looked at Mike questioningly, awaiting a response.

At last, Mike understood. They were not going directly to the crash site, but instead to a vehicle, *la troca*, likely stored elsewhere for use by the area's inhabitants. Supposedly they would use it to travel the remainder of the distance to rescue Reynaldo.

Only another mile had passed when they reached a narrow dirt road. Judging by its general north-south direction, they surely had crossed it last night, but failed to notice it in the dark. Alberto steered them left and followed the road about a half mile to an old shed that blended in so well with the surrounding area, Mike didn't even see it until they were within a hundred yards of the weathered, sagging structure.

Alberto dismounted and pulled back a tarp covering one end of the shed. Inside was an old pickup with tall tires and four-wheel drive, the perfect desert buggy. Amazingly, it cranked up with a few spins of the starter. Alberto pulled it out onto the road and left it idling while he motioned for Mike and Sandra to leave the horses in the shed.

"Good thing we didn't stumble across this last night," Mike said, swinging his leg over the saddle to dismount. "I would have been tempted to take it and drive off."

"I'll bet the first little town we pulled into, we'd have been branded as "*los bandidos Yanquís,*" having stolen the community vehicle," Sandra observed. "I'd hate to face the punishment for that offense."

"I guess *Señor* Gomez is the *Patrón* for this area, this *ejido*. He supplies his community with enough to keep them satisfied and away from Mexico

City, where they could petition to have his land divided among them. This vehicle is for everyone's use—except two *gringos*, of course."

Sandra took the reins of both horses and tied them to a rickety railing attached to the inside wall of the shed. She and Mike stiffly climbed into the idling pickup with Alberto at the wheel, and he pulled away, back in the direction they'd come from.

"I'm surprised there's not a vehicle at the ranch, a nicer one than this," Sandra said, edging over in the seat to avoid a protruding spring poking her in the butt. "Judging by his other transportation, he can certainly afford it."

Mike shook his head. "This one's reliable for local use, that's all that matters. He probably wants to keep the ranch as remote as possible. Besides, if he kept a better vehicle for his ranch use, it might draw attention or someone might be tempted to steal it. This way, it's just basic transportation, but everyone benefits."

"I guess so. Even with the landing strip, the ranch is plenty remote. Did you see this road last night?"

"No, but I was beyond seeing much of anything by the time we got this far. I felt pretty good for nine or ten miles, then it hit me all of a sudden. The rest was pure hell for me."

"Me too. I've had enough walking for a while."

Mike had pulled the map again and tried, with Sandra's help, to determine where they needed to turn off to proceed to the crash site. "This map's used for aviation, so roads aren't shown," he said. "But I'd bet there's not a map in existence that depicts this one, anyway. Cartographers probably don't over-research this area."

Sandra peered over at the map. "I don't see how this is going to be much help, then."

Appearing unconcerned about their chatter, Alberto continued driving, slowing from time to time to look at the left edge of the dirt track. When they had traveled about two miles, he slowed again, this time pulling to a full stop. He got out, beckoning for Mike and Sandra to join him beside the road. He was already pointing to the ground when they came around the truck, their footprints fairly evident in the deeper dust of the roadside. The sharp-eyed rancher had spotted the tracks from their trek made hours before—a distinct advantage in speeding up the search for Reynaldo. Mike marveled at the tracking feat and gave Alberto a thumbs-up, finally getting a smile from the taciturn foreman in return.

Encouraged, Sandra smiled too. "I guess back-tracking toward the canyon from here is our best shot for finding Reynaldo quickly. Alberto is plenty good at tracking and getting around in this area, but he's going to be tested this time."

"Yeah, it would be nice to go straight to the crash, but just getting in the vicinity of the canyon will have to do. I don't think our compass routine would do much good going in this direction, except to follow the reciprocal heading from the twin mountain peaks. Alberto probably will just want to follow our tracks."

Alberto pulled off the road to the left, whereupon he immediately had to steer in and out of vast patches of cactus and catclaw. Mike couldn't see how he could possibly dodge the obstacles and still follow the path of their previous night's journey. However, the rancher evidently knew the general direction to the canyon, and he pressed on in his winding drive.

An hour later, the cactus began to thin out, and the land became rougher, gouged here and there with rambling arroyos. It looked familiar to Mike and Sandra, but it was impossible to know if they were near last night's route—it looked the same for miles in every direction. Alberto stopped several times to get out and look for more footprints, but the ground was too hard and gravelly to be of much help. Only once did he find what appeared to be a couple of footprints, but when he motioned for Mike and Sandra to look, none of them could be sure of the faint imprints in the hard material.

Again discouraged, Mike and Sandra could only watch their overall path of travel and hope that Alberto would discover some clearer tracks that would lead them to Reynaldo. Once, when Alberto had driven toward the north for a good while, Mike pointed to the map and motioned toward the east. *"Creo que está mas allá,"* he said in his imperfect Spanish, hoping he was right. Alberto nodded and steered a more easterly direction.

After another half hour of working across the land, Sandra spotted a grove of cottonwood trees to the south. They were on a small rise when she happened to look out toward the right, or she wouldn't have seen the tree tops poking up from an arroyo. "I remember seeing a grove of trees last night!"

"Are you sure?" Mike asked. "I didn't see anything but the ground in front of us."

"Yes, I'm sure, because I was surprised to see anything except cactus. I wondered if there might be water near them, but when I mentioned it to you, you said, 'keep walking.' Oh, and when I saw them, they were to our right, so we're way too far over this way. We need to get to the other side of them."

Mike pointed out the grove to Alberto, but he had already intuited their excited exchange and pointing. It took about a quarter hour to make their way to the cottonwood stand, which was larger than it had appeared from the rise. Sandra began to express doubts as they neared the trees. "These trees are a lot taller than I recall. But I was seeing them by moonlight at a distance, and our position may have made them appear lower in this arroyo."

The trio got out to look around the grove, a pleasant contrast to the harsh landscape surrounding it. Sandra led the way down the winding ditch, looking back occasionally to see when the trees would appear to her as they had the night before. At about two hundred yards, she was satisfied the trees looked the same as she remembered. They began looking around for footprints, but it was another forty yards before Mike triumphantly spotted both their shoe imprints in a sandy area. He got a thumbs-up from Alberto for his find.

They hurried back to the pickup and veered to the south, confident they were back on course. Another few miles and the land changed again; rougher, less vegetation, and some rolling rises. Arroyos thinned out, but the rockier landscape eliminated their spotting any more traces of their passage.

"Good thing you saw those trees," Mike said. "We were way off course."

"Yeah, because we're not going to find any tracks in this rock pile. Sure hope we're getting close, but you couldn't prove it by me."

CHAPTER 18

▼

Jack edged closer to the *cenizo* bush, trying to stay in its scant shade while cursing and swatting at the tiny flies that torment every living thing in the desert. The unmerciful sun was almost directly overhead and the hot breeze blew incessantly, though not enough to disrupt the flies. He couldn't see Reynaldo, but earlier he had crawled to a higher point and watched as he leaned motionless against the embankment, exactly where Mike and Sandra had placed him.

Observing the injured man, Jack realized that he could turn this situation to his advantage. Clearly, the upper hand had shifted away from Reynaldo Gomez—his hitmen were both dead, and he lay injured, unaware of Jack's survival. It had been a long time since Sandra and her boyfriend had left for help, and Jack wondered if Reynaldo was still breathing. Things would be much simpler if he were not, because Jack Pearson had undergone a recent transformation.

It had begun in Gomez's office in Wichita Falls, when Reynaldo questioned him about the handling of Mike and Sandra's escape, and had increased on the trip to Del Rio when Reynaldo launched into another verbal tirade about the matter. Jack had never before questioned Reynaldo's position as boss, but something in his boss' tone had sounded churlish and dismissive, as though he had lost faith in Jack's ability. Troubling doubts began to form in Jack's mind, along with vague thoughts of a long-needed change.

Then, Jack's transformation had become a full-fledged concept with the appearance of Dan and Vince, the two hard-edged men that Reynaldo had not even bothered to introduce. Indeed, it seemed that his boss had seen fit to bring in a couple of slick guys in whom he *did* have faith. That had played poorly with Jack, who was accustomed to being a big shot, at least in his own little world. Reynaldo's actions pointed out that he, Jack, was an insignificant part of the operation, and though Jack had known all along that he was being used to launder money, he had benefitted sufficiently to overlook the occasional slight. In fact, he had skimmed enough from the operation to make it quite lucrative, and Reynaldo had never suspected.

He'd also never suspected that Jack had given an occasional thought to taking over the drug portion of the business, a plan that he had even hinted to Eva during a particularly close moment. But these latest humiliating reminders—along with an increasing desire for Eva over the past few months—had created an atmosphere for change in his career path trajectory. The pivotal moment came when the helicopter crashed.

In addition to being acutely aware of his own fear at the time, something else had occurred to Jack—a revelation that he was just as capable as the hitmen, or even Reynaldo himself. He had seen Vince crushed like a rabbit by the Land Cruiser, while he, Jack, had survived. He saw the fear in Dan's face as the chopper was going down and had witnessed Reynaldo's tight grimace during the seconds just before the impact. Clearly, none of them was impervious to fear and pain; nor were they indestructible.

In the instant before the crash, Jack vowed to change his life and—if he lived long enough to get back on the ground—do something to erase the feeling of subservience that had been building for months. He would not only have Eva, he would have Reynaldo's empire. At this moment Dan's head was crushed and Reynaldo lay badly hurt. Meanwhile, Jack was sitting here under a bush, alive and well, contemplating his new ally—the desert.

The desert was the great equalizer. It cared not if one was wealthy, powerful, or had important friends back in civilization. In the desert, no amount of money would buy water, nor would it protect one from the heat and sun. It respected only the animal instincts of survival; not necessarily survival of the fittest, but of the most clever, the most ruthless.

Its remote vastness would shield Jack from the results of his plan by providing a hiding place for the bodies. The rest of them must die, and by the time anyone found the corpses, the coyotes, buzzards, and heat would have obliterated any evidence other than an unfortunate helicopter crash. And back in civilization, the only survivor would be Jack Pearson.

The wind was now increasing, along with the noise it produced as it whipped the branches of Jack's meager shelter. Thankfully, it brought a respite from the tiny desert flies, and Jack savored the moment, leaning back and listening to the wind. After a few minutes, he became aware that it wasn't just the wind but a new sound; an engine, the sound of it coming and going as the vehicle traversed the ridges of the rough countryside.

The approaching vehicle wasn't entirely unexpected; he just hadn't been sure when it would be coming. He bolted upright, straining to hear, trying to determine how far away the car was. Watching Jack and Sandra talk with Reynaldo earlier, Jack had surmised that they were going for help—probably the ranch foreman, and old man named Berto or something like that. It was likely that they were returning with him, which didn't surprise Jack at all. Even the rancher couldn't find this God-forsaken place without being shown the way, he thought.

He visualized the upcoming confrontation, weighing the options. Should he approach them, feigning injury at first, say that he had been knocked unconscious until a few hours ago? Maybe they would save him the trouble of finding his way out of the wilderness. Or should he just ambush the returning party, kill them all and drive away in the vehicle? Before deciding, he'd have to see how the vehicle approached and who emerged.

And what about Reynaldo—was he already dead? If not, should he be left to die of thirst? As inviting as that solution seemed, Jack had doubts about that method. Gomez had shown amazing resilience in business, legal and otherwise, and Jack had witnessed his toughness over the years. This was no time to be squeamish; he had to know for sure that Reynaldo Gomez would never again be a factor in the life of Jack Pearson.

He pushed the limbs aside and crawled out of his hiding place in the bush. Staying on hands and knees, he made his way to higher ground where he could see Reynaldo, still propped against the embankment, not moving. He rose and sprinted to his left to get out of Reynaldo's line of sight, then gasped as he was forced to slow to a painful hobble. Falling out of a moving aircraft, followed by hours of lounging in the shade of the *cenizo*, had resulted in stiff muscles, and he chastised himself for not moving around more during his long wait.

Cursing his inability to move quickly, Jack also realized he should have made sure Reynaldo was dead earlier. Only upon hearing the sound of the vehicle had he been prodded into action, and now he was pressed for time in eliminating the most dangerous obstacle to his future—Reynaldo Gomez. Watching him earlier, he had been almost certain that he was dead, or would be soon. Now he wasn't so sure.

Staying out of Reynaldo's line of vision, Jack walked to a rocky ledge jutting out of the gravel and selected the biggest rock he could comfortably carry, roughly the size of a football. Cradling it against his side, he continued walking parallel to the ledge for a few more yards, then angled back toward Reynaldo's position, looking for another way into the gorge. He spotted a shallow arroyo that looked as though it might lead to the injured man and he quickly stepped into it, stooping to remain undetected as he followed its winding path toward the main ditch. As he progressed, it deepened and he no longer had to crouch to remain out of sight, but he was unsure if Reynaldo would be to his right or left when he emerged from the tributary ditch.

After following the serpentine gully for another thirty or forty steps, he felt he had to be getting close. Slowing and walking softly, he wished he had studied the area around his prey more carefully from the confines of the bush instead of snoozing and contemplating the long-range results of his revenge. The gravel beneath his feet was crunching too loudly and he couldn't take a chance that Reynaldo would hear his approach, so he moved to the side of the ditch where softer dirt and silt had been deposited. His footsteps quietened, and he proceeded carefully to avoid stepping into the open too soon.

Around the next bend, the gully opened up and Jack crept forward, listening for any sound that would give away Reynaldo's position. He no longer heard the faint sound of the vehicle approaching, but he knew it might arrive soon. In the quietness of the desert, the engine had sounded two, maybe three miles away, but even allowing for time spent skirting around cactus patches, it wouldn't be long.

Straining to hear, Jack thought he detected a stirring ahead, and he held his breath, struggling to pick up any telling sound. Reynaldo must have moved slightly, because he heard a soft moan, then a loud cough followed by a groan of pain. Damn! He's still alive, Jack thought, his own heart pounding so loudly he was afraid Reynaldo could hear it.

The sounds had been just ahead to his left, and very near, so his caution had paid off. He eased forward, gripping the rock tightly until his fingers hurt. He peered around a break in the embankment and saw Reynaldo still leaning in the same spot as before, nothing else around him except an overturned

Coke can. From his vantage point ten feet away, Jack could see that Reynaldo's eyes were closed and his breathing so shallow it was scarcely noticeable.

Why the hell didn't he just die?

Jack hefted the rock with both hands and raised it over his head, rushing the man seated on the ground. Reynaldo heard the approaching footsteps, opening his eyes just in time to see Jack bringing the rock toward his head as though slam-dunking a basketball. Reynaldo jerked his head back instinctively and threw up his right hand to deflect the blow, but the rock landed with a sickening smack just above his right ear.

Reynaldo never uttered a sound. His head slumped to the left onto his shoulder, then his entire body relaxed and folded over in a heap like a sack of grain dumped onto the floor. The bloodied rock rolled off his arm and stopped in the dust beside him, a tiny tuft of hair still attached to it. The hair stirred in the hot breeze, but otherwise, the entire scene was deathly still.

Jack straightened and held his breath, looking down at the body. Suddenly, he heard the vehicle again, closer now, and he realized that he would have heard it sooner if not for the sound of his heart thundering in his ears. He forced himself to begin breathing again, and for the next several seconds he was gasping so hard from exertion and excitement he thought his lungs would burst and his heart explode. For a minute, he was afraid he wouldn't live to see his plan work.

As his breathing slowed a little, he heard the vehicle again, now drawing closer by the second. He grabbed the bloodied rock and carried it far back into the arroyo, where he buried it in the gravel and smoothed the area with his hands. To anyone investigating the scene, it would appear that he had suffered a head injury in the helicopter crash, but managed to crawl to the shade of the embankment, where he drank a Coca-Cola, then died of heat, dehydration, and head injury. The pilot, still strapped in his seat, had obviously died in the crash.

As to the crash itself, the flight certainly had not been reported or documented in any way. There had been no flight plan, no passenger list. The discovery of a crashed helicopter containing the body of a man who surely had a criminal record, accompanied by a wealthy Hispanic with known, or at least suspected, ties to the drug business couldn't cause much of a stir, certainly not in Mexico. The incident would be recorded as an unfortunate end to an unofficial flight—low altitude to avoid detection by radar, dangerous wind shifts among the desert canyons, two dead drug dealers. End of investigation.

Jack now had firm plans for the approaching rescuers, too. Plans that became increasingly simple after he remembered Dan's and Reynaldo's reputations. If nothing else, Jack's connection to Reynaldo's industry had taught him the realities of the trade. Putting himself in the position of some unfortunate law enforcement official sent out here to investigate, he decided that anyone found dead at this scene, by *any* means, would be viewed as a victim of his—or her—own lifestyle. Even if the bodies were discovered with bullet holes, so what? The authorities would simply shrug it off as a drug deal gone badly. And whatever their findings, Mexican authorities wouldn't spend a lot of time with forensics trying to decipher why they were now short a few drug dealers. Some would quietly appreciate the event. Others, being on the take from their own connections, would applaud the gesture and welcome the decline in competition.

Glancing back at his recent handiwork, Jack's confidence grew. He quickly determined he would handle the approaching rescuers by taking out the strongest first, the boyfriend, who had embarrassed him in front of Reynaldo. Now, contemplating the upcoming reunion, Jack looked forward to killing him. If Sandra showed up with him, he'd have to deal with her too, but neither she nor the old ranch hand would be a problem.

CHAPTER 19

▼

Mike handed the canteen back to Sandra, who took another long pull. They were on their second canteen since leaving the ranch house, and both were still thirsty. Alberto had turned over three canteens to their care, and they wouldn't last long at this rate.

"We'd better save one for Reynaldo," Sandra said. "He's got to be plenty dehydrated by now."

"He's gonna be worse than dehydrated if we don't find him soon."

As the old pickup bounced over the rough ground, Mike sensed they were nearing the area of the crash, though he couldn't be sure. They were in a maze of ravines and gravel washes caused by flash floods washing the softer material from between a series of long, rocky ridges. Tires spinning, Alberto finally managed to goad the pickup to the top of one such ridge that ran toward the general direction of the crash site for several hundred yards. The increased elevation gave them a better view of the adjacent gorges.

"We didn't go through many of these arroyos before we broke out onto flatter ground," Mike observed. "So we needn't go too far in this direction. We've got to be close. Look, isn't that the ridge where we stood to take our first compass reading?" He pointed to a ridge a hundred or so yards to their left.

"Looks like it. But all this stuff looks alike to me, so I'm not sure," she replied, pointing out the spot to Alberto, who nodded and turned the wheel slightly, angling off their current ridge and following her pointing finger.

As they climbed the next rise, Mike began to doubt his memory, but wanted to check the adjoining gorge and its tributaries anyway. *"Alto aquí por favor, Alberto."* He got out and walked to the edge for a better view.

Sandra had followed him for a few feet, but turned and headed toward the right, where a point jutted out, giving a view to the east. Mike jumped when she suddenly shouted, "There's the helicopter!"

She was pointing to the tail boom, which had separated from the main cabin on impact. The cabin had come to a rest some distance from it, but at least they were close. Mike scrambled down the ridge and climbed partway up the next one, where he spotted the main cabin wreckage and the top of the embankment sheltering Reynaldo. He waved to Sandra, then pointed toward the find before heading higher up the hill for a better view.

Alberto had shut off the engine, but started it when he saw Mike signaling to Sandra. He motioned for her to get in and started toward Mike to get as near the wreckage as possible. He found a narrow passage across two arroyos, then bounced down a steeper hill near the wrecked aircraft and pulled to a stop. Sandra jumped out and was already dashing to the bottom of the embankment just as Mike arrived at the top and looked down at Reynaldo.

Something was wrong. He lay curled on his side in the sun, with one arm flung out as though clutching the gravel. He looked dead. By the time Mike descended the embankment, Sandra was already kneeling beside the injured man. She gently raised his head and saw the gash just above the ear. It clearly was not the wound she had treated, the one he'd suffered in the crash. When they had left, he had been resting comfortably against the embankment, and despite his injury, his speech was coherent and he seemed clear-headed. Now he was unconscious, his eyes closed and his breathing ragged. Sandra stared at Mike with disbelief for a few seconds. Then her eyes darted around the surrounding area, trying to spot the source of her patient's new injury.

Mike felt for a pulse, but couldn't detect one. Just as he was reaching for his neck to feel for heartbeat at the carotid artery, Reynaldo moaned and tried to push him away, feebly slapping with his left arm. "Reynaldo!" Mike shouted, leaning back to avoid the weak attack. "It's us, Mike and Sandra! Who did this?" He didn't respond, except to continue flailing away and moaning.

Sandra grabbed his arm and grasped his hand tightly. He apparently sensed the touch of his earlier caretaker and ceased struggling. Alberto stooped down at his side to examine the head wound more closely. By his expression, it was apparent that he thought his boss' injury was serious.

Mike and Sandra's eyes met. They knew Alberto didn't realize this new wound was a mystery. "How do we explain this to him?" Mike asked, nodding toward Alberto. "He thinks it's just from the original accident."

Sandra shook her head. "It's still bleeding, so it happened recently. Is it possible that bandits roam around here looking for victims?"

"Maybe so, but not too likely. Where the hell would they come from? Where would they go? Maybe he got up to move to a better spot, then got dizzy and fell down. But I don't see what he could have hit his head on to make that gash."

"Let's get him back in the shade first. Then we'll check to see if his wallet's gone."

Together the two of them managed to move Reynaldo back into the shade of the embankment and prop him up in what seemed to be the most comfortable position available. Alberto produced a handkerchief and Sandra poured some water from the canteen on it and dabbed at the new wound. Her charge stirred again, but as she proceeded to wipe his face, he seemed to relax a little. His breathing was still shallow, but more regular, and Mike tried again, unsuccessfully, to determine if his pulse had strengthened.

Albert took his turn at examining the wound and declared it "*malo, muy malo.*" Very bad indeed. However, his breathing had steadied, an improvement from only moments earlier. The gash was ugly and blood was still seeping from the wound each time Sandra removed the cloth, but the flow was definitely slowing.

Mike and Sandra were at a loss to understand the bizarre finding. Their ordeal had been going on for almost three full days, with only a couple of hours of fitful sleep, minimal food and water, and miles of punishing desert travel on foot. Their exhausted brains, like their bodies, were not operating at full efficiency, and there seemed to be no explanation for Reynaldo's new injury. The answer came in the form of a question from about ten feet away.

"Just what the fuck are you doing back here?"

Mike was startled for a second by the sound of the voice, any voice, and he had to play the question over again in his mind to realize what had been said—and who said it. Sandra recognized the voice immediately, but even so, it didn't fully register for a brief moment as to what was occurring. Alberto, having had his share of surprises for a while, was shocked. All three whirled around to face Jack, now having reappeared and clearing up a lot of mystery in doing so.

Mike recovered first. "Where the hell have you been?"

"Don't worry about it. I've been around. And I've been waiting for someone to come out here and save my ass. I kinda' figured it might be you two, but I can't imagine why. If I was y'all, I'd have hooked 'em and let ol' Berto come out here by himself to get him." Jack was pointing the gun at first one, then another of the three, all the while shifting his weight back and forth from left leg to right.

It was the same movement he'd done before, soon after their first encounter, and Mike wondered if there was a weakness in his nervous actions to be exploited. Besides, he was tired of this loud-mouthed jackass waving a gun at him. "What are you shifting back and forth for?" he asked. "If you gotta pee, go find a bush or a cactus."

Pointing out Jack's nervousness only enraged him. "Shut up, Wiseass!" he screamed. "One more word out of you and *you'll* have to find something new to pee with, 'cause I'm gonna shoot your pecker off!"

At that instant, perhaps brought on by the loud voice, Reynaldo moaned, then opened his eyes long enough to see Jack holding a gun. It was also long enough for Jack to see that he had failed to eliminate his boss. His baffled expression told the three rescuers that he was responsible for Reynaldo's new wound and had certainly intended to kill him. It also told them that he would have to finish the job and kill all the rescuers, too.

While Jack was staring in disbelief at Reynaldo, Mike slowly eased his hand toward his pocket. There was no longer a choice; he'd have to use the pistol. Jack's plan had gone awry, and the maniacal look on his face told Mike he would likely do anything in the next few seconds. He looked as though he were seeing a ghost, as indeed he almost was. It was a miracle that the crushing blow from the rock had not found a vulnerable spot on Reynaldo's skull, yet he lay there badly hurt, but still breathing.

Earlier, during the hike back to the helicopter, Mike saw that Jack had been afraid of Reynaldo Gomez and the power he wielded over his empire— and over Jack himself. And just when Jack thought he had finally defeated that power, killed it, it was now back, still alive, watching him through fluttering eyelids. Eyelids that moved and evidenced life still beating inside a man who would kill a traitor at the earliest opportunity. Clearly, Jack couldn't afford to fail again. He raised his gun and pointed it at Reynaldo's head. His finger tightened on the trigger as he aimed, but a movement to his right caught his eye and he swung toward it.

Alberto had produced an ancient revolver from somewhere and was thumbing back the hammer on the single-action relic when Jack shot him, spinning him around and placing him in a heap against the embankment, not far from Reynaldo. Sandra shrieked and turned to stare at Alberto now lying beside her first patient. Open-mouthed, unable to utter a sound, Mike was astonished at the cold-blooded murder of the old man. Even with all they had been through in the past hours, seeing the old ranch hand who had befriended them gunned down from a few feet away evoked a whole new level of emotional shock.

Mike turned to Jack, who was staring stupidly at Alberto's still form. Taking the opportunity, he jerked the little automatic out of his pocket and quickly fired it at Jack. The round missed, and Jack swung his pistol in Mike's direction just as he was squeezing off a second shot. This one caught Jack in the upper arm, causing him to fire without taking aim. The shot went wide, but Sandra shrieked again just the same.

Howling with pain, Jack spun and crumpled to his knees. Then, realizing he wasn't seriously hurt, he staggered to his feet and ran toward the pickup. Mike let him go, instead turning to grab Sandra and checking her for injury. Her eyes were wide with fright, but she was unhurt, except for uncontrollable shaking. Mike pulled her to him and rocked her in his arms, trying to stop her quaking and thankful she had not been hit with a stray round from either of the inexperienced shooters.

Meanwhile, Jack had reached the pickup, started it, and proceeded to over-rev the tired old engine. It backfired, causing Mike and Sandra to jump again, just as he engaged the clutch and roared off. It was a few seconds before Mike realized that Jack had just left with their only means of transportation. But at least he was gone, the immediate danger of ending up like Alberto, dead in the dust, was past. Mike continued to rock Sandra, wondering what they would do now, how they were going to escape the desert this time.

Their state of shock was interrupted by a gasp from the old man, and they rushed to his side. Gently rolling him over, Mike saw blood on his side and thought for a moment it was a stomach wound, a sure way to slow death out here. Closer inspection showed the bullet had only grazed the old man's rib cage, slicing open the flesh and causing a fair amount of bleeding, but not much real damage. The bullet had struck a rib and turned to cut a path through the skin, rather than entering the body. At that range, it couldn't have been a very powerful round, or else Alberto had been incredibly lucky by turning sideways at the instant the bullet was fired. Maybe it was a combination of both, Mike thought, or the old man had the good judgement to fake a worse injury until Jack was gone. Either way, both he and Sandra were delighted that their new friend was alive. Now the problem was *keeping* him and Reynaldo alive—and getting all of them out of the desert one more time.

It took a half hour, time they didn't really have to spare, but Mike and Sandra finally calmed down enough to assess their new dilemma. Even though stranded in the desert again, they were fine physically, having had some food and water, and even a little rest. But both knew that the two wounded men couldn't survive their injuries and the desert heat for long. Reynaldo needed real medical attention and more water, soon. Neither could walk, so it was back to the same situation they'd had the day before, except now they had two injured instead of one. At least they knew where they could find transportation, such as it was. Like it or not, the buggy and horses would have to suffice—but those were ten or twelve miles away.

They had dragged Alberto beside Reynaldo in the shade, where Mike got him out of his bloody shirt and fashioned a bandage from it, using his belt to hold it tightly in place against the wound to staunch the bleeding. Then he and Sandra propped them up against each other and the embankment. Reynaldo seemed to be slipping back and forth into unconsciousness, but now that he wasn't baking in the sun, his breathing and heart rate seemed okay. Alberto sat quietly with his eyes half-open and breathing evenly.

Mike stooped and spoke quietly to the ranch foreman. *"El pistolero ha tomado su troca. Voy a conseguir los caballos."* He hoped that his limited Spanish was enough for Alberto to understand that the gunman had taken the pickup—or did he just tell him that Jack had *drunk* the pickup? Plus, he was going to get the horses...at least he hoped that's what he'd said. In any event, Alberto nodded and reached to squeeze his hand firmly, definitely a good sign.

Mike rose and stepped away, taking Sandra's arm and walking away from the embankment, out of hearing distance, just in case Reynaldo was conscious. "Your patients don't look so good. I never thought we'd be running a field hospital. I should have listened to all that first aid crap they tried to teach me in the Army."

"Alberto doesn't seem to be too badly injured," she said, "but I don't know about Reynaldo. That gash on his head needs stitches, and he's probably got a concussion."

"One of us has to get that buggy and the horses. It's not ideal for hauling wounded people, but it's all we've got. You want to stay here with them, or trot on over there about twelve miles to the horses?" Mike asked with a grin on his face.

"You're the horse expert," she answered, laughing. "So you can just waltz over there, get them and ride back here, hell bent for leather!"

"I was afraid you'd say that. Sorry I asked."

Suddenly Sandra's face clouded and she looked up at Mike. "You think Jack will come back?"

Mike shook his head. "He just wants to get away. He's terrified of Reynaldo, and seeing that he isn't dead shook him up. But he's also certain that we can't walk out of here again. He's sure the desert will do his dirty work for him." Squinting as he looked out over the surrounding desert, he continued. "He may be right. It's a long way to the horses, plus the return trip. Then we've got to load these guys and hope they survive the trip." The observation got him a worried frown and he quickly added, "At least we got some water and food in us. I don't imagine Jack gave any thought to that, and it's a real plus for our side."

"I wish we had some water for them," Sandra said. "Reynaldo did manage to sip down the rest of that canteen, but it wasn't much. I used some to clean the gash. I guess I should've kept it for him to drink, but I wasn't counting on being bushwhacked before we could start back."

"Maybe there's another canteen in the buggy. I don't remember if Alberto put all the stuff into the pickup. Anyway, the horses are bound to know the fastest way back. They're getting thirsty too, by now."

Sandra opened her mouth to say something, then stopped herself as though thinking better of it. She tried again. "Guess you better get started, Horse Whisperer."

He grinned at her joke. "I know. I hate leaving you here, but hold onto this, don't put it down for a minute." He handed her the pistol and gave instructions. "The first shot is double action. Just push this safety down and pull the trigger," he said, demonstrating the motion. "It'll seem a little hard to pull, but don't worry. The next round will automatically load and the hammer will be back, so when you pull the trigger the second time, it'll be real easy, and so will every shot after that, until the clip is empty. There are five rounds left, but that's plenty for defending yourself against anyone. Just point, shoot, and keep on shooting till it quits."

Neither spoke for a moment, knowing that he was talking about the unlikely, but possible return of Jack Pearson. Seeing the troubled look on her face, Mike asked, "Want to come with me? We can leave them here," he suggested, gesturing to the two injured men. "There's not much you can do for them anyway, except be a reminder that I'm coming back for all of you."

"No, you're right about that part," she answered. "They need to know we're trying to get them out. If we both walked away, they might give up hope, regardless of how you try to explain it to Alberto."

He tried another tack. "You could go get the horses, and I'll stay here. Horses like you better anyway."

She shook her head emphatically at that. "You're better at navigation than I am, so you need to go for the horses. I might get over the first rise and panic when everything looks the same for miles."

I'm certain that he won't come back," Mike said. "But if he does show up, don't let him get close to you. You've seen firsthand what his intentions are, so no matter what he says, start shooting when he's still ten feet away."

"Yeah, I know now what Jack is like, I really do. Mike, please be careful."

"I will. You too." He lingered for a second as though he wanted to say something else, but didn't. Instead, he hugged her tightly for a minute, burying his face in her neck. Then he pulled back and looked into her eyes. "I'd better get started. I won't get there by standing here talking. I'll be back in a flash. *Adiós.*"

CHAPTER 20

▼

Jack's arm hurt, but the wound wasn't bleeding much, so he could at least drive the battered old pickup around the cactus patches. From seeing the pickup approach earlier, Jack knew to drive to the southwest, and he crossed Alberto's tire tracks often enough to verify he was on course. Eventually he would reach a road or civilization of some sort, even though he had no idea what he would do then.

Driving along the rough ground, he cursed his bad luck. His entire plan had gone wrong, and all because of Sandra's damned boyfriend. Where the hell did he get a gun? He pondered the gun battle and thought about his hasty retreat, wondering now if he should have stayed to shoot it out. After all, how lethal could that little gun be? It had sounded like a .22; or worse, maybe a .25, a damn pimp gun—probably chrome-plated! Going back and killing all of them would fix it, a final bullet in each of their heads to make sure. Jack, in his typical fashion of fancying himself the tough guy, almost turned around right then.

But something about that tall guy's smart mouth and cavalier attitude, and the way he'd magically produced the little pistol had scared Jack witless— just like earlier, when he and his cronies had looked up to see a big Land Cruiser bearing down on them. That had been a ball-buster...and what other tricks did the guy have? Whatever they might be, Jack was reluctant to experience any of them. The one lucky shot he'd made, even hitting him in the arm, stung like...well, like being shot. And the next one, had he stayed around, might not have hit his arm. He'd made the right decision in high-tailing it out of there, of that he was certain.

The other side of tough-guy Jack Pearson was emerging during this mental exercise, a justification process to place a stamp of approval on his questionable actions. Running out in combat might have been viewed as cowardly by many observers, but Jack preferred to think of it as survival smarts. In his mind, he'd done the right thing. He had to survive, get away to figure out how to mend this mess—and without giving that guy a chance to pop him again with that little pimp piece!

Pushing the old truck much faster than Alberto had, Jack reached the dirt road in just under an hour. He stopped and looked both directions, wondering where it went…in either direction, since both ways looked identical. He rummaged through the glove box, but found only a pair of fencing pliers and two boxes of staples, plus some rags and various plumbing fittings. The sight of the plumbing fittings reminded him of how thirsty he was, so he got out and looked for a canteen or water jug among the rolls of barbed wire and tools in the back. Nothing there. Finally, under the seat on the passenger side, he found two canteens, and one still had water. He drained the canteen of the lukewarm water and looked again under the seat for more. He didn't find any more water, but he did find an old road map. When he spread it open on the seat, he saw that it was a California map dated 1968—not much help.

He leaned back in the seat, continuing to scan the dirt road as though his salvation might appear at any moment. He began to assess the situation more carefully and decided it wasn't as bad as he'd first thought, except that his arm hurt. Looking at the wound, he saw the bullet had only skimmed along his skin for about two inches and not entered the flesh of his arm. He took off his shirt, tore both sleeves off and made a bandage from the one that had no bloodstains.

Confident now that he would survive the gunshot, he mulled over the likely fate of the group he'd left behind. As for Sandra and her boyfriend, they could either try walking out again, or just die of thirst. The second trip would be more difficult; they would be tired from their recent effort, and this time they didn't have Berto to rescue them, as he must have done earlier. No way that pair could have walked straight to the ranch house; the ranch hand must have been out checking on things and run across them.

Furthermore, while Reynaldo was still breathing, surely he was too badly hurt to survive a trip out of the desert. He couldn't walk, and he would only burden the survivors. And although the rock had failed to finish him off immediately, Berto, the group's only chance at guiding them out of there, was dead. Now, if anyone was found to blame for the deaths of the two Hispanic men, it would be the two *gringos* staggering around in the desert—if they lived long enough.

Jack's mental gymnastics bolstered his confidence and he decided to get back to Del Rio, where he'd ordered Dirk and Sarge to stay and wait for his call. Recalling the time and speed of the ill-fated helicopter flight from the canyon, he realized that he might be eighty or ninety miles from the border town, a lot of miles over unknown territory with few roads, driving a stolen vehicle, no map, and in a foreign country. At least it's Mexico where everything's screwed up anyway, he thought. It wasn't likely that a police bulletin would be issued for the stolen pickup; who would report it? It had probably been stolen years ago in California, judging by the old map. Besides, he could always rely on its belonging to *Señor Gomez* while he drove it in this area, telling anyone he encountered that he was performing an errand for *El Patrón*.

He decided to turn left onto the dirt road, which bore to the south. After a few miles, he noticed it veered to the east-southeast, generally angling back toward the border, though farther downstream on the Rio Grande than going due north. North would be the shortest path to the border as the buzzard flies, but the old pickup was stuck with taking the road, which was primitive, but smooth enough.

Looking ahead, he saw it was going to be a long haul; there was no sign of civilization as far as the eye could see. And while the gas gauge read almost full, he knew better than to count on its accuracy. He would need to nurse it along, hoping to reach civilization and get his bearings (and fuel) before approaching the *aduana*, or customs station located on every major road fifteen to twenty-five miles inside Mexico's borders.

The *aduana* worried him. He didn't want to risk some over-zealous customs officer questioning him about not having a stamped visa, or over-researching the ownership of the pickup. Besides, he was still carrying the gun, a definite no-no in Mexico. He had to find another way to get back across the border and decided he'd try to find a village with telephone service and call Del Rio. If he could reach Dirk and Sarge, they could rent a car and come get him. Then they could re-enter the States easily and resolve the problems that were brewing. Luckily, he'd retrieved his passport from his pickup before he and Reynaldo had started out from Wichita Falls. It would make things a lot easier than trying to use his driver's license and a sad apologetic story about forgetting the new documentation requirements. Those two dumbasses better be at the Super-8, he thought. And they'd better have *their* passports.

Jack had always prided himself on being able to think on his feet, remember the details, and recent events required just that. Quick thinking—and well-delivered BS—had enabled him to get by reasonably well all his life. Moreover, he thought himself an entrepreneur, an adventurous business experimenter, whereby he could justify any action and any consequence thereof as being just another component of life as he chose to live it, anyone's viewpoint to the contrary be damned. Braggart and blowhard that he was, he could fend for himself in dicey conditions, always finding a way to survive. That characteristic would have served him well, perhaps made him a success in a more socially acceptable lifestyle, had things been different earlier in his life when, whether by choice or thrust on him by circumstances, he veered toward a grifter's existence. But as it turned out, leading life on the edge—sometimes merely skirting legality, other times involved in outright criminal activity—suited him, and Jack Pearson was forever stuck being just what he was.

Jack had been driving on the dirt road for almost two hours before he saw a collection of huts on the horizon. As he drew nearer, he could tell that it was a village—but could see no human activity, no utility poles or wires. That probably ruled out finding a telephone, unless one of the inhabitants had a cell phone, which didn't seem likely.

Pulling into the village, he stopped in front of a commercial establishment, possibly a store or a cooperative for trading agricultural products. Two elderly men sat out front with sacks of grain piled high on either side of them, holding court with several bystanders. None of the crowd reacted with more than a curious glance at the big gringo in the old pickup, one they had already identified as the Gomez Ranch truck.

Jack's Spanish was woefully deficient, especially for one who had spent the better part of his life working around job sites where Spanish was used as much as English. Rather than try to communicate with those workers, Jack had always looked up the head honcho and related instructions through him. As a result, he had never bothered to learn much of the language. Now he dreaded trying to get any information from this bunch, but decided to try his luck anyway, and possibly find out how far it was to the nearest telephone service.

"Hola Seeñoreez," he addressed them, exiting the pickup. *"Dondee este uno telefonero, por favor?"* he asked, butchering the accent, as well as the words.

"There's no phone service here, but it's only a few more miles to Tule. I think there is a public phone at the store and also one at the Pemex station," one of the younger men answered, with only a trace of an accent.

Jack was stunned to hear a Mexican National who spoke perfect English here in the wilds of the Chihuahuan Desert. He'd spent years around migrant construction workers who couldn't grasp a word of English, although they lived year round in Fort Worth, hundreds of miles from the border. What next? This day was just full of surprises. "Well, uh, thanks," he stammered. "I 'preciate that."

One of the other men murmured something to the spokesman, who nodded and turned toward Jack, who was already climbing back into the pickup. "Isn't that Alberto's pickup?" he asked, his tone and demeanor suspicious.

"Uh, yeah, I was out at the ranch and decided to see if I could find a phone. He let me use it."

"You would have saved time by just riding into Tule from the ranch instead of going all the way to the shed for the pickup," the spokesman said, making the statement almost a question.

Jack thought quickly and did a good job of covering. "I may have to use it to go on from there. Can't ride a horse all the way to Del Rio."

The response seemed to satisfy the speaker, who nodded slightly and turned back to his companions. Jack was somewhat relieved; he hadn't anticipated being questioned about the vehicle this soon. He had relied on the language barrier as a handy, logical tool to bluster his way through any confrontations with locals and was now suddenly bombarded with unanswerable questions— in English, no less. But of course, he had no idea of what, or where, "the shed" was, or what it had to do with Alberto's pickup. What Jack also didn't know was that the old pickup, residing in its shed beside the area's only road, was for *ejido,* or community, use when it wasn't being driven by Alberto.

So the curious inquiries were innocent enough; anyone was welcome to use the pickup, and it was certainly available to this gringo who had obvious ties to *El Patrón* himself. But Jack's ignorance and resulting nervousness over the questions weren't missed by the villagers. He would have liked to get something to drink, but thought better of it. He just wanted to get out of there, so he cranked up the engine and quickly pulled away from the group, not looking back. Only when the village was gone from his rear view mirror did he breathe easier.

As informed by the English-speaking man, the tiny town of Tule was only minutes away. It had few streets, most of them dirt, but the main street was paved, and it seemed to be the only road out of town. Jack pulled into the Pemex gasoline station, wary now of his inability to hide behind his lack of Spanish.

He needn't have worried; this time, it took several minutes just to get across the fact that he needed change for the phone booth. At first the clerk thought the gringo wanted to buy the telephone and was adamant in refusing to entertain such a transaction. The confusion was caused by Jack holding out a twenty-dollar bill, reciting *"para telefonero, para telefonero,"* omitting the verb *"usar,"* meaning "to use." Despite the language barrier, the clerk made it known that he didn't want to sell the telephone. Then, after figuring out the gringo wanted change, the clerk was even more amazed; how could any store keep enough change on hand to satisfy customers who waved around such huge denominations of money? And even if the business had kept enough money on hand to change it, Jack would have needed a wheelbarrow to carry that many coins. The clerk's resolution to the problem was to continue saying *"No, Señor."* Clearly, the North American Free Trade Agreement hadn't solved all international trade problems.

Finally, Jack recognized the problem and dug around in his pockets to find a wrinkled five and some ones. Seeing the lesser amount of U. S. dollars in his hand prompted the clerk to action. He quickly calculated an inflated rate of exchange and forked over a double handful of pesos without counting them back to Jack. He'd straighten out the register later, relieving it of those extra coins in order to balance at the end of the day. For now, he was satisfied to watch the gringo studying the intricately engraved coins of various denomination, squinting closely, trying to determine their value.

Lucky for Jack, he already had the phone number and managed to get an English-speaking operator on the second try. The motel shift manager answered and put the call through to Dirk Benson's room.

"Uh, hello?"

"Dirk, I need you to rent a car and come down into Mexico and get me," Jack began without preamble.

"Uh, okay, uh, where you at?"

"*I'm in a little town called Tule, T-U-L-E. It's southwest of Del Rio, I dunno, maybe eighty or a hundred miles in. I don't have a map, so I don't even know what damn highway number it's on. Get a good map of Mexico, rent a car, and be sure and buy insurance that allows you to drive on into the interior, past the aduana checkpoint. If you don't have all your shit in order, you can't go beyond them, and I'm way the hell inside of that. So talk to the rental place and make sure you got everything you need, 'cause I need you here, pronto,*" he instructed. "*Bring your passport, but leave your piece over there. We'll get it later.*" He'd have to figure out something on his own pistol before they approached the border. Maybe he'd just bluff it, hide it in his boot. I can get away with that, he thought, but if Dirk tried it, his foot would start itching.

"*Jack, where's the others?*" Dirk asked. "*Did you catch those two? And how the hell did you end up stranded in Tooley, Mexico?*"

"*It's Tule, Dirk. And it's a long story, but we'll have plenty of time to talk on the way back.*" Jack sounded irritated. Then he added, in a milder tone, "*Hell, I'm just glad y'all got back to Del Rio.*" Which indeed he was. If he hadn't been able to reach Dirk, he would have been forced to rely on the old pickup and bluffing his way through customs and back into the States. Dirk, for all his shortcomings, at least came through this time.

"*Hey, Jack, we ran across those two again at the RV park on Amistad, but they hauled ass again like fucking rabbits. Sarge and I ran as far and fast as we could, but they're like chasing cats. Hell, I never seen anybody could just run out across the damn pasture for miles like that. Why, they run faster than shit through a pet goose!*"

"*Well, where do you think they went this time?*" Jack asked, rolling his eyes at Dirk's vivid description.

"*I guess they're still out there wandering around somewhere. Anyway, we just came on back to Del Rio like you said,*" Dirk offered solicitously. "*I didn't want to miss your call in case you needed us.*"

"*It's probably just as well. I think I know where they ended up. And I'm going to pay for both of you fat fuckers to get some running lessons,*" Jack laughed, omitting the fact that he, too, marveled at Mike and Sandra's ability to run away from pursuers with seemingly little effort—for miles. "*Anyway, a lot has changed in this deal,*" he continued. "*I've got a whole new plan. Just get down here and pick me up at the Pemex station in bee-yoo-tiful downtown Tule, 'mos rikki tikki' as Sarge would say. He there with you?*"

"*Yeah, he went to get us something to eat. He'll be back in a minute and we'll get started.*"

Without further discussion, both men hung up and Dirk began to scurry about the room, gathering up their belongings. As soon as Sarge arrived, they'd eat and get moving, he thought. He'd been afraid that Jack would be pissed about losing the pair yet again, but apparently, whatever had changed had eclipsed that failure. Dirk was relieved that Jack hadn't even seemed concerned about it and he wanted to make sure he didn't screw up again. He finished cramming the few items they had bought at Walmart into a trash bag and grabbed the phone book to look up the nearest car rental.

CHAPTER 21

▼

At first, Mike set a rapid pace toward the southwest, but he hadn't covered two miles before the fatigue returned. Despite the food and water Alberto had given them, he had not rested nearly enough to start this journey again, and his muscles tightened in protest to the renewed torture. He was forced to slow down, shorten his stride, and concentrate on steadily covering ground rather than getting to the horses quickly, as he had hoped. Despite the meandering trail, which was now composed of two sets of tire tracks, Mike knew that following them would get him to the road at a point near the shed. It was a relief to know with certainty where the tracks led, unlike the night before when they had relied on sheer guesswork with the compass and every step could have been taking them farther from help.

The sun was blazing now, the heat building on the hard, baked ground. It was already hot, and Mike was sweating slightly. But for now, the light breeze kept the air currents moving over the ground and evaporation was doing its part to keep him reasonably cool. Later in the afternoon, the breeze would cease to cool; instead, it would feel like a blast furnace, scalding the skin and searing one's eyes.

As he walked, Mike's thoughts turned to Sandra and their relationship, along with how this misadventure in the wilds might affect it. He couldn't deny that he enjoyed her company and was far happier when they were together—even now, staggering around the Chihuahuan Desert trying to survive a botched kidnapping/murder plot. That thought prompted him to wish he had insisted on her coming with him, but he knew from their discussion she felt strongly about staying with the two injured men. Besides, throughout their time together, he had made a point of never *insisting* on anything, and this time was no exception. Occasionally, when pressed, he would resort to pointing out advantages and disadvantages to the subject at hand, but he resolutely refused to direct her on anything and seldom even offered advice.

But from recent comments she had made, he realized the tightrope he was walking with that outlook. Sometimes she apparently wanted him to take a stronger stand or express a stronger opinion. That might prove to be a hard thing to change, he thought. Even before this current drama, he had heard enough snippets about her ex-husband's controlling personality to reinforce his steadfast policy. And recalling his own recent encounter with know-it-all Jack Pearson and Sandra's reaction to him, Mike thought she ought to appreciate the contrast. He wanted to be as different from Jack as possible, but he couldn't help but wonder if that was what she wanted. He surely hoped so, because Mike Conner could only be himself.

In mid-afternoon, he reached the dirt road and turned right, toward the shed. He walked for another half hour before he spied the rickety enclosure only fifty yards away, well-camouflaged against the backdrop of the area's scrub mesquite and creosote bushes. Whether by design or accident, the low visibility of the structure made him glad he had seen it. He was exhausted again, and the last thing he needed now was to pass it by and have to backtrack to find the horses.

As he neared it, the horses picked up his scent or heard him and began to shuffle around restlessly, probably eager to move around after being held captive for hours. Recalling his ineptitude with the beasts, Mike hoped they wouldn't be difficult about this. He needed them to cooperate and get this job done. Besides, he'd never live it down if one of them ran off and he had to face Sandra, short by even one horse. He untied them and led them outside where he securely hitched the three mounts to the back of the buggy before climbing in. Slapping the reins on the buggy-puller's rump elicited nothing but a lazy turn of its head and a baleful stare, so he tried again, a little harder. No dice. He tried again, and even embellished his effort with a silly-sounding clucking sound, just like in the movies. Something worked, because the horse moved out, heading down the dirt road just like it was supposed to.

I didn't know I could cluck in Spanish!

Tired as he was, he had had the foresight to tie a strip of his shirt to a bush at the cutoff point, not wanting to waste time looking for tire tracks. He had to get back to the crash site as quickly as possible so they could be on the way to the ranch before darkness overtook them. He wasn't going to depend on their good fortune of the previous night, with its early moonrise and cloudless sky. Hopefully, the horses knew the way, but Mike didn't want to rely entirely on that, either. Instead, he wished for his Land Cruiser—which was sitting a hundred miles or so away in the bottom of a canyon, riddled with bullet holes. It made him wonder once again why he was rescuing Reynaldo Gomez, the chief architect of all this mess in the first place.

The return trip progressed better than he had hoped for, with the lead horse dutifully picking up the pace to a fast walk through the landscape. Mike made an effort to steer around the thorniest areas, but occasionally the horse pulled the buggy and the horses tied behind right through patches of spiny vegetation, seemingly oblivious to the thorns that had to be pricking its lower legs. He made a mental note to check all the horses' legs to make sure there was no impending disaster there in the form of a lame animal. Better yet, he'd get Sandra to do it—Mike couldn't recall any time he'd escaped dealing with horses without being pitched off, dragged off under a tree limb, or stepped on, in addition to having his butt beaten numb by the rough ride.

By early evening, he was nearing the crash site, recognizable by the now-familiar gullies and dry washes. The setting sun's light was more subdued than the harsh light of midday, and the effect on the appearance and colors of the land was stunning. What had earlier been a scene composed entirely of hazy, shimmering off-white was now separated into several shades of pale tan, ochre, browns, pinks and yellows. In the shadows of the gorges, muted gray tones lent a prominent contrast, giving the landscape definition and depth. Only at the extreme ends of the day did the desert abandon its harshness. Early morning and late evening in the desert unleashed a beauty unseen and unknown to most people. In an environment better known for its hostility, those times of day briefly provided a stark contrast to unforgiving heat and blinding white light. Mike savored the scenery for a few hundred yards, pleased with knowing he was nearing the crash site, ending the hard journey, and getting closer to Sandra.

All Sandra had been able to do for the injured men was make sure their wounds were protected from dirt and flies and that they weren't exposed to the hot sun. She couldn't treat the wounds and didn't have water for them to drink, but she could watch over them, hoping that her presence would comfort them until Mike returned with transportation. She looked forward to his return, not only for the rescue effort, but for the sense of well-being she felt while in his company. She was happiest when he was near, a feeling that had intensified during this trying experience, and she wondered what, if anything, it signified for their relationship.

In between periods of watching over the men she leaned against the embankment and managed to fall asleep, but her naps were continually interrupted by fits of panic brought about by short, violent dreams in which the gunfire started again. The trauma of the past few days' events was seeping into her sleeping thoughts. The dreams had no real beginning and no end, and she couldn't even determine who the gunman was; she simply seemed surrounded by loud gunfire, constant and unrelenting, suspended there with no help or relief until she jerked awake each time. Tired as she was, the fitful sleep did little to ease her fatigue.

She heard the horses and buggy coming well before their arrival. She stood groggily, rising stiffly from her resting place beside her patients with more than a little effort. Alberto was now fully conscious, but in some pain from the gunshot wound. Reynaldo, surprisingly, had regained consciousness on two occasions and once mumbled something in Spanish, but now had slipped back into a deep, peaceful sleep. She checked his breathing again, pleased that it seemed regular, then stepped away from the shade of the embankment to see the buggy lurching around the end of the ridge.

She was so glad to see Mike she couldn't stop the tears that came to her eyes. As he pulled to a stop, she reached up for him and hugged him tightly even before he could get completely off the buggy. After a long moment of embrace without a word said between them, he stiffly clambered down and turned to the injured men to plan how to load and transport them in relative comfort.

Sandra dug around in the saddlebags and found a half-full canteen, which she quickly carried over to Reynaldo. Splashing a small amount onto a strip of cloth, she wiped his face, eliciting a groan from him, then a fluttering of eyelids. "Can you drink?" she asked.

"Yes. Yes, I think so," he whispered hoarsely.

She held the canteen to his lips and he drank, tentatively at first, then trying to gulp down more as he felt the water on his parched throat. "Easy, easy, take it slow," she cautioned, recalling Alberto's admonition to her only hours before.

Reynaldo nodded and leaned back, his eyes closed, but the expression on his face more relaxed and pain-free than it had been.

Mike had been at Alberto's side, but turned to Reynaldo. "Do you think you can stand up, Reynaldo? We've got to get both of you into the buggy, and you've got to help us by trying to stand, okay?"

Again he nodded, and after a slight hesitation, rolled to his right. With a lot of effort and Mike and Sandra's help, he stood shakily and tried to move forward, taking his first step in almost twenty-four hours. They steered him to the buggy, and he reached with both hands for the rail in front and managed to pull himself into the vehicle. The movement seemed to improve his state and he sat up, quiet, but alert.

Alberto presented no problem; Mike practically carried the thin man to the buggy, taking care to avoid his wounded ribcage. With assistance, the tough old man climbed in and groaned as he settled into the seat beside Reynaldo. But he, too, seemed alert, which Mike and Sandra took as a good sign for themselves as well as their patients. The ranch hand would be able to direct them to the ranch, even if darkness overtook them.

The injured men loaded, it was time to leave. Mike and Sandra wasted no time walking their horses to either side of the buggy. Alberto sat up straight on the seat and said something, motioning for the reins, which Mike had draped around to the front in preparation for pulling the buggy horse behind him. Mike shrugged and handed him the reins. The old man smiled, pleased at being able to help further his own rescue.

Before mounting up, Mike told Sandra about the horses walking through the thorniest vegetation and helped her while she checked their legs for embedded thorns. They found several and Sandra pulled them out, laughing at Mike's nervous reaction each time one of the animals flinched or snorted.

"What's the matter with you?" she asked with an impish grin, knowing full well what the problem was. "You're pretty jumpy, aren't you?"

"Just making sure I don't get stepped on, that's all."

"Well, hold this foot up for me, and quit jerking every time the horse moves. It scares them. Come on, we're almost done."

"It scares *me*, dammit! I wish I'd never mentioned it. Hell, they've got to be used to thorns out here."

"Get out of the way, then."

To Mike's relief she finished the last one by herself and declared the animals ready to go. They mounted up, and Alberto clucked to the buggy horse, slapping the reins to get the procession moving. With Mike and Sandra riding behind the buggy, the four began what all hoped was the last journey across this stretch of desert—at least under these conditions.

"I am *so* glad to see you," Mike told Sandra as they clopped along a few yards behind the buggy.

"Me too. I was wishing I had gone with you, but now I'm glad I stayed.

I think Reynaldo may have hung in there trying to stay conscious because he knew you'd be back."

"Yeah, you were right about staying with them, but I missed you anyway."

After a few minutes of riding in silence, Sandra brought up a subject she had obviously been worried about during Mike's absence. "You were right about Jack just wanting to get away. I wonder where he went. And what will happen to him now?"

Mike shook his head. "His future probably isn't very promising. Reynaldo doesn't seem like the type to take disloyalty lightly. And he's got the resources to see that punishment is carried out, especially if he's still here in Mexico."

"I hate to say it, but it couldn't happen to a better guy, whatever he gets. I see that now."

Mike looked over at her, but she kept looking ahead, so he said nothing in response to her observation. The silence continued for another few minutes, both of them engrossed in thoughts about what this turn of events might mean for them, as well as for Jack Pearson. Had they compared thoughts, they would have agreed that their future looked a lot brighter than Jack's.

When she spoke again, it was a much lighter subject. "Didn't have any trouble with the horses, huh?"

"Nah, nothing to it! You know me, the Horse Whisperer. I just showed them who was boss, and they jumped at the chance to do what I told them."

"Okay, boss," she laughed. "I'll remember that the next time I need a horse saddled. You can probably get the thing to saddle itself and just wait for me to cinch it up, right?"

"Sure, no problem."

"Well, tell me, Horse Whisperer, what do you do when your mount gets skittish on you?" she asked, moving closer to him.

"Huh? What do you mean?"

With that, she gave his horse a gentle kick in front of its flank, causing it to jump sideways, nearly dislodging him. He grabbed the saddle horn to avoid being dumped on the ground. As soon as he regained his balance, he leaned out to grab her shirt, but she eluded him, dancing her mount just out of his reach, laughing the entire time.

"Just wait. Just you wait!" he hissed at her.

Her laughter caused the two men in the buggy to look at each other and smile, despite their pain. Reynaldo said something to Alberto, and he responded with a string of Spanish that included the phrase *"gringos locos."*

CHAPTER 22

▼

The trip back to the ranch was bumpy and thirsty. As the group neared the ranch house, the horses started picking up the pace because the ranch meant shedding saddles and blankets for a roll in the dust of the corral. Combined with the smell of water, it took a lot of restraint from the riders to keep their mounts reined in to a manageable pace. Alberto continually strained against the reins of the buggy horse, slowing it to ease the rough ride and lessen the danger of upsetting the rickety contraption it was pulling. The rigors of the trip showed clearly on the faces of both the injured men, and Reynaldo was slumping over against his employee, doing his best to hang on a while longer. Meanwhile, Alberto leaned against Reynaldo and gritted his teeth against the pain in his side caused by pulling on the reins.

True to every horse-riding experience Mike had ever had, it quickly became a test of wills, his versus the horse, exacerbated by the contest among the homeward-bound animals. When the buggy sped up, the trailing mounts stepped up their pace, refusing to allow their companion hitched to the buggy to beat them home. They even tried to pass the buggy, sometimes bolting through thorny bushes, an uncomfortable proposition for the rider. It took all of Mike's attention to keep his horse reined in behind the buggy. By the time Alberto had managed to slow the buggy, Mike and Sandra had invariably ridden near the back of it, pressuring the buggy horse to take off again, creating yet another burst of speed and a race for home. The accordion effect of the group was maddening to Mike, but Sandra merely smiled and acted as if everything were normal.

This beats walking, but just barely!

Mike and Sandra had never seen a more inviting sight than the ranch house, at least not since early that morning when the same little house and its single light had first appeared in the darkness. Though not as exhausted as the night before had left them, they were plenty tired, hungry, and thirsty. And this time, they had to care for the two injured men.

They were greeted in the yard by a younger man and a woman, presumably another ranch hand and his wife. Following a few words from Reynaldo, they helped lift Alberto from the buggy, and supporting him on each side took him to the nearest bunkhouse. They eased him onto a bed, whereupon the woman immediately began removing his shirt to examine the wound while Sandra looked on. Meanwhile, Mike and the young man repeated the process with Reynaldo, but with a lot more effort. They finally got the bigger man into another bed in the bunkhouse, where he settled back and groaned in obvious pain, but remained conscious, his eyes shut.

Sandra moved to his side and removed the crude bandage from his head, then proceeded to cleanse the wound with the shallow basin of water placed at bedside by the man. After doing the same service for Alberto's side, the young woman, who introduced herself in reasonable English as Henrietta, moved over to help her. She first examined Sandra's handiwork at cleaning the gash, then produced a poultice for the wound and finished by winding a clean bandage around his head.

Mike helped the young man, who spoke only a little English, with the horses and buggy. They unsaddled the mounts and placed the tack on racks in a barn, then released the horses to the corral, where they cavorted and rolled in what Mike thought was typical horse behavior. After watching for a minute, he turned to the young man and introduced himself as Miguel. The young man's name was Agapito, and he seemed genuinely pleased to make Mike's acquaintance.

Together they trudged back into the bunkhouse, where Alberto was propped up on pillow, bright-eyed and alert. Cleaning the wound had been painful, as well as application of a disinfectant and the poultice, but Henrietta had skillfully wrapped his mid-section just tightly enough to support the damaged rib, allowing him to move around a little. For now, he seemed content with sitting up in bed, conversing with Henrietta, who was interpreting for Sandra.

Looking over at Reynaldo, Mike thought he was sleeping peacefully, but had no idea if that was a good or bad sign. Turning to Agapito, he spread his hands, palms upward, as if to ask "what now?" Agapito shrugged, said something Mike couldn't quite catch, but "who knows?" was obvious from his expression. He said something to Henrietta, who looked up and responded, first in Spanish to him, then turning toward Mike, she interpreted. "We must wait and see. He has a bad injury for his head, but he is awake some. That is good."

Mike, too, thought it a good sign that he was conscious for the most part; had he slipped into a deep coma, he wouldn't even have been able to drink water, and if he couldn't rehydrate, his health wasn't going to improve.

As if reading his mind Sandra said, "Next time he wakes up, we'll try to feed him some soup. He needs some nourishment, and I don't know what more we can do for him except keep his strength up. With food, water, and being out of the heat, he's got a good chance at recovery, I think."

Henrietta, who had gone outside for another bucket of water, re-entered the room at that moment and said something to Agapito, gesturing toward Mike. To Sandra, she said, "I have some clothes for you to wear if you want, and Agapito can find for Miguel some clothing. The other bunkhouse has a shower and some beds. You are very tired, yes?"

Sandra smiled at her. "Yes, we are. And we'd be most grateful for a shower and some clothes, but we don't want to impose on you."

Henrietta seemed baffled by the unfamiliar word, but it was clear that imposition would never apply anyway, not to these two people who had arrived carrying with them the wounded *ranchero jefe* and, of all people, *El Patrón* himself! Whatever had taken place out in the desert, it was evident to her that her two benefactors would not be alive had the gringos not cared for them and delivered them to the ranch house.

The shower was a crude affair, no more than a pipe nipple sticking out of the wall, turned on by a handle more suitable for the garden hose. There was no hot water, but in the heat of summer, the cool water felt just fine cascading down their head and bodies. Washing off the grime and dust of three days and nights spent slogging through the wilderness was a reward beyond belief. Even more satisfying for both of them was the delivery of two new toothbrushes and a tiny tube of toothpaste. Henrietta had slipped in while Mike showered and left them on a small washbasin in the corner before smiling at Sandra and quickly ducking out of the bunkhouse. Sandra pointed out the precious delivery to Mike when he stepped out of the shower, and he responded with a big grin and a thumbs-up for their new hosts without saying a word.

This is first class, no doubt about it! A toothbrush is better than cable TV!

As for Sandra, she marveled at how the simple things in life, like food and water, even a shower, could put things in a whole new light. She toweled her hair and slipped on the jeans and T-shirt, thinking "Thank God, a toothbrush!" That made things heavenly, she reflected as she stood at the basin, brushing hard enough to endanger the enamel on her teeth.

When they were both done and sporting their borrowed clothes, they immediately headed over to check on the patients. Alberto was sitting up in bed eating, and he smiled broadly as the two entered the house. He extended his hand to Mike, and he crossed the room to shake it. While Alberto grasped his hand in both of his, he babbled away in rapid Spanish to both of them, and gestured for Sandra to come to him. She walked over and joined the handshake, and the old man's eyes lit up as he smiled even wider at her. Neither could understand much of what the old man was saying, but the word "gracias" was repeated several times, so the message was clear.

Embarrassed at the attention, Mike attempted to divert the conversation. *"Como está Señor Gomez?"* he asked, trying out his Spanish and fearing the results as he looked over at Reynaldo, who appeared to be asleep. Sure enough, Alberto answered with a fast, unintelligible string of Spanish that Mike couldn't catch.

Luckily, his furrowed expression prompted Henrietta to smile and help him out. "He is better. He awoke for a few minutes, and I fed him some soup. Then he fell asleep again."

"Can we do anything more for him?" Sandra asked. "Or should we try to get him to a hospital?"

"I think he is better to rest here already," she answered in her imperfect English, then bustled about to get food for them.

They pulled up chairs to a wooden table by the window and dived into the big plates of beans, cornbread, and squash. Henrietta had brought them two icy bottled Cokes, and both thought they'd never tasted anything so good. They ate ravenously at first, but even before finishing, fatigue settled over them like a fog, and they barely stayed awake to finish the meal. After thanking Henrietta for the food, they were shooed away in their attempt to help clear the table and retreated to the other bunkhouse, where they collapsed into the beds fully clothed.

Unbeknownst to the exhausted pair, Henrietta peeked into the bunkhouse a half hour later, then hurried back to the ranch house, where she gently shook Reynaldo and reported their status. Reynaldo smiled and thanked her, issued some instructions, then closed his eyes again.

CHAPTER 23

▼

Jack strode over to the old-fashioned cold-drink box that sat humming along under a window unit water cooler and raised the lid. There was a good selection of *Jarittos*, the popular national brand of soft drink, along with Coca-Cola, all in bottles and all ice cold. Hefting a couple of Cokes, he scouted around the meagerly stocked shelves until he spotted some cheese crackers and peanut brittle. Carting his meal over to the counter, he let the clerk take a slightly inflated amount from his remaining handful of change. Jack figured he was getting clipped on the snacks, but what the hell—it was still a cheap price to get something in his stomach. Not worth a confrontation, especially since he didn't want to be noticed here in Tule. Besides, Dirk and Sarge should soon be on the way, and he'd get out of this dump forever.

He went outside and climbed in the old pickup and pulled it around to the rear of the station where it was not so visible. He propped his feet on the dash and proceeded to munch his meal, such as it was. Not great, but since he hadn't eaten in two days, it tasted pretty good. Then he pulled his hat over his eyes and tried to take a snooze. Like the meal, it wasn't all that great, but it beat trying to sleep in a *cenizo* bush. It wasn't as hot and there were fewer flies.

Jack awoke with a start at the noise; it sounded like Morse code being tapped out on the side of the pickup. He pulled his feet from the dash and pushed back his hat. He turned and looked out the driver's side—nothing there. Sliding across the seat, he looked out the open passenger window, but again saw nothing. Listening intently, he heard the noise again, but not as loud this time. He exited the pickup and limped around behind to see a little boy, about five years old, slapping on the tailgate with a stick, apparently playing a tune known only to him. Jack smiled at the kid, leaned down to tousle his hair, and got back in the cab. He tried unsuccessfully to go back to sleep and finally got out to stretch, hoping it would make him feel better. He hadn't bathed or shaved in three days, and he felt like death. He hadn't eaten real food, and the cokes had only increased his thirst, so he went back in the station and spent the last of his pesos on two bottles of water.

As he twisted off the first cap, he smiled, remembering the part of Dirk's story about Sandra buying the water in Laredo before she and Mike had escaped. Pretty smart thinking on her part, he admitted to himself grudgingly. Dirk hadn't realized it until later, but she had known that they must have water before trying to escape in the desert. What they consumed or carried with them had undoubtedly made the difference between survival and death. Well, by God, they didn't have any water now, he thought as he chugged the last of the bottle, so the smart bitch and her hotshot boyfriend could just curl up and die of thirst out there in the desert, along with Reynaldo and his ranch hand.

The train of thought prompted Jack to decide what action to take once Dirk and Sarge arrived. He felt confident that the desert would finish off the survivors of the helicopter crash, but how to retrieve the shipment from the shop in El Paso? He hated to walk in and pay retail price for the items, even though that method was used occasionally in collecting the drugs from various little shops, the ones Morales hadn't cut in on the deal. It served to quell any suspicions of others in the trade, since the pricey Morales brand gave the small shops a financial boost. But full retail price in Conner's shop would amount to a larger sum of money, a purchase that might provoke suspicion from whomever Conner had operating the shop.

Jack was also worried that the shop might be shut down if Conner failed to show up there soon. If the bodies were discovered and identified, the entire inventory might be sold in settlement of his estate. Or Conner might have debts that would result in a court-ordered sale, carried out by the Sheriff's Department in order to satisfy creditors. That thought sent a chill through Jack. He'd been in enough legal scrapes himself to have a fair working knowledge of such matters, and the possibility of losing the huge shipment to some third party outbidding him made him very nervous. About two million dollars' worth of cocaine-holding pottery might end up sitting around growing Aunt Bertha's geraniums or Uncle Johnny's prize petunias. It would give new meaning to the term "hidden treasure."

There were too many loose ends to figure out the best approach right now, but Jack had an inkling of the best method to recoup the shipment— and it certainly didn't entail paying for it. The first step was to get to El Paso and check out the shop, if those two bone-headed helpers of his would just show up.

And show up they did, albeit three hours later, when it was almost dark.

"Where the hell y'all been?" Jack demanded as Dirk got out of the rental car, while Sarge remained planted in the passenger seat.

"Shit, Jack, we was held up at the border for a while, then at the *aduana* station for about an hour. Those assholes wanted to look at every piece of paper on the car rental, but not a damn one of them could read it. They studied it like it was the Dead Sea Scrotums or something."

From the front seat Sarge gave a snort of derision, and Jack considered correcting his numb-skull helper on the difference between male genitalia and ancient parchment writing material, but thought better of it. Something so complicated would be a further waste of time. "Alright, alright. Let's just get the hell out of here. I've had all of Tule, Mexico I ever wanted, and then some."

Jack got in the back seat and Dirk turned a full circle around the now-abandoned pickup and pulled out onto the main street. "Sure you don't want to bring that old pickup?" Dirk chided him. "It looks just like you, Jack, kinda' ragged and beat up. It fits your image!"

"I can't knock that old rattletrap, by God. It got me here, got me away from a hell of a gunfight. I was on the verge of getting my ass shot to shit when I managed to get in that thing and haul ass," Jack began, already embellishing the story of his retreat from the crash site. "The way lead was flying, I was lucky to escape with only this little scratch." He pulled the bandage down for Dirk and Sarge to inspect.

Sarge turned in his seat to look and Dirk was peering into the rearview mirror, straining to see the wound in the quickly fading daylight. "Hell, Jack, I didn't know that was a bandage. I thought you was playing Rambo or something!" Dirk quipped.

Jack proceeded to tell the entire saga of the past two days, conveniently placing himself in the hero's role in every scene, from the helicopter chase to the recapture of Mike and Sandra, to the crash, and finally, the gunfight with Alberto and Conner. "Reynaldo got real pissed after the crash when those two got away. He blamed the whole thing on me—in fact, on *us*—just for knowing them," he explained, shrewdly drawing Dirk and Sarge onto his side of the fray. "He went crazy and came after me with a big rock. We fought like hell for a while, me tryin' to talk sense into him while he swung a boulder at my head. I finally got it away from him and tagged him with his own weapon, just to quieten him down. Guess I hit him harder than I thought."

"Damn, Jack, are you serious?" Dirk asked. "What happened then?"

Jack continued his story, leaving out some facts, replacing them with slightly altered details. "Then the Meskin ranch hand pulled a big piece, so I plugged his ass, right 'tween the eyes! But that damn Conner guy whips out a barker and cranks off five or six rounds. I was lucky he's a piss-poor shot, and only one grazed me. He was reloading, but I was out of ammo and had no cover, so I hauled ass for the pickup, figuring they could just die of thirst out there. Or if somebody finds them before they die, it'll look like they killed Gomez and ol' Berto. Hell, the Meskin *policía* will lock their gringo asses up and throw away the key, especially after killing a big *patrón* like Gomez. Or they might just kill 'em on the spot. Either way, we're shut of those fuckers."

"That's the best news I've heard lately," Sarge said from the back seat.

"Damn straight it is!" Dirk agreed. "I was tired of chasing those two."

Jack was so caught up in regaling his minions with his own story he failed to admonish them or even bring up their earlier ill-fated kidnapping and Mike and Sandra's escape. As for Dirk and Sarge, they were both relieved at that; besides, after hearing Jack's wild tale, they would have had a reasonable defense for their failure. After all, if Jack and two professional henchmen, along with Reynaldo himself couldn't recapture the pair, how could they have been expected to fare better?

Pleased with the reception to his narrative, Jack began explaining what had changed, carefully editing the tale to suit his needs and informing the pair on how the arrangement would benefit them. Dirk and Sarge, who had had little direct contact with Reynaldo anyway, interpreted the new description of business as a promotion for them, as indeed it was. With Jack taking Reynaldo's place, all the players had moved up one notch—but it was that and more. He needed them to carry out the most important and the most dangerous part of his plan—retrieving the shipment of Morales merchandise.

As for future business, Jack knew all the details of purchasing from Morales and would have no problem in continuing the arrangement. He also knew the downstream contacts with whom Gomez had done business. Their distribution system was in place, and they didn't care whether they bought product from Reynaldo Gomez or Jack Pearson—or Joe Blow, for that matter, so long as he wasn't a Drug Enforcement Agency operative and the price was right. In fact, some of the largest drug deliveries from Gomez had been made by Jack personally, and he had been entrusted with the money for the return trip, so there was no reason to think that the buyers wouldn't deal directly with him now.

The players in the drug business weren't the type to inquire of Gomez's health or wonder why he hadn't contacted them. When they received word of his demise, no tears would be shed. All they wanted was delivery; they weren't running a personality contest. In short, Jack thought, they didn't give a damn; the perfect environment for Jack Pearson and his revised business plan.

CHAPTER 24

▼

Two more days passed while Mike and Sandra slowly regained their strength and caught up on sleep. Under Henrietta's care, Alberto improved remarkably and was able to walk around for a brief time before the stiffness of his gait and the injured rib forced him to rest. But Reynaldo, still bedridden, complained of headaches and dizziness between long periods of sleep.

Mike and Sandra, being active by nature, quickly tired of sitting around and pitched in to help with the operation of the ranch. Mike went out with Agapito on his rounds to check on small herds of cattle located around the ranch. They also fixed a broken windmill and patched a break in a fence, both routine maintenance tasks around a working ranch. Mike learned that Agapito had not been in the employ of the ranch very long, and while his knowledge of horses and livestock was adequate, his ability with maintenance tasks was limited. Apparently, Alberto had usually tended to those items, leaving the livestock management matters to the younger man.

Meanwhile, Sandra helped Henrietta with standard household chores, learning about washing laundry on a scrub board and hand-crank wringer. Sandra was an excellent cook and managed to show Henrietta a thing or two, even with the ranch kitchen's sparse supply of utensils and basic ingredients. They shared duty looking in on their patients every hour or so, tending their wound dressings and delivering meals. Reynaldo mostly slept, awakening only for limited eating and drinking. Alberto, true to his self-sufficient character, was embarrassed by the women's attention when pain and fatigue forced him to recline and accept their help.

On the morning of the third day at the ranch, Mike and Sandra entered the main house kitchen for breakfast and were surprised to find Reynaldo already seated at the head of the table. He had showered and shaved and was immaculately dressed in starched khakis and a white shirt. Gleaming cowboy boots sat nearby; although the swelling in his right ankle had subsided considerably, he still couldn't pull on the boots and would have to be content with padding around in socks for a while longer. And under his shirt, his ribcage matched Alberto's—tightly taped to restrict movement of his torso. A small patch covered his head wound, and the cuts on his face and forehead were down to a couple of small Band-Aids. But with his dark hair carefully groomed, the handsome man looked a lot more like *El Patrón*, rather than the bedraggled, semi-conscious figure who'd been carted in from the desert.

"Good morning!" he said cheerfully, rising stiffly for Sandra's sake and pulling out the chair to his left for her, while smoothly gesturing with his other hand, palm up, inviting Mike to take the chair to his immediate right.

"Well, good morning to you! It's nice to see you up and about," Sandra said, taking the offered chair.

"It is for a fact," Mike agreed. "We were beginning to worry about your recovery. You took a big lick on the head, but after two days, we'd hoped to see more progress. You're feeling better today?"

"Much better, thank you. The ribs are still very tender, but not unbearable." He gingerly probed his side. "The last two days have been bad, very bad. Blinding headache and dizzy. Sleep was my only refuge. Anyway, when I woke up early this morning, I felt much better and wanted to give you both my heartfelt thanks, so you wouldn't think I was rude."

Sandra smile at the remark. "You needed your sleep much more than we needed thanks. Besides, we only did what we told you we would. Things just changed a little when you ran into trouble after we left."

Her words created a moment of awkward silence, finally broken by Mike. "Can you tell us what happened?"

After a brief hesitation, Gomez said, "Jack somehow must have been thrown from the crash and escaped serious injury. He obviously hid somewhere in the area while you were helping me out of the chopper, or maybe he was lying unconscious in the brush. Either way, after you two left to come here, he crept up on me and bashed my head with a rock. I looked up in time to see him swinging it toward me and could only try to deflect it from my head.

I didn't do a very good job, though," he added, wincing as he touched the bandaged wound.

"Well, on the other hand," Mike countered, "he didn't do a very good job of finishing you off, which is apparently what he intended to do."

"Why did he do it?" Sandra asked.

"Greed, Sandra, human greed. He intends to gain control of my business, particularly the portion of my, um…activities that Jack and I have in common. It is quite lucrative, a cash arrangement that would benefit Jack greatly upon my demise."

"I'm sorry," Sandra said, embarrassed by putting him on the spot. "I didn't mean to pry into your personal life, but I assumed it had to do with your business and we thought Jack did your bidding in that area. At least that's what we've been led to believe throughout this whole mess."

"Yeah," Mike added, "since you didn't disagree with your guys' methods of sticking guns in our faces and kidnapping us, we assumed you ran the show and Jack was your guy." He felt that Gomez wasn't telling the whole story, but it eluded him as to what might really be playing out between the two men. Something in Gomez's voice had indicated a deeper rift than business greed, but Mike chose to let it lie for the moment.

"I'll not mislead you on that part," Reynaldo replied. "At first, I wasn't aware of who you were, or Sandra's previous connection with Jack, but when I received word that you two were being difficult, I instructed him to dissuade you from further involvement with the Morales Company. In retrospect, I would have tried different methods first, but Jack took over, then delegated the job to his two workers with no thought to the consequences. He also severely underestimated your capabilities—as did I.

"After you proved so troublesome and elusive, I rashly directed that you be eliminated. I cannot deny that. You are both fully aware of the violence in this business. But had I talked to you instead of entrusting the task to Jack, I think violence could have been avoided in this case. I am certain that Jack's previous connection to Sandra made it personal for him, especially with her new, uh…*friend* being present," he said, gesturing to Mike.

"Furthermore, it appears that you two have interesting views on illegal drug trade. While you oppose it, you have a *laissez faire* attitude about my involvement and a realistic outlook on taking out a single participant. So a discussion between the three of us in the beginning might have prevented all this," he said, gesturing toward his own battered body, then toward them."

He settled back in the chair and briefly closed his eyes, as though the explanation had taxed him. Mike and Sandra sat still, absorbed in their own thoughts regarding the past several days, remembering the nightmare of the initial kidnapping and being chased and shot at, as well as the terror of the crash. A sobering moment for all of them.

"Or maybe it was destined to happen this way," Reynaldo said suddenly, sitting upright again. "As I said, Jack's former connection with Sandra made him want to appear tough and decisive against Mike. But I take full responsibility for ordering your deaths and what has happened since."

The frank admission left all three at a loss for further words—what else was there to say? Mike still had a nagging feeling that Reynaldo was not telling all he knew, but he remained quiet. What difference did it make now? The impasse was finally broken by Mike, who asked Gomez how they could get back to Del Rio.

Reynaldo thought for a moment, back in his element of being in charge, making decisions. "Agapito will arrange for you to be delivered back to Del Rio, where you may wish to file a claim regarding your vehicle. I suggest that you simply report it as stolen. The authorities will have been notified by now and it has probably been towed to town. I shall pay for all damages you suffered. In fact, I shall be happy to buy you a new vehicle."

"A new one's not necessary," Mike said. "But I would appreciate your help with repairs and greasing the wheels with the authorities if any problems or questions arise. I'm sure you can help me avoid a lengthy explanation of what I was doing here, how my vehicle happened to get stolen, why it was under the Pecos River Bridge with bullet holes, and so on."

"Certainly. That will not be a problem, I assure you. I know you want to get on with your lives without ever seeing me again, and I understand that. But first, there is the matter of the shipment of Morales merchandise, which I would like to purchase from you at your regular retail prices plus any premium you wish. You surely have earned a premium on that shipment."

"I don't want a premium. Just my standard price and your guys pick up the entire shipment, all at once, at my shop in El Paso. Then I want your assurance that we'll never hear of the matter again. In return, we won't reveal this story to anyone, ever. As we mentioned a while ago, we don't approve of your occupation, but we're not so naïve as to think jamming up one shipment changes anything. And we're not the world's policemen or moral authorities, so we have no interest in causing you any problems, believe me."

"I am delighted that we are in agreement. You are a most gracious couple. Even though I allowed, even condoned, endangerment of your lives, you risked your safety to save me and my trusted employee. There are not many people of your caliber in this world. I regret that we cannot continue our acquaintance, but I certainly must respect your wishes.

"There is the possibility of a complication, however, now that I think about the situation at hand. Jack is still at large and apparently seeking to take over my business. He knows of your shop and that Morales shipped the goods there. He may try to get the merchandise first and, given his propensity to shenanigans, he may not wish to pay for it."

Mike thought of the Hanson couple, innocently running the shop, oblivious to any of this. It had been almost three days since Jack drove off in the old ranch pickup. Had he made it back to the States and re-grouped with Dirk and Sarge? Were they on their way to El Paso? They could even be there right now. Mike chastised himself for not thinking through the possible scenarios after Jack fled the scene. He had been too caught up in getting the injured men back to the ranch and undergoing recovery for all of them. His face must have revealed his concern and Sandra picked up on it.

"Do you think he might be there already?" she asked Reynaldo.

"It's possible, but I doubt it. He would need time to get back and organize before he barges into your shop. He'll need a truck and helpers. I guess he would round up Sarge and Dirk, if they've made it back to civilization. Anyway, I'll direct that your shop be guarded against any violence. I have people at my disposal in El Paso who can pose as shoppers and watch out for your employees. We can go into the little town of Tule, about ten miles from here, and use the phone to get things arranged."

"That would be great," Mike said, hopeful that the Hansons would be under protection sooner rather than later.

Gomez rubbed his ribs and moved gingerly in his chair, contemplating the situation further before continuing. "Of course, if he walks in and just buys the merchandise, then you have no need for concern. I shall deal with that later, on my terms," he added grimly, touching his head.

"That would be a good outcome, but I think the gash on your head is a good indication of Jack's business practices. I'm really worried about the older couple who run my shop, so I really appreciate your arranging someone to watch things until we can get there."

"Very well, let's go now," Gomez said, rising from his chair with some effort. "Agapito can get horses ready for us."

Horses? Why does it have to be horses?

"Can you ride?" Sandra asked Reynaldo.

"I may have to wear house slippers, but I can manage. Anything but that miserable buggy," he added, smiling. "Also, you can leave from there if you wish, and go directly to El Paso. I can provide a vehicle at Tule and you can be driven to Boquillas del Carmen and taken across at La Linda, a little town near Big Bend National Park. From there, you can drive to El Paso. It's better than going back to Del Rio first."

Mike knew about La Linda, the tiny mining town on the Rio Grande near Big Bend's eastern edge; he'd been there several times while visiting the park. He also knew it was indeed much closer than going all the way back to Del Rio. Crossing into the States at La Linda, it was a mere two hundred miles to Van Horn, a truck stop town on Interstate 10, then another hundred miles to El Paso. And it would be nice to have help getting back across the border if they had to pass through an *aduana* station on the way. They hadn't exactly been documented as legal visitors to Mexico when the helicopter crashed, and exiting the country to re-enter the States might prove tough without Gomez running interference.

Alberto had recovered sufficiently to venture out to the corral and help Agapito with the horses. Within minutes, they were saddled and ready to ride. Sandra hugged Henrietta and thanked her; Henrietta, confused as to why the American was thanking her (after all, it was *la gringa* who had saved two important men), smiled and wished her *buena suerte*, good luck. Likewise, Alberto was effusive in his thanks to both Mike and Sandra; it was their turn to be embarrassed by the attention.

Good-byes completed, the four mounted up and started for Tule at a brisk walk. As usual, Mike's teeth were rattled by the gait until a pleading look at Agapito prompted him to laugh and increase the pace to a smooth canter. It wasn't great, but it was better. Mike wondered how in hell Reynaldo was coping with this, given his damaged ribs, but he saw no sign of pain on his face. Either he was one tough bastard or Henrietta had done a superb job of wrapping him, he thought.

Probably both.

They reached Tule before the day's heat had fully set in and rode abreast into town. Mike thought they must look like four desperadoes looking for trouble, but the few bystanders smiled and waved at the approach of Reynaldo Gomez, who returned waves and shouted greetings to some of the older men. A couple of kids ran away, presumably to inform the rest of the townspeople of *El Patrón's* arrival. By the time they had ridden the short distance to the Pemex station, a small crowd had gathered there to greet the town's benefactor. As they dismounted, some approached timidly, shaking hands with *Señor Gomez* and directing animated conversation at him and Agapito simultaneously. The rest were enthusiastically jabbering among themselves, casting sidelong glances at the strangers, who appeared entertained by the spectacle. After a few minutes of talking, the glances turned into direct looks, then admiring stares. Agapito clearly enjoyed his role as storyteller, informing the people about the drama of the past few days. For Mike and Sandra, it was another embarrassing moment.

Meanwhile, Gomez had stepped aside to talk to two older men, and Mike noticed the grave expression on all three faces. One of the men pointed to the side of the building, and the three stepped around behind the structure, with Reynaldo limping along between the other two. He now was holding his ribs, a sight which somehow gave Mike a perverse sense of security. Seeing Gomez again evidencing human frailty, like he had exhibited after the crash, returned him to mere mortal status. His near-miraculous recovery this morning had unnerved Mike, a feeling exacerbated by his insistence on riding, bruised and broken, into Tule on a horse—just to handle this business personally. And limping or not, he still exuded an aura of one tough *hombre*, a man who had not always led a privileged and wealthy existence.

The old ranch vehicle was brought around from behind the building and filled with gasoline. Then, one of the men who had spoken quietly with Reynaldo now emerged from the station carrying two large gas cans which were placed in the bed of the pickup and filled with fuel. Another quiet conversation took place, with Reynaldo nodding soberly in response, a grim expression on his face. Apparently, the private conversation had served to inform Reynaldo of the details concerning the arrival of the big *gringo* a couple of days ago in the pickup and his departure that evening with two other *norteamericanos*. It didn't look like the news was well-received.

Gomez turned abruptly toward Mike and Sandra. "Paulo here will drive you to La Linda," he announced. "Don't worry about the appearance of this old pickup. It's quite reliable. Paulo himself sees to its maintenance, and he is an excellent mechanic as well. He will deliver you to La Linda as quickly as possible and arrange for a vehicle for you to drive on to El Paso."

"Thank you," Mike said. "We appreciate your help with this and with Jack, but I still want to get back there as soon as possible and check on the old couple. I'm not sure what I can do, but I don't pay them enough to deal with—"

"I will make some calls and arrange to handle Mr. Pearson within the next few minutes," Reynaldo interrupted. "And as soon as I have completed my preparations, I will come to your shop and buy the merchandise. Until then, I wish you the best of luck and thank you again for seeing to my safety."

He extended his hand to Mike and shook it. Then, turning to Sandra, he took her hand in both of his and thanked her profusely for staying with him after Jack's attack. "I don't remember much about that time, but I knew you were there, which meant that Mike was coming back. You are truly my angel of mercy and salvation."

"I'm glad we were able to get to the ranch and get help for all of us," she replied. "It didn't look too good for a while, though, did it?"

"No, indeed it didn't. Given this bizarre past several days, it is fortunate that we are all alive and well. At least nearly so," he amended, grimacing as he touched his ribcage.

"I don't know how you rode a horse with your injuries, Reynaldo," Mike said, laughing. "I get injuries just trying to mount up."

"Ah, my young savior, you should learn from Sandra. She is an excellent horsewoman. Perhaps she will teach you."

An awkward silence set in, finally interrupted by Gomez. "Well, I would like to talk more, but we all have our business to attend, especially the phone calls I promised I would make. So *adios*, and again, *muchas gracias*. I'll see you soon."

He turned to enter the Pemex station and Paulo reached across to open the door of the pickup for Sandra. She and Mike hopped in, slammed the door and they were off. A few of the crowd waved, and Mike and Sandra returned their salutes before Paulo turned onto the main street and pulled out of town to the south. A few miles on, the road forked, the right turn heading west, into the most desolate portion of the northern Chuhuahuan Desert, and toward the large loop in *El Rio Bravo* known as the Big Bend.

CHAPTER 25

▼

Jack left his pickup and trailer with his cohorts at a motel near El Paso's outskirts and drove Sarge's car to find Conner's Imports. The address turned up at an attractive storefront located in a former warehouse district, and he slowed almost to a stop to look at the colorful showroom windows. Cleverly arranged displays of attention-grabbing curios were grouped in room-like settings, an effective way to appeal to the wealthy clientele necessary for marketing such pricey merchandise.

But attractive merchandising wasn't the focus of Jack's attention. He knew that the store's inventory now included fifty to sixty thousand dollars' worth of Morales brand Mexican pottery. That was the face value. Hidden within compartments of many of the pieces were neatly sealed plastic bags containing high-grade cocaine worth two million dollars at the next level of distribution.

He also knew that not all of the items contained cocaine. By examining interior and exterior dimensions of a particular Morales piece, it was possible to determine if it housed a hollow compartment located, say, in the bottom of a large pot or the back side of a *chimenea*, which could hold up to ten sealed bags. But that method was not foolproof in determining if the piece actually held cocaine. Morales had included hollow pieces into production so easily that he felt it wise to distribute a few that had compartments, but no contraband. They were placed in each shipment—conveniently near the door—in case a customs inspector broke into a piece for inspection. Another clever twist to confuse the issue.

Jack had thought long and hard about the best approach to recover the Morales shipment now sitting in Conner's Imports. He had also talked a lot. Conversation during the ride back to Del Rio and down to Laredo to get Sarge's car had been dominated by Jack's plans to get his hands on the shipment. He had become so fixated with it he spoke of nothing else. Dirk and Sarge had to listen to a long list of reasons why Jack deserved the goods. After all, he declared, he was the successor to Gomez's drug business, and that "greedy-assed Meskin Robles" had prematurely shipped the merchandise to the wrong buyer. Gomez' ongoing business arrangement with the Morales Company provided for the batch to be added to his account, and Jack felt he shouldn't have to pay for the pottery again. Certainly not by paying full price, and *especially* from Conner's shop, not after all the trouble he had caused. Above all, Jack was determined that neither Mike Conner, nor his estate, would profit from this deal.

"It's high time *we* cashed in on all that money those fucking drug dealers have," he told his captive audience. "If we can grab this batch of goods, we'll be richer than four foot up a bull's ass."

And on it went, all the way back to North Texas. But not all of the talk was just "Jackbabble," as Sarge liked to call his boss' periodic tirades. By the time they reached their home base they had actually devised a plan.

Retrieving Jack's pickup and trailer, the three men left for the border city the next day. Sarge followed Jack and Dirk in his car, in case they needed alternative transportation. Just as the trio was pulling out of Graham, heading southwest toward El Paso, Paulo, Mike, and Sandra were leaving Tule, Mexico, bound for the same destination.

Despite Jack's self-serving raving and ranting, he was no fool when it came to crooked scheming. He couldn't stand to see anyone else profit from him if he could find a way around it, but beyond his natural greed and reluctance to walk in and buy the goods, his reasoning was sound. He didn't want to spend a lot of time inspecting each item for the Morales trademark, along with the dimensions, indicating only a *possibility* of bags of cocaine. And even though no one in the shop could connect him to the shop owner's girlfriend, he didn't want a security camera putting him, Sandra Payne's ex-husband, in Mike Conner's shop soon after the couple's untimely deaths in the Mexican desert—certainly not while buying a huge amount of merchandise for cash. He couldn't send Dirk and Sarge into the shop; they weren't well-versed enough to pick out the Morales brand, much less the right pieces. They might spend thousands on the wrong ones. Even if buying the goods outright went perfectly, it would still be a big price, and that meant flashing big money, cash money. He couldn't very well whip out a Visa card and sign for fifty thousand bucks worth of flower pots. That left only one viable method: Steal it.

And it needed to happen soon. Since the merchandise was surely already in stock, Jack had a recurring, horrible thought of some snotty soccer mom from San Angelo waltzing in and picking out a nice *chimenea* for her patio, unaware that she would spend cool winter evenings sipping white wine and warming her ass while baking a hundred grand worth of nose candy.

Jack drove around the block, examining utility easements, alleys, fire hydrants, and power lines, using his experience in the construction business to plan the job. He was looking for a way to cover his tracks while making the biggest heist of his life, something that would cause a lot of confusion and misdirection for investigators.

He parked well down the street and ambled back toward the store, noting the distance from the nearest side street to the front door in order to pinpoint the shop's rear door in the alley. He cautiously approached the import shop, glancing at the plate glass window this time, rather than the merchandise. No burglar bars, but the tell-tale thin metallic strip around the outside perimeter alerted him to an intrusion alarm system, at least on the showroom windows. It might also have a motion detector, but the sensors would be located at strategic points inside. And were the systems powered by a separate source? If so, cutting off power at the circuit box wouldn't disable the alarm; in some systems, a power failure would automatically set it off. He had installed many alarm systems and knew what to look for, but it would entail a closer inspection of the premises.

Jack had vowed not to be seen in the shop, but as he approached Conner's doorway, he had a sudden change of heart. He had originally planned on sending in Dirk or Sarge for what they had excitedly called a "recon mission," but after seeing the alarm system and no burglar bars, he decided to look at the inside layout himself. The absence of burglar bars alerted him that the internal alarm system might be tougher to overcome than some. This could be a little more complicated than snipping a wire or two and prying off some flimsy, decorative burglar bars.

Although he justified the risk with his perceived need to see the alarm setup, he also wanted to look for the Morales merchandise. Just a peek, he thought, a quick look. Donning sunglasses, he walked in, immediately focusing on the job at hand by evaluating the store's protection. He glanced up to see a sprinkler system routed throughout the main showroom; hanging from the exposed beams, it would cover any back storage area as well. He assumed that the open double-width doorway in the middle of a partition wall led to such an area. The wall equally divided the shop's floor space, and it occurred to him that there might be a firewall partition extending into the attic. If so, they would need to distribute flammable material throughout to ensure burning the entire place.

A chirpy voice startled him. Turning around, he had to look twice to spot a small woman who had emerged from behind a blanket display. Remembering his sunglasses, he reached to take them off, but thought better of it.

"Hi! I'm Bernie Hanson! May I help you?"

"Uh, yes ma'am, I was just looking at your, uh, stuff," Jack stammered. Recovering swiftly, he fingered the fabric of the blanket and said, "This is nice, real nice." Looking around, he continued, "I see you have a lot of clay products. Do all of them come from Mexico?"

"Almost all the pottery does," she chirped. "Now, the blankets come from Ecuador and Peru, as most of our fabric products do. And we have some paintings from Colombia, both watercolors and oils. And our hats, our Panama hats, now where else would we get them? Panama, of course!" The geography lesson was followed by an extended round of chirping laughter, sounding like an entire cage of parakeets at feeding time.

"Of course," Jack laughed. "Where else?" At least her whacky demeanor made Jack more comfortable as he moved around the store. It was difficult to imagine the daffy little woman spotting anyone casing the shop for a break-in.

He moved over to a *chimenea*, touching its surface at the lip of the chimney as though gauging its thickness, then leaned over to look inside. He couldn't see, of course, with his sunglasses on. He took them off and peered inside, but still couldn't determine if the depth was considerably less than its outside height indicated. His research was interrupted by the clerk, who had moved beside him, and he gave up, turning his attention again to the outside paintwork.

"That's a new brand we've only just started handling," came the bird voice. "It's from a company called Morales. They're reputed to be the very best."

"Oh, really?" Jack responded, trying to sound only mildly interested, while his heart rate picked up considerably at the mention of the manufacturer's name. After a moment's pause while he further examined the piece, he asked, "How long have you had this Morales stuff?"

"Just got a shipment of it two or three days ago. It's really beautiful. Highest quality all the way. Isn't it just lovely? Oh, I just think that's such a divine *chimenea*!"

"It does look nice," Jack agreed. Warming to the challenge ahead, he ventured, "Do you have a lot of the Morales stuff out here in the showroom, or is it still in the back?"

"We placed quite a bit of the shipment out front as soon as it arrived. We've already sold some nice pots, some of the bigger ones, like that one over there. Now, we do have some of the vases still in the back, but the bigger pots always attract people. Why, two ladies from Odessa came in yesterday and just went crazy over them! When they left, their Suburban was crammed full."

Jack's spirits sank. As he had suspected, the Morales line would entice buyers to snap it up. They had to get in here and grab the rest, or risk having garden club members from all over Texas and New Mexico growing ivy on top of high-grade blow instead of peat moss.

"A Suburban?" he asked, feigning amazement. "Goodness, how many pots did they buy?"

"Oh, just three, but they were quite large. The pots, I mean. Well, so were the ladies, now that I think about it! Filled up the back of their car. My husband helped them wrap quilts around each of them to make sure they didn't break on the way home. Of course, I'm still talking about the pots." Her inside jokes prompted another bombardment of laughter, chirps and tweets in equal parts.

"That's nice," Jack said weakly, still shaken by the news of three possible caches of cocaine heading for Odessa, Texas. Of course, the buyers of the three pots might easily have been rich enough to buy every pot in the place, plus pay for the cocaine—at full price. Odessa might not be known as the garden spot of Texas, but many of its residents had enough money to burn a wet mule. He was glad they hadn't been pulling a trailer.

Jack wandered off to look at the rest of the store and get a feel for the place, as well as to escape the chirping lady. Starting at one corner and working slowly around the room, he had covered nearly all the wall space without seeing where the electrical circuit breaker box was located. No conduit, no pipes, nothing that looked helpful. Finally, at the back of the showroom area, he spied a narrow door behind a rack of floor tiles. Looking around nonchalantly, he spotted the clerk on the other side of the floor talking to an older couple, waving her arms and chattering.

He gripped the door handle and opened it a crack, peeping inside. He spotted the breaker box and a junction block on the back wall with telephone wires poking from it. Another square apparatus with several sets of protruding wires was mounted on the side wall, higher up. He recognized the alarm control box as the type used with the metallic strips on the showroom glass. It was powered by a separate battery, evidenced by the glowing red light, and therefore unaffected by a power shut-off. He was relieved—so long as the glass wasn't broken, the alarm wouldn't sound.

But still no sign of a shutoff for the sprinkler system. Jack glanced out; the clerk was still with the customers. He opened the door a little wider and stuck his head in. There it was, a cut-out section in the sheetrock, behind which should be the sprinkler shutoff. Everything in one spot, nice and tidy, just the way he would have installed it. Unable to see more without flinging the door wide open and turning on a light, he shut it and continued his leisurely shopping tour.

He moved to a tall display of hand-painted tiles with street numbers embossed in bright yellows, reds, and oranges. Looking up as though viewing the top pieces, he was able to look for motion detector sensors across the ceiling. He saw none of the little dome-shaped sensors, which was good; they would have been a real problem to overcome. He wished he could go into the back storeroom, but that would be pushing his luck.

He made for the door, stopping once more to look at the *chimenea*. "How much?" he called out to the chirpy clerk.

"Three hundred, seventy-five dollars. Plus tax."

"Hmm. It's very nice, but that's more than I can pay right now. Thank you for showing me around."

He walked out, a little disappointed that he hadn't at least bought the one piece. But it was three blocks to the car, and he didn't want to carry it that far. Besides, he would get it tomorrow night. For free.

Leaving the store, Jack turned the opposite direction he'd come from and circled the block until he reached the entrance to the shop's alley access. He strode through the alley, glancing up every few yards to check out potential pitfalls to his plan. The alley was uncluttered, and he couldn't see any sign of outdoor security cameras mounted on the rear walls or roofs of the buildings.

As he passed the mid-point of the block, he began gauging the distance to the street, comparing it with the position of Conner's front door. When he reached the third overhead door from the west end, the distance looked about right. This has to be it, he thought, eyeing the twelve-foot roll-up freight door.

The lock mechanism was a standard design, easily disassembled from outside by drilling out the two round mounting bolt heads. By doing so, it was possible to release the lock, allowing the bar shafts to spring out of their lock holes. After unlocking the door, insert two new bolts and re-assemble the lock mechanism to re-lock the door from the outside when the job was done. Sweep up the drill shavings and old bolts. In and out without a key and no visible break-in.

He proceeded to the end of the alley and turned to follow the electric line to the back of the import shop. He had seen the city's electricity supplier's breaker box and meter mounted to the right of the freight door; the padlock securing the handle in the "on" position would be no problem for bolt cutters. Once the power was turned off, they could enter the store and replace some wiring with a sub-standard gauge that would heat up without tripping the inside circuit breakers. To guarantee that a fire started soon, they could strip the insulation from the wire that contacted something flammable, like cardboard or packing material. With flimsy, bare wire, the tampered circuits would quickly overheat and ignite the fuel material and some wall paneling, maybe inside the closet containing the water heater or air conditioner unit.

When they had finished loading the merchandise and were ready to leave, Jack would turn on the juice again and install a padlock identical to the one now in use. He thought it would be a final classy touch to have Sarge re-key the replacement lock to match the original—it took about three minutes and could be done sitting in the car with a flashlight tucked under his arm. That part wasn't really a big deal; but the firemen might have the correct key in order to shut off power to a burning building, so he wanted everything to look normal, just in case.

An investigation would be started as soon as the fire trucks pulled out. Before the ashes had cooled, a sharp investigator would find the cause of the fire. It would likely be written up as an electrical overload caused by sub-standard wiring or a malfunction of the circuit breaker box. Then the contractor who wired the building would be blamed, followed by the inspector who signed off on the job, or possibly the breaker box manufacturer.

Actually, the cause of the fire was of little importance, even if arson were proven. Hell, we could pour five gallons of gasoline around and torch it, Jack thought. An investigation would reveal that in about two minutes. But it would be a lot cleaner if the investigation of the fire pointed to a simple case of negligence by disinterested third parties like the electrician or inspector. While arson usually involved the owner and indicated insurance fraud, Jack wasn't interested in that angle—not that he cared about Mike Conner's reputation. In fact, with Conner missing, a fire in his shop would be another piece of the mystery. It might begin to look like a life insurance scam, especially if someone didn't soon find the bodies in the desert. And if his body *was* discovered, the policy beneficiary would be the likely suspect. All those possibilities were interesting, but Jack wanted the fire to cover the break-in.

He had given a lot of thought to the best method for a cover-up. He'd first considered breaking into the clay items while inside the store and removing the cocaine, then using an explosion to destroy the interior of the store. That would obliterate the broken Morales pieces, and he wouldn't have to haul the pots back to Graham. It would eliminate the risk of some curious cop inquiring of the clerks exactly what was missing, even before the insurance investigators did. However, that method was far too time-consuming; a destructive cover-up was the best way.

Without a cover-up, the clerks would immediately see that only the Morales goods were missing. Flower pots not being high on the list for burglars, investigators would surely suspect that something else was involved, and an inquiry into the Morales line might be launched. Not only would the hollow-compartment scam be endangered, every cop in Texas and New Mexico would be alerted to check for trucks and trailers with pottery.

Everything pointed to the need for a cover-up, a diversion from the burglary. An explosion would be dramatic, but harder to make and control. Ultimately, Jack figured a good hot fire going through these old wooden warehouses, followed by firemen wielding gushing water hoses and pickaxes, would effectively prevent an accurate inventory count of the store. Ideally, no one would suspect anything was missing. Besides, Jack really wanted to burn Conner's Imports.

As he drove back to the motel, he thought about the things they needed to do the job. Most were already in his pickup toolbox—everyday items and materials that a skilled builder could easily put to good use. He would only need to pick up a padlock like the one on the exterior box and have Sarge get it ready to be re-keyed. He'd noticed that the alley was clear of the usual stacks of pallets and cardboard boxes full of packing paper, and barring a recent trash pickup, there was certain to be plenty of flammable material inside that could be placed around the wires to ensure that the fire took off quickly.

By the time he arrived at the motel, he was satisfied with his mental checklist. He had been successful in the building business due to his skill and attention to detail. He had always made sure he had the right tools, the right materials, the correct permits and licenses. He knew the building business, inside and out. Whatever his shortcomings in the morals department, the tasks looming tomorrow night would present no problem for Jack Pearson and his crew.

CHAPTER 26

▼

The road out of Tule was paved, sort of, and Paulo pushed the old pickup up to fifty miles an hour. As the miles slid by, the countryside became even more barren. This area was dry most of the time, and the terrain showed it. The soil was rocky, and there was little evidence of weathering from water flow, such as the gullies and washes that were numerous to the east. Before long, the Sierra Del Carmen mountain range appeared on the horizon, marking the edge of the ranges that run the length of the continent. The Sierra range borders Texas, towering nine thousand feet or more over the Rio Grande where it flows out of Big Bend National Park, providing relief from the flat, featureless desert floor.

Paulo spoke a little English, and as he drove, he told them stories about life in Tule. Apparently, he didn't know the whole story of how they had become acquainted with Reynaldo Gomez; he seemed to think they had been friends of his for some time. He proudly related how *Señor Gomez* was the highly respected *patrón* of the area. No direct mention was made of what *Señor Gomez* did for a living, but it was clear that the locals thought him a kind, benevolent man.

Mike and Sandra exchanged glances, but said nothing, wondering what his admirers would think if they knew he was a distributor of illegal drugs on a massive scale. Or, how heroic would he look directing his helicopter pilot to swoop in on two innocent people while a professional killer shot at them with a high-powered rifle? Hell, probably no different than they do now, Mike thought. He provided essentials for them, and that was really all that mattered.

He had long thought that Americans were foolish in their notion that foreign countries like Mexico and Colombia were responsible for the proliferation of drug usage in the U. S. They were even more foolish to think that the citizens of those countries, even the authorities, were interested in doing much about it. It was easy for Americans—well-employed, well-fed, well-entertained—to worry about such idealistic matters. Americans could afford to spend time thinking about social problems and their long-term impact.

In poor countries, the only period of time worth worrying about was between now and the next meal. And if that next meal meant suckering a few more Americans into a dangerous and expensive habit to make them feel good, that would be arranged, right or wrong. Sure, a little violence might occur. As Gomez had needlessly reminded them, his was indeed a violent business. Perhaps it was this, the final stage of the adventure—now being escorted home by Gomez's man, unhurt, with Sandra sitting safely beside him, assurance that his vehicle would be repaired and returned—that had cooled Mike's anger toward the crime boss. He had been enraged while it was going on, but he was no longer angry at Reynaldo Gomez; he just wanted never to see him again.

But, he thought, Sandra's jackass ex-husband is another story, and his two flunkies are classic jerks...no sleep will be lost worrying over those three. All of them are about to get paid back for their part in terrorizing us. Gomez will deal with them; he surely has a reason to now. And if they all kill each other in the process, so much the better.

As to Gomez's chosen field of endeavor, Mike had never held strong feelings about the illegal drug business or those who were involved in any part of it: users, suppliers, or carriers. He hadn't used anything stronger than Coors himself, but his friends in the military, and afterwards, in the oilfields, used illegal drugs. Some users were purely recreational (or so they said). Others couldn't seem to carry on without the crutch of the next high. They became addicted, and their lives were eventually ruined, either medically, psychologically, or legally. Among users he had encountered, there seemed to be no middle ground. In any event, Mike Conner refused to believe that it affected him, so long as he steered clear of them and their habit.

Sandra seemed to share his outlook. It wasn't a topic they'd discussed, so it had surprised him when she boldly confronted Gomez after the helicopter crash, telling him that, while she opposed illegal drugs, she didn't care what business he was in, so long as it precluded her and Mike. Clearly, she was wise enough to recognize the problem lies with the individuals who use drugs, not the trade itself. Without willing—even desperate—users, there would be no trade.

Her outspoken attitude went one step further: nothing she or anyone else did to stop one shipment was going to make a difference. Living in El Paso, she could see the poverty right across the river, two hundred yards away from the richest nation on earth. She witnessed it enough to know what Mike had determined long ago—the drug trade was too profitable to go away. Despite the combined efforts of the Border Patrol, Highway Patrol, Sheriff's Patrol, Rat Patrol, the DEA, INS, IRS, FBI and all the other letters in the alphabet, it was here to stay. It was astounding that a lot of people, *smart* people, just didn't get it. They were apparently too far removed from reality, too naïve to see the hard facts. Sandra did, and her practical viewpoint was just one more thing Mike admired about her.

His thoughts carried him all the way to La Linda, and Sandra dozed on his shoulder until they pulled into the little settlement late that afternoon. After some honking and socializing by Paulo, he parked the old pickup and walked with them across the bridge, unlocking the official-looking gate with an ominously-worded sign atop it with a key from his pocket.

So much for border security provided by Homeland Security!

Paulo led them directly to a 1976 Ford Galaxie; not exactly what Mike would have chosen to set out for El Paso, but he figured it had as good a chance as any. All his adult life, he had seen cars running around in Mexico that looked as though they couldn't possibly even start. Recalling the just-completed trip in the ancient pickup, he quit worrying. That old Ford will probably be running after I've stopped, he thought.

Paulo must have noticed his apprehension though, because he laughed as he retrieved the keys from under the floor mat. "*Señor* Mike, I know this old *coche* doesn't look like much, but it has current license plates and runs very well. It is reliable and will get you to El Paso, *no problema*."

"Thanks, Paulo, I'm sure it will. And we're really grateful for it and the ride here. We thank you, and please thank Mr. Gomez again."

"He will see that your car is delivered to you. He may have me bring it to you after it is repaired. I can pick this one up at that time. If so, I hope I will see you again."

Mike couldn't help but notice a marked improvement in Paulo's English here late in the visit. Paulo was aware of the repairs to be made to the Land Cruiser, so he obviously knew a lot more than he had let on during the trip. During the drive, his contribution to conversation had been carried on with adequate, but limited, heavily accented English and Mike and Sandra's sparse Spanish. Maybe that was by design, Mike thought.

Pretty slick. Sends us off in the care of a poor peasant with sombrero in hand, limited communication ability with Americans, happy to be delivery boy of the famous gringos. Now he sounds like a boardroom executive.

Oh, well, no matter, Mike thought, dismissing the change as a mere curiosity. He had never intended to delve into the machinations of the drug business and its hierarchy of workers, anyway. Right now, he just wanted to get back to El Paso and check on the Hansons and his store. Hopefully, Gomez or Paulo would show up soon with his vehicle, buy the Morales merchandise, and this mess would be over. And while he would never voice it to Sandra, his earlier thoughts about Gomez dealing with Jack Pearson and his helpers in a very permanent manner would be a bonus.

They climbed into the old Ford, cranked up and pulled out to Ranch Road 2627 leading to the northern boundary of the national park, and on to the small town of Marathon, a hundred miles away. From there, they would pick up U. S. Highway 90 west to IH-10 and El Paso. Mike settled in for the drive, feeling safer and more content than he had in several days. It had been an action-packed trip, more so than either of them could ever have envisioned. It would be nice to get back to regular hot showers and a soft bed. It would even be nice to go back to work.

Two hours later, Mike wheeled into the Chevron in Marathon, where he topped off the Galaxie with gasoline and called the shop. Ralph Hanson answered on the first ring, indicating he wasn't very busy.

"Conner's Imports."

"Hey, Ralph, what's going on?"

"Mike! Hey, I was getting worried about you. You okay?"

"Yeah, Ralph, I'm fine. Just had a little car trouble and some other stuff happened, so I haven't had a chance to call. In fact, I was out of phone service completely for the last four days. Is everything okay there?" he asked, trying to keep his tone casual.

"Sure, everything's fine here! Not real busy, but steady enough for this time of

year. Oh, we got that new stuff in. It came in on some independent trucking firm out of Laredo, about three days after you left."

"Really? The guy I dealt with was the warehouse manager, a guy named Robles. He didn't waste any time shipping it, did he?" Mike shook his head, recalling how the Mexican's surprising efficiency in closing the sale had nearly cost him and Sandra their lives. *"I actually didn't intend for him to do it that quickly."*

"Well, it sure is fine-looking stuff. We've already sold some."

"Oh, yeah? That's great!" Mike said, trying to sound enthusiastic, although he was experiencing a vague sense of discomfort, almost dread, at the mere mention of the tainted shipment. Who were the buyers? he wondered. And what would they think if they accidentally broke a vase and cocaine spilled out? What would be his legal standing in such a case? He wished he could tell Gomez so he'd come get the rest immediately. Reynaldo Gomez surely didn't want the shipment of cocaine-stuffed pots sold to little old ladies for growing flowers. But Mike couldn't instruct Ralph not to sell the merchandise without doing some explaining, which he was not prepared to do right now.

"Yeah, we sold a few of the big pots to some ladies from Odessa. I used that price list that came with the packing invoice. Boy, that stuff is expensive! You'd think it was filled with gold!"

"Who knows, Ralph? Maybe those special ingredients Morales uses are really special!"

The two talked on for a minute, touching on various aspects of the business. Mike ended by cautioning him to "keep a close eye on things around there," and telling him he'd be back sometime tomorrow.

When Mike hung up, he was relieved and worried at the same time—everything was okay at the shop, but the Morales stuff was being sold off. Surely Gomez wanted to get his shipment, so he would get someone up there within the next day or so. So might Jack, he thought, and that worried him even more.

He got in the old Ford and pulled onto U. S Highway 90, the same road they had fled on foot after running over the hog, albeit a couple hundred miles farther west. This time they were heading back to El Paso by themselves. Hopefully, no unwanted parties would be there to greet them. Mike thought briefly of calling the police, but the same problem of potentially having to explain why he had a load of cocaine in his pottery inventory cropped up.

Sandra must have been having the same worries. "Don't you think we could just tell the police that the Morales stuff is very expensive and might represent a high theft risk?" she asked.

"Possibly, but I don't want to alert them to anything odd about this merchandise. I'd probably have to tell them something about why I anticipated someone grabbing my goods. How often does someone ask for increased patrols for their flower pots?"

"I guess you're right. I wish Gomez would come get that stuff and we'd never hear of it again."

"I'm counting on that. I also want him to deal with Jack and his buddies, on their own turf and on their own terms. I don't like them or their lifestyle."

Sandra got quiet after that, and he wondered if she were contemplating Jack's fate. Mike couldn't suppress his jealousy of her ex-husband, but he said nothing more. She has to know it won't go well for old Jack, he thought, recalling the look on Reynaldo's face when Sandra had let loose her remarks concerning his wife and Jack. As a man, Mike better understood the effect of those words, and he wouldn't want to be in Jack's shoes.

CHAPTER 27

▼

At that moment, Jack's shoes (boots, actually) were off, and he was comfortably propped up in bed watching TV. Dirk and Sarge were sprawled across the other bed, Dirk's feet on a chair and Sarge's on the nightstand.

Jack hit the "mute" button on the remote and turned to his companions. "I know we've been over this a dozen times already and we've got what we need, but let's go over the main points again to see if I've missed anything. I worked out the timing, and we'll just have to stick to the schedule without a practice run. I don't want to go back down there to walk through it, 'cause we're gonna be there again at two o'clock the next morning. Can't spend too much time in that area, somebody might remember us. As much as we've worked together, I know how long it takes to do this stuff without being in too big a hurry. All the same, don't fuck around."

"You know we wouldn't do that, Jack," Dirk said solemnly.

Jack ignored the promise and launched into his instructions again. "At two o'clock straight up, y'all drive through the alley, east to west. Dirk hops out and cuts the lock off the breaker box. Throw the switch and get the hell out of there. Go to the coffee shop we saw down the street and park out front, not too close to the door. Re-key that new lock with the guts out of the old one, then go into the coffee shop, get something to drink. Keep an eye on the shop and see if anyone shows up. Cutting off the power might cause an independent power source to kick in and automatically set off an alarm that I missed when I was in there."

"Say somebody shows up and goes inside the shop. What happens then?" Sarge asked. "We won't have a chance to get the stuff."

"If that happens, security guards or cops will be all over the place and we're shit out of luck. Call me immediately, I don't want to drive into the alley with fifteen cops standing there. I checked around the neighborhood, and there's not another all-night eating place for blocks, so the cops on that beat will probably be in the same coffee shop at that time of the morning."

"How we gonna know if the alarm is silent?" Dirk asked, surprising Jack with the pertinent inquiry.

"You'll know if the cops get a call on the alarm. If they get up and leave any doughnuts, they just got a 'code one,' or whatever the hell a priority call is. Call me the second they hit the coffee shop door. But if there're no cops in the place, just watch the shop until two-twenty, then drop Sarge at the west entrance to the alley to do his thing."

"I'll drill the bolts on the roll-up door lock. It'll take about three minutes," Sarge interjected.

"Right, gotta get that done pronto, so make sure you have that cobalt drill bit and the drill battery is fully charged. Again, if no cops in the coffee place and no action at the import shop by two-twenty, we move on it. I'll pull the trailer through the alley from east to west at two-thirty sharp. Use the extra time to have the door open a few inches and the lock re-assembled.

"Dirk, you *back* the car into the alley from the east end. If anybody shows, we hop in the vehicle that *isn't* blocked and haul ass. The vehicle we leave behind will block them from pulling through and coming after us for a minute or two. They'll have to back out of the alley, giving us time to turn a few corners and lose them. We'll have to report the vehicle left behind as stolen, but that won't cause us a problem. Understand?"

Both men nodded, and he continued. "When we open the door, we need to move fast. Dirk, you have the wire and shit ready and get on it. I'll start picking out stuff for Sarge to load. You should have the wiring job done in fifteen to twenty minutes. There will be some packing material or cardboard in there to place around the bare wires. There should be plenty of it in the shop, 'cause that shipment just came in and there's none in the dumpster or anywhere out back.

"We'll get all the Morales stuff from the back end of the store first. I don't want to shine the light around too much up front with those showroom windows facing the street. I only saw five or six pieces in the front showroom area yesterday, so we'll wait until last to get them. Anybody got any questions?"

"It'll take you longer to pull the trailer around the block and hit that street that leads to the freeway," Sarge said. "You want me to wait until I see you go by before I pull out of the alley?"

"No, just pull on out and watch for me in your mirror. Drive slow, and if you don't see me within about six blocks, turn left and go around. You'll be behind me for sure, then. If anything's gone to shit, we'll be on foot so you can pick us up. All we can do then is try to make the border."

No one spoke for a moment. Jack idly pushed the "volume" on the remote, and Dirk immediately returned his attention to the TV. Jack frowned and angrily punched "off," lest his underlings become too interested in the program. Dirk turned to face him, a hurt expression on his face.

"Dammit, you guys need to think this over!" he snapped. "We can't fuck up tonight, or our asses will be cooling it in Huntsville for the next twenty years."

"We got it down, Jack, we really do," Dirk whined.

"Yeah, we know what to do," Sarge quipped. "This ain't like chasing those fuckers across the prairie. This stuff we can do better than anybody."

That was true, Jack thought, calming down quickly. They might not be the brightest at everything, but when it came to performing hands-on construction work, Dirk and Sarge were plenty good and fast. On balance, he preferred to have it that way. If he had helpers with too much imagination, they might be tempted to alter the plan when something changed or went wrong. Excessive imagination would not be a problem with Dirk or Sarge.

CHAPTER 28

▼

Mike and Sandra pulled out of the motel parking lot in Marfa and turned left on Highway 90, to the west. They'd been tired the night before, too tired to continue on. By spending the night in Marfa, they could easily make the two hundred or so miles into El Paso in time for a late lunch. Afterwards, Mike planned to go to the shop for a while, and Sandra wanted to stay at the apartment and get ready for going back to work early next week. It was her last vacation day before the weekend, and she needed to catch up on all the things she had planned to do before getting side-tracked. She reminded Mike (with the familiar poke to his ribs) that she hadn't been shopping a single time while on vacation, a record for her.

Some vacation, she thought…but it certainly hadn't been boring. In the past few days, she and Mike had experienced and endured more than some people do in a lifetime. And not only the physical part, she recalled, reflecting on Mike's reaction to meeting her ex-husband, her recent social connection with him, and her disclosing to him about Mike buying from Morales…not to mention the resulting ordeal, which could have been their last. Although Mike hadn't said anything else about it since his tirade while being pursued by Dirk and Sarge, she sensed that it still nagged at him.

And a new concern about their relationship had developed. Not since this drama had begun at the Laredo airport had they made love. Was that the reason? Not that there had been much time or opportunity, at least until last night in Marfa. But he had kissed her goodnight and fallen asleep immediately. Obviously, he was tired, and so was she. Plus, she knew he was worried about the illegal merchandise sitting in his shop. She told herself that things would be a lot better when the stuff was gone from their lives forever, but she worried that her duplicity had caused a permanent rift in their relationship.

As a test, she tried to view the situation fairly by reversing their roles in the drama. She speculated about Mike revealing to her that he had recently met with his ex-wife at a party and had been introduced to all the details of her illegal criminal enterprise. What would *her* reaction be?

She couldn't deny that she would have felt betrayed, angry, and hurt— and she would have shown it a lot more than Mike had. After her tearful explanation to a visibly angry Mike on that eventful night, he hadn't mentioned it again. He'd simply concentrated on getting them out of danger, a tactic that had saved their lives.

Besides being a lot more emotional if the situation had been reversed, Sandra knew she would have been more frightened by the possible consequences of dealing with dangerous people, especially if she had viewed them as Mike had, as a bunch of violent thugs. But until the last few days, she hadn't been able to see Jack Pearson and his two buddies as outright killers. Abusive, yes. Dangerous, maybe. But not murderers. Some of the others in that realm, she could envision as killers. They really scared her, but that was another…secret.

In the beginning of the kidnapping episode, she wasn't really afraid, just angry, both at Dirk and Sarge as well as herself for not telling Mike about this mess earlier. Because of her failure and the resulting anger, she had missed the fear in Mike's face and voice early in the ordeal. Mike's only knowledge of kidnappings was from news stories, mostly accurate, that supported the fact that most kidnappings, whatever the motive, ended in murder. And later, when he learned about the hidden cocaine, his fear probably multiplied, given the well-publicized lengths that drug dealers go to in order to protect their profits.

That's how it almost worked out, both of them in real danger of losing their lives for the last several days. Sandra concluded her silent analysis by resolving to make amends for the mess she had caused. She'd do whatever was necessary to regain Mike's trust and affection. She even considered bringing it up now, while two hundred miles of highway stretched before them, but decided to wait. Mike would probably be more receptive to her promises when the legal danger of contraband in his shop and dealing with Reynaldo Gomez one more time were both past.

They arrived at the apartment parking lot a little after one and emerged stiffly from the old Ford. Mike went straight to the manager's office to inform them his parking place would be occupied by the Galaxie for at least a few days. Sandra went inside and immediately took a long, hot shower, something she'd craved for days. She was toweling her hair when Mike walked into the bedroom, stripping off his borrowed shirt. The hot shower idea had hit him too, along with a need to shave and wear some clean clothes that actually fit him for a change.

"I told the office manager that I had a different car now, and it would be in my space for a few days," he said. "She gave me a temporary permit so it wouldn't get towed."

"Did she ask where you got such a dream car?" Sandra asked from the closet.

"Yep. I told her it was my new girlfriend's car, and that you were leaving. I told her I traded girlfriends and cars at the same time and got money to boot on both, a great deal."

A thrown shoe from the closet was her response.

"Aw, come on now, you pretty thing! I promised the office gal there wouldn't be nearly so much ruckus from this apartment now, because you're a lot nicer than that mean ol' Sandra I used to have!"

The second shoe followed the first, then a giggle when it found its mark.

"Ouch! Guess I lied to the office manager. This new girlfriend's even meaner than the last one. But at least I finally got a good car, dents and all."

"I don't know about the car, but I'll show you all about your new girlfriend if you'll take a shower."

Mike quickly complied. When he came out of the bathroom, her hair was almost dry. The towel, having done its job, lay across the chair, while she lay across the bed without a stitch of clothes. He dropped his own towel on the floor and stared. "Wow! I really like this new girlfriend. Now what were you going to show me?"

During the next hour, Sandra implemented the first phase of her plan to recapture Mike's full attention. It worked pretty well, because her concerns about that facet of their relationship faded away like last year's suntan.

Two hours later, Mike strolled into Conner's Imports and admired the showroom displays as he headed toward the office area in the back. The stuff looked great, artsy-craftsy little pyramids erected here and there, everything color-coordinated. Plenty of stuff, but not too crowded. Ralph and Bernie

Hanson did a fine job arranging the displays and ran the store day-to-day, while Mike handled the business end of things. It worked well for all parties.

Several hors d'oeuvre trays were positioned strategically near the priciest goods—that had been Bernie's idea. Mike scarfed a couple of jalepeño cheese balls and smiled to himself as he chewed the snacks and contemplated his customer base. Pretentious, self-important—moneyed, to be sure—yet always trying to show more affluence than they really had. He knew it was a good thing he had the Hansons to run things. Without Ralph and Bernie to handle the snooty customers, Mike would have soon been selling velvet paintings to college kids for their dorm rooms, or huge sombreros to drunken accountants from Cleveland.

"Oh, hi Mike!" Bernie Hanson squealed.

"Hi, Mrs. Hanson. Good to see you. How's everything going?"

"Oh, my! Fine, just fine. Ralph's in the back, building a rack for some new Peruvian blankets. I thought we'd fold them into the shape of condor wings and have them suspended between a rack shaped like the body of that *magnificent* bird and the ceiling. You know, like spread wings, when the bird is soaring. And for the tail, I thought maybe the hand-made flags from Ecuador might look nice."

"I'm sure it would, Mrs. Hanson. Does Ralph have all the materials he needs to build what you want?"

"I think so. He hasn't said a word to me all day, he's been working away back there, so I suppose he has everything he needs"

He's got peace and quiet back there. That's what he needs.

Shelving his private thoughts, he said, "I'll check on him. I can go get him something if he needs it."

Grinning to himself, he sauntered to the back area where Ralph was measuring pieces of pine trim molding laid out on the floor. "So that's what a condor looks like, huh, Ralph?"

"Yep." Ralph stood up slowly, flexing his legs after being in a stooped position too long. "At least it will when I'm finished. What do you think about it?"

"Ralph, I think condors are *magnificent* birds. And you and Bernie have never been wrong when it comes to displays. So I have no problem with your building condors or pterodactyls, or buzzards, for that matter, if Bernie thinks it looks good. You need anything here?"

"Nope, got plenty of wood from those packing crates. I can fashion at least two condors from what I have. Maybe that'll be enough for Bernie. She's set on making the wings out of those new blankets and hanging the ends from the ceiling."

"That'll be real eye-catching. You fix it up right for Bernie, okay?"

"Sure. Hey, check out that new stuff from Morales. All those pieces lined up by the office are part of the shipment. I put some more out on the floor this morning. The big pots and *chimeneas* are over by the packing area."

Mike walked back to a corner of the storage area used for preparing large orders to be shipped out on freight company trucks. Several of the big portable fireplaces were lined up there, gleaming under the warehouse lights. The paintwork was excellent, beautiful pinks, reds, and greens forming rosebushes on one piece, rich browns and tans depicting a desert scene on another beside it.

He tilted the rosebush one toward him and peered into the bottom. It appeared to be of normal thickness. He reached for the desert scene job and carefully hefted both of them; the weights seemed the same. Tilting the desert scene one toward him, he compared the floors of the two. On this one, the floor was noticeably shallower, but the overall height was the same for both items. So this one either had a floor about five inches thick or a hollow compartment between the floor and the interior bottom. He knew which it was and involuntarily shrank back from it. For an instant, he even considered wiping his fingerprints from the surface, but discounted the thought as silly.

Come on, Mike. Get real.

Checking the rest, he found five that had the false floors. Due to the overall size and diameter of the *chimeneas*, a compartment of that size could easily hold eight or ten sandwich baggy-style pouches. Or so he thought. He could only guess at what the packages of contraband looked like based on watching *Miami Vice* re-runs.

Hell, it could be packaged in goat bladders or Prince Albert Tobacco tins for all I know!

Grinning to himself and whistling *Smuggler's Blues*, he ambled out onto the showroom floor and looked at the Morales pieces there. He found four more that clearly had room for the hollow storage space. As he picked up another one, a voice behind him interrupted his thoughts.

"Those are very pretty. I haven't seen them before. Did you just get them?"

He turned to see a gorgeous Hispanic woman, about his age, with huge brown eyes and pouty lips. Beautiful dark brown skin, with just the tiniest trace of eye makeup. Fingernails of medium length, perfectly matched with the lip color, of course. It was impossible for Mike to ignore her well-proportioned figure, though she was bigger than what he was normally attracted to.

His eyes automatically dropped to her breasts, which were pushing against some kind of silky material, threatening to escape. He felt like Lot's wife trying to resist looking toward Sodom…or was it Gomorrah? Like that poor foolish woman, he failed to avert his eyes. *Unlike* her, sinful Mike Conner didn't even *try* not to look. Instead, his thoughts ran to Dragline in *Cool Hand Luke*, watching the girl wash the car and pleading with the Lord not to strike him blind, at least not at the moment.

"Did you just get those?" she repeated, a quizzical smile on those gorgeous lips.

"Uh, yes, we did, as a matter of fact," he answered trying to recover his composure. "It's a new line for us. The Morales Company, out of Monterrey makes this line. Pretty, huh?" He held out the flower pot, one with a rosebush design much like the *chimenea* he had just examined in the back.

She took it from him with a smile. Red fingernails played over the intricate paintwork, gently tracing the pattern, the movement of her fingers over the piece almost sensual. She could have been the artist with the brush, tracing the pattern. "It's beautiful. I have a rose bush that looks very much like this, so it will be a clever addition to that area of my patio, near the bush itself, don't you think?" Without waiting for a response, she added, "And these colors will harmonize perfectly with my other things. I'll take it."

"An excellent choice. May I wrap it for you?" he asked, returning her gaze and forcing himself to concentrate on her eyes, rather than her chest.

"Yes, please do. I have quite a long trip, and I wouldn't want to get home and find it broken."

Mike walked to the back to the packing area and found a suitable box to hold the pot, plus a substantial amount of packing material to cushion it. As he placed the pot in the box, he saw that it had the disproportionate measurements indicative of a hollow compartment piece. He briefly considered damaging the piece and pointing it out to her in an attempt to switch her to another pot, but abandoned the idea as too risky. She had looked at it pretty closely and she had like this particular design. To hell with it, he thought, I'm going to make a sale. Reynaldo had better get here and take the rest of this stuff before it sells.

He completed the boxing job and carried it out front. By now, Ms. Gorgeous was looking at other items, so Mike set the box on the counter near the register and ventured in her general direction, discretely keeping his distance so as to be there if needed, but not so close as to crowd. She browsed for a few more minutes, then strolled to the register, pulling out her wallet as she walked.

"Anything else, Ms....?"

"Please call me Eva."

She extended her hand and Mike took it. He resisted the urge to kiss it and firmly shook it instead. "Mike Conner," he said quickly, before he forgot what his name was.

"It's a pleasure to meet you, Mike Conner. So, you are the proprietor of Conner's Imports?"

"I am indeed. And the pleasure of this meeting is all mine, I assure you."

"I always enjoy having the owner himself take care of my needs. This is the way I prefer to do business, so perhaps I'll come again." She paid cash for the pot and pocketed her change. As she lifted the box and turned to leave, she said, "My, but this is heavy! Could you carry it to my car?"

"Certainly." He took the box from her and gestured for her to precede him.

"I'm right here in front," she said, holding the door open and pointing to a new Jaguar at the curb.

I would have known that was her car. Looks just like her.

She opened the passenger door and he deposited the box on the floorboard, then straightened from the task and turned to face her.

"Thank you so much," she said, smiling.

"You are quite welcome. And do come again."

Mike turned away—reluctantly—and re-entered the store. As luck would have it, Ralph was strolling by the front entrance, condor wings trailing in his wake. His sly grin told Mike he'd checked out Ms. Gorgeous too. "Boy, she was a looker, huh? Was that her new Jaguar out front?"

"Sure. What else would she drive?"

"Drive me crazy, that's what. Well, back in my younger days, that is."

Mike laughed and headed back to go over sales records and checkbook entries made during his absence, leaving Ralph to condor construction. He met Bernie on the way, looking for Ralph, of course. He pointed in the general direction of the condor's flight and ducked into his bookwork.

Business looked fairly good, even for this time of year. He had built a good cushion of operating cash, and the regular deposits of sales proceeds were mounting up nicely. His profit margins were adequate if not stupendous, and he watched expenditures closely. *Now, if I could just get rid of that tainted Morales crap,* he thought, *things would be great.*

After first being dismayed that the pretty woman had chosen a pot with a hollow compartment, Mike had thought of a way to reduce sales of Reynaldo's nose candy containers (for flower pot prices), at least for a couple of days. Hopefully, the crime boss would have it picked up by then. He considered coming back to the shop tonight to work on his plan, but right now, he had other things on his mind. He bade Ralph and Bernie good-bye and started for home, stopping off for a bottle of wine on the way.

Hours later, they lay watching television, Sandra sprawled across Mike's chest, sipping on the wine. "Let's go out for a late supper," he suggested.

"Okay. You shower first and get the water warm. If you're a good boy, I'll join you."

"Deal. But first I've got to take a little nap."

"*Nap?* You slept through the crocodile show and half of that other crap. You're still sleepy? Did this afternoon wear you out?" she asked with a mischievous grin.

"I think so. I'm not as young as I once was, you know. You know what they say about younger women."

"No, what?"

"Oh, I don't know, I was hoping you knew."

"Go take a shower. And where are we going to eat at this time of night?"

"I dunno. What do you want?"

"Food. I'm starving. It must be one of those younger women things, I've burned a lot of calories this afternoon."

Mike laughed at that. "Me too. How about that all-night diner dive down by the shop. We never go there."

"Okay, so we can get a good, healthy, make-mine-a-triple-meat cheeseburger with extra grease? That's why we never go there, Mike."

"Right, I knew that. But we're going there tonight. Afterwards, I want to go over to the shop and move some of those Morales pots around so they won't all get sold before they're picked up."

"Tonight?"

"Yeah, I'd rather do it when Bernie's not there to quiz me about what I'm doing. By the time I have to explain anything, maybe it'll all be gone anyway."

"Maybe Gomez will show up tomorrow or Saturday."

At the mention of Reynaldo's name, a fleeting thought crossed Mike's mind about the handsome drug trafficker, but he didn't concentrate on it. He was thinking about where to place the Morales pieces to get the least possible customer exposure and what to tell Bernie when she asked what he had done.

CHAPTER 29

▼

Jack turned the corner and headed north on the side street just east of Conner's Imports. He glanced at the dashboard clock. Two-thirty sharp. He swung wide, allowing for the trailer and turned into the alley. Idling along under the dim streetlights, he barely noticed Sarge, who stood in the shadows by the door, almost hidden from view. Jack inched forward until the rear of the trailer was even with the door, then jumped out, looking in both directions for any sign of activity. A car passed the east alley entrance and stopped, its backup lights coming on as it reversed and backed into the alley. He watched long enough to make sure it was Sarge's Ford Taurus. Dirk backed in close to the trailer and got out.

"Already drilled and ready to raise it, Chief," Sarge whispered.

"Okay, just enough to put the new bolts in. Get that part finished, in case an alarm goes off and we need to haul ass in the next few minutes."

Sarge grasped the bottom grip handle and pulled the door up even with his waist with one steady pull. Jack held his breath, hoping his two numb-skull helpers had remembered their assigned tasks. He needn't have worried.

Inside, the shop was completely dark. As instructed, Dirk had already cut the lock and switched off the breaker, and Sarge had re-keyed the new one and hung it on the box, ready to be re-locked when they left. Jack began to gain confidence; his men had done well, and the plan was off to a good start.

The men listened intently for a few seconds, but no sound came. Sarge quickly put the cover plate in place and inserted the new bolts while Dirk tightened the backing nuts. Then he raised the door to the full open position while Jack grabbed the broom and swept away the filings from the drill operation. He pocketed the two old bolts that had fallen inside the door and shined his flashlight around for any other evidence of the drilling job, but saw nothing.

Jack motioned for Sarge and Dirk to stay put while he stepped into the storage area, where he immediately spotted several pieces of Morales goods. Five big *chimeneas* and two sun face sculptures were lined up against an interior wall to his right, and he moved to inspect them. Four of the *chimeneas* and both sun faces had the suspect inside dimensions, and he motioned for Sarge to start loading them while he and Dirk prepared to alter the wiring and water systems.

All the planning and discussion of the past few days came into play, and the three went to work. Sarge hefted two of the big *chimeneas* and headed for the trailer in a trot. Dirk already had the wire and some tools, and he quickly moved into the shop to look for the hot water heater and air conditioner. He and Jack had agreed it would be better to install faulty wiring in a couple of areas, just to be sure. Both of those systems drew a lot of current when operating, making them good spots to place weaker wiring. A couple of quick adjustments just before leaving would crank up the demand for amperage.

Meanwhile, Jack moved to disarm the sprinkler system. They had discussed the control panel for the sprinkler system that he had seen during his earlier trip into the store and decided it would be best to shut off the system's water supply, rather that tamper with the control itself. That would be quicker and surer than manipulating the control settings, which could be an iffy proposition without testing.

He shielded his flashlight beam with his hand and went to the closet containing the sprinkler control. A rectangular piece had been cut out of the closet wall sheetrock to expose the pipe, and a shut-off valve had been installed just in front of the pressure regulator for the sprinkler. This was a piece of luck, since they wouldn't have to go to the front sidewalk to shut off the water at the meter box. He hadn't wanted to take that risk, even at this time of night. The original installer had done all the work for him, including placing a neat panel cover over the opening in the sheetrock wall.

Using a crescent wrench, Jack turned the valve ninety degrees, stopping the flow of water. He carefully replaced the panel cover and turned the slide hasps into place to hold it neatly in the wall. What little water was already in the lines might spew out when the sensors picked up the heat, but it would only dribble out, stopping long before it extinguished even a small fire. He played the beam of his light around the closet, but saw nothing else of interest, so he closed the closet door and focused on getting the Morales pieces moved toward the door so Sarge could load them.

Within fifteen minutes, Sarge had almost all the chosen pieces loaded when Dirk ambled back to the storage area, his electrical work finished. "Get that one, Dirk," Jack ordered, irritated at his helper's nonchalant movement. He pointed to a big, sun-face sculpture. "And the three big *chimeneas* by the corner of that office enclosure go, too. I'm going to the front and check the showroom."

They had loaded about thirty-five or forty pieces already, but he recalled seeing the pieces in the showroom, and greed prevented him from leaving them. After checking for a few minutes, he found only three more "maybes," of which he carried two and left the third sitting in the middle of the floor. "I left one vase, same size as these two, sitting in the middle of the aisle by the cash register," he told Sarge as he headed toward the back of the trailer. "Get it and just put in in your car. I'm locking the trailer right now. Did y'all get those three big ones, Dirk?"

"Yeah, we got 'em. I'll close the door when Sarge comes out. I got to throw the breaker switch and put the lock back on it."

"Okay, I'm pulling out now. You ride with Sarge." He quietly shut the trailer doors and climbed into the pickup. He decided to watch his mirror while Sarge exited with the last vase and Dirk closed the door. He left his door open, interior light off, and listened for several seconds after the door was shut and locked. He watched Dirk throw the switch and lock the new padlock, then started up his pickup. He pulled through the alley and turned left onto the street, driving slowly so Sarge could catch up to him before they entered the freeway.

Mike finished Sandra's fries with the help of a little more catsup and swallowed the last of his coffee. "You want dessert?" he asked.

"Are you kidding? I've eaten enough for three days."

"Yeah, I'm full as a blood tick too, but the pecan pie sounds good. I'd better not, though. Come to think of it, you'd best not either. I was going to mention that you're getting pretty hefty. You keep eating like this, you'll be fatter'n the town dog."

"Oh, you think so? Well, my other boyfriend doesn't mind. He comes over

every time you leave, and he never makes remarks like that. In fact, he thinks I'm a bit thin."

"He must like hefty women. And I'd better not catch him over there, or you're going to be punished—most severely."

"Ooh, I can hardly wait! By the way, that's what he says too."

"As a matter of fact, you're going to be punished right now. Let's go over to the shop, and you can help me move that stuff."

"If you weren't so afraid of being punished by Bernie, you'd wait till normal business hours to do this, you know."

"That's true. I may be the owner, but I don't want to cross swords with her. I'll leave that risky behavior to poor old Ralph."

"Coward. My other boyfriend's a lot braver than you."

"You must be seeing Ralph on the sly, then."

"You'll never know."

They drove the long block to the shop. Mike drove past to the next intersection and made a U-turn on the deserted street so he could park at the curb near the entrance. As he unlocked the door, he realized it was completely dark inside. Normally, a couple of small lights were left on up front to illuminate the showroom, and a big overhead light was left on in the storage area. The double door leading to that part of the shop always remained open, so passing police patrols could see inside.

He felt along the wall for the switch to the main showroom lights. He flipped the switch, but nothing happened. No juice, he thought; that explains it. But glancing outside, he saw a light shining in the store directly across the street and the glow from street lights, so that ruled out an area-wide power outage. The problem had to be right here in the store. He eased toward the cash register where a flashlight was kept under the counter. Moving slowly to avoid bumping into some new obstacle course erected by Ralph, he had almost reached the counter when the lights came on. At that moment, an engine started outside the rear of the shop. He turned toward Sandra, but she had already run to the back and was pulling up the freight door before Mike caught her.

"Wait!" he shouted, but not in time to prevent the door from fully opening after her initial tug on the pull-rope. He grabbed for her wrist to pull her back, then reached for the rope to re-close the door, but it was too late. Once again, Mike and Sandra were staring down the barrel of Dirk Benson's gun.

After Dirk pushed the lever to the "ON" position and slipped the re-keyed lock into place, he turned to head to Sarge's car. Jack was already pulling forward in the pickup, and Dirk watched as the trailer swung to the left then disappeared from view. At that instant, he heard the roll-up door move slightly and jerked around toward the noise. Startled, he saw that the door was rising, allowing light to spill into the alley. At first, he prepared to dash for the car, but stopped when he saw a familiar pair of running shoes appear as the door rose higher. He pulled his gun just as Sandra was joined by Mike, who reached for her hand and yelled something indecipherable at her.

The three stunned people stood looking at one another for a few seconds before Dirk exclaimed, "Well, looky here! I guess you two don't die as easy as Jack thought!"

Mike considered jerking Sandra's hand and diving to the side, away from the door opening, but Dirk was too close. They couldn't possibly pull the door down quickly enough, and Dirk would shoot them both before they could escape to the storage area or out the front door. The stare-off continued for a few more seconds as each contemplated the next move.

Dirk, obviously remembering his last encounter with the pair in front of him, broke the silence. "Get your asses in the car. I bet you don't do so good this time around. I'm going to see to that myself." He cocked the gun and aimed it at Sandra's face, an easy target from only three feet away.

Mike and Sandra had to pass even closer to get through the door opening and follow the order to get in the car. Dirk never budged, but kept the gun trained squarely on Sandra's face as she walked through the door, followed by Mike. They stepped into the alley and walked toward the car as directed, Dirk right behind them.

The driver's door opened and a surprised Sarge emerged, watching the scene over the car's roof. Mike had opened the rear door for Sandra and started to get in behind her when Dirk lashed out with the gun barrel, clipping him just above his right ear. The blow wasn't hard enough to do real damage, but it stung enough to make Mike so angry he could barely control himself. He fought down the fury, knowing there was nothing he could do about it without getting killed. He shook it off and got in the car, slamming the door quickly to avoid another blow.

Dirk already had the front door open and was entering the car with his knees in the seat, facing them in the rear, while his finger danced dangerously on the trigger, pure hate showing in his eyes. Observing him, Mike was afraid Dirk was not only expressing his frustration and anger over their earlier escapes, but providing a macho preview of what would take place later. Mike also knew they had to act very carefully to prevent the enraged gunman from killing them even before he intended. He was so agitated he could pull the trigger accidentally, and at the point-blank range between the gun's muzzle and their faces, someone would surely die. Not that it would make much difference—now, or an hour from now, out in the desert. But the basic human drive to stay alive kept Mike's mind racing to come up with a plan to escape.

Sarge pulled out of the alley and accelerated north on the side street. Ahead, about three or four blocks, Mike could see another vehicle's tail lights, the only other one on the streets at this hour. As Sarge closed the gap and slowed, Mike saw that it was a pickup pulling a trailer. The trailer's right turn signal flashed and Sarge followed, both vehicles entering the on-ramp for Interstate 10, leading back into the desert. It was then that Mike realized who and what was in the vehicle in front of them.

CHAPTER 30

▼

Jack set the cruise control on sixty-five and glanced in the mirror. Sarge and Dirk were hanging back about a quarter mile, just as he'd told them, so he settled in for the long drive. As the miles clicked by, he mentally recapped the long night's events. So far, he was pleased with the operation. They had loaded over forty pieces of pottery that might contain cocaine, and past experience indicated that such a shipment should result in over two million dollars. And the kicker was that Reynaldo Gomez had already paid Morales, so whatever the take, it would be pure profit. Jack figured it was a great way to start a new business: get rid of a greedy boss, an ex-wife, her boyfriend and his shop— while picking up a couple of million bucks. Cash, tax-free.

By now, the faulty wiring should be heating up the cardboard and newspapers nicely. With the weak wiring installed in the hot water heater and HVAC system circuits, a surge of current would overheat the wires quickly, an event he'd insured by turning on the hot water taps and setting the AC thermostat to sixty degrees. There would be a fire before dawn, long before anyone noticed in that relatively quiet area of town. A good night's work, he thought.

In the car behind Jack, the situation was not so pleasant. All of Dirk's plans for Mike and Sandra ended with bullets in their heads, and he was more than happy to share those plans in great detail. Without taking his eyes or his gun off Sandra, he turned halfway in his seat where he could watch both of them while talking with the car's driver. "Sarge, find us a spot outside of town where we can pull off and rearrange our load. Seems we're a little heavy on this trip, about two passengers too many. And this pistol is too heavy, I need to lighten it by a couple of rounds. Maybe I could just plug the lead into the back of their damn heads, let them carry it for me."

"Let's pull Jack over and check with him first," Sarge suggested. "He wanted us to stay right behind him, not pull off until he does. Besides, he'll want to be briefed about this, and he can decide what to do with them."

"I already know what I'm going to do with them—and since Jack thought they was dead when he left them, I don't think he'll mind if I just finish the job for him."

"Just the same, I want to pull him over after we get way out of town so we can ask him. He didn't want to stop to eat until we get to Pecos, so he's gonna be pissed at pulling over this soon. Remember what happened last time."

Dirk didn't know exactly what part of "last time" Sarge was referring to, but he hadn't thought any part had worked out satisfactorily, so he reluctantly agreed. "All right. Another half hour or so, we'll be beyond all the shit-hole outskirts of this burg. We'll be far enough out that Jack won't mind stopping for a minute."

The next forty miles or so were a continuation of Mike and Sandra's previous ride with Dirk, his mood changes child-like in their mercurial swings between temper tantrum and carefree, jocular sarcasm. Cartoonish as he seemed on the surface, Mike was growing scared of this maniac who couldn't keep one thought for more than ten seconds. On the plus side, he was sure that Sandra had learned never to deal with people of his ilk, not for the rest of her life. However, right now, it occurred to him that the rest of her life, or his, didn't look to be a long time. No matter how desperate, or even foolish, he had to think of something to change this scene.

His dark thoughts were interrupted by Dirk's abrasive voice, launching again on Sandra about her seductive actions in Langtry. "You left a little early from our rendezvous. You could've enjoyed yourself, but I guess you didn't realize what a stud I am."

"I realized you're a *creep*."

"Aw, you should've stuck around, Baby! You just don't know what you missed."

"What I missed was *you*, running down the sidewalk when I drove away. I should have sacrificed the paint job to run you down."

Clever as her comebacks sounded, Mike wished she would just shut up and try to avoid further conflict with this nut, but she continued to meet every comment with one of her own. But rather than infuriating him even more, as Mike feared, Dirk seemed to thrive on the verbal jousting, at least for a while. Finally tiring of the game, he asked Sarge what the next exit was.

"The last sign back there said 'Fabens, ten miles.'"

"Fabens? Never heard of it. Pull up behind Jack and flash your lights so he'll pull in there. We got to figure this out."

Sarge glanced in his mirror, then looked over at Dirk. "I'll remind you again, Dirk, he's gonna be pissed at that. If you hadn't left your cell phone in the hotel room, you could just call him."

"Well, no shit, Sarge! If you had brought your phone charger, *you* could call him! But I'd rather use it to call that worthless fucking radio station you got tuned in and request some Willie or Hank, Jr."

The two bickering, phoneless men didn't think to take their captives' phones; in any event, they didn't have Jack's number in anything other than their own phones' directories. Sarge was bright enough to predict that Jack would be angry when he learned that neither of his henchmen managed to hang on to phone and charger, the main reason for his reluctance to pull Jack over with flashing headlights.

About forty miles southeast of El Paso, Fabens lay just off the freeway, a truck stop and a couple of stores available from a single off-ramp. As they approached the exit, Sarge began flashing his headlights, and Jack signaled to pull off. From the access road, he spotted a convenience store a quarter mile up and pulled into the parking lot as far from the store itself as possible. Sarge pulled in behind and stopped directly behind the trailer, while Jack was already out of the pickup and stalking back to the Taurus, ready to strangle his employees for not simply calling him. As he neared the car, he was astonished to see the dim shapes of two people sitting in the back, although he couldn't see who they were. Phone communication forgotten, he was ready to blow his top at his idiot helpers for picking up hitchhikers in the midst of a huge burglary operation when the driver's door opened.

Sarge got out and met Jack by the front of his car. "Jack, we got a little problem here. It's that guy Conner and your ex-wife. They came out the back door just as we were leaving."

Jack met the information with incredulity. "*What?* Are you shittin' me?"

The news hit him like a sledgehammer. He bent forward and jerked his head toward the back seat, straining to identify the occupants, then staring in disbelief. Whereas most people would have known that simply leaving someone in the desert was a shaky method to get rid of them, Jack, in his self-absorbed frame of mind, had convinced himself that no one could survive a second brutal trek through the wilderness. Clearly, he hadn't taken them seriously enough, despite ample evidence that the pair were resourceful and physically adept. The occasions he had witnessed Mike and Sandra's capabilities, he'd either dismissed it as luck, or the episode had later changed in his mind, like the gunfight.

But now, it dawned on him that it was time to eliminate the pair for good and not leave anything to chance. He pondered the problem for a moment, recalling the route back to Wichita Falls before responding. "Dammit, I can't believe they've showed up again! That sonofabitch must've been faking it out there in the desert, but I'm gonna fix their asses now, I guaranfuckintee you."

"What do you want us to do with them, Chief?" Sarge asked.

"Just keep 'em in the car and don't let them get away again. We're gonna take a little side trip to finish this shit for good. Take the first exit into Pecos and turn north on that road that goes to Carlsbad. About twenty-five miles or so out of town there's a turnoff to the right that goes to Mentone."

"Jeez, there's nothing up there until you get to Carlsbad Caverns, is there?"

"Right. That's why we're going there. I worked on a ranch in Loving County when I was a kid. I know a place on that road that's so remote, the road department has forgotten it, so stay close behind me."

"I'll take care of them when we get there, Jack," Dirk interrupted, having maneuvered over by the driver's door to get in on the conversation.

"We'll see. Y'all just stay behind me and keep an eye on those two. I'll decide before we get there exactly what's going to take place." Then, as an afterthought, he added in a voice loud enough for the captives to hear, "But if they move, or make any trouble, kill them."

Walking back to his pickup, Jack wished he had more faith in Dirk and Sarge. He hated to leave the crafty pair in their custody for another two hundred miles, but he couldn't bring himself to trade places with either of his helpers for the drive. The reappearance of Conner and Sandra was an embarrassment, after he had regaled Dirk and Sarge with his tale of single-handedly taking care of all the problems out in the Mexican desert. That the pair had survived Jack's abandonment in the desert was bad enough, but popping up during the execution of his clever burglary of the shop was worse.

He was determined to make them pay for their smug attitude about their escape and untimely reappearance.

Watching out for the trailer's wide turn radius, he made a sweeping turn in the parking lot, then angled left, back onto the access road and signaled for re-entry onto the freeway. He glanced in his mirror, making sure Sarge had followed him and hoping he would stay close behind. He also hoped Dirk guarded the pair better than the first time he kidnapped them. Surely they could handle it until they reached the barren area near Mentone where he planned to kill them. If he kept his speed to sixty-five miles an hour, at least they couldn't jump out and run away this time.

Miles slid by, and despite his shock and anger, Jack's resolve to do the killing himself was already wavering. He began to wish they would try to escape, or otherwise piss Dirk off, so *he'd* shoot them. That would save him the embarrassment of confronting them, even though he'd have to get rid of the bloody car *and* the bodies. That unpleasant task was preferable to facing the pair for any reason—even to execute them. What if they taunted him in front of Dirk and Sarge about his clumsy retreat during the shootout?

Hey Jack, hope you don't trip and fall like the last time you waved a gun at us!

But Jack reminded himself that whatever they said, they wouldn't be telling the story—or any others—for long. Besides, any snide remarks from those two would make it easier to pull the trigger. He could always convince Dirk and Sarge later that their comments were lies, just more of the pair's clever diversionary tricks. The thought soothed him, and he settled down. In fact, he looked forward to it.

CHAPTER 31

▼

Ramón Vallenzuella watched the scene unfolding from behind the dumpsters in the alley, about thirty yards from the back of the pottery and import shop. His shift had begun at midnight, and now, two hours later, he had witnessed exactly what he had been instructed to watch for. But not only had he seen the theft of the pottery; just as he started to leave his station and report to Arturo, another event took him by surprise.

The taller of the two *gringos* had just switched the power back on and padlocked the breaker box when two more people appeared, opening the warehouse door from the inside. Silhouetted in the doorway by a light behind them, Ramón could only see that it was a man and a woman. After a moment of the three facing each other and carrying on a verbal exchange he couldn't quite hear, the departing *gringo* pulled a gun and ordered them into the getaway car.

As soon as the car left the alley and sped away, Ramón ran to the pay phone and informed Arturo of the shocking news. The burglary had been anticipated, but neither of the men knew what to make of the kidnapping and spent no time discussing it. *Jéfe* had given them specific orders about the lookout, and that was all they needed to be concerned with; that, and using pay phones rather than their cell phones for communication.

Arturo hung up and immediately dialed another pay phone, dutifully passing along the detailed sequence of events to the listener, as well as a description of both vehicles. He was instructed to call the police anonymously from yet another, more distant pay phone and inform them that Conner's Imports should be checked for a possible break-in.

Within minutes of Arturo's first call, two vehicles pulled into the east-bound access road of Interstate 10. As soon as the occupants spotted the pickup being followed by a Ford Taurus, both cars entered the freeway at the next ramp and kept far enough back to avoid drawing any attention. Unbeknownst to the two lead vehicles, their little convoy now consisted of four cars.

An hour later, when the Taurus signaled to exit, one car pulled to the shoulder and the other took the Fabens exit. When the pickup rig and the Taurus stopped in the parking lot, the car pulled up to the convenience store, and one occupant got out and went inside. Unnoticed by Jack or Sarge having their conflab, the lone man stood just inside the store looking through the magazine rack while the two men discussed what to do with their captives. Meanwhile, the second following car had pulled back into traffic and advanced to the entry ramp just beyond Fabens where it pulled over again, its emergency flashers indicating just another motorist with car trouble.

The man in the store watched Jack get back in his pickup and pull onto the access road, closely followed by the Taurus. He chose a magazine, paid at the counter and stepped into his waiting car. Even at this time of night, the interstate carried enough traffic that neither Jack nor Sarge paid any attention to the car pulling out behind them. Nor did they notice the second car dousing its emergency flashers and pulling in behind the first soon after they re-entered the freeway and merged with east-bound traffic. The four-car convoy was again intact.

CHAPTER 32

▼

Holding his speed to just under seventy, Jack glanced at the dashboard clock and reset it to Central Daylight Time, having left the Mountain Time Zone near Van Horn, eighty miles back. He saw the exits ahead for Pecos and slowed to take the first one, Highway 285, which led to Carlsbad, about a hundred miles to the north. He had planned to stop here for breakfast, but the business with Conner and Sandra had to be completed first. His appetite would be better when that business was done.

Jack drove slowly through the town, catching a red light at the first intersection before he turned left toward tiny Mentone, in Loving County. With only a hundred or so residents, most living in Mentone, the county's six hundred square miles provided exactly the environment he needed to eliminate the problematic pair in the car behind him.

Traveling north out of Pecos, Mike and Sandra watched the sunrise, both wondering if it would be their last. The flat land became more barren with every passing mile. The scant vegetation consisted of dry, brittle bushes and sparse clumps of grass. In some areas, the vegetation played out completely, exposing a dry expanse of gravel stretching off toward the horizon, broken occasionally by gullies and rocky ledges.

Mike noticed buzzards sitting in clusters on fences, their wings half-spread to soak up heat from the rising sun. As the day heated up, the vultures would take to the Texas sky, soaring in circles encompassing hundreds of square miles of land, buoyed by thermal currents rising from the desert floor. Sharp eyes could spot carrion several miles away, but the real tool was the over-developed olfactory sense system. Aided by the big nostril openings in the beak, a highly developed sense of smell enables the birds to detect rotting meat from even greater distances than their keen vision.

The grim reality of the situation hit him as his mind flitted over the terms "carrion" and "rotting meat." In a few hours, he and Sandra would be exactly those things. Buzzards would swoop down for a closer look, wary at first because the bodies were human, the buzzards' only real enemy. After more hours under the Texas sun, the odor of putrefying flesh would overcome natural fear, and the first brave one would land nearby. The first tentative pecks would be to the throat, eyes, and lips. Later, if the coyotes didn't complete the chore of ripping clothes off, the bolder vultures would do so in an effort to expose other soft areas, such as the genitals.

Mike nearly puked at that thought. He felt flush all over and he began to sweat, fear coming out of him, palpable and visible on his shirt. If he didn't do something, he and Sandra would soon be *dead*, a term that took some getting used to.

But first the terror of *dying*. Not by the gunfire of the old movies, putting the victim on the ground with a peaceful, sleeping look on his face. No; instead a loud crack and a piercing, shocking sting, immediately followed by a spurt of blood and tissue, with more of the same from the exit wound. Shards of lead and splintered bone gouging into the soft tissue, fraying nerves and inducing shock. And not dying immediately, like in the movies, with a gasp and a gentle exhalation of the final breath; nothing that quick and easy. No matter how horrendous the wound, the human body is tough, and it survives for at least a few minutes, twitching and gasping, bleeding and frothing and shitting. And worst of all, *aware*. Aware that it's dying.

Mike knew the time had come to live or die. His entire life, and Sandra's too, coming down to the next few minutes. Their lives were sliding away like sand through an hourglass. Like blood from a gunshot wound. Or, he thought, to put it in the colorful vernacular of a Texas upbringing, like shit through a goose.

His mind was racing so fast he couldn't keep all the thoughts, serious and silly, straight. He forced himself to calm down and concentrate. If he could get out of the car and make a break, Dirk would think that he was abandoning Sandra to escape, an event that would bring the wrath of Jack down on him. Not very chivalrous, to be sure, but neither was sitting here letting them *both* die without doing anything. Dirk would be forced to follow him, leaving Sandra behind, where perhaps she could get away from the overweight Sarge by herself.

As Mike went over the plan again, he wished he could signal his intentions to Sandra, get her to make her break at the same time, greatly improving their chances of escape. Two targets fleeing in opposite directions would, hopefully, cause enough confusion to allow them to put distance between them and the killers. Dirk had only a pistol, as did Sarge. Mike reasoned that not many shooters could hit anything running over a few yards away with a handgun, but the reasoning did little to quell his fear. He took a deep, slow breath and reminded himself they had no choice in the matter.

The car slowed, shaking Mike from his morbid thoughts. He saw the trailer's light signaling for a right turn and a sign informing drivers the road led to Mentone. He grew even more anxious—they certainly weren't going to Mentone to see the sights. It was completely deserted out here, and Mike knew why this place was their destination. He and Sandra would not live to see Mentone—or anywhere else. He glanced over at Sandra and saw her big blue eyes brimming with tears of fright.

Soon after turning off, the road crossed the Pecos River, only a stream at this point, a trickle of water meandering to the south. Salt cedar saplings stood in tight groves, covered with brush and debris from long-forgotten spring storms. Just beyond the bridge, a dirt road to the right bordered the river downstream for a quarter mile or so before disappearing between a series of gravel ledges that blocked the view of the road's purpose or destination. Seeing the dilapidated path, Mike realized it for what it truly was: a dead end.

Jack pulled off the highway just beyond the dirt road turnoff and parked well off the pavement. Sarge pulled up behind while Jack sat in the pickup, waiting, watching his mirror. A lone car slowed, then passed by heading toward Mentone, but the occupants paid no attention to the vehicles beside the road. Jack had not seen another car since leaving Pecos, and this one was possibly the only one that would travel this route all day. He watched as the car increased its speed toward the horizon, then checked his mirror for other traffic. Nothing. He waited a few more seconds before he got out and strode back to the Taurus. He reached for the door handle, but when he pulled it the door remained locked until Dirk managed to find the manual control to override the auto-lock feature.

Watching, Mike saw that his own door was locked, and it struck him that the car's automatic lock system apparently locked all the doors when the car was put into a forward gear. Hoping the information would prove helpful, he glanced over at Sandra, then down to his right hand with the index finger pointing to the door lock. She nodded almost imperceptibly, and Mike knew she wouldn't be taken by surprise when he bolted. He glanced toward her door lock, but couldn't see her reaction because Jack had now taken Dirk's place in the front seat and turned to glare at them, displaying a pistol for effect. Mike kept his eyes straight ahead and hoped that Sandra would do the same until his attention waned.

Though unexpected, the change in front seat occupants made no difference in Mike's plan to jump and run at the first opportunity. The only chance they had was to bail out, taking their captors by surprise, whether it was Dirk or Jack in the front seat. It looked as though Dirk would stay with the pickup and trailer, so only Sarge and Jack would escort them. While Mike didn't know about Dirk's or Sarge's marksmanship, he had witnessed Jack in action, and he hadn't appeared very handy in a gunfight. Unfortunately, this wasn't going to be a gunfight; it would be a close-range execution, of that he was sure.

As if to verify that unpleasant speculation, Jack said, "We're going to take a little ride down this road a few miles. I want you two to just sit there and shut the fuck up."

Neither had uttered a word, but chose not to comment on the absurdity of his order. When Sarge pulled the gear selector down into "Drive," Mike heard the click of Jack's door locking again. He'd been right; the locking system was automatic. This might give them the margin of time needed to save their lives.

The car rocked over the first rough potholes in the road within a few yards, and the view ahead didn't promise to be any smoother. Good, Mike thought; lurching around inside the car might create enough distraction to make a break. Relying on high school drama class acting lessons, he turned his head toward Sandra in an exaggerated movement to draw the audience's attention to that character. Jack, being the sole member of the audience, noticed it and looked at her also. Mike had opened his mouth as if to say something, but instead leaned forward in the seat as though the rising sun outside Sandra's window had suddenly caught his eye. The tricked worked; Mike was able to move his right hand to the door lock button.

He turned to look directly at Jack. "It's pretty early in the morning for a side trip, Pearson," he said with more boldness than he felt. "I'd think you'd want to get on down the road. Leave Dirk with the goods, and he may be gone when you get back."

"Don't worry about it."

"Tell you what, I'll offer you the same deal we did Gomez. Just pay me for my merchandise, and you can have the cocaine without ever hearing from us again." He knew the offer sounded lame, but he wanted to draw Jack's attention away from Sandra's hand. And the remark about Dirk, though unlikely, just might break his concentration.

"I've already got your merchandise and in about five minutes, I'll never hear from you again, anyway. So shut the fuck up."

So much for my career as a hostage negotiator.

Mike let it rest for a minute, watching for any change in the scenery that would offer a small advantage. The road got worse, and they crossed a wide gully about eight feet deep, went over a rise, then back into another ditch. This one was filled with soft dirt, and Sarge revved the engine to keep the car moving forward. Clearly, this was not the terrain Ford engineers had in mind for the mid-size family sedan Taurus. For Mike, it was a godsend; the more gullies and ridges, the better for escaping from view quickly.

Knowing they might be nearing the end of the road—in more ways than one—he decided that he and Sandra had to break soon, at the bottom of the next gully or low spot in the road. If either of them could reach the slightest bend in a gully, they would be out of sight immediately and completely out of pistol range soon thereafter.

The land leveled out for the next two hundred yards, and Mike wondered if they'd missed their only chance. Then a slight rise gave way to a steep dip into another dry wash feeding into the riverbed, now some fifty yards to their right. Not as narrow and twisting as he would have liked, but it might be their last opportunity. It was time.

He waited for the car to hit a pothole and was rewarded by one so big it made Jack lurch toward the dashboard. He had to turn and put both hands forward to steady himself, while Sarge cursed and leaned on the steering wheel for stability.

"Now, Sandra!" Mike yelled. In one motion, he flipped up the door lock release button and grabbed the handle, hoping it wasn't disconnected from the internal linkage or otherwise inoperable, like door handles in a police car. It worked fine. He pushed the door open with all his strength and bailed out before Jack had fully recovered his balance. When his feet hit the dirt, it was so loose he almost lost his own balance, so he leaned forward like a running back, churning ahead and angling slightly toward the front of the car, the hardest area for Jack to get a clean shot—if he ever got his door open. Mike could hear him cursing as he jerked on the door handle, nearly pulling it off trying to get the locked door to open, but to no avail. He took a quick glance over his left shoulder to see the other rear door open and Sandra's blonde hair streaming behind her as she bounded up the gully in the opposite direction like an antelope. Encouraged by her quick movement, he knew that she would be beyond the range of the average pistol shooter in a few seconds.

The automatic door lock fiasco had worked perfectly. Although Sarge had finally jammed the transmission into "Park," releasing the locks, Jack was still fumbling with the handle, unable to exit the car. By the time he got the door open, his captives were no longer captive; far from it, in fact. He pulled himself from the car and let loose two quick shots at Sandra, who was quickly disappearing from his view. She was already twenty or thirty yards out, and the shots missed by a mile.

Meanwhile, Mike had hit some firmer ground and stretched out to about thirty yards in front of Jack, who stumbled and swore as he made his way around the front of the car and sent a wild round in his general direction. Mike felt elated until he heard two different shots, obviously from Sarge's gun. He couldn't turn around to check on Sandra, since Jack had opened up again with two more rounds; a pause, then two more. The next round from Jack sounded farther away, but he put on still more speed and hoped Sandra was doing the same. Sarge's gun fired only once more, and Mike took it as a good sign that she had also successfully eluded her pursuer.

Sandra's heart hammered as she followed Mike's lead, inching her hand up to the door lock while the road surface jostled everyone inside the car. Jack was having trouble steadying himself, since he remained turned in the front seat to watch them, unable to see the road and anticipate rougher sections. Sarge was trying to dodge one large pothole when the right front tire fell into another one. The car lurched forward on its suspension, throwing Jack backwards. He turned away to grab the dashboard and failed to notice their hands creeping toward the door lock buttons, so when Mike yelled, her hand was almost touching it. She pushed the door lock up with her left thumb and jerked the door open with her right hand, then hit the ground running. She juked left, then right a couple of times while putting distance between herself and the car. At about twenty yards out, she leveled down and sprinted in a straight line, away from the car, away from the gunfire.

It took Sarge several seconds to figure out what was happening, and by the time he put the car in "Park" and exited the car, she was too far away for all but the best pistol shooters. After two hastily fired rounds, Sarge saw the range to his rapidly moving target and fell back on his long-past military training. He steadied his gun hand on the top of the open car door and took aim at the center of her back, concentrating on holding his sight picture. Ignoring the confusion and uproar behind him, he carefully squeezed off the next round.

CHAPTER 33

▼

When Jack signaled for the exit to Highway 285 in Pecos, the two trailing cars dropped back. Only after the pickup and trailer had turned north did one of them pull up to about three hundred yards behind Sarge's car and hold the position. The other car followed a few minutes later, bringing up the rear a couple of miles back on the desolate stretch of highway toward Carlsbad. No observer would have seeen the two following cars as working in concert.

Cell phone service was spotty in this part of the state, so the pursuit cars remained in contact with powerful walkie-talkies, infrequent murmurs passing between the cars for the first several miles out of Pecos. A longer transmission occurred when the front car notified the other as Jack signaled to turn toward Mentone, prompting the driver of the rear car to pull over immediately. The car remained motionless for several minutes, its engine idling in the morning stillness. Then two figures emerged from the rear doors carrying parcels and began running due east, toward the river bed.

After taking the right turn toward Mentone, the lead pursuit car had continued beyond the parked pickup and Taurus, none of its occupants even glancing out of the tinted glass as they passed by. Not until it had traveled beyond a rise almost a half-mile away did the car pull over to the right and make a U-turn in the deserted road. Two figures got out, one carrying a tripod, the other, a camera with a huge lens. The pair carried the bulky items back up the rise until they could see the vista to the west, the pickup and trailer still parked beside the road. By now, the Taurus was moving parallel to the riverbed, leaving a plume of dust in its wake.

One man quickly set up the tripod with a camera and telephoto lens, allowing him to use the camera equipment as a makeshift telescope. With the rapidly rising sun at his back, any curious observer would assume him to be taking photographs of the desert landscape, catching the best light of the day. What might have seemed a little mysterious was the constant stream of conversation over the walkie-talkie by his assistant, conversation with two other men who were definitely not nature photographers. In any event, observers, curious or otherwise, were in short supply this morning.

CHAPTER 34

▼

Sandra heard the next shot before she felt the sharp pain in her right calf. At first, she thought she had badly strained the muscle, sprinting as she had without warming up. Two steps later, the leg refused to work at all and she realized she must have been hit. Still, she lurched forward trying to get to a bend in the gully that would put her out of the gunman's line of sight. The next step with the wounded leg was clumsy and landed her foot on a rock, rolling her ankle over with a resounding pop. The weakened leg gave way, and she went down hard. When she hit the ground, she was momentarily stunned, and the pain in her leg grew intense. She knew she couldn't stay down, but before she could overcome the pain and rise to a standing position, Sarge was standing over her, gasping for breath and holding the muzzle of the pistol steadily on her face. Neither moved for a few seconds, both trying to catch their breath, difficult for Sandra because of the pain and fear, and nearly impossible for the overweight, out-of-shape Sarge.

Sandra felt the throbbing pain in her leg, but was afraid to look. Of course, she'd never been shot before and had no idea what to expect next; whether the bullet had hit bone or artery, passed through with minimal damage, or was imbedded in her flesh. None of the possibilities lessened the pain emanating from her calf, but the pain in her ankle, though bad, was familiar. It had happened before, and it would heal within days. But from her helpless position on the ground, seeing the savage look on Sarge's face, she knew she didn't have that long.

Then Jack appeared, running up the gully, huffing and puffing, his face red and contorted with hate. He had given up on Mike, mostly because he had run out of rounds and his spare clip was back in the pickup, over a mile away. He had stumbled back to the car, then followed Sarge's footprints in the gully's soft dirt. Enraged by once again being foiled by Mike, he needed to take his anger out on someone. "Fucking bitch!" he screamed. "You fucking bitch! I'll teach you a lesson you'll never forget!" He bolted forward and slapped her across the face.

The blow was hard, and she shrieked with real pain. Bright flashes of light streaked across her vision and her senses dulled. For a few seconds, she thought she would pass out. Her vision was blurred from the blow and with tears of pain and terror, but she could plainly hear Jack's ragged breathing. Knowing that his pulse had to match his sky-high respiration rate, she closed her eyes and had a vague hope that he would have a stroke.

Jack stood over her until she opened her eyes, clenching and unclenching his fists, gritting his teeth and breathing like a laboring steam locomotive. He moved toward her as though to hit her again, and she cringed away in fear. But at the last second, he stopped, straightened, and cupped his hands to shout. "Conner, I've got this bitch of yours here on the ground! Get your ass over here, *now!*"

Mike had changed his course to run in a large arc around the car, hoping to join up with Sandra far in front of the pursuers. He thought he was getting close when he heard Jack's shout to his left, sounding fairly close, maybe fifty yards away. He was stunned; it made no sense that those two fat-asses could have caught her, not with the way he'd seen her rocket from the car, but he had to check.

Picking up the pace, he angled toward the source of the shout. After a few dozen yards, he topped a small mound overlooking the gully and looked down. Sandra lay on her side, with her leg bleeding. Her face was red and twisted with pain, and blood trickled from her mouth. Sarge stood to one side, still panting, and Jack loomed over her, clenching his fists and gritting his teeth like a madman. The sight nearly made Mike sick with anger.

As in the confrontation with the helicopter pilot, Mike again lost all sense of fear or restraint. No matter the consequences, he was going to kill Jack Pearson. *"You sonofabitch!"* he screamed. *"I'm going to tear your fucking head off!"*

He ran to the edge of the embankment and launched himself down the steep gravel slope at full speed. Jack wheeled and pulled the trigger too quickly, and the shot missed. Mike was almost on him, arms outstretched and hands in position to perform exactly what he had threatened when Jack's head disappeared—simply *disappeared*. In its place, a pink and gray shower of blood, bone, and brain tissue spewed up in a horrifying spectacle. Mike felt the gore spatter on his face an instant before he heard the sound that caused it.

Mike stopped in his tracks. The sound of the big-caliber rifle was still echoing through the morning air when Sarge's arms flew out as though he were making a grand welcoming gesture, his pistol flying from his outstretched hand. It landed at the same time Sarge did, both plunking unceremoniously into the gravel. Then the sound of the second deadly round registered on Mike's ears, causing him to flinch. He stood stock still, wondering what was going on, while his breath came in ragged spurts. Absurdly, he wondered how his threat to take Jack's head off had resulted in that happening, but without even touching him.

Several seconds passed before he heard Sandra whimpering. He knelt beside her, cradling her head in his bloody arms, saying nothing. She was trembling, but Mike didn't notice due to his own shakiness. "It's okay, it's okay," he told her, over and over. It was the only comforting thing that came to his jumbled mind at this point. He still didn't understand what had occurred, but at least they were free of the two men intent on killing them.

Sandra's trembling gradually ceased, and Mike moved to see to her wounded leg. As gently as he could, he rolled up the leg of her jeans above the wound. The bleeding had slowed, but he tore the sleeve off his shirt anyway and wrapped it firmly. Then he saw that her cheek was badly bruised and her lip swollen to twice its normal size. "Open and close your mouth, see if everything works okay," he instructed.

She complied and flinched, raising her hand to her mouth. "I think it's okay, nothing's broken. My lip feels huge, though."

"Yeah, it's pretty swollen, but I was more worried about your jaw being broken. You look pretty good for a girl with a fat lip."

She tried to smile at the remark, but broke into tears as she relived Jack's demeaning physical attack. Minutes, or maybe hours later, Mike was gently rocking her when a familiar voice interrupted the silent, terrifying scene.

"Mike and Sandra...we meet again."

CHAPTER 35

▼

Reynaldo Gomez stepped forward, followed by two men carrying rifles with huge scopes. He was nattily dressed in light gray slacks and a charcoal blazer, a blue silk tie knotted snugly at his throat. For some reason, the incongruity of the situation—a dapper man stepping calmly into a gruesome murder scene out here in the wilderness—struck Mike as being terribly funny, and he started laughing hysterically.

Reynaldo looked puzzled at first, then broke into a smile as he realized Mike's odd reaction was simply an involuntary release of emotion brought on by the intensity of the moment. He had told Mike and Sandra only a few days before that his was a violent business, and most people couldn't be expected to act rationally under these circumstances.

He leaned down to look at Sandra's wound, nodding in satisfaction at Mike's earlier work. He said something in rapid Spanish, and one of the men hurried over with a small medical kit. Using a razor blade, Reynaldo cut off the leg of her jeans and removed the shirt-sleeve bandage. He carefully cleaned the wound with antiseptic, then replaced Mike's makeshift bandage with the real thing.

When he had finished dressing the wound, Sandra smiled up at him weakly. "Where did you learn those nursing skills?" she asked.

"Oh, I had some lessons just last week, and I'm a good student. But I didn't realize I would need to practice medicine so soon."

Standing, he said something to the men. They looked surprised, and one began to protest. Reynaldo stopped him with a wave of his hand. He turned back to Mike and Sandra. "Please forgive my companions. They are a bit distraught that I am on such friendly terms with you, after having ordered the elimination of those two." He gestured toward the bodies with a dismissive nod. "They have worked with those two in the past, so they were surprised at the order. However, in this business, nothing should come as a surprise. Not even that I am saving her life," he continued, looking at Sandra.

"What do you mean," Mike asked, "about saving *her* life? You saved mine, too."

"True enough. And my companions were quite impressed after hearing of you two doing the same for me a few days ago in Mexico. But they have only recently become aware that your friend here, the very pretty Sandra, is Cassandra Payne, an accomplished confidential informant for the United States Drug Enforcement Agency. Persons of that position are generally not well-received by men in my employ."

Mike was dumbfounded—again. Once more, he was feeling like a complete idiot, like the night in the Land Cruiser, just before hitting the hog, when Sandra had revealed the hollow compartment trick. Now he realized why she had been so well-informed. It was her *business* to be well-informed about transporting drugs, not the result of overhearing some ill-kept secret at a party. Without looking at her, he asked, "Is that true, Sandra?"

She didn't respond, and when he looked down, he saw that she was crying again. It took a minute for her to regain her composure and talk. "I didn't mean to mislead you, Mike," she began. "But I was recruited just after I left Jack, when I reported my suspicions about his involvement in the drug business to my divorce lawyer. She encouraged me to complete the divorce and then turn him in. Turns out, that was terrible advice, I guess." She touched her lip and winced before continuing. "He'd been at it for quite some time, I was sure of that, but after we separated, he didn't even try to hide it—"

"So you used me because I was in the same business, importing pottery," he interrupted, "which is what these guys *pretend* to do."

"No! Mike, that was pure coincidence. When we met at the race that day, I didn't know what you did. And you didn't tell me very much about your business until we'd gone out a couple of times. And soon after we started seeing each other, I resigned from the Agency. I hadn't found out anything useful anyway, except that Jack was having an affair with Reynaldo's wife, and that didn't help the Agency much. Committing adultery didn't mean they were dealing drugs. Besides, I knew that no matter what I did, it didn't slow down the flow of drugs across the border. Or stop adultery," she added with a bitter laugh.

"They must have thought you could find something to bust Jack with, but I didn't know they used ex-spouses in anything short of a murder investigation."

"They use whatever and whomever they can, because it's a hopeless numbers game—how many arrests, how many pounds of contraband seized. It's done mainly to placate those few who think the key to stopping drugs is to stop the dealing. Even if I could have helped bust *twenty* Jack Pearsons, nothing would change. There would always be someone to take his place. Or *his* place," she said, indicating Reynaldo, who stood by quietly, a passive look on his face.

"I was kind of surprised to hear you say that, right after the helicopter crash. I didn't know you felt that way. Of course, drug trafficking isn't a subject I'd ever discussed with you until a few days ago. I wasn't aware you were an *expert* on the subject until now."

She looked up at him, hurt by the last remark. "After I moved to El Paso and started my new job, I thought that part of my life was over. Then, about a year later, the Agency contacted me because they'd received some information about large shipments coming into the North Texas area, specifically into Graham and Wichita Falls. They asked me to take one last shot at finding out how Jack and Reynaldo were doing it. I agreed to do it, providing it was the last time they would call on me. So I went to the party, and Jack was more than willing to brag to me about how it worked."

Mike had turned his gaze to the bodies lying nearby and nodded in their general direction. "I always thought those guys were smarter than that. Guess I saw too many movies."

"Jack was smart about stuff like that, but maybe enough time had passed since our divorce that he didn't need to be on guard, or lie to me any longer. He'd lied to me constantly during our marriage, mostly about other women, but also about what he did for money."

"I can see why he'd lie about work, if he was involved in something that would put him in the slammer for twenty years."

Sandra shook her head. "He lied about *everything,* even when he didn't need to. Sometimes he'd make a remark about dealing in drugs, but I thought it was to cover more lies, to cover for the time he spent with women, or just trying to sound more glamorous than remodeling houses. But after a while, I realized we had too much money for the construction business to account for, especially since he just worked for Reynaldo. Jack didn't own the company."

"Is that when you bailed on the marriage?"

"Yes, that was the final straw. I was sure it involved Reynaldo Gomez or his wife, because he spent so much time with them. I'd already been humiliated by affairs with other women, but going to prison because of illegal business with another woman was too much. By then, I'd decided to leave him, so all communication was done by our lawyers. It wasn't a subject I cared to discuss, but I brought it up with my lawyer, because I was afraid I'd be hauled off too, if they caught him before the divorce was final." She hugged her knees and put her head down on them. Mike was afraid she had started crying again, but when she continued, her voice was strong. "Then, at the party, he comes right out and tells me about the hollow compartments that Morales builds into some of the pieces. He'd already heard that you were in the import business, and I had mentioned that you were going to buy some stuff from Morales. I didn't dream at the time there was a connection, or that you'd get caught up in his mess."

"So he told you to get me to change my plans, buy from somebody besides Morales?"

"I told you already, I didn't know what else to do. If I refused, they would have a reason to think I had ulterior motives, and that I was going to tell someone about it. I was so stunned and confused, I couldn't think straight. It seemed impossible that the very thing I'd been sent to find out involved the pottery importing business, the same business you were in."

"So you agreed to wave me off the Morales purchase." Mike's statement had more bite to it than he intended.

Her voice changed from defensive to plaintive. "I just couldn't think of another way, especially since I'd already told them you were planning on buying from the same manufacturer. At the time, Jack said he would have Dirk talk to you and leave me out of it. I was as vague as I could be, I told him where you usually stayed in Laredo and what color your car was, hoping Dirk would play it like he just ran into you by accident. I also thought there was a good chance that it would all fall through, or that Jack was just pricking with me because he'd found out you were in the import business. The best that could have happened was the Agency arresting all of them before they confronted you. Of course, none of the good solutions happened. It had to come down to this."

"Why didn't they arrest them? Did you give them the information they needed?"

"I reported everything as soon as I got back from Wichita Falls, but I wasn't privy to the schedule for taking action on it. I was instructed to go on about my business, that the information would be passed along through the proper channels and used appropriately. That's government talk for 'thanks, now butt out.'"

"Makes sense now, but I wish you hadn't butted me out of the loop. I would've been sure to carry a gun everywhere, and I'd have been watching for anything suspicious, like when they grabbed us at the airport. That little scene would have ended a lot differently, then and there."

"I didn't want you to be angry with me, or think that I had used you because you happen to sell pottery, and I needed a connection to the industry. When they showed up at the airport, I knew it was too late. And when I told you all—well, most of this—in the desert that night, I still couldn't tell you about my connection with the Drug Enforcement Agency."

"Why not? Why couldn't you have just come clean right then?" he asked, an edge creeping into his voice again.

"Because I was afraid you'd react just like you are now, dammit!"

She started crying again, and Mike gave it up. There were still a lot of unanswered questions, like why had she continued to play along with his concerns over having the tainted shipment in his shop? As an agent, she should have been able to turn in the stuff and probably receive a commendation for making a big haul, the kind they show on the late news broadcasts. Of course, without any arrests, it would look pretty bad for the agent and her boyfriend to be in possession of such a shipment. But she could have told *me*, so *I* could do something, Mike argued with himself. A lot should have been done differently, but standing here with a drug kingpin and a couple of shooters and their victims wasn't the best venue for fact-finding.

He turned to look at Reynaldo and asked, "Well, what now?"

"I think we should leave. This is very remote, but we don't need to take a chance at having to explain this," he said, gesturing to the bodies. "We can discuss things later."

Flies were already buzzing around the bodies, and Mike was swatting at them also. Suddenly he realized they were after the gore spattered on him, and he was nearly sick. Reynaldo noticed and took a canteen from one of the men. He handed it to Mike, along with his handkerchief, and he began wiping his face and arms, using the entire canteen in the process. When he finished he turned to hand the canteen back to Reynaldo's gunman. Turning to Reynaldo, he smiled weakly, still nauseas from the grisly chore. "No matter how bad this is, we wouldn't have wasted that much water last week, would we?"

Reynaldo smiled back and repeated the quip to his men, who grinned appreciatively and made some comments, apparently agreeing with Mike's statement on water conservation. "We learned a lot about the importance of water, didn't we? In fact, we learned about the importance of a lot of things."

"That we did, Mr. Gomez."

Reynaldo said something else, and the men lay down their rifles and dragged the bodies around the bend in the gully, presumably to a better spot in which to bury them. It wouldn't matter, though. The coyotes would find them unless they were several feet deep. The next day, the buzzards would finish the job.

Mike noticed Sandra watching her ex-husband's body being drug unceremoniously through the gravel, his boots digging twin furrows in the bed of the gully. He went to her side and cradled her head in his arms, trying to shield her from the view. Eyes closed, she willingly lay her head in the crook of his arm and stayed there until both bodies had disappeared around the bend.

Reynaldo, who had been standing quietly nearby, knew that despite the hatred that had grown between her and Jack, it was hard to witness such a violent death and ignoble ending to any human life, but especially one she had known—and supposedly loved—at one time. He helped Mike hoist her to her feet and supported her on one side with Mike on the other as they walked back to the Taurus. The men with rifles didn't reappear.

As the three slowly made their way out of the gully arm in arm, Reynaldo looked around the area one more time. "We were fortunate to be able to see down into this ditch. Had you been positioned beyond that bend, my men might not have had a vantage point from which to make the shots. But they are extremely competent, and they moved quickly when Jack turned toward you. It was apparent by the look on Mike's face that they would have to intervene," he said, smiling.

"How did you know?" Sandra asked.

"Oh, we've been following you since El Paso. Some people in another car pulled ahead when you stopped. They were watching and reporting your progress to us. When you started down this dirt road, it was no secret what was going to happen. My men had to hurry to get into position at a high point to make the shot, but as I said, they are quite good.

"We suspected it would happen here in this deserted area, but if they had not turned onto this road, I would have had my men force the car off the highway before reaching Mentone. Then we would simply try to extract you from danger."

Mike mulled over the last statement, *"try to extract you from danger."* A phrase that should have been followed by *"and hope you didn't die in the process."* So clipped and precise, like a military operation. A plan with *"acceptable loss of life levels,"* another phrase he recalled from his military stint that would have fit the current situation. It had worked out, but it had been another close brush with death, and he was getting tired of it. Would their luck continue to hold? Did this *finally* mark the end of the terrifying ordeal that had begun days ago in the airport parking lot?

They reached the Taurus and lowered Sandra into the back seat. Mike got in beside her, and Reynaldo got behind the wheel to drive them back to the highway over the rough surface. As they neared the road, the pickup and trailer were sitting in the same spot, but Dirk was nowhere to be seen.

Reynaldo followed Mike's gaze and said, "No need to worry about Dirk. He has been taken care of by the people in the other car."

Mike marveled inwardly at the cultured voice with its veiled message of assurance.

So Dirk's head was blown off, too.

Reynaldo noticed Mike's silence and he looked in the mirror to catch his eye before speaking. "Mike, this business is filled with unsavory characters like Dirk and those two back there. I know you don't approve, but it was necessary to handle things the way I chose—"

"I'm in no position to question how you handled things. If you hadn't handled things the way you did, Sandra and I would probably both be dead. She and I used our only skill, which was making a break for it and counting on outrunning Jack and Sarge. We nearly made it, too, but a lucky shot from Sarge changed everything. We're thankful that you were watching over us. I'm just concerned about getting this thing over completely and returning to life as we know it."

"With all that happened and all that continues to happen, I know you are apprehensive. But I assure you, this business is done. You and Sandra are no longer in any danger.

"By the way, my sister reports to me that your shop is intact, and the couple who work for you are both safe and sound. They were notified by the authorities soon after the police arrived to check out a telephone tip. It seems someone left the back door open and lights on inside—"

Mike interrupted and shook his head. "Oh, man, I can't believe I'm just now thinking about my shop! And the Hansons must be worried to death after getting a call like that, because they're listed at the police and fire departments as secondary point of contact in an emergency. Which reminds me, my phone is lying on the counter by the cash register…anyway, what happened after we left?"

"Relax, Mike. I had men watching your shop, as I said I would. They knew from the activity at the breaker box that something electrical was being tampered with, so the telephone tip included that piece of information. Jack and his men set up your shop for an electrical fire after the burglary, but it was reported quickly, and the fire department shut off power before it got started. So there is almost no damage, other than you will need to have your wiring repaired."

"What was that about your *sister*?" Sandra asked incredulously, ignoring the information about the fire.

"Yes, my sister, Eva, whom you thought was my wife. I have a wife, but she stays in Mexico quite a lot in the hottest months of the summer. It is pleasant in Cuernavaca at this time of year."

"But didn't Eva and Jack—"

"She is very clever, my sister Evangelina. She has worked with me for months to uncover the devious Jack Pearson. It was she who discovered that he had been stealing for quite a while and had planned to take over my operation. Alas, she went to lengths I would have preferred she not undertake, but that is her nature. She will do whatever is necessary. Not only is this business violent, it is, uh…shall I say, *demanding*."

Sandra sat very still, embarrassed by her tirade in the desert and again a few moments before, when she alluded to Jack's affair with Reynaldo's wife. Sensing her discomfort, Reynaldo dismissed it with a wave of his hand, smiling at her in the mirror. "It is not important, Sandra. We all have our little secrets, yes?"

The remark embarrassed her even more, but she smiled back at the mirror. "You're right about that."

Something stirred in Mike's mind and he asked, "Your sister's name is Eva? Is she a very pretty woman, about five-nine, with…uh…*long hair* and uh…gorgeous skin? Did she come into the shop just…when, yesterday? And buy a big flower pot?"

"Yes, she did!" Reynaldo responded, laughing at Mike's clumsily edited description of his well-endowed sister. "And she said you were quite a nice man."

Mike shook his head again and fell silent as Reynaldo pulled up to the pavement, stopping just behind the trailer. He turned in the seat to face Mike and Sandra. "I have some things to do here. Why don't you two just take the pickup back to Pecos and have Sandra's leg attended? Then you can take it on to your shop in El Paso. You will probably wish to unload the merchandise and get it back on your shelves as quickly as possible. Eva reported to me that business with the Morales product was brisk, so you don't want to miss any sales."

Mike stared at him incredulously. *"Are you crazy?* I don't even want to be near that stuff! It's already loaded in the trailer, so you can take it wherever you wanted it to go in the first place. Our deal is the same. We'll never mention anything about you, and you take this stuff off my hands. Just pay me what I gave for it, no profit on my end. Or hell, better yet, just *take* it. *Free.* When Robles submits my draft, I'll gladly pay it, so long as I don't have anything to do with drugs or pottery containing drugs."

Reynaldo Gomez burst out laughing. "Mike, there are no drugs in this batch. Sure, many of the pieces have the hollow compartment, a method that will now have to be altered or delayed for a while. But not a single one contains contraband. I spoke with Ernesto Morales soon after you two left Tule. He had worried that Robles might sell some of the pieces to the wrong person, because he is new at the Laredo warehouse and has already proven to be an aggressive salesman. So Ernesto had Robles set aside my shipment, but I only found out a couple of days ago. It made no difference in my plans to expose Jack Pearson as a traitor and get rid of him."

"This was all a plan to uncover a problem in your organization?" Mike asked.

"Not in the beginning. But after he bashed my head, I saw this shipment of pottery—your pottery—as good bait to catch him, while Jack saw it as his just spoils, his reward for treachery."

"He got his reward, all right."

"Yes, he got what he deserved. And so should you. The shipment has already been added to my business account, so your draft will be returned to you, not submitted to your bank for payment. Robles has been instructed to mail it back to you. Given the timing of international mail service, you should get it back in a week or so."

"But I can't accept the shipment without paying you for it, then," Mike protested. "That's not the way I do business."

"I know that, but this business has been unusual from the start, Mike. Look at it as *your* reward, *your* spoils, in return for this adventure in the desert. *Please.* Take it back to your shop and make a handsome profit, I insist."

"So you're sure there are no drugs in this shipment?"

"I'm absolutely certain, believe me. If there were, I'd take them, because a shipment this size would amount to a huge sum of money. That's why Eva went into your shop to look at the pieces, and to buy one to make a closer inspection. Sure enough, as the batch numbers indicated, these pieces are empty. That trailer is loaded only with fine pottery."

For the third time that day, Mike Conner was stunned.

Fine pottery indeed. No kidding.

He sat there a minute, then pulled on the door handle. Reynaldo had left the car in gear, engine running, so of course, the door was locked. Sighing, he turned to Gomez, tried to smile, and stuck his hand over the seat. "Mr. Gomez, I can't help but admire you, admire your operational abilities, and your power and influence. And I appreciate your saving my shop and saving our lives, I really do, and I'm overwhelmed that you paid for this shipment. But to paraphrase a line from an old movie, I hope this is the *end* of a beautiful friendship."

Reynaldo nodded and shook his hand. Mike unlocked the door and went around to help Sandra get out into a standing position. She got an arm around him, and together they stepped to the driver's window.

"Good-bye, Mr. Gomez," she said, offering her hand. "Thank you for saving us."

"Ah, good-bye to you, my pretty nurse," he responded with his brilliant smile. "And best of luck to both of you. By the way, Mike your vehicle is at your apartment and the Ford is gone. When you get the goods unloaded, just leave the pickup and trailer in the alley. It will be removed quickly."

Mike supported her weight as they hobbled the few yards to the pickup. He lifted her into the seat, then got in and started the engine. "I hope this is the last episode of this story," he said. "I've had about all the entertainment I can stand for a while."

"It was a bit much, wasn't it? I agree with you, let's leave this kind of excitement to him. All I want is to get my leg fixed, then Mike Conner can take me home and take care of me."

"Well, coincidentally, that's exactly what I want, too."

He turned the rig around in the deserted highway and looked to the left, raising his hand for a final wave, but Reynaldo Gomez had disappeared from sight.

CHAPTER 36

▼

Mike swam to the side of the pool and smoothly launched himself up out of the water. Turning around as he plopped down on the edge, he promptly fried his hands and backside until the water cooled the tiles.

Watching from her chair, Sandra laughed at the expression on his face. "You're supposed to splash some water up there *first!*"

"Nope. Real men just get out of the pool," he insisted.

"Real men fry their hands and butts, you mean."

"Uh, yeah, something like that."

"Want something to drink?"

Mike stood and started for her chair under the umbrella. He walked quickly, dashing the last few feet on the hot surface. "Wow! I'm staying here in the shade. Too hot for me out there. Is there a beer in here?" he asked reaching for the cooler.

"Fresh out. I drank the last one," she replied, yawning nonchalantly, then bursting out laughing when the lie failed to fool him.

She quickly shifted her feet to the cooler lid, almost catching Mike's fingers in it as it slammed shut. He grabbed her left ankle and started tickling the bottom of her foot. Predictably, she screamed and started kicking with her free foot, but Mike had placed himself on her left side, so she couldn't get more than a weak side-swipe at him. "Okay, okay! I quit! Mike! *Stop it!*"

"Where's my beer?" he asked, grinning. He ceased to tickle her, but kept grip on her ankle and his fingers poised over her foot. "I'll bet there's one more in the cooler, but you had it all planned out to drink it, didn't you?"

"You can have it! Just don't tickle me, you know I hate that!"

He released her foot and reached into the cooler for the last Coors Light. Pulling it out, he commented, "It's not very cold. Here, you can have it."

"Forget it, Buddy. You drink it and then take me to dinner and buy me some wine. I've had enough beer—two. That's my limit."

Mike sat down on the towel beside her chair and sipped the beer, deciding it was cold enough after all. "Okay, I'll do it. All the wine you want."

"You're only agreeing to it because you know I can only drink one glass before I get silly. Then I get sleepy. So it won't cost you much."

"I was counting on a different reaction, maybe, before you get *too* sleepy," he said, reaching up to stroke her hair.

"Oh, you were, huh? We'll see."

Mike looked up at her expectantly, and she turned her head to hide a smirk. "What's *that* look for? You want a good foot-tickling?"

She sprang upright in the chair as though she'd touched a live wire, swinging her feet away from him, out of range. "Don't even think about it! Not if you want that different reaction you're hinting at," she warned.

"You win. Let's go in and shower."

"Later. I'm sleepy. Just a snooze, then we'll go in. Can we go to Barney's to eat?"

"Suits me. In fact, whatever pleases you just *tickles me pink*!" he answered, almost shouting the last three words and reaching again for her foot.

"Mike! Don't!"

"Okay, but I mean it."

"Mean what?"

"Pleasing you really does make me happy."

Camouflaged in the middle of his clowning, she had missed his vague reference to his fondness for her, and now he was embarrassed to have to explain it. Sandra was quiet for a moment, playing over in her mind the statement he had made. "Sometimes I realize that, Mike. I know you do a lot of things to please me. But then, other times we're not very close to each other, and…well, I just can't tell—"

"I know. That's why I'm telling you now. So you'll know."

She thought about that for a while, saying nothing, picking at the label on the beer bottle. Mike stayed quiet too, and remained very still, as though waiting to see if she would react before he had to elaborate. They watched in silence while a couple of teenage boys appeared and started horsing around on the other end of the pool, until the apartment manager came out and rousted them.

Sandra finally broke the silence. "I want some *things* in life. You know, like a house, maybe even a family. And that requires a commitment, to do that stuff. I don't know if you can do it, Mike, and still be happy. I'd be the last person in the world to want you to be unhappy, just so I could have what I want."

"I know that, and I appreciate it. That's why I realize I should do everything to keep you. But you're right, long-term arrangements entail a commitment, and that's difficult for me. Let's face it, Sandra, neither of us has a stellar track record in the relationship department."

"But at least you know that about me," she argued, "but I don't know anything about your background. You never bothered to tell me. That's what I mean when I tell you we're not close enough."

Mike propped himself up on his elbows and pulled his sunglasses from his forehead onto his face. The gesture caused Sandra to cast a furtive glance at him, as though whatever he was going to say or do next would somehow be masked by the dark lenses. Mike caught the glance and recognized that he had sub-consciously done exactly what she suspected: pulled the glasses down to hide his eyes and his thoughts, not because the sun had suddenly become brighter.

Turning to face her, he raised the shades back to his forehead before speaking. "There's not much to tell. My life's been pretty uneventful, which is not a bad thing. Normal parents, regular childhood, average grades in school, a little college, short time in the military, got out and went into business. But I've told you all of that.

"I'm somewhat of an exercise fanatic, which you already knew, and I like to travel. Travel and exercise are my only hobbies, and you're involved in both of those, plus my work. So, since you're involved in all of those things with me, what more could I say?"

"I guess you're right," she admitted. "But you never spoke of anyone or anything *special* from your past." Her voice was defensive, almost accusing, as though it trumped Mike's attempt to explain himself, and she regretted the tone before the words escaped her mouth.

Mike didn't seem to notice, and he continued as though he had intended to get to that part without prompting. "I've never been married, but I've been close a couple of times. It just didn't work out, either time. We just didn't pull the trigger, for whatever reason."

"And you don't think that's important enough to tell me about? Some insight into your personal life, even if it was in the past?"

Mike shrugged. "It didn't happen, so there didn't seem to be any need to air any of that with you. Besides, if you were one of those women, would you want to be the subject of a conversation with the next 'significant other?' Not even be able to tell your side of the story?"

"I guess not," she replied. "I hadn't thought of it that way, but that is considerate of you."

Mike wasn't quite done. "Anyway, there was nothing to tell. At least not anything that was going to impress you, good or bad." As he reached the end of the explanation, he reached again for his sunglasses, but stopped himself.

"I didn't need to be impressed, Mike, just *informed*, I guess. To me, that's how people really *know* each other. It would have seemed more personal, more like we're a couple, more like you really cared for me and trusted me with everything about you and your past."

"Well, I *do* care. A lot more than anyone else who drifted through your life, I'd say. By the way, you didn't exactly enlighten me about your entire past." He let the last comment hang, knowing it might sting, but convinced that it was true, which she confirmed with her next statement.

"I know. You don't have to remind me of the bad decisions I made."

Mike immediately wished he had phrased his earlier comment differently, true or not. "Sandra, I'm not pointing out bad decisions. God knows I've made enough of them for both of us. But everybody makes decisions based on what you know at the time." After a pause, he added, "Everybody's got twenty-twenty hindsight, and it doesn't do any good to second-guess your decisions after more facts come to light. That's cheating."

She laughed at that and reached out to touch his hand. "Well, I certainly don't want to be a cheater!"

They sat quietly for a while after that, watching the sun sink, finally going behind the privacy wall and putting the pool in the shade. Sandra snoozed and Mike lay back on the towel, going over in his mind the uncomfortable conversation—uncomfortable because of his inability to open up to her as much as she wished, but...it would have been difficult for him, even without the saga of drug-filled pottery, her ex-husband, her past life's contacts with slimy drug dealers, and the deception concerning her confidential informant status with the DEA. As it was, all those things had served to push him further into himself in order to insulate his feelings against the possibility of failure in the relationship. As much as he cared for Sandra, it was going to be hard to overcome his self-imposed barrier against permanent emotional ties.

And how could she be critical of his secretive attitude about his past? She hadn't exactly come clean about hers, not until circumstances forced the issue to the surface. Reynaldo Gomez had learned information about Sandra that she might never have volunteered had it not been for the final showdown in the desert, when her connection to the federal agency was revealed.

His reverie was interrupted by a sharp jab in the ribs, and Sandra's giggle. "Wake up, Sleepyhead! Want to run a few miles before we go eat?"

"Um, okay. If you insist. I sure need to, although I didn't drink as much beer as I might have—if I had a more thoughtful girlfriend who would put enough ice in the cooler to keep it cold."

The remark cost him another dig into his ribcage, so he got up and helped her collect towels, sunscreen, and the cooler. Stopping by the apartment, they changed into running gear and headed for the track at the park across the street. Their regular starting point was the kids' playground near the entrance. Four laps gave them six miles and always called for resting on the swing set afterward to cool off.

As they walked toward the starting point, a middle-aged man stood next to the slide, looking around as though he expected something or someone. He was dressed in cream-colored slacks and a yellow, open-collar shirt, but the heat had brought him out of his chocolate blazer. Slung over his shoulder, hanging by one finger, it ruined the casual look he was trying to effect. Besides, standing next to a deserted gym set, not a single kid in sight, made him stand out like a Chevrolet pickup at a Ferrari dealership.

As they neared the man, Mike noticed him staring at Sandra. Just as he turned to ask her if she knew him, she stiffened in mid-stride and stopped short. He looked over at her to see the troubled look in her blue eyes that he had become adept at spotting. "What's wrong?" he asked her. "You know him?"

"Hello, Miss Payne," the man said before she could answer. "I'm Frank MacAuliff, from the local office. The Fort Worth office wanted me to visit with you."

"About what? How did you find me here?"

"We need to have you sign a release form and a confidentiality agreement. That will finalize your contract employment with the Agency. As to your second question, I figured you'd rather do this somewhere besides your place, in front of neighbors. I've been watching, waiting for you to leave your apartment."

Sandra didn't respond, and he pulled a sheaf of papers from the inside of the jacket. He extended them to her, but it was a long moment before she reached for them. She held them away from her body, like someone's pet python, the troubled look still on her face. Finally she spoke. "I need a pen."

"The Fort Worth office really appreciates your efforts," he said, searching the blazer pockets for a pen. "Your information was correct. Unfortunately, some bozo got his wires crossed, and they tried to knuckle Gomez without a warrant. They didn't have probable cause, but went to his house anyway, pushed their way in and looked around. I guess they thought he'd have the evidence just sitting in the hallway closet.

"He called his mouthpiece in San Antonio—guess they have better drug lawyers down there—and a local judge made the preliminary ruling in his favor. The Tarrant County DA notified the Wichita County DA and advised him not to file charges. Same for the federal prosecutors, they knew better. Naturally, Gomez walked, just like he knew he would. But not before having a long private talk with Anderson, the AIC in Cowtown."

He handed her a pen, and noticing the questioning look on her face, filled her in. "AIC. Agent in Charge. They talked for a while, and Gomez denied using the hollow pottery scam. But he knew you were the one who reported it. And he said your ex-husband had a big batch of it. He didn't know where it ended up, but that the Agency could forget trying to find it. So the Fort Worth office has been searching all over North Texas for a guy named Jack Pearson for the past six weeks."

He watched her expression for any sign of recognition at the mention of the name, but she remained blank. Ignoring the fishing expedition, she looked down at the papers and found where she was supposed to sign without reading a word of the agreement. "Oh, and there," he said, pointing to another signature line. "That should do it. Thanks."

He folded the papers and took the pen from her hand before continuing. "You know, Gomez told Anderson the strangest things during their little pow-wow. He said we ought to find Jack Pearson—he's your ex-husband, right?—and his buddies. He said they could fill in all the blanks about how it worked. But you know what I think?"

Sandra looked at him blankly, clearly not caring what Frank MacAuliff thought.

"I think those guys are history. And I think Reynaldo Gomez was responsible. And I also think you know more about it than you're ever gonna tell."

"Are you done with your business here, Sandra?" Mike asked, not even glancing at her interrogator.

Before she could respond, MacAuliff spoke again. "You're Mike Conner, right?"

"Right."

"I thought so. Because the strangest thing Gomez said was at the end of his chit-chat session with Anderson. Of course, Anderson was pissed, and he told Gomez so. Gomez laughed at him, told him not to be such a sore loser.

"That Mexican drug dealer had just beaten a rap that would've rolled him for twenty, maybe thirty years, and gotten away with it. Just because of a technicality. How lucky can you get? So anyway, Anderson told him he was the luckiest man alive. And you know what Gomez said?"

Mike didn't respond and continued to look at him without expression. Sandra stood looking out at the running track as though seeing it for the first time, studying the route.

MacAuliff looked back and forth between Mike and Sandra as if he actually expected them to know the comment Gomez had made two months before, at a meeting three hundred miles away. After several seconds, he supplied the answer. "Gomez said, *'No, Mike Conner is the luckiest man alive.'* Now, I wonder why he said that. You got any idea?" The question hung in the air a minute while he inquired with his eyes.

"Let's go, Sandra," Mike said, breaking the uncomfortable silence. He took her hand and headed for the track. They were almost to the starting point before they heard his voice again.

"I'm glad I got to meet the luckiest man in the world!" MacAuliff called after them in a tone that implied he didn't believe Gomez's assessment. "And thank you again, Miss Payne!"

He turned and walked away, but they were already on the track, bending and stretching, not saying a word. Sandra finished and took off at a jogger's pace, still hobbling slightly from the bullet wound. Mike fell in behind her, but called out to her before they'd covered a quarter mile. "Slow down, will you?"

"Sorry."

She slowed her pace and he pulled up beside her. "Let's walk. You're wobbling all over the track. Is your leg hurting?"

"Yeah, some. Guess I started out too fast."

They slowed to a walk, which suited both of them. The mood was wrong for a relaxing run, ruined by the unexpected meeting with the federal agent. But the sun was setting, and the air was finally getting cool enough to enjoy being out-of-doors. They walked a full lap before either spoke.

"Did you know that guy?" Mike asked.

"No, but when I saw him standing there, looking at me, I knew he was from the Agency. He had that look. And all that crap about meeting with me out here, instead of at the apartment, they just want me to know that they can watch me, find me anywhere. Makes them feel like big-time spies or something. They're more like Peeping Toms."

"And that little scene brought it all back, didn't it? The last two months have been nice and quiet, too good to last."

"I'm sorry, Mike. I can see that you're the one who was left uninformed. I was—I *am* interested in your past, because really knowing someone is what makes a relationship. But I left you in the dark about important stuff, stuff they nearly got us both killed."

"It sure made for an adventure, though, didn't it?" he asked. "Hopefully, signing those papers ends this mess...doesn't it?"

"Yes, that finished my business with the Agency. They told me a long time ago that's how they finalize their business relationships with informants; making them sign a promise to never reveal any part of the information to anyone, like to write a book or do a movie."

"Well, that's a relief. Who'd believe this story, anyway?"

They walked another lap while the sun disappeared below the horizon. The September air was still warm, but it would cool off before morning, making mornings for the next two months the most pleasant of the year. They talked about the moderate weather and running, and how they needed to concentrate on increasing their mileage before races in the spring. It was completely dark before Mike spoke again of the matters between them.

"I know this is difficult Sandra, for both of us. It's sure not going to be easy for me, but I'm going to do my best." He stopped and turned to look at her. "Because Gomez was right about lots of things."

She looked up at him in the darkness, but couldn't see his face well enough to tell if he was joking. "I thought you didn't approve of anything he represents."

"I don't, but that doesn't mean he's not right about some things; you know, like Jack being a traitor, and knowing that you'd take care of him in the desert, and knowing that somehow we'd survive. And he obviously knows how to survive in the legal climate his line of work creates."

"He does have a knack for judging people, doesn't he?"

"Yes, and he saw in you what I need to see, and that makes him right about something else."

"What's that?"

"Mike Conner is the luckiest man alive."

Printed in the United States
By Bookmasters